Lynn Steigleder

DALON CON

THE ESSENCE OF TIME

DALON CON, The Essence of Time
by Lynn Steigleder

First Edition © July 2024

Published by
Soul Fire Press / Christopher Matthews Publishing
Gleneden Beach, Oregon 97388

ISBN-13:
978-1-944072-43-8 (hbk)
978-1-944072-42-1 (pbk)
978-1-944072-93-3 (ebk)

The events, peoples and incidents in this story are the sole product of the author's imagination. The story is fictitious, and any resemblance to individuals, living or dead, is purely coincidental. Historical, geographic, and political issues are based on fact; the stories of the children of Central America are based on truth, however, the names have been changed to protect the innocent.

Every effort has been made to be accurate. The author assumes no responsibility or liability for errors made in this book.

Cover / book formatting & design by Suzanne Parrott
The Essence of Time, ©Suzanne Parrott (Midjourney)

Printed and bound
in the United States of America.

Dedication

To Mari Dyer, my physical therapist.
Her enthusiasm on my behalf and
her constant encouragement remain a source
that inspires me to forge ahead.

Thanks Buddy.

BOOKS BY
LYNN STEIGLEDER

RISING TIDE SERIES
Rising Tide
Eden's Wake
Deadly Reign

* * *

Terminal Core
Dalon Con

* * *

CHILDREN'S BOOK
Papa "N" Lil' Ed

NOTE FROM THE AUTHOR

You are about to delve into a work of fiction . . . at least that was the original intent. Of course, now that I have opened the door of doubt, a tiny shiver worms its way up the back of my spine.

"Why?" you ask.

With the menagerie of creatures I have brought to life within the pages of this novel, if any have a chance of existing, we have trouble on a monumental scale looming on the horizon . . .

Read quickly for who knows what tomorrow brings.

Lynn

CHAPTER ONE

Drade

Drade was tall for an Odobi, which was an overstatement, considering the average height for this clan was a quarter of an inch. He strode past several new eateries in favor of his old standby, CATT's. The food wasn't great, and the place was noisy, yet it had a calming effect, enabling him to work. He never felt bothered by hypotheses or theories. Why waste time? Instead, he bypassed suppositions for practical solutions. It was his calling and one he chose to bear alone.

"Idiots," the Odobian mumbled as he entered CATT's restaurant. "If they don't act soon, it'll be too late." Distracted, Drade initially failed to notice the restaurant's altered state.

"What the . . .?" Drade blinked several times as he looked around the eatery, which appeared to have been abandoned for decades. "This has got to be some kind of joke. Where is everyone?" He walked outside and checked the signage, hoping he was in the wrong place.

Anyone with good sense would turn around and leave, but curiosity is something a scientist runs toward, not away.

Deposits of dark red debris littered every corner of the restaurant. Stained floor tiles curled as cracked vinyl booths and broken chairs sat empty. Drade crouched, running his fingers over the floor covering's edge.

Last night, this place was spotless with new floor tiles, but now . . . no term other than 'death' fits this setting. Swatting at an errant piece of something, Drade glanced up, running his fingers through his short strawberry-blonde hair. Faded blue ceiling paint hung in sheets, and bits of color floated down like leaves. A thick layer of dust sat atop every horizontal surface, and the surrounding air smelled musty with the faint odor of copper.

A faint glow filled the diner. Stepping up to a window, Drade wiped away years of dust. Gasping, he tried to absorb the scene.

"It-It can't be," he stammered, "it just can't be." He stumbled toward the front door, falling forward as he reached for the handle. Opening the door, the sun rode high above lush green flora, signaling a warm, pleasant day for Burrus Plax. Near midday, the dwarf sibling's light was absorbed by the larger of the two. This was overlooked by the mass of humanoid lives that rushed past as the dwarf star's meager output floundered. Drade stood in the doorway glancing between the everyday world outside and the chaos inside.

Re-entering the restaurant, he dashed back to the window. The scene was that of a desert. *No trees. No grass. Nothing green in any direction. The topography reeks of death.*

Two worlds existing simultaneously. No, not two worlds, *two times.*

A noise caught his attention and he turned. Slowly, Drade moved toward the kitchen, pushing through the double door hoping to find something to explain these delusional episodes. He cursed as the sticky remnants of a mammalian carcass clung to the underside of his boot.

"No need for boisterous speech," a deep voice said as Drade scraped his gut-covered sole across the floor.

"Who's there?" Drade seethed, continuing to scrape off the guts. "Are you responsible for this illusion?"

"Yes, and no. This is no illusion, I assure you. You are Drade and we have an immediate need for your services."

"My services?" Someone was hiding in the shadows. He glanced toward the long-dry sinks overflowing with dirty dishes. Mingled with the musty odor was apparently enough to attract the three-foot wooly slug rat — just not sufficient enough to sustain its life. He carefully slowed his breathing. "I don't speak to shadows. Show yourself. Now."

A dark, undulating, shapeless figure backed into the highest corner of the kitchen. "Does this form meet your approval?" the deep voice asked.

Drade trembled while attempting to maintain his composure. The formless creature radiated an alluring energy that he felt to his core.

"You may call me Deep Sink," the thing offered.

I MAY? Drade thought angrily as he kept a watchful eye on the creature and his possible escape. "Fine, Deep Sink, but I have questions before your interrogation."

"Of course," the thing replied. "You may ask anything you wish ahead of my questions to you."

"I ate here yesterday and today this place looks as if a meal has not been prepared in over a century."

"One-hundred thirty-two years, to be exact."

"Why? What happened to throw time askew?"

"Bear in mind," Deep Sink articulated, "the significance of time, as theorized by entities beyond our galactic realm, holds no weight. The key factor, which I refer to as 'relevance,' remains unaltered with each individual leap through time, often leading to the derailment of these temporal ventures. In such instances, time rewinds, erasing any memory of the mishap, and the traveler is returned to the starting point to attempt the time journey anew. This cycle may repeat itself multiple times until the journey reaches completion or is abandoned as unfeasible. In your situation, it's possible that this is merely an attempt by a former associate to capture your notice." Deep Sink emitted a sound resembling laughter, echoing omnidirectionally, enveloping Drade before fading as if torn into fragments.

"Who might be orchestrating these temporal voyages?" inquired the Odobi. Drade, aware of the council's prohibition on time travel, could only conjecture the involvement of two individuals daring enough to undertake such forbidden endeavors.

"No doubt you remember your former classmate, Hayden, and

professor Wakke, from the first three years of your rudimentary instructional group, and then the final years of advanced temporal vortex theory."

Drade clenched his fists. "Yes, I remember Hayden and Wakke. Hayden was a good friend until we fell out over a notion concerning time travel. Simply stated Hayden believed temporal travel was theoretically possible . . . I did and still do not." Drade paused, furrowed his eyebrows, and grimly smiled. "Though I must admit the happenings of earlier today have forced me to reconsider."

Drade redirected his thought process and moved to answer Deep Sink's second question. "Professor Wakke, while being a great educator, fell by the wayside when my studies advanced beyond his understanding."

"What of the Consortia Awakening of Temporal Travel?" Deep Sink asked.

"The Consortia is what drove the last nail, ending my and Hayden's friendship. Just suppose this Consortia is real. Where is it and how can such a thing exist, remaining undiscovered for all these years?"

"You are standing in the Consortia itself," Deep Sink said. "Take time to think and have a glass of refreshment, courtesy of CATT's."

Drade turned as a frosted glass containing a light-colored carbonated beverage slid across a counter, slowing as it neared his position. Ignoring the lack of sanitation, he grasped the container and drank. *Unbelievable.* Questions and answers began to plow through his brain.

"Of course!" Drade said, "the acronym, this restaurant I've been coming to for years and never made a connection . . . CATT's, it's the perfect cover."

"Stay your excitement. Throughout the centuries, not one soul has noticed, which is where you come in."

"Your friend, Hayden, and educator, Wakke, have reawakened temporal travel." Drade paused. "I see my words have piqued your interest. Most assuredly you will want to stay."

"Go on," Drade said, slowing turning.

"Hayden and Wakke claim there is some nonsensical malevolent being that has taken over dozens of worlds and now has our planet, Placene, in its sights," Deep Sink said. "In fact, their claims insinuate Burrus Plax, a world unknown to me, could be gone within days, leaving Placene the next in line, which is why they wish to reinstate time travel."

"How will opening something as dangerous as a temporal vortex assist a planetary crisis, even if there were such a thing?" Drade said. "Suppose they can travel backward in time; even the slightest variant in the timeline could cause disaster for what we now know to be normality.

"Hayden and Wakke have recruited a handful of dissidents to help in this plot to bypass the Consortia's permission and proceed with temporal travel, no matter what the cost," Deep Sink said. "This is why you will infiltrate their small group and thwart their plans whether it is through sabotage, mass destruction or whatever means you deem necessary."

CHAPTER TWO

Hayden

Two eyes entrenched within a newly formed stone ridge stared at the cave entrance containing the Odobi scientists. This being was a physical branch of Burrus Plax, a planetary anomaly, a constant, no matter the timeline. The eyes blinked, patiently waiting for the happening to occur.

****

Hayden stood before the temporal doorway, the last eighteen years of construction running through his mind. A slight sniffle followed by a sneeze broke the silence. Even after many years, Hayden could not shake his allergies to the moisture present in the cave. He dressed in a skintight black undergarment that kept its wearer clean, cared for bodily functions, and regulated body temperature for comfort in the most severe weather. Wakke entered, handing Hayden a bundle of garments: a neutral-colored, long-sleeved pullover and form-fitting pants.

The final piece Wakke held appeared as a square bag with six straps. "This is a travel bag pre-packed with basic items you will need while away." He quickly used the six straps to anchor the unit to the traveler's back. Hayden ran his thumbs underneath the straps, eyeing every portion visible of this unknown technology.

"This is your propulsion system," Wakke said, "and if this has piqued your curiosity, and as well it should, you *will* be able to attach and remove the pack." Wakke winked. "Consider this first time as an instructional introduction."

"What's *this* form of propulsion?"

"It was made explicitly for this mission," the scientist said. "It is totally intuitive, meaning it will follow your commands and your commands only, whether issued orally or mentally."

"The device uses air," Wakke continued. "Each time you command the system to operate, intake ports will emerge from the top of the pack and curve ninety degrees over your shoulders. Thrust cones will exit the pack near the bottom and operate independently of one another. Altitude and velocity are solely determined by you, and this system is powered by a Dalleon cell which will continue long after you and I cease to be."

Wakke handed Hayden a palm-sized black box. "All controls are on one side of the rectangle," he said. "The circular screen on top is to speak into. There are three buttons below the screen. Push the first to begin a vocal communique, the second to send a signal, in case the first option is down, and the third button if you are unable to return home."

Placing his hand over the box in Hayden's palm, Wakke looked firmly at Hayden. "Guard this, for without this technology, we have no way of knowing what has become of you or me." Wakke opened the back of the box. "This is a scale that will be useful when judging your time jumps. It measures in years. Unfortunately, a single year is as close as we could hope to measure our journeys through time."

"Not all options that I would choose," Hayden said. "However, I suppose we must make the best of this situation."

Wakke stepped up to a panel and pressed a palm-sized button. An orange light began to move around the portal, increasing in speed until it appeared as a solid entity traveling from left to right, winding around the frame as it moved.

"Notice the frame itself," Wakke said, "by the sheer nature of time travel this portal will expand or shrink to accommodate virtually any size being, for a temporal vortex does not discriminate." Wakke smiled, "I thought you might like to know."

Hayden bade Wakke farewell and stepped toward the doorway. A hole opened amid an orange lightning show that filled the temporal entrance. Once Hayden pushed through, the entrance closed with a loud sucking pop.

CHAPTER THREE

Gabriel and Mama Byrnes

Defeated, a city stewing in inequity had lost any desire to identify crime, even murder. The most heinous infractions went unpunished due to an apathetic view of life. Some took it upon themselves to act as judge, jury, and executioner but used this premise as a game, defying any rule of law. Few chose to live outside the city, instead opting for an exciting and profitable existence within Defeated's boundaries, even if death was a common byproduct. Unfortunately, the young suffered, paying for their elder's misdeeds.

"Gabby!" Mama Byrnes squalled. "Where ya be, ya good fer nothin' cuss? I done and telled ya the next time ya touched my things, I were gonna wear ya out." Gabriel, only six years old when Byrnes had lured his family to their deaths, was savagely abused for the ten years that followed. His clothes withstood being patched, let out, and added to over the years to match his growth cycles. Running his fingers over numerous holes that spanned several repairs brought back memories—*but memories from this hell are never pleasant.*

Removing a self-rolled cigarette wedged in the nook between her ear and head, Mama Byrnes sucked the dying smoke into her mouth—the scent of tobacco and burning wax-shavings filled the air. She set to chewing on it turning it into a disgusting wad of wax, tobacco leaves and paper, until swallowing, then nimbly lit another with nicotine-stained fingers.

After lighting the new cigarette, she took a long drag and continued her tirade as tendrils of smoke escaped her mouth.

Gabriel discovered asylum within his self-appointed sanctuary, doing just enough over the past ten years to keep the old shack from collapsing. In doing so, he found an area between the walls, and with a few minor additions, Gabriel could come and go unseen like a ghost among shadows. The boy safely watched the old woman seething with anger. Despite the imminent threat of another beating, he savored these fleeting moments of solitude. However, time was short; he would need to leave before she unleashed the hounds that could sniff out his sanctuary.

"Now, if ya don't want to double the beatin' ya already got comin', I spect ya show yerself and rat now." Gabriel watched as Byrnes unknowingly wiped guilty hands against her filthy, tattered dress, symbolically removing the blood from a lifetime of sins against humanity. Dark brown feet, so colored from lack of hygiene, plotted her course as she padded down the hallway.

Gabriel remained hidden in the ephemeral spine-chilling silence as tormenting memories surged through his consciousness. Horrifying events filled his mind with unwanted clarity as the experiences of his six-year-old self unfolded.

"Gabby," Mama Byrnes screamed, "I down telled ya the next time ya tried to runneded way from me I were gonna sick my hounds on ya . . ." Mama Byrnes dropped her voice to a mumble. "Ha, ha, ha. Keep runnin' boy . . . yeah, you just keep a runnin."

Two mangy four-foot high canines displaying elongated muzzles and teeth too large to be contained within their mouths dragged the boy back to Mama Byrnes. The animals growled and moved in circles, working themselves into a frenzy, desperate to eat the scarred and bleeding carcass they'd just retrieved. The stench of wet dog encased in death permeated the area. Gabriel was silent, nearly comatose from blood loss.

"Maybe you be a listenin' to me next time," the old witch said. "Course next time I spect there weren't be nuff 'o' ya left to talk at." Mama Byrnes whistled, signaling her bloodthirsty hounds. "You two get this here youngin' up to the house. He be a bloodin' ever where. And don't get no ideas 'bout eatin' this here boy . . . take one bite, and I'll skint ya plumb to the bone." The dogs dragged Gabriel toward the old woman's abode.

"Gabby!" Mama Byrnes' shriek jolted Gabby back to the present.

Living in the past does no good; I've got to stay grounded in the here and now. Let her try to find me. Just let her try. My momma and daddy named me Gabriel, and that trashy old bat turned it into garbage, just like her. "Gabby!" he mumbled, then followed with a guttural noise and a ball of spit. *I'll see her choke on that name . . . or maybe I'll do the choking.*

Gabriel moved along the corridor, doing his best to match her every move on the other side of the wall. He'd created this haven courtesy of the old lady's failing eyesight and the recent downturn in hearing. Even though sights and sounds were not as sharp as in the past, her other senses enhanced her awareness. At the same time, sensations outnumbering her standard five began to emerge.

"I'm not going to take it anymore," he promised himself in a whisper ending with a hiss. A decade-long stint with this heartless witch caused Gabriel to turn inward, suppressing any goodness he once had into a deep, dark abyss.

Mama Byrnes relentlessly yelled as rage continued growing within the tortured young man. Gabriel cringed. "Shut up, old woman or you won't see another day," he mumbled.

Through another small fissure in the poorly constructed wall, Gabriel's nemesis stood just inches away. "That little good-fer-nothin' will be the death 'o' me yet," Mama Byrnes said, then she became quiet, moving her body sideways and pressing an ear against the partition. With one swift action, she slammed a meaty fist through the wall, the punch landing several inches from Gabriel's face. Grabbing the woman's bleeding appendage, Gabriel's hatred boiled over.

The injuries on Mama Byrnes' right-hand knuckles were bone-deep, several fingers broken and disjointed as they pushed through the wall, searching for her quarry; Gabriel pulled, dislocating her elbow. Surprised at his newfound strength, his adrenaline steadily increasing, Gabriel snapped her wrist, rotating her lower arm until the joint gave way. He kicked through the wall, finding himself face-to-face with his nemesis. Mama Byrnes fell to the floor, screaming from her destroyed elbow, a heavy flow of crimson fluid spilling from her knuckles. Gabriel moved toward the old woman, seething with each step.

"Why ya wanna hurt me?" she whimpered between bouts of pain. "I done took ya in and raised ya from a scat." She clutched her wrinkled bicep with her good hand as another wave of agony wracked her body. "Ya stay back, ya hear, or I'll put ya to bed with no supper." Using her feet, she pushed along the floor in a futile attempt to escape the crazed youth standing over her.

Gabriel placed his right foot on Mama Byrnes' left ankle and then grabbed a piece of wood leaning against the wall. "You call what you did to me raisin'? You didn't raise me up! You beat me up!"

She felt the first of many blows sink deep into her forehead. Long after her ability to feel fled, the downward strikes of the 2x4 continued.

The metallic odor of blood wafted through the air. The boy stumbled backward, staring at his handiwork; the steady drip of blood onto the wooden floorboards broke the silence.

"Never again," he whispered, "never again." Then the boy slowly turned, dropped the bloody plank, and left his prison for the last time.

****

A serpent-like shadow rose from Mama Byrnes's lifeless body in the now-silent house. The anomaly paused, watching until the boy disappeared into the storm. Then, it slithered through a crack in the floorboards.

CHAPTER FOUR

Dalon Con

An elderly man sat tending the fire to the crude spit. Drippings from a small mammalian carcass sizzled as they hit the hot coals, the fragrant smoke traveling upward. This scenario had played out for years—waiting for the sign. Hungry as the old man was, he failed to notice the inviting aroma; other matters lay heavy on his mind. *I hope the young man who stumbled upon my encampment made his way to the light,* he thought as he stirred the coals robotically. *For the life of me, I cannot recall his name. We dined on cabot, and then he departed, never revealing from wince he came or his final destination.* This, in turn, brought another worry to mind. *Did my grandson find the weapon I left to assist him in the battle against the Azurians? Forged from caladium, a mineral exclusively found on the planet Aon, the indestructible rod would decimate all it encountered.*

The man known to many as Dalon Con was at least an anomaly, at most a mystery, and to all an unknown. He was kind, helpful, honest, and devoted to the Great One. When asked about the Great One, his eyes would widen, a broad smile spread across his face, and his entire persona began to glow.

I have played many small but pivotal roles, yet I know the outcome of none. He sighed. *As soon as I complete this battle for the inhabitants of Burrus Plax set before me by the Great One, I will return home for a much-needed rest until called again.*

He began to chuckle as he noticed a pile of clean bones at his feet. *I ate the entire cabot with no recollection. Truly, the Great One possesses a magnificent sense of humor.* Dalon Con sucked against the roof of his mouth with a grateful tongue. *Tasty, indeed; my usual jovial spirit has returned. Blessings, many blessings, I receive each day.*

His thoughts once again turned to an earlier time. *I can only suppose I will follow a similar trek as the young man when on his journey.* Breaking from his reverie, he sighed. "But that was a world away from where we are now, on Burrus Plax."

Suddenly, an orange light that left a trail across the night sky caught his attention before disappearing. The man smiled at the diversion, as this gave him a brief hint of things to come.

Dalon Con extinguished the fire and cleaned the area, saving the bones for a later meal. The old man turned toward the pinhole of light in the distance, unsure of what he would find when he arrived.

The man inhaled deeply. "It is time," he said and then vanished.

****

Another set of eyes, born from soil, also watched the orange streak move across the darkened sky. The creature, Max, shared a profound connection with the planet, allowing him to metamorphose into any substance, be it soil, stone, water, or any other element. As the orange glow receded, Max assumed a bipedal shape and embarked toward the site of the enigmatic anomaly.

****

The familiar sound of human pain and violence surrounded Dalon Con as he stood in the city of Defeated. How could a vibrant township turn into such a cesspool of evil? When the authorities rob the citizens of everything under the guise of giving plenty to all, it opens doors to further reduce the meager belongings. When nothing remains, malevolence is given an easy inroad.

The glow behind him faded, revealing a brick wall lined with foul-smelling containers and oozing refuse. Although he wore a fur cloak and carried a staff, Dalon appeared to others as a professionally dressed thirty-something. This appearance transformation was a protective measure, preventing those who might recognize him from prior encounters over the decades, thus safeguarding his true identity.

An acid drizzle hung in the air, and Dalon Con crouched and touched a puddle of water, feeling its acidic sting. He gazed at his reflection. *I sense the beard hanging from my weathered face, yet I see a clean-shaven young man with a smooth complexion.* This would be the persona most would see. Then, the old man sighed. *Still, there are rare times when a handful will see me as I truly am. Even I do not know when these instances will occur.*

His staff appeared as a walking stick with an ornate brass handle and a twisted, blanched wood shaft. He rubbed his hand along the polished surface. *Undoubtedly, I must appear to have an infirmity to require such a device.* Taking several steps, his legs seemed to function normally, yet in the reflection of the water, he observed a noticeable limp in his new persona's right leg.

"What's 'a matter, crip?" a gravelly voice said. "Ya done an bought yerself a peck 'o' trouble bein' out on this here night."

"I wish for no trouble," Dalon Con said, "but perhaps you could assist me in locating a particular individual."

"Sure, but the first thing I'm gonna do is take a pound a meat outta ya fer every credit I want and ya ain't got."

Dalon Con wrinkled his forehead. "Do as you wish, though I cannot guarantee your retention."

As a small chuckle turned into a boisterous laugh, the large man with the gravelly voice regained his composure and spoke, "Retention—mighty big word yer a usin.' Just what is it I'm s'posed to retain?"

"Body parts, of course that choice is yours; however, take care that you choose wisely." Dalon Con paused and then continued. "Some decisions last a lifetime, while others reflect that same life's early demise."

A small yellow stone set into the butt of his cane started to glow.

"Ahhh," the gravelly voice man snarled. His large fist sliced through the air toward the head of Dalon Con.

"Another fails to listen," Dalon Con whispered. Standing his ground, the old man raised his staff, diverting his attacker's arm before contact.

The gravelly-voiced one stepped toward the old man, slicing his blade through the air. The attempt fell short, yet the attacker sliced again, making contact with Dalon Con's cane.

"I wish you no harm, please." Dalon again blocked an attack, taking several steps backward. "You must understand, it is not my wish to harm you."

"But it *is* mine."

He again attacked, throwing his bulk toward the old man. Dalon Con easily stepped aside, watching the man slam into the brick wall.

"Another fails to listen," Dalon whispered. He raised his staff, slicing his attacker's arm before contact. The man froze, mouth agape, as he slowly turned to watch the blood flow from his shoulder.

"Stop now, before you lose more," the old man warned.

The man began to laugh wildly and lunged. The staff was raised again, and then the man howled in pain—a severed hand lay on the pavement. Undaunted, the man picked up his blade with his left hand.

"You'll die for that."

"Son, you will lose more than a hand," Dalon Con held out his hand. Softness filled his voice. "You know me."

The gravelly man took several steps, then faltered, his weapon clattering onto the stone street. The man's eyes grew wide, and then he slumped to his knees, head hanging low, his eyes glowing as moisture began to collect.

"I-I remember you," the man whispered. "I met you . . . a long time ago."

Dalon Con approached the trembling figure. "The Great One still wants you as one of his own," he said, placing a hand on the gravelly-voiced man's shoulders. "Are you ready to accept the one who died, but now lives for all of our sakes."

"I-I don't know how. I don't deserve. . ." the man crumpled into sobs.

Dalon Con knelt next to the man and continued to speak for the next hour.

CHAPTER FIVE

Broan, Jence and Murph

A nightly ritual had commenced in the city of Defeated. A trio of human rats combed back alleys, searching for anything to survive one more day. Threatening, rigid, and verbose, Murph, the self-appointed leader, instructed his pack of "scrubbers" to scour the garbage bins for items of value.

Broan, a born follower, seldom displaying a thought of his own, preferred to hang back, awaiting Murph's instructions. Jence, however, would murder his mother for the most meager of profits. Traitorous, he searched for any opening to enrich himself, no matter the cost. Any rational intelligence these men possessed from their former lives was absorbed into oblivion as they acclimated to the moral desolation that was Burrus Plax.

As the three continued down the alley, they spied an elderly figure cloaked in fur and set out in pursuit.

I sense a familiar nuisance from three misguided individuals, Dalon Con thought. *Before this comes to bloodshed, I shall put it to rest.* Out of sight, the old man switched from fur to silk, reversed his direction, and then lost his beard, becoming again the thirty-year-old suit in the eyes of his pursuers.

Jense and Broan rushed into a large, well-lit area, followed by Murph a few seconds later. They turned in circles in a befuddled search for the old man.

"There's nothing here," Broan said, "but a suit." At that, Dalon Con pushed back into the shadows, quickly making his getaway. "He's gone now."

"What?" Murph turned in the direction Broan was looking. "How many times are you two gonna lose one old man? Tonight makes three. We could have sold that shiny stone in his staff and been eating like kings tonight. Instead, we're crawling around in dumpsters." Like his two cohorts, Murph was shabbily dressed, barefoot, and sported a full beard with long mussed hair.

"That thirty-year-old-suit was totin' a cane with a shiny stone," Broan said.

"He's the same guy," Murph bellowed. "And I'd be willing to betcha, he's the one they call Con . . . Dalon Con."

"I heard about him," Broan said, "but didn't take much stock in a man they claimed could move faster than sound itself."

"Or change his appearance, like he just demonstrated," Murph said, "always touting something called a 'Great One,' from what I hear."

"It's like he just disappears," Jence said, "And I'm here to tell ya that I ain't so sure we ought to be chasing this 'Con.'"

"What kind 'o' fairyland are you livin' in?" Murph asked. "People don't just disappear."

"Well, they do wherever this guy 'Con' comes from," Broan said. "One minute he's this old guy in a fur cloak, and the next we can't find nothin' but a thirty-year-old-suit. I'm siding with Jence. We need to leave this old man alone. Ain't no telling what else he can turn in to."

Murph looked at his two cohorts and then nodded. "You may have a point, for once," Murph said, "but since I ain't the one who's gonna be doin' the actual chasing, I don't believe that's gonna happen."

"Every day we hear something new about this Dalon Con, and it ain't in our favor," Broan said.

Murph glared. "If you think that little bit of information is going to stop me, think again."

Broan opened his mouth to speak—

Murph waved his hand. "Enough already; we'll sort this mess out later. It's gettin' dark, and we still have to rustle up supper. Whatcha got a taste fer tonight?"

"The same thing that's got a taste fer us," Jence replied.

"Outta all the critters 'round here that are an easy kill," Broan said, "you gotta go and pick the one that comes with a fifty-fifty chance of us being eatin' or gettin' et."

"Mucus rat?" Murph said. "A twelve-foot-long blob of hairy snot that can chew stones to dust, really?"

Several moments passed. Then, a broad smile spread across Murph's face. "Good choice," he exclaimed, "dang, fine choice."

****

"Whew!" Broan said from within the refuse container. "Ain't found our supper but done found me a dead jader, and she stinks to high heaven." The jader was three feet long, half of it a leathery tail with random-length spikes that could pierce steel. "You's mighty purdy fer such an ugly cuss; a plum shame you ain't no better fer eatin'."

Broan reached down and touched the plush multi-colored fur, with a ridge of bone beginning at its nose and ending at the base of its tail. "This here head's worth more than eight year's wages, if 'n I was the type to get a job. But Trader ain't never gonna go that high."

The jader's head was made from a precious stone, with tufts of hair randomly spread across the skull. "Ya sure got some nasty fangs pokin' every whicha way outta ya." Broan slipped a large knife out of its sheath. He grabbed the animal by its horizontal fangs and put the knife to its throat.

"Ain't this a hoot," Broan smiled, "the jaders is usually the one doing the killing. Looks like I'm on top this time." A growl told him this animal wasn't as dead as he'd thought.

"Just hurry and carve up that smelly booger's carcass, so's we can sell that head," Murph barked, "the prices for them jader heads changes by the hour."

Suddenly, an unnatural "squee" broke the lull, followed by "bam, bam, bam" as the struggle to escape the metal container ensued. A voice, "AHHH," as if being torn apart one bite at a time, joined the fray.

Then, silence.

"Broan? You dead yet?" Jence yelled and then chuckled.

Four mutilated fingers appeared, grasping the top edge of the metal container. A forearm smeared with lime-green blood followed, holding the large jewel. Random tufts of hair pushed through the blood that coated the stone.

"Broan?" Murph asked. "Broan, is that you?"

A scarred face, nearly devoid of hair and missing most of its right ear, popped up from inside the dumpster. "Ya better hope it's me, cause if it ain't, you boys are headed fer a world 'o' hurt." Broan tossed the jader's skull to Murph. "Check it out and make sure ya tell me it worth it."

Murph, busy wiping the clotting green slime from the jewel, neared completing his task by the time Broan joined him. *It was definitely worth it*, Murph thought.

"Well, what we got?" Broan asked, coughing up a ball of phlegm.

"Not bad," Murph said. "Looks like top-notch stuff." Murph glanced at Jence for a moment and then toward Broan. "You look like you've been chewed up and spit out."

"Good to know," Broan said, "cause that's just about how I feel."

"Also, good to know," Murph replied. "Kinda makes things easier."

"What ya talkin' 'bout?" Broan asked.

Jence walked up and placed his chin on the man's shoulder. Broan jerked, and his eyebrows shot upward. "Nothin' personal, just a simple matter 'o' numbers," Jence said, withdrawing the eight-inch knife from Broan's gut.

"Why?" Broan gurgled.

Murph held the jewel at eye level in front of Broan. "Divide it three ways or divide it two ways. Like Jence said, nothin' personal, just a simple matter 'o' numbers. And by the by, even though this is a moot point it bears sayin' . . . I told you to quit hackin' up them hunks of snot, cuz I gotta tell ya, it's disgusting."

Broan slowly slid to the ground, landing on his back like a large, bloody rag doll.

"That dirty stiff done and ruint my duds," Jence said, inspecting the blood stripe on his front shirt. "I'll teach him to bloody up my clothes. He drew back his leg—

"You move that leg forward," Murph warned, "and I won't have anyone to split this jewel with."

"Look what he done to me," Jence said.

"Look what you done to him!" *Maybe I had the wrong one killed.*

****

Two bare feet were dragged through the alley under another's locomotion. A dull thud ensued, followed by heavy breathing. "Thanks for all the help," Jence said sarcastically. "I don't believe I coulda done it without ya."

"You killed him. You haul him," Murph said.

"Am I gonna get any help heavin' this dead weight into the metal container?"

Murph shook his head. "If you drop him more than once while you're trying to push him over the edge, I'll consider it. Ain't like you're gonna hurt him if he hits the ground a couple times."

"You're all heart," Jence said, standing over Broan's corpse. "Well, here goes nothin'." Jence lifted Broan into a sitting position, then tossed the dead man's right arm over his shoulder.

Murph smiled and chuckled to himself. "Don't forget to lift with yer legs."

"Don't forget to lift with yer legs," Jence mumbled. "I'll show him how to lift." Wrapping his arms underneath Broan's armpits, he managed to heft the body onto his shoulder. Pressing the lifeless man's butt against the metal container, Jence pushed to hold the corpse in place.

"Ya know," Murph said, "I might just keep ya around. If fer nothin' else, the entertainment's priceless."

Jence fumed. An increased flow of adrenaline allowed him to hoist the body into the dumpster. Then, he placed his hands on his knees and gasped for air.

"Not bad," Murph said. "Maybe you're not as useless as I thought."

An unearthly cry resonated from Jence.

"Enough whining," Murph said, tossing the jewel into the air. "C'mon. Let's get a move on."

As Murph drove his knee into the wailing man's ribs, a knife began its journey upward, the tip protruding just right of the spinal column. Jence pushed the blade, slicing through ribs, organs, and the clavicle before exiting the body.

Standing over Murph, Jence watched his victim's eyes blink until they remained in the open position. Reaching down, he pulled the jader's skull from the lifeless hand. "If ya need any help gettin' into that smelly container, I'll give it some thought. Just remember—it won't hurt if ya fall a couple times."

He lifted his prize until it was backlit by the waning sun. A red aura emanated from the jewel, and then, like dusty red smoke, it entered the man through the only windows available—his eyes. With each passing moment, Jences' eyes bubbled a dark crimson, accepting all until the jewel and Jence were no more. Instead, a new creature was born, the likes of which this world could not imagine.

A chilling, beastly howl resonated through the desolate night, piercing the silence as the creature broke free from the confines of the city.

****

Purple eyes with a red iris reflected out of the darkness. They blinked several times, tilted to the right and then left.

"Mighty strange," a voice sounding like Broan said.

"I'll have to be agreein' with ya," a voice that sounded remarkably like Murph replied, followed by an identical pair of eyes opening beside the first.

"How'd we end up here?" Broan asked, "Wherever here is." The first pair of eyes to arrive glanced in numerous directions, then stopped, realizing the futility of its actions.

"Can't see a thing, can ya?" Murph said, "Least wise nothing but dark and a pair of weird looking eyes."

"That's about it," Broan replied, "ceptin we ain't the only two here."

"Not bad for a dummy," an old woman's voice cackled, "but that'll be jest fine, cuz Ima gonna learn ya." A long, vaporous black cloud arose, absorbing Broan and Murph, compressing their essence into a tight ball, then blotted any remaining luminescence from sight.

"Ha, Ha, Ha." Mama Byrnes' cackle faded into the night.

CHAPTER SIX

Gabriel

The young man trudged through waist-deep snow, each effort advancing him only a few inches. The biting cold tempted Gabriel to return to Mama Byrne's for his father's coat and hat. However, that possibility was no longer viable as he was hopelessly lost.

He tightened his tattered shirt collar, attempting to fend off winds laden with a swirling mass of ice crystals. His chest tightened with each frozen breath. Gasping, a dark shape appeared through the haze—a line of immense trees that provided shelter from the storm.

Weakened from the cold, Gabriel pulled his way to the timberline, where travel was relatively easy for several hours. Then, the terrain changed from rocky soil to larger stones that stretched up hillsides, holding the air of mountains soon to come. The trees thinned, and within moments, the storm's fury returned.

Gabriel struggled through the deep snow. Exhaustion and cold seeped into every muscle. He again berated himself for not taking any provisions or warmer clothing. Yes, he was free, but at what cost? To freeze to death?

She was a witch of the worst kind, but at least I had a warm place to stay and food to eat, though it was barely tolerable.

His breath labored, his feet frozen. *I may just as well lie down and let the storm cover me.*

As the sky began to dim, the boy took several more shaky steps until collapsing onto the snow. He attempted to rise.

No more left . . .

Gabriel looked upward at swirls of snow drifting down from a violet sky. He reached back to his early years, before Mama Byrnes. His family around the dinner table, and the blessing of giving thanks.

"Thanks." he snorted. "If you're all-knowing and all seeing, why did you let me endure ten years of hell?" Torrents of tears froze on his face. He shook his fist toward the blizzard. "And why did you let my family die at the hands of someone like Mama Byrnes? You know she made their last moments as painful." Their screams echoed in his mind.

"Why didn't you let me die too?" The howling wind blew stronger, and Gabriel slammed his fists onto the packed snow. "Got nothing to say, huh? I always figured if you did exist, that you would practice kindness and take care of the ones you supposedly created. Guess that isn't the case. I suppose you just don't exist — at least not to me. So now, you're free to help somebody else. Go on! Get out of here! I don't have any use for you."

The boy crumpled onto the snow, letting the storm take him.

****

Gabriel felt like he was floating. The storm had passed, and through blurred vision, stars sprinkled the sky.

"Hold on, young man," a voice said. "A fire to warm, food to fill the stomach, and nourishment for the soul awaits."

Gabriel turned his head toward his savior. Unable to produce an articulate sound, he nodded. When Gabriel felt a warm hand touch his forehead, a living entity entered through this touch and settled deep within the boy, awaiting a time to come forth.

CHAPTER SEVEN

Dalon Con and Gabriel

Gabriel awoke next to a crackling fire and the enticing aroma of cooking meat. The stone fortress surrounding him was small but adequate. In fact, had it been any larger, its comfort would have been lost.

"Awake, I see," an older man said, "and due to the condition in which I found you, also famished, I imagine."

Gabriel bolted upright, looking for the doorway and escape.

"No need for worry; I was sent for you."

"S-Sent?" Gabriel's heart pounded in his chest. Did he just leave one hell for another?

"Calm, young one. I am here to help you. All will be revealed in good time." The old man set to tending the fire and the animal carcass hanging above. Gravity and heat worked together to extract moisture from the cabot, while droplets of fat sizzled into the fire, releasing an enticing culinary aroma.

The old man's eyes twinkled. "Take heed. This is but an appetizer for the meal yet to come."

****

Despite being a stranger, the man had a calming aura, which Gabriel welcomed. It nourished him as much as the meal he devoured. Remaining cautious, his unease gradually subsided, giving way to curiosity.

"Great place to weather the storm. How did you find it?" Gabriel said between bites of cabot.

"Not find," Dalon Con replied, "constructed."

Gabriel tossed the last bone into the fire and then sucked his fingers to remove every trace of flavor possible, glancing at the man who appeared to be seated in an oversized stone chair.

"Take care in your zeal not to injure yourself," Dalon Con said, smiling as the young man stared back, puzzled. Then, a wide grin of understanding spread across Gabriel's face.

"You built this?" Gabriel glanced at the blending of stone and organic material. The boulders alone had to weigh several tons.

"The basic shape was already in place, formed by the large boulders you see spread throughout the walls. I cut and placed the smaller stones to fill in and bring each wall up to the same height."

"And how did you construct the ceiling?"

A wide grin spread across Dalon Con's face. "The solution is not as difficult as it first appears. I spanned from wall to wall a series of heavy, living vines, shearing them long enough to plant into the ground on either side of the structure, once they crossed overhead. I repeated this, forming a hatch work pattern completing the roof for now."

"I don't understand," Gabriel said, "I look up, and your description is nothing like what I see."

"As I said, 'completing the roof for now' meant laying the groundwork, and leaving the structure for a single growing season. This would allow the vines to take root, forming a fortified structure to hold the final roofing components.

"The vines took root, stretched tight and filled in each square with a system of foliage. It was then a simple matter to cover the roof with broad leaves, several inches of soil and multiple layers of flat stone."

"Wouldn't that cause the ceiling to cave in?"

"Each layer, once reaching maturity and pressing against other strata would strengthen, allowing it to stand alone. In turn, each level would reinforce the one it touched, bringing the whole to a formidable structure able to withstand great weight."

"I can see your large supply of firewood, and the fire that keeps this enclosure warm, but how do you rid this area of the smoke, it most certainly produces?"

"The large stone stretching from floor to ceiling has been hewn into the wall. The firebox at the bottom holds the fuel for the flames while the remainder of the structure is hollow. This along with the draft provided by this room ushers the offending air to the outside."

Dalon Con removed a twig from the fire, touching the ember to the bowl of his pipe, and drew until its contents glowed, sending an inviting aura of lavender throughout the living area.

He signaled for Gabriel to sit on the boulder to his right. Much to his delight, Gabriel discovered that the stone provided unexpected comfort, offering him relaxation he seldom experienced.

"Why would one so young be out in a storm such as this, alone?"

The idea of kindness was foreign to Gabriel, but he wasn't ready to share his past. He found himself staring at the composite floor.

"Your silence is understandable," Dalon Con said. "Yet, your behavior leads me to believe you are running from someone, something, or perhaps, a situation involving both."

Gabriel's eyes connected with the old man's. "I want to thank you for saving me." He paused, gathering his words, making sure they sounded believable. "The food was especially good, not what I'm used to. I was with my family and got lost when the storm turned."

"I would think it perilous to be out in such a squall in the first place."

The boy shrugged, staring at the fire, his brain inundated with excuses from the viable to the outlandish. "We were waiting for our wagon to be repaired . . . ohh," he moaned. *I would have to pick that.*

"Strange that your father would choose this time of year to plan such an extensive move," Dalon Con said, "and wagons are not a preferred mode of travel with heavy snowfall."

"Daddy said we had to leave and fast." Gabriel paused, tears creating pathways through the dirt layer on his cheeks.

Dalon Con spoke. "I can't help unless you tell me the truth."

Gabriel nodded. Wracked with sobs, the boy pressed his face into the old man's fur cloak. For the first time in ten years, he could be a child.

****

Dalon Con handed the boy a drink of water. "Feel better?"

Gabriel nodded, his eyes swollen but his heart lighter from the torrent of pain he'd held onto for so many years.

"You slept several hours, assumably still exhausted from your ordeal. However, your sleep was uneasy. The release burdens is crucial, and you have many for one so young. I can help you, but you must be transparent, truthful."

"I have been."

Dalon Con leaned back, his face calm. "I believe your declaration that you were lost in a storm. That is true. Yet, that happened many years ago, did it not?" Dalon Con said. "Ten years, to be exact, as you are now sixteen."

"H-How could you possibly know that?" Gabriel stammered.

"As is my knowledge of you. My eyes see you are about sixteen years and you are troubled. But, it is not I, but He who shares with me. A true vessel can only be filled by the winemaker."

Gabriel frowned as a low-pitched whistle emanated from another room.

"I will return shortly."

The boy watched the old man disappear into an adjoining room. He continued to watch the dark entryway for several moments. Gabriel now realized that the dwelling was more than just a stone cave with a comfortable living area and several rooms. *It would take more than a year to construct. Who was this man?*

Dalon Con re-entered the room carrying two large mugs, handing one to Gabriel. "This is not merely a drink," the old man said, "but an entire meal you are about to ingest. Drink slowly and take small sips, until you are used to its effects."

It's like things appear when needed, Gabriel thought as Dalon Con sat.

"Please," the old man said, "drink."

The boy lifted the mug to his lips, inhaling the inviting aroma. He sipped. Then he froze, his eyebrows furrowed in thought. It was more than taste. Something tugged at a memory, lost, almost forgotten. "It reminds me…" the boy inhaled again, and a smile started to grow. "It smells like home."

Gabriel never thought of Mama Byrnes' hovel as home. This was a deep memory, of family and love—a memory that brought tears of longing.

An inner voice urged him to drink, and Gabriel complied. Taking another small sip, he let the liquid linger in his mouth before swallowing. Once again, he heeded the direction of an inner voice, and his mouth filled with the tastiest tender meat he had ever encountered. He never imagined food as anything but a life-giving necessity, not a soulful experience.

"I'm happy to see you are enjoying my humble offering." Dalon Con sipped his meal and then proclaimed, "Though they are few and far between, amenities are a worthwhile indulgence."

Humble? Gabriel thought this was a feast for kings, having just swallowed something akin to a potato. Then he paused, asking. "What is 'menities? If it's got anything to do with what I'm drinking," he raised his head and wiped the flow of broth, which had migrated to his chin, "then I like menities."

Dalon Con reached out and rubbed the young man's head. "Yes," the old man said, "menities *are* very likable."

****

Gabriel sighed. "Don't believe I could eat another bite, or, should it be, drink another bite?"

Dalon Con chuckled. "Either one is acceptable; however, there are important issues that require our attention."

Even though a smartly dressed thirty-year-old sat upon Dalon Con's chair, Gabriel saw through this guise into the eyes of a wise old man, his previous thoughts of distrust fading into oblivion.

Dalon Con inhaled, and then turned his pipe upside down and tapped the bowl, emptying its contents into a round stone container. "Let's resume your tale before our intake of nourishment."

Gabriel sank. "What do you mean? I told you all I remember."

"Please, repeat your tale," Dalon Con said, leaning slightly toward the young one. "This time, employ the truth."

The boy deflated further, lowering his head in shame. "I couldn't bear to tell you the awful thing I did."

Dalon Con knelt beside Gabriel, placing his hand on the young man's back. "Confessing one's shortcomings is good for the soul, and I am one who delegates his essence to listening."

"I was lost during a storm while traveling with my momma and daddy. But that's where the truth ends." He raised his head and began to talk with greater fervor. "I wandered off. I suppose I could blame it on being young, but I knew better. I made my way through the storm until I found a rundown house." He began to shake his head. "I thought I was saved; boy was I wrong. I'd have been better off passing the house and trudging on deeper into the storm."

"What could have brought you to such a decision?" Dalon Con asked. "With the ferocity of storms, such as is roaring outside this very moment, why would you deny yourself shelter over certain death?"

Gabriel sighed. "Sometimes I think death would've been better than living with that witch for the past ten years."

Dalon Con's eyes welled. "Please explain. Your comment disturbs me greatly."

"Her name was Mama Byrnes," Gabriel said, a storm beginning to grow inside this tortured boy.

"Calm yourself, young one," Dalon Con said. "Even though what you have endured I can only imagine, you must remember what is done is done. It cannot be changed; however, through the grace of the Great One, your past will become exactly that— your past."

Gabriel looked at the old man and smiled.

"I see His work is already beginning within your tormented soul. I want to hear everything you can recall over the past ten years," Dalon Con said, "and leave out nothing."

CHAPTER EIGHT

Jack

"'It was the best of times, it was the worst of times, it was the age of wisdom, it was the age of foolishness.'" Jack slammed the hard-covered novel shut. *Yeah, right—somebody is a fool if they think I'm gonna read that mess. Sorry, Mr. Dickens, but about as close as I'm gonna get to one of your books is something they used to have around called a TV show with that Scrooge dude.* He shook his head, releasing a blast of air. *If they are determined to pilfer books and technology from other worlds, would it be so bad to lift something that a small percentage of the population would read?* Jack stood, opened his closet door, and reached under a stack of blankets. Removing a high-tech experimental skateboard found in the ruins of a city due east, he beamed. *There's my baby.* He ran his hand down the ultra-thin sillian fiber base. *Black as night, fast as lightning, and wheels so thin they're nearly invisible.* He folded the wheels flat and slid the board along the edge of his belt, positioning it against his right rear pant leg. As he pulled the door closed and bounded down the steps, a familiar voice rang out as he headed for the front door, stopping him in his tracks.

"Where ya headed, son?"

Jack leaned his forehead against the door. *Five more seconds, just five more seconds, and I would've been on the other side.* Jack sighed. "Nowhere in particular, Dad; just out." He held his breath.

"Don't be long, it'll be dark soon."

"I won't," Jack called out, racing down the sidewalk before the door closed.

****

"Get off the ground," Dub said, pushing against the asphalt to gain more speed on his conventional skateboard. He drew his leg back and, on his second trip around, rammed his steel-capped boot into Rave's side, attempting to drive ribs into the boy's lungs.

"Aargh," Rave groaned, emptying the contents of his stomach.

"Comin' 'round again," Dub warned. "I wanna see if you got anything left in that gut of yours."

"Aaah," was all Rave could muster.

"Still comin'," Dub repeated. "I don't want you to be surprised when I blast your gut wide open." Using his leg for thrust, Dub increased his speed. Just before making contact with his victim, Rave rolled, grasping the offending boot, and began to twist. Ankle tendons and ligaments gave way, leaving nothing but twisted flesh.

"Whatcha think now, you sadistic slug?" Rave gurgled through a steady flow of blood.

The attacker-turned-victim did a double twist as Rave held tight to the boot, causing Dub to do a face plant and then roll onto his back. Rave ensured his accomplice would never walk again, to the point that when Dub's boot was removed, his foot flopped unnaturally to one side—not that it mattered to Rave.

Rave struggled to stand. Raising his boot above the semi-conscious teenager, he slammed it down, reducing Dub's IQ. Then Rave collapsed, dead before hitting the ground.

* * * *

Rave opened his eyes to darkness. Moments later, a second pair joined him.

"Dub, is that you?" Rave asked. Attempting to touch his side, wanting to feel the extent of damage, Rave found he had no hands.

"I think so," came Dub's disembodied voice. "Where am I?"

A low cackle echoed in the void. “Don’t worry ‘bout things that ain’t your business no how. Jest hush and keep it thata way,” the voice of Mama Byrnes boomed. The essence of Murph, Broan, and Byrnes engulfed Rave and Dub, all five destined for completion at a later time.

****

Jack continued rolling down the sidewalk, anxious to meet his cohorts at the old gasworks parking lot. Pulling onto the asphalt, he saw someone lying on the ground and another lying several feet away. Jack lived in the small township of Thayron, ten miles north of Defeated. It had not yet degraded to the depth of its neighbor but, within several years, would sink to an equal level. At one time, Thayron was a suburb of Defeated and carried the same name. This ended when intentionally placed explosives created two settlements, destroying ten miles of structures and permanently separating Defeated and Thayron.

Nearing the lot’s end, the scene quickly turned bizarre. Dub lay on the ground with a halo of blood about his head. Rave lay an arm’s length away, the massive amount of blood flowing from his mouth just beginning to clot.

****

Jack tentatively approached the scene and paused, swallowing hard to keep his last meal down. He cautiously moved toward the body of Dub and knelt. “His skull,” were the only words Jack could muster. Crawling over to Rave, he lingered but a moment. Without a word, he stood and began backing away. Then, Jack mounted his board and fled from what he perceived as a double homicide.

****

Jack slammed his bedroom door and started to ransack his room; why, he didn’t know. Just finding two dead friends, he should tell someone, but who? There was no one left in authority. Death and bodies were commonplace in Thayron, but he'd never lost friends, not like Dub and Rave. He stopped and furrowed his eyebrows. "What *am* I looking for?" He stood for several moments, not moving. *This world is collapsing around me . . . closing in . . . death is the only way out, but into what?* Jack's truly rational fears, building in an irrational world, began to tear his consciousness to shreds. Then, a small white light grew from out of the dark recesses of his mind—a light he could not see but knew was there. As it grew, it brought along with it a 'something.' When the light faded, the 'something' remained. Jack squinted his eyes, trying to identify what was taking place.

Jack shook his head, then raised his arms defensively. "AHH," Jack screamed, falling across his bed, then onto the floor, rolling and holding his head. "Stop…please, stop!" The 'something' pushed its way from Jack's subconscious into his conscious thought process. Jack sat up, leaning against his bed. The pain was gone. The 'something' was finally clear. "Nexus," Jack whispered. Standing, he began changing his clothes and gathering a few essential items. Stashing them into his backpack, he left. When Jack reached the bottom of the front steps, he paused and glanced back, unsure if he would ever see home again.

****

Moving quickly down the center of the street, Jack found himself purposely in Defeated, his skateboard easily navigating the pockmarked surface. Traversing the usual crowd of degenerates wandering the streets, he kept his eyes wide open for any opportunity to exploit the weak. Jack could see a small group gathering just ahead. Nearing the crowd, he slowed and swerved to avoid the group. Just as he passed, two of the men lunged in his direction. *Not this time.* Jack maneuvered his board just out of reach of the first assailant. This caused the second would-be thief to trip over the first, resulting in a pileup. Preoccupied with the comical scene he'd just witnessed, Jack failed to see the third goon lunge and take him to the ground.

"Aww," the man said, "looks like the little feller took a tumble offin' his board." He walked toward Jack. "Hey there, little feller, the name's Merk." He raised one hand to his mouth and took a long drag from his cigarette, flicking the butt away. Merk drew in a deep breath and commenced to cough, depositing several green lung cookies on the ground.

Jack slowly rose, gathered his composure, and retrieved his skateboard during Merk's coughing fit. He glanced at the man, then at the gelatinous deposits on the ground. "Nice work. Get out much?"

Standing with his hands on his hips, Merk wore a silver-colored necklace with permanent green runs staining his chest. Wiping his mouth with the back of his hand, he reached into a pocket cut into his abdominal skin. "I made it maself, along with three more jest like it. When ya ain't got nothin' more than a single pair of tighty-whities, ya gotta have somewhere to put stuff." Removing a long stiletto from the organic pouch, he smiled, revealing a mouthful of yellow and black teeth. "Ya got a messa killin' comin', boy." Pushing a button, a blade the size of a small machete extended from the end of the case.

Jack was terrified but determined not to let it show. "Nice stick," he said. "Whatcha reckon you're gonna do with it?"

Merk growled. "Stand still, ya little snot and I'll show ya."

"Oh, so you want me to stand still," Jack said. "I hope you brought a lunch, fat boy, cuz you're gonna need it after a couple hours of chasing me."

Lunging for the boy, Merk sliced the air in front of Jack. Missing his target, he fell hard on his face, losing his breath in a massive diaphragm collapse. His next loss occurred seconds later as his stiletto-on-steroids left his hand.

Commandeering Merk's weapon, Jack moved slowly around the inner circle of degenerates that formed, waving the stiletto above his head. The human blockade started to disassemble, allowing Jack to escape without injury.

CHAPTER NINE

Hayden

A pulsing, orange light appeared following a barely audible "crack," echoing throughout the cave. Because of its diminutive scope, visibility and audio were virtually impossible. The anomaly grew in size and volume until its diameter reached twelve inches. The orange light spiderwebbed out, contained by a shadowy rectangular doorway. A blue orifice opened in the center of the brightly colored light, and seconds later, a tiny being appeared in the breach, pushing through the doorway. A thunderous clap resounded as the orange anomaly collapsed.

"What a ride!" Hayden exclaimed. Pushing an index finger into each ear, he attempted to scratch the temporal itch while opening his mouth and moving his bottom jaw from side to side. After several minutes, he abandoned this technique, electing to bend over, place a hand on each knee, and let the annoying tickle run its course. Once the irritation subsided, he retrieved the remote communication device from his backpack and pushed the button, signaling to Wakke his safe arrival. The response was instantaneous but came across as a garbled message. Straining to hear Wakke's future voice, the static faded to silence. Then, a dizzying moment of panic racked Hayden as he grasped the possible consequences of participating in this world.

He witnessed the presence of an entity, visible in a beam of light amidst the surrounding darkness, harboring no ill intent toward him. One glance told Hayden this One's kingdom would never end. This vision lasted less than a millisecond but left Hayden with an undeniable peace.

Hayden pulled himself together, concentrating on the task at hand. *There was no way to precisely gauge the amount of time I traveled into the past. The portal was set as closely as possible to the precise year. I just hope we were close enough.* He tossed the device into the bag, slipped his arms through the straps, and secured the clasps. Hayden walked toward the cave entrance. He stopped and took several turns, scrutinizing the cave's configuration.

Continuing his trek toward the entrance, several hours passed, and he was no closer to the opening. He quickened his pace, then suddenly stopped. *After eighteen years of living and working in a natural stone structure, you'd think I'd remember. . . It took us months to reach this spot in my time.* He could hear Wakke's light reprimand, "Propel in, propel out." Shaking his head, a feeling of loneliness overwhelmed him as he began strapping on the propulsion device. Hayden sighed. *I do hope all is well with my comrades.* Embodying a new sense of resolve, he rose several feet off the ground and flew toward the cave opening.

****

The area is different from what I remember before leaving.

I am grateful to Wakke and the fabricators for this apparatus, which allows me to move at a great rate and soar with the flying creatures. Traveling well above the trees, Hayden noticed the foliage was beginning to thin. The forest ended abruptly, giving way to brick structures laid out in a grid pattern. *At last, there are buildings made by human hands.* He knew this to be true, for the numerous bipeds were milling throughout the city streets. *This single factor indicates the need for a closer look.*

He descended, heading for the cobblestone road and landing near the corner of two adjoining buildings amidst a multi-tiered flowering display where two people were conversing.

"Any thoughts on where to have lunch?" a well-dressed gentleman asked.

"It's up to you," his female companion replied.

There is no degradation of society at this point, at least no more than would be expected in a law-abiding town with a moral code. Hayden took a seat, making himself comfortable among the greenery. Observing the town folk for several hours, he rose and stretched.*I should delve a bit deeper into the personal lives of a few select individuals.* He pursed his lips and wrinkled his forehead. *As much as I hate invading someone's privacy, I can see no other way to confirm their true intent. So often, people are not as they appear.* Hayden traded his terracotta fortress for a spot hovering above the streets, looking for a likely candidate.

****

Hayden postured, diving toward the ground, pulling up inches from his target. He hovered to make a soft landing, touching down on a flowered hat. Hayden was grateful to Wakke for the neutrally-colored clothes, knowing they would help him blend into most situations.

"And here we are," the man said, leaning over and kissing his female companion.

He reached into his pocket, removing a ring of oddly shaped brass objects. All were octagonally fashioned on one end and flat with a straight protrusion extending from each octagon. A lengthwise groove was cut on either side of the extension. Jagged cutouts had been made along one edge of the protrusions that left what appeared to be triangular-shaped teeth.

"David, not in public," she said, smacking him playfully.

"You're behind the times, my dear Susan," David said, pushing one of the octagonal protrusions into a slot that fit the grooves perfectly. Making a half turn with what was actually a key, David began a process by rotating a round object that held the slot and octagon. The door opened, and the two and a tiny stowaway entered the residence.

Hayden observed the young married couple go through what had become (unbeknownst to David and Susan) a nightly ritual, settled into a concealed vantage point, able to see and listen.

"How was your day, dear?" Susan would ask. This would initiate a response from David detailing his interactions and events of the day. David would then ask Susan the same question while opening a bottle of wine. Susan would respond. After an hour or so passed, she would begin dinner while David relaxed. Following dinner, the couple bathed and prepared for bed.

Nothing unusual here. They have water and means for cleaning and relieving themselves and electricity for lights, cooking, and environmental controls within their domicile. Hayden hovered, stroking his chin. *All things look proper, yet something is amiss. A presence? . . . no, I believe it to be an object, one that does not belong.* He began a slow turn. *The thing I seek exudes familiarity.* Hayden continued his methodical exploration. *Fortunately, it bears no malice.* He was about to close the circle, having traversed the 360°, then paused for a moment. *It cannot be.* Hayden moved across the room, hovering in front of a gold-colored disc about the size of his head and the thickness twice that of a fingernail, with handholds cut laterally across from one another.

"A Dalleon cell," Hayden whispered, "but how?" He placed each of his hands in the corresponding slots. What he expected to be a simple lift would not budge. *I do not understand; these cells are incredibly lightweight.*

Hayden tried to move the gold-colored disc again, calling upon all his strength, with the same results. Intensifying his grip, he used his propulsion system to move the disc. As the thrust increased, his fingers uncurled, and his hands pulled away from the Dalleon cell. *Whoever put the disc here placed it in stasis. It cannot be moved until the selected time.*

To most, *stasis* was a scientifically advanced process. The planet's core was utilized in chorus with the gravitational pull of the solar system's sun. With the addition of centrifugal force created by the planet's rotation, these three critical energies could stabilize an object. In essence, the planet would then rotate around the object.

To a select few of the surviving ancients, *stasis* was a state of mind surrounding the three critical energies and the object, achieving identical results on a biological plane.

Thinking through the entire scenario, Hayden reached a conclusion. *I must let the couple know, for their own safety, without causing undue alarm . . . but how?* Hayden pondered this conundrum while moving into David and Susan's bedroom. Circumnavigating the couple, David lay on his back and Susan on her right side. Hayden put down, ever so lightly, at the entrance to Susan's left ear. With her head propped up on a pillow, he began walking into her ear canal, bracing himself by grasping the cilia. Hayden spoke softly, conveying what he deemed the most helpful information to Susan. Hopeful that he was placing this entirely into her subconscious, he finished, moving toward then ultimately into David. After completing his self-appointed task, he left the residence through a gap under the front door.

****

"Did you sleep well last night?" Susan said.

"It's funny you asked," David said. "Something seems a little off, and I don't know anyone named Hayden."

"Curious," she agreed, "that name keeps running through my head, also."

He took a sip of coffee. "If there's anything to it, I guess it will come back to us." Susan raised her eyebrows, nodded, and continued to eat her breakfast.

CHAPTER TEN

Dalon Con and Gabriel

Dalon Con watched Gabriel with compassion as the youth began his story.

"I was separated from Momma and Daddy in a raging storm just like the one when you found me. The snow was just beginning to fall, so Daddy and I were walking beside the wagon." Gabriel straightens and then dips, swinging both arms to the left, one atop the other, palms out. "Swish," as he brings them back to the right, demonstrating to Dalon Con the blast of frigid air that separated father and son in a total whiteout.

At first, I thought it was by accident, but the old bat told me she used my family to get to me."

"Why?" Dalon Con responded.

"My momma, daddy, and brother were too old to train into slaves; at least, that's what Mama Byrnes said. She kept me because I'd be easy to train and no good to anybody else. When I asked her what happened to my family, she said, "Them varmints tweren't no better 'n you, so I told 'em I ain't seen no young'uns and sent 'em on their way." Gabriel paused to collect his thoughts. "I found out a couple years later when I started building my hiding spot that she was lying when she told me she'd sent my family away."

"I found Momma's jewelry, along with Daddy's hat and clothes, spread out on top of a pile of bones in the attic." He continued to stare at Dalon Con while clenching and unclenching his fists. "There were three skulls on top of the pile. I knew then my family was gone, and it was up to me to make things right."

Dalon Con refused to allow his true feelings to surface. "Did you?"

Gabriel slowly shook his head. “I faced Mama Byrnes and asked her about my find.” She brought a fist across my face, and down I went. Each time I came to, she would crawl on top of me, pull my head up by the hair, and beat me until everything went black. How long this went on, I don’t know. I woke up and covered my face, expecting her fists to put me back to sleep. When the beating didn’t come, I could only see an empty room through swollen eyes. I tried to roll to my side and work my way onto my knees, but I fell on my back, and the darkness took over.”

“Gabriel, did this have any effect on your decision to ‘make things right’?” Dalon Con asked.

Gabriel nodded. “It shames me to say so, but I was afraid she’d kill me if I brought it up again.”

Dalon Con placed his hand on Gabriel’s shoulder. “Tell me what happened next.”

“It’s not real clear. I remember waking up, but I’m not sure. At least not ‘til I saw food and water when I opened my eyes. I was so hungry and thirsty I threw myself on top of my first meal since who knows when. Shortly after I finished, my head began to pound and my swollen eyes started to water, and then closed, I guess because of my recent intake of water. After a while, I became able to stay awake longer, and my eyes finally got to where I could see clearly. Not long after I started feeling better, Mama Byrnes came back.”

“You say she came back. Was she different in any way?”

“I’ll say, the beatings slowed, but she kept them in her arsenal, prompting me to be afraid of doing or saying anything against her.”

“Anything else?” Dalon Con asked.

Gabriel began gnawing on his fingernails. Suddenly, he stopped and stared at Dalon Con. “She was starting to lose me. That’s why she tried to get back the power she held over my life with her last attack.”

Dalon Con smiled. “Your ability to overcome the hardships in your life is inspiring and, no doubt, guided by the Great One.”

Gabriel's expression turned to one of peace. "Now follow me to a place you have never known or even heard mentioned," Dalon Con said. "And remember, the Great One is with you always."

****

"We've been walking for hours," Gabriel said. "Things are starting to change."

"We are nearing the dregs of society as it exists on this planet," explained Dalon Con. "I say this because the inhabitants have plunged to a new depth, far below what could be called depravity."

The pair walked on in silence until Gabriel ended the quiet. "What's that smell?"

"That is our destination, young one, It is what is left of the city, Defeated."

"Defeated," Gabriel echoed, "that's just about as depressing as a name can get."

Dalon Con nodded. "You will find this city to be much worse." He made for an open doorway and signaled Gabriel to join him. Stepping into the building was like walking into a dark past.

"The air here is so thick," Gabriel said, "I'd almost swear it needs to be cut into pieces before I can breathe."

"It is the evil residing here that makes the very air oppressive. Stay close to me." Gabriel nodded and placed a hand on his friend's fur-covered cloak. The pair wove their way around tables where patrons sat eating and drinking.

"I find it hard to believe that anyone could eat something that releases an odor like I smell," Gabriel said, "On top of that, they're mumbling and pointing, and I'm pretty sure it concerns us."

"You are correct. Above all, I hope that each one in this place will recognize danger and shy away."

"Who be you, one with the fancy Dan suit," a fat man taunted, "and the one who travels with ya?"

"I am Dalon Con and this is my companion, Gabriel. We wish for no trouble and would greatly appreciate the answer to several questions."

"Well, Dalon Con and companion Gabriel, ain't nobody here gonna be answerin' nothin', and I do believe ya jest might wish ya hadn't wandered up into this here place, cuz I got me a feelin' that gettin' in here ain't yer problem." The big man began to laugh and then stopped. "Yer problem's gonna be gettin' outta here." A dozen men stood.

"Gentlemen, I have expressed my desire to avoid trouble at any cost," Dalon Con said. "May I count on your participation in this endeavor?" The street filled with hysterical laughter.

"I do believe that thar be yer answer," the big man replied, "and jest so's you and yurn understands the answer . . . it be 'no'."

CHAPTER ELEVEN

Jence

Jence returned to his original image. Every time this malevolent transformation would occur, his appearance changed slightly. He began to look around, surprised at seeing Murph's split corpse lying between his legs and an underlying recollection of having thrown Broan into the trash receptacle. "See you guys later," Jence said. "Sorry you couldn't join me."

Jence made his way out of the cobblestone alley. He paused and glanced from structure to structure. "Hmm, I never thought about the buildings that way before." He turned right at a rusty, old street sign labeled 'Hackenshire'; most of the sign face, now eaten away, simply said 'Hack.' Jence enjoyed his stroll down the cozy little thoroughfare, passing numerous open doorways with people milling about. Jence, smiling as he ambled by, waved his hand and then pushed it down into the pocket of his jeans. Even though atrocities were being committed everywhere he looked, Jence smiled and waved.

One man noticed Jence's calm demeanor amid the surrounding chaos. His sudden recognition released a domino effect of heads, and within seconds, a mob had surrounded the smiling stranger. "Ya gonna dance or whistle us a tune, fruitcake?" a fat man said. "'Cuz ya got us in the mood fer some entertainment."

"No need to get up in arms, friend," Jence said. "I'm just enjoying a nice walk through the city."

"Listen, and listen real good. I ain't yer friend, I ain't yer daddy, and I ain't yer mama. What I am gonna do—is rip yer head off."

The crowd had grown in size and tightened in a circle around the two, who were having a battle of words, knowing that only one would leave the arena alive.

"I told ya, friend—" Jence said, "I'm not looking for trouble."

The fat man stood there smoking a cigar, then knelt like a defensive guard, pulling his tank top above his urine-soaked boxer drawers. Like a horned Blanchard preparing for attack, the fat man carved several deep scratches. Talon-like toenails, protruding through his stockings, made contact with the ground before he spoke.

"You ain't been lookin', but you sure 'nough done a passel 'o' findin'." The fat man's claws dug into the ground, bearing down on the friendly bystander.

"You keep this up, and that name 'friend' is going away in a hurry," Jence said.

"Send er away," the fat man roared. Attempting to speak and run in tandem. "Don't make me no never mind anyhow." Jence easily sidestepped the big man for a second time. The cigar smoker made his third round and again set his sights on Jence.

"Three strikes...ya know what they say, fat boy," Jence said.

"Tell me all about it when ya see me," the big man said.

"I don't have that much —"

The two collided. The upper half of the big man disappeared.

"—time," said Jence. "There never seems to be enough of it." What remained of the fat man twitched, wobbled, and then fell forward with a dull thud and a whoosh of foul-smelling air pushed out of the empty cavity.

Jence nudged the body with his foot, pushed his hands back into his front pockets, and continued his stroll, this time whistling an unknown tune. His eyes had taken on a slightly orange hue, his skin a leathery texture, and his stature increased several inches. The circle parted, allowing the whistling stranger room to pass. *What could that jader want with me? I'm not the one who killed it, and I'm not about to assist the one who did.* A deadly presence began to engulf the inner portion of Jence that lingered. Realizing this manifestation led his mantra to spread. *Neither friend nor enemy will look to me for help.* The one called Jence would soon no longer remain.

****

Slag / Jence

Hack Street ended abruptly with wooded foliage pushing through the displaced cobblestones. The stitches in Jence's shirt popped as his body continued to enlarge. His midsection contorted as he bent toward the ground, becoming a four-legged creature. His face elongated into a canine-like snout with exaggerated top and bottom fangs. Both hands and feet twisted into freakish avian toes. Talons extended from each digit, pushing into the ground. The beast freed each, in turn, shaking off the dirt.

"No longer Jence," the creature growled. "Now Slag," he released with a mortal scream. The squall of man-turned-monster soon lost any human characteristics in the voice. The mutant bore a comical facade as it walked. One pant leg encircled a rear ankle, causing the former Jence to drag the entire pair of shredded pants behind him. His shirt clung to his neck, giving him the appearance of a drunk canine crawling home. But the crowning glory was his underwear still in place, elastic stretched to the point of bursting. This scene gave the animal an almost docile look until he turned and swiped his front appendage across a large ironwood tree, removing a twelve-inch-deep swath.

Slag gnawed his way into the hole, disturbing a six-foot cleft serpent. He maneuvered the writhing viper around in his mouth, attempting to swallow it whole. But the cleft snake had other ideas. It twisted its body around Slag's muzzle several times, sank its fangs into the mutant's head, and clamped his mouth shut. Slag clawed at the muscled constrictor around his snout. He wobbled, the venom beginning its trip through his nervous system. The cleft serpent tightened its embrace, causing the cartilage to crack and give way. Slag dug his claws into the serpentine organism in a frantic attempt to free himself. He ripped through steel-like strands of musculature, mortally wounding the serpent. Then, with one shake of the mutant's head, the dying snake fell to the ground.

Slag sniffed the carcass, pushing the cleft serpent to strike one last time. Slag wailed as the fangs penetrated the membrane under his tongue. With one snap of his jaw, he removed the cleft serpent's head, the amputated cranium still pumping venom into the soft tissue of Slag's mouth. He stumbled further into the foliage, his mouth producing enough foam and slobber to overflow down his chest, oozing onto the ground. Slag rose and shook his head violently until the serpent's head released and flew from his mouth. He began to stagger sideways, falling over the edge of a stone bridge into a shallow stream. His body acted as a dam until the water flowed over him, moving the fluids from his mouth downstream.

CHAPTER TWELVE

Dalon Con and Gabriel

Sixteen-year-old Gabriel, wearing oversized heavy cotton pants, leather boots, a cotton shirt, and a heavy coat, paused in the short foliage. Beside him stood Dalon Con, dressed in a suit and tie. This mismatched pair stepped onto one of the many streets leading into Defeated. As Dalon Con and Gabriel moved deeper into the city, another figure, just a single block over, left town.

"Why are we here?" Gabriel asked. He stepped closer to Dalon Con, experiencing a moment of fear.

"Even though your childhood was fraught with evil, I have brought you to this place for a reason."

"I don't understand."

"Humans have a great capacity for love and forgiveness when they abandon selfishness for selflessness. There is no end to the good they can attain when focused on the perfect example."

"But what is the reason you brought *me* here, and what is the perfect example?"

Dalon Con smiled. "The Great One, the further humans gravitate away from the Great One and his edicts, the farther they fall."

Gabriel's forehead furrowed. "Is that the lesson you want me to learn?"

"Indeed, you must guard with all diligence what you know to be good and true."

"I want to understand," Gabriel said, "because living with Mama Byrnes, I learned to incorporate hate in my treatment of others. I can remember a few good times with my parents, but just bits and pieces."

Gabriel rubbed his eyes. "And now you're showing me a whole new way to live."

Dalon Con stopped walking and turned to face Gabriel. "Explain to me why this bothers you so."

Gabriel looked into Dalon Con's eyes. "It's like I'm being pulled in too many directions at the same time." Gabriel hesitated, "But something inside is telling me that your words are true."

Dalon Con hugged the boy. "You are a very astute young man."

"I made a promise to myself that I would speak like my parents taught me and never butcher my language like that witch, Mama Byrnes," Gabriel said, then scratching his head, asked, "Who is this Great One you keep talking about?"

"I've been waiting for you to ask that very question." Dalon Con beamed as he moved off the road and sat on the ground. "Please, young one, take a seat so that we may converse."

In the fading light, the boy knelt to join his seated friend. Before his hand touched the ground, Gabriel was gone.

Dalon Con jumped to his feet. He spun in a circle, surveying his surroundings, then closed his eyes and retreated into his memory. He wasn't there long before his eyes popped open.

"Of course, there is another, and this one carries the Nexus." An image began to develop in Dalon Con's mind, the vision of the one most likely to have seized Gabriel. Yet, the path taken to conceal the boy was unclear.

"It will not be an easy task tracking the two I seek," Dalon Con said. "The aura of evil in this vile town is so thick it is difficult to reach beyond." After much deliberation, he decided on a direction. Before he could act, a notion of the one who carried the Nexus entered his mind. He stumbled as a wave of vertigo brought him to his knees.

"The Nexus and its owner are being hunted by Slag," he whispered, picking himself off the ground. "The Nexus will have to wait. My first priority is Gabriel."

****

Smort

"Defeated," Dalon Con said, "it lives up to its name and then some." He walked through the vile odor of human excrement intermingled with the stench of death, rotting meat, and mounds of garbage. Small streams of blended fluids flowed throughout the city, bubbling with a deadly cocktail of bacteria. "I am unable to sense a definitive location for the boy . . . in some way, speak to me Gabriel."

"Why'd ya want a Gabriel when ya could have a Smort," A large newcomer eyed the smaller Dalon Con imagining monetary gains.

Dalon Con stood tall. "And who might you be?"

"Well, I might be the king of Defeated," Smort said, laced with sarcasm, "but I ain't. In fact, I don't know any fool who'd wanna rule this hell-hole." He blew his nose into his hand and ingested the contents. "And ta answer yer question, I ain't a Smort, my name be Smort." He stared at Dalon Con. "Now it's yer turn."

"That's a lovely name," Dalon Con replied.

"Tryin' to blow smoke up ma shorts, eh," Smort said. "Enough of this back and forth; let's just cut to the chase." Smort stood atop a mound of trash, his hands clenched into fists and firmly planted on his hips. He sported a pair of ragged overalls and bare feet so dirty they were black. His mussed, long, brown hair provided an identical match to his matted beard.

Wrinkling his forehead, Dalon Con tried to process what Smort said. "I am not endeavoring to fill your undergarment with smoke, nor would I lacerate this one you call Chase."

Smort smacked his knees and broke into a fit of laughter. After he calmed down and wiped his eyes to remove the tears, he continued to chuckle. "You ain't gonna fill ma underdrawers with smoke or anythin' else 'cause I ain't wearin' none." This started another round of laughter, which didn't last as long. "And when I said 'cut to the chase,' I meant let's get down to business." Smort glanced up and then at Dalon Con. "Make it quick, ain't got time ta waste,"

Dalon Con exuded an expression of sarcasm. "Do you not have time to waste due to the business you wish to, in your words, 'get down to' …?"

"Well, it seems to me that someone as young and well-dressed as you got to be worth quite a sum. And if you ain't got nothin' worth nothin' on you, then you'll make a mighty tasty meal right down to the bone."

"You have failed to answer my question."

"It be like this hard head. Even though I'm a living on the streets like a filthy no account scab, I's still gots me a job ta do. Now that job requires me to keep a check on the population of defeated to make sure they get everything they need to live a long and fruitful life." Smort bent over, placed his hands on his knees, and laughed. As his spell came to an end, he continued to speak. "Kinda ironic, don't ya think." He coughed several times, then wiped his mouth with his hand. "Well, I'll let ya in on a little secret. I still keeps up with the population, but nowadays it's more for nutritional value, if you get what I's sayin'."

Dalon Con stared at Smort, his eyes beginning to well, not wanting to injure his present nemesis. "In your best interest, I implore you not to do anything foolish. Walk away and forget our meeting."

"Now why would I do a fool thing like that?"

"To retain your own life, as purposeless as it is."

Smort slid down his throne of trash and approached Dalon Con. The overall-clad man stood several feet taller than his opponent. He poked the well-dressed Dalon Con with a single finger. "Near as I can tell with all that fancy talk spewin' outta yer mouth, is you's plans to hurt Smort with that little body 'o' yorn."

Dalon Con shook his head and spoke solemnly. "Please, do not pursue this."

"Okay, little man, I won't pursue whatever 'this' is, but first, I'm gonna show you a world 'o' hurt." Smort reached down and picked up Dalon Con with one hand, holding him at eye level, then drew back an enormous fist. "Sleep real good, little man." Before Smort's fist could move, Dalon Con's hands connected with each side of Smort's head, popping both eardrums. Smort released his captive, then dropped to his knees in anguish.

"Will they ever learn?" Dalon Con said over the agonizing cries of his latest opponent. He wiped away a tear. "I must concentrate on the task at hand, the whereabouts of Gabriel, and those responsible for his disappearance." Dalon Con stepped around the body of Smort, now flat on his back, writhing in pain, having cracked through the pavers and carved out a divot in the earth underneath. He came to a smaller passage on his right, so narrow he nearly passed the egress by.

"Ahhh," the tortured creature yelled. Smort wrapped two hands around Dalon Con's ankle.

A powerful arm quelled all forward motion, the fist on its end plowed through Smort's hair, stopping short of crushing his skull. Dalon Con pulled his punch, allowing the one called Smort to remain in the realm of the living. "It is evident you are only looking for relief." He dragged the large man's body, still trembling in pain, to an area less traveled. The old man appearing as a thirty-year-old-suit, searched through a stand of wooded vegetation. *This should do nicely.* He raked the fingernails on his right hand down the bark of a sanare tree, catching the shavings in the palm of his left hand.

"Sleep and heal, impulsive one," Dalon Con said, sprinkling the wood pulp into Smort's mouth and across his eyelids. The healer completed the treatment of his patient, mixing the remainder of the wood shavings with clay he obtained by thrusting his cane into the ground and rolling the components into two earplugs.

"I will return, please know the Great One will place you within his protection."

Dalon Con paused, staring down the dark alley. Unclear bits of information filter through, emanating from the narrow access. Out of the gibberish, he reckoned Gabriel had traveled this thoroughfare. Before following this notion, he heard, "Bile stole not to have, but Gabriel was too fast." This sent Dalon Con down the narrow corridor faster than any human could move. *Strange, but the voice supplying this mishmash of information seems to be coming from the earth itself.* He cocked his head, hoping to obtain a different perspective from this disorganized voice. *The phrase changed to that of one touting the name of Max.*

CHAPTER THIRTEEN

Jack

Unaware of the battle that had just taken place, Jack remained oblivious that he was following the same path as Slag. He approached a bridge where the disabled mutant lay in the stream below, obscured by dense foliage. Slag opened an eye in recognition and closed it again. Any attempt to capture Jack would have to wait for the ailing monster to recover. Jack continued, each step taking him further from the city and into the wilds. His belief that the wooded area would be safer than the city was a severe error in judgment. *Good to be out of that hole. Every time I left my house, I wasn't sure I'd be going home.* He stopped, looked around, and then sighed. *At least this way, I'll be safe as long as I can find food.* Then, an unnatural roar echoed within the dense patch of forest. Jack resumed his original trek, this time at a faster pace, while a hint of doubt took root and began to grow in the recesses of his mind.

****

Sim and Slag / Jence

As Jack moved deeper into what he hoped would be his new home, the scenery changed from a densely wooded area to an open field with waist-high grass. *This place doesn't know what it wants to be, but at least it's less claustrophobic, and I didn't like the idea of something hidden in the trees jumping on me.* Jack took several more steps when what he dreaded most brushed past his leg. He jerked sideways, catching himself before falling, and then froze as dark thoughts raced through his mind, making him panic.

Slowly removing his backpack, Jack grabbed the confiscated stiletto and walked in a tight circle. "If you want me, then come and get me," Jack said half-heartedly.

In answer, something wrapped around his leg. Taking a blind swipe, Jack sliced through the grass, nearly cutting his leg as the creature swiftly retreated. No stains on the steel indicate he had hit anything other than grass, *but the grass could've wiped it clean.*

As Jack stood firm, his eyes darting in all directions, pieces of soft rope-like tendrils pushed through the ground and curled around his ankles, working their way upward. Unable to move, he raised the stiletto and screamed, "Show yourself!"

One tentacle-like appendage, colored a mottled red, emerged from the grass. Jack swiped his blade through the tentacle, causing a gush of fluid and a quick retreat of the offended limb. As he felt the organic chains around his legs release, he bolted with no set course, only to immediately come to an abrupt halt.

"What now?" he mumbled. He squinted in an attempt to focus on the setting unfolding ahead. *A large section of ground is beginning to rise.* Jack shook his head. *Can't wait to find out how this ends.* Once the earthen works reached a height of thirty feet, it erupted like a volcano save for dirt, spewing aloft instead of molten rock. And out of the dust and debris, a large, toothless mouth appeared.

"I am Sim, and you are mine, boy."

Jack stared at the subterranean aberration and began to seethe. He raised his oversized stiletto and exclaimed, "Then come and get me, you dirt-eating freak!" Jack moved toward the newcomer. Multiple tentacles pushed their way into the air in anticipation of Jack's assault. Sim consisted of a head with little visible thorax. The head was shaped like an obelisk with rounded corners and a bulge in the middle. *Not much bigger than a good-sized man.* Jack's expression changed to one of disgust. "To call you a dirt-eating freak was being kind, in fact I'd say it was a compliment."

Sim was covered with rows of six-inch sharpened nodules, twisted horns jutted from the top of the head, forming the conical shape of a drilling implement. "I will remove your belligerent mouth and feed it to whatever orifice is left."

The appendages are used to bore through the earth, so I guess it's my turn. Jack knelt, plotting his course, then ran, slicing tentacles flush with the height of the grass. When he reached the base of the creature, Jack scaled the dirt mound created when Sim arrived, then leapt into the air, the stiletto grasped with both hands held high above his head. Jack's target: one of the beast's eyes set into deep sockets.

A tentacle knocked Jack facedown onto the ground. The creature pushed himself up as a large set of leathery wings unfolded. Sim rose from the crater, revealing numerous tentacles protruding from a thick ring of stiff hair. At its center was a cavernous hole filled with untold rows of lethal teeth that spiraled inward until lost in the darkness.

"As I expressed earlier," Sim bellowed, "you are mine, boy, and time will not save you, for time is a friend to no one, save for a select few!" The hovering abomination began to lower over the young man. Jack watched as the creature's teeth moved in unison, then he curled up into a fetal position, waiting for the end to come.

An ear-numbing thud and a squall of pain but not from Jack ensued. Sim was in the air, his limbs circling. Slag clung to Sims's back, tearing out chunks of flesh with his mouth and digging furrows with his claws. Jack shoved his stiletto into his backpack and ran.

Sim wrapped two tentacles around Slag, with a third reserved for his throat. As Sim applied pressure restricting the quadruped's oxygen intake, he removed the creature from his back. Sim released two tentacles, allowing Slag to dangle by his neck. He jerked the long appendage several times, watching the limp body until it unceremoniously flopped about. Satisfied, Sim released the carcass, increased his altitude, and was soon out of sight — loosed to pursue his reason for existing, the likes of which were an unknown of the highest order.

Slag shuddered, and then gravity took over. As his lifeless body made contact with the earth, all that remained was a mutilated biped named Jence holding the jeweled skull responsible for his metamorphosis. This change into a malignant creature was courtesy of the dwindling population of jaders. Sim was loosed to pursue his reason for existing, the likes of which were an unknown of the highest order.

A sizeable gray rodent slipped in and consumed any flesh remaining on the jeweled skull, leaving one more strand of evil awaiting its time to grow. Sim roared as he awaited the next victim falling into place as a warm meal.

CHAPTER FOURTEEN

Gabriel and Bile

"Hold on, boy," Bile shouted over his shoulder. "Taint much further now." Gabriel felt himself slipping toward the ground. The large man moved so fast that the mortar joints between the cobblestones blurred. Grasping a suspender, Gabriel wrapped his legs as best he could around his captor's waist, and attempted to pull himself up to Bile's shoulders. When the suspender's clasp on the front of Bile's pants slipped free, the boy grabbed the other elastic strap before falling and then scrambled back up the man's shirt, wrapping both arms around Bile's thick neck just as he slowed.

"Good thing that second strap held fast," Bile said, "cause the next thing holdin' you up would have been this here pig sticker." Bile glanced downward, then motioned with his head for Gabriel to do the same. Inside a sheath attached to a specially made harness was a knife, the size of which he had never seen. The boy shrank back, terrified. Then, a nauseating odor assaulted his nasal passages. He gagged, losing the meager contents of his stomach. Just when he felt every vein in his head would explode, his nose became so stuffy he was unable to smell the offensive odor, and his stomach spasms ceased.

"Off me, boy," Bile commanded. Pulling Gabriel's embedded legs from his sides and jerking his suspenders taut, he flung the exhausted boy from his back. Gabriel landed facedown, knocking the wind from his lungs and causing his diaphragm to seize. Bile knelt beside the gasping youngster, then flipped him onto his back. "What's a matter, boy, ole Bile's stench too much fer ya?"

"Hyaaah," was all Gabriel could muster as he gasped for breath.

"Well, now, let me 'splain it to ya," Bile said. "See these here brown pants I'm wearin'?"

Gabriel nodded.

"To get this perfect color, I never take 'em off, and I mean never, 'ceptin to dump 'em out every week or so. This here shirt ain't been off ma back since I put'er on many year ago. Now yer real kicker to gettin' this sweet smell is all in yer head." He stretched out a foot of matted hair, where numerous insects, furry vermin, and scaly reptilians scrambled for cover.

"See them critters?" Bile said. "They's all ma friends when they ain't ettin' each other."

Bile jerked Gabriel to his feet. "Time to move, boy. Lead the way so's I can keep an eye on ya."

"But I don't know which way to go," Gabriel protested.

Bile gave the boy a push, causing him to hit the ground a second time. "I'll tell ya which way to go," Bile said. "Now git up and git to steppin'." Gabriel stood, headed in the same direction they'd been moving. After the boy took several steps, Bile rose from his kneeling position and followed, yelling, "Faster, boy." Bile's knee was in Gabriel's back in an instant, urging him to increase the pace. Gabriel boosted his speed to a slow jog. "That's better," Bile said. "See that ya don't slow down."

Gabriel glanced behind, noticing Bile's size. "He's at least 7 feet tall and about that wide," Gabriel mumbled.

"Who ya talkin' at up there?" Bile asked.

Before Gabriel answered, a towering fur-covered creature jumped out of an adjacent alley, landing in front of the pair. Gabriel heard a sound like metal rubbing against leather and then a slight 'ching.' He turned around, but Bile was not there. When Gabriel turned back toward the newcomer, he saw the animal being systematically dismembered. Each time a part would fall, Gabriel would catch a quick glimpse of Bile before he'd disappear again. As Gabriel observed the process, he noticed a blur between momentary still images of the noxious man. After several moments, Bile stood over a neatly placed stack of butchered meat.

"Best close that mouth 'o' yers," Bile said. "Somethin' ya don't want is liable to crawl up in a right big hole such as that."

Gabriel immediately slammed his mouth shut.

"Come here, boy," Bile said. "I wanna show ya somethin'."

The boy reluctantly moved toward his undesirable companion.

"Looka here, boy," Bile said, "and see whatcha missed." He stood over a pile of fur-covered pieces. Reaching down, he retrieved the head and slid his knife from its sheath.

"That's the ching sound I heard," Gabriel blurted.

"Ah," Bile said, "he does talk." Bile drove his knife into the top of the creature's skull. "This here, boy, is what we call a scabmaker. Don't rightly know what the thing's real name be." He moved the head until it was directly in front of Gabriel's face.

Gabriel winced and took a step back. The scabmaker's facial features were subtle at best– small, round, black eyes and a wide nose and mouth that extended from the face just enough to form a muzzle. Bile slammed the head onto the cobblestones. Hundreds of sharpened six-inch bone spikes seemed to instantly emerge from the head. Its mouth flew open, exposing razor-like teeth curving inward. A spike-covered tongue, so long it comically lolled out of the mouth, came to rest on the ground. As Bile twisted his knife, the skull cracked, allowing him to remove the blade. "How'd ya like to have that in yer face, boy?"

Gabriel grabbed his throat and swallowed hard. "No…no thanks."

Bile chuckled. "Didn't think so." He nudged the scabmaker's head up against the wall. "Follow me, boy." Gabriel complied. They stopped at the pile of skinned meat. Bile picked up what appeared to be a tenderloin.

"That's gotta be twenty pounds of meat or more," Gabriel mumbled.

“Thirty-two,” Bile said, “thirty-two even.”

“I didn’t think you could hear—”

“I can hear most everthin’,” Bile interrupted. “Now, how big a slab ‘o’ this here thing ya want?”

Gabriel looked at Bile, then at the meat in his hand, and then back at Bile while uttering, “No. No. No!”

“Gotta et, boy,” Bile said. “Gotta keep up yer strength.”

Gabriel continued to shake his head. “I can’t.”

“Take a seat, boy. Once I get ‘er cooked up, the smell’l make ya wanna et.” Bile tossed several pallets into a pile. Gabriel found a bucket and used it for a chair. Bile began to search in earnest, looking behind objects, through piles of trash, pretty much anywhere he could fit his head.

“What’s he looking for?” Gabriel whispered.

“I’ll tell ya when I find it,” Bile called. He stopped dead in his tracks, staring at Gabriel. “And I just found it.” He moved so quickly toward Gabriel the boy had no time to move aside. The strike from Bile’s hand was much lighter than anticipated but strong enough to knock him off his seat. “Good find, boy.” Bile picked up the bucket and moved to the stack of pallets. He plunged his knife into the side of the container near the top. The cutting was complete within seconds, and Bile was busy pouring out the black, acrid contents. When finished, he tossed the empty bucket to the side, then slid his hand into his right pants pocket, pulling out a thin, one-inch square piece of stone. With each strike of his knife against the stone, a shower of sparks rained down on the liquid-coated pallets.

Gabriel watched with interest, and, known only to his deep subconscious, a fondness for the strange giant began to grow.

CHAPTER FIFTEEN

Jack, Link and Johnny Boy

Jack ran until his stride began to fail, forcing him to walk. Again, he was out of the open field and into a dense forest. The sunlight started to wane, compounded by the thick canopy overhead. *Well, ain't this just great.* Jack peered upward, watching the last vestige of the sun disappear. *If the claustrophobia weren't enough, it brought a friend along with it. Hello, darkness. I guess you dropped by to make sure I can't see where I'm steppin' or what I'm steppin' on.* Jack moved gingerly, one small step at a time.

After several hours, he noticed a faint glow ahead. *Hope that's what I think it is.* He increased his pace. *A campfire.* He started to jog.

Two heads turned to see a terrified teen moving in their direction.

"Whatcha think, Johnny Boy?" Link asked.

Johnny Boy spat on the ground. "Looks to me like a young man runnin' at us." He took a moment to scratch the side of his face. "I don't reckon we ought to kill him til we find out for sure what he's up to." Johnny Boy wore canvas shorts, a tattered tank top, and sandals, while Link sported a pair of long pants with suspenders and was barefooted. He'd taken the time to shave and cut his hair with a piece of flint while Johnny Boy's bushy hair grew wild on his head and face.

"I reckon not," Link agreed. They both watched as Jack neared their location. They saw a smile spread across the young man's face, and then suddenly, he was gone.

Johnny Boy jumped to his feet, pulling an 88 mag with a ten-inch barrel out of his side holster, and scanned at the ground in a purposeful pattern.

Simultaneously, Link fell to the ground, brushing aside the dead vegetation, and then placed his ear on the bare earth. "Cursed hatcher, move just once—" He clamped his mouth shut, daring not to take a breath.

Link twirled his right index finger above his head, then pointed at the ground, indicating two spots ten feet apart. Johnny Boy acknowledged Link's signal and slowly moved between the two designated points.

Link again put his ear to the ground. Then, his hand gestures became more erratic, with a sense of urgency. With his sidearm in hand, he jumped to his feet and yelled, "There!" He pulled the trigger, followed by Johnny Boy discharging his weapon, throwing a plume of dirt into the air.

****

Jack advanced to a fast jog, smiling as he neared the two men. Without warning, his world turned black, moving in a downward spiral. Vertigo robbed him of any chance to determine his location. He stopped, reversed and, turned down alternate tunnels. He moved unpredictably, his frame simultaneously elongated, shortened, and bulged from side to side. A wave of nausea threatened to overtake him. Four hands and a sudden burst of light, followed by a face full of dirt, ended to his surreal journey. Jack's body returned to normal, save for the nausea. He dropped to his knees and vomited.

****

Link and Johnny Boy had ropes attached to the creature by barbed harpoons fired from their weapons. The snake-like hatcher was eighteen feet long, and the end of its tail was similar to a double-bit ax.

"Here," Johnny Boy yelled, "take this." He moved closer to Link and handed him his rope. Johnny Boy drew his 88 and took aimed at the quarter-sized spot deep underneath the creature's head. "Hold still, ya sludge-suckin' varmint, whilst I get a bead on ya."

The hatcher rose another six feet into the air, bobbing and weaving like a serpent ready to strike. Down each side of its body from head to tail were six legs equipped with three claws, allowing the creature to bore through the earth as easily as it moved above ground.

Bang! Zing!

The echo of a ricochet as the projectile skipped off the hatcher's body armor. The serpent hissed, and a diamond-shaped protrusion made of bone and leathery skin opened, protecting its head.

Bang!

This time, the bullet struck the membrane of the protective umbrella. Yet, it simply absorbed the kinetic energy, causing the projectile to fall harmlessly to the ground. The creature retaliated, swinging its ax-shaped tail back and forth, narrowly missing Link.

"We can't kill it!" Johnny Boy yelled. "The skin has some kind of invisible protection."

The hatcher's body was covered with undetectable armor, appearing as smooth, tan-colored skin. This animal's epidermis was as vulnerable as any human's. The notable difference was that the threatened area would contract when its cells detected danger in close proximity, warding off the impending strike. In contrast to the hatcher's otherwise drab color, the only prominent features were the sunburst pattern on its diamond-shaped appendage and the striking green color that originated at its nose and began fading several feet down its neck.

Link said. "I can't hold this thing much longer." Another gunshot rang out, followed by another ricochet.

Johnny Boy reloaded his 88, cocked the hammer and aimed. "I can't hit what I can't bear down on." He glanced at Link. "Can ya hold him still for just a second so's I can get one shot off?"

"Sorry, J.B., but the little I got left is fadin' fast."

A small bipedal broke through the void behind Johnny Boy and Link, hands wrapped around the oversized stiletto. He approached the hatcher from the rear, bringing the blade down cleanly, removing half of the serpentine's ax-shaped tail. The tormented creature began to wail, jerking the ropes from Link's hands. The last the three saw of the hatcher was a bloody tail disappearing down a three-foot-diameter hole.

"Well now, young feller," Link said, "you got a mighty special blade there. S'pose I can take a gander at 'er?"

Jack looked at the blade, then glanced at Link. "Sure, at least I think so." He reluctantly passed the blade to Link.

Link pushed the button, opening and closing the stiletto several times. "Johnny Boy, take a look at this. Don't believe I ever seen anything like it."

Johnny Boy ran his fingers down the handle and then carefully along the blade's spine. He took great care to avoid the honed edge after seeing the damage inflicted by the unfamiliar weapon. He handed the knife back to Jack. "Where'd ya come across that blade, son?"

"Got it from a fat man in Defeated."

Link crossed his arms and nestled his chin between his right thumb and index finger. "I heard of such a blade a few years back."

"Well, ya gonna tell us about it," Johnny Boy asked, "or we gotta pull it outta ya?"

"Ain't a lot to tell," Link said, "ceptin' it were forged by somethin' called the Nexus."

Jack's mouth dropped open as the stiletto hit the ground.

"Sure does appear your words hit the nail square on the head with at least one of us here," Johnny Boy said.

"I believe ya got somethin' there," Link replied.

CHAPTER SIXTEEN

Dalon Con

Dalon Con stopped at a crossroads within the tunnel system he'd traversed for nearly an hour. He began to listen intently. The voice was back and now evident to Dalon Con, here on behalf of the Great One.

Bile has taken the boy, the messenger said. *The one you call Gabriel is beginning to regard his captor as a benefactor. He knows no other way, lacking anyone to give him direction as he grew.*

Gabriel subconsciously searches for guidance and approval from a father figure, but makes no distinction between good and evil. You must reach the young one soon, for Bile is the worst of the worst, and time works against you each moment you delay.

"Show me," Dalon Con said.

Follow and know this is the last time we will palaver.

"Understood."

Wisps of vapor moved away at an accelerated rate, and he adjusted his speed to follow. The vapor gave the impression of one taking steps along the cobblestone walkway. After a time, the mist faded away. Dalon Con stood very still, his eyes squinting as he searched for any sign of the unseen guide, but the messenger was gone.

Dalon Con surveyed his surroundings. Three-foot square openings with steel grates had been cut through the tunnel ceilings. However, the illumination was intermittent, as the streetlights appeared to be spaced more than thirty feet apart, causing ominous black voids within the tunnels. Dalon Con moved cautiously, listening to muffled voices. The messenger was gone. Then, a movement in the tunnel up ahead grabbed his attention.

"Hey, Krabb," a scraggly short man wearing denim shorts and high-top tennis-like shoes with no toes said, "looks like we got us one 'o' them thar zecutives." He began to chuckle. "Whatcha spose he's doin' in these parts?"

"Don't rightly know," Krabb said. "Maybe he's searching for one 'o' them whatchamacallits…ya know, one 'o' them things. C'mon Sketch, help me out."

"I ain't got no idea whatcha goin' on about," Sketch said.

"Intern!" Krabb blurted. "All them fancy Dan zecutives gots an intern. The man called Krabb stood just over three feet tall. He'd honed his physique through years of lifting inanimate items—stones, logs, and the like—along with battles fought against animate beings, much larger in size. His chosen attire was a soft leather wrap that covered Krabb from his waist to several inches above his knees. He had one distinguishing characteristic—his total lack of hair. He used a strong pair of pinching fingers and fingernails to remove each hair as it sprouted.

He turned to face Dalon Con. "We ain't much on fightin' fair, so's I guess this ain't yer lucky day, Mr. Stranger. If'n that be yer intention."

"My friend here do like to be polite," Sketch said, "even if we is gettin' ready to tear you a new one."

Dalon Con raised both hands in front of him, palms out. "I desire no trouble with either of you."

"Then whatcha doin' so deep in the bowels 'o' Defeated?" Krabb asked.

"I'm looking for my ward and the gentleman accompanying him. He goes by the name of Bile."

"Bile!" Sketch and Krabb said simultaneously.

"I wouldn't zactly call Bile a gentleman," Sketch said. "Fact is, I'd call him anythin' but a gentleman."

"Most folks is tryin' to get away from Bile," Krabb said. "Now, here you is lookin' to find him. What gives?"

"He kidnapped a very close friend of mine," Dalon Con said, "and in the words of your vernacular, 'he's all mine'." Dalon Con lifted his cane and brought it down to the ground. A strange vibration originated from its tip and spread throughout the cobblestones.

Krabb glanced at Sketch, and then both stared at Dalon Con. This man was not to be trifled with.

"Mister," Krabb said, "me and Sketch don't much care fer Bile, and we…" he paused for a moment, "we got four good hands that'd take a peck 'o' pleasure helpin' you get that friend 'o' yourn back safe and sound."

Dalon Con nodded. "I receive faint impressions on the boy's whereabouts, but nothing concrete."

"We knows where Bile feeds," Krabb said, "and the rocks he crushes to mix with water," Sketch added.

"Sketch, here, likes to leave out stuff when he's tellin' a story," Krabb said. "Bile searches for this soft yeller rock. He crushes it to a powder, that he mixes with water. Bile drinks it to call what he's doin' gettin' stoned. Sometimes he gets mean, but he always falls to sleep, and I figure that's the best time to swipe that friend 'o' yourn."

Dalon Con glanced at Krabb. "Good to know."

"You says you get pressions on the boy," Krabb said, "but then he gets stuck in concrete?"

Dalon Con smiled. "You may forget what I said earlier; however, remember this: there will come a time when I will need your help retrieving my young friend. When this happens, I will let you know and instruct you on what to do."

"Now let me git this right," Krabb said. "Ya want me and Sketch to ferget what ya said afore?"

Dalon Con nodded.

"Then what it is you . . .?" Sketch started.

"Hold on a doggone minute," Krabb interrupted. "Sketch, I be a wantin' you to shut yer mouth." Krabb said, looking at Sketch, "sometimes I'd get more outta a rock if I took a mind to talk at it. So's listen at me and don't say nothin' til somebody says somethin' to you…got it?"

Sketch shifted his weight back and forth, his head hanging low. "Okay," he replied.

Krabb turned his attention back to Dalon Con. "Now, here's the way I see it: yer a lookin' fer a kid. When ya find him, yer gonna' need our help to wrangle him, and afore we wrangle him, yer gonna' tell us zactly how."

"I could not have expressed it better myself," Dalon Con said.

"Then it seems like we be agreein' on somethin'," Krabb said.

"Indeed," Dalon Con replied, "we should use the daylight to our advantage and leave with all haste."

"We's followin' you," Sketch said. He stood there scratching his head. "See, I ain't as stupid as you thunk I was."

CHAPTER SEVENTEEN

Bile and Gabriel

Gabriel continued to ponder this one-sided relationship between Bile and himself. His mind drifted back to Dalon Con. *How could I ignore my first benefactor? A stranger who found me during a blizzard and took me in. He nourished my body, my mind, and my soul.* "This man saved my life." He clamped his hand over his mouth, realizing in his zeal he had blurted his last words out loud.

Until then, Bile had been kneeling over a flat rock supported on each end by piled stones. A small fire heated the makeshift griddle, releasing a stimulating aroma. Then, the giant man rose and moved toward the boy, knife firmly planted in his right hand. Gabriel's eyes widened, imagining the carnage with each step that brought the loathsome one closer. Bile stopped and tapped the young man on the shoulder.

"No need to thank me." Bile raised his knife, "Here, try this." A small piece of medium rare scabmaker had been pierced by the tip of Bile's blade. Gabriel glanced at the meat and then looked at Bile.

"Go ahead, give it a try." Gabriel reluctantly poked the piece of meat. "Et!" Bile thundered, pressing the point of the knife closer to the boy's mouth. Gabriel jumped at the order, grabbed the meat, and pushed it into his mouth. As he chewed, a smile slowly crossed his face.

"More," was all he said. Bile supplied the boy with meat until Gabriel waved him off. "That was some of the best food I've ever eaten." He wiped his mouth with his shirt sleeve. "Mama Byrnes never let me have meat. In fact, the first time I tasted animal flesh (Gabriel caught himself before he mentioned Dalon Con and the cabot they shared) was when you fed me just now." Bile noticed a hint of hesitation in Gabriel's statement. The big man cut off another chunk of scabmaker and tossed it into his mouth. He chewed slowly, then spit out a piece of gristle, all the while glaring at Gabriel.

"Don't lie to me, boy. That twisted tongue 'o' yourn'll land you in a world 'o' hurt."

"No, sir, wouldn't do it."

"See to it." Bile paused and looked at Gabriel. *The kid called me sir.* Bile puffed up his chest and curled one corner of his mouth into a smile. He stood. "Time to go, boy."

"Where are we going?"

"Let me worry 'bout that." Bile extended his arm. "Get aboard. If I have to wait on you, we'll never get there." Gabriel took Bile's hand, climbed onto his back, and situated himself behind the big man's suspenders. "Clamp hold to somethin' good 'n tight 'cause we fixin' to fly close to the ground." Bile drove the heel of his foot into the edge of a nearby manhole cover. The heavy round piece of steel flew from the opening, permitting access to the world below. Bile dropped through the breach, landing in several inches of water. He then moved as a blur through the storm sewers of Defeated's underground. Even though Gabriel was held to his transportation's back by elastic straps, he maintained a death grip on the suspenders.

Everything's a blur; I can't tell where I am, where I've been, or where I'm going. The drop-inlets that permit water to trickle into the sewer apparently allow in light, which appeared as one constant blurred window.

****

Bile walked through the degraded sewer as casually as one would stroll through the countryside on a beautiful sunny day. When a six-foot long-haired ran toward him, Bile extended his left fist and shoved it into the snarling rodent's mouth.

Bile began to laugh as the rat's jagged teeth pierced his fingers to the bone. "Guess ya don't know 'bout ole Bile." He lifted his hand until the two were eye-to-eye. "Well, I'ma gonna learn ya." Steel slid against leather, followed by the sound of ripping hide, vertically splitting the rodent from stem to stern.

"How'd ya like that?" Bile's mouth spread into a wide grin. "Then yer gonna love this." A quick horizontal slash and the bifurcated body fell cleanly from the head. Bile used his knife to pry the teeth loose and shake the rat's jaws from his hand.

"What's goin' on?" Gabriel asked, the anxiety evident in his voice.

"Nothin' much, jest a critter I had to put in its place. Now come on down and help me get supper ready."

****

"Betcha never thought sludge rat could taste so good," Bile said.

"Nope," Gabriel replied, "especially when it's cooked over dried poo."

"It's the only thin' down here that'll burn," Bile said, "and there's plenty to be had."

"There were creatures everywhere when you first brought me to this place. What happened to them?"

"Once they seen what Bile do to that sludge rat, they know it best to stay outta sight."

"What's next?" Gabriel asked.

"I show you even better places than here," Bile said. Once again, he extended his arm. "Hop on." Gabriel took Bile's hand and noticed the big man smile. Gabriel returned the gesture and climbed aboard.

"Ya know," Gabriel said, "he doesn't smell so bad after all."

CHAPTER EIGHTEEN

Jack, Link and Johnny Boy

"Whatsa matter, young feller?" Link asked. "One mention of the Nexus and you act like you've seen a ghost."

Then the ground shook, throwing the trio down and showering them with dirt. The hatcher briefly reappeared, then quickly slipped underground.

"That carn sarn devil is back," Johnny Boy said as he slid his 88 from its holster.

"Where is it?" Jack bellowed. "I was standing right over the area where that overgrown snake pushed through the ground."

"Where's what?" Link asked.

"My stiletto," Jack screamed, "it's not just a knife; it's part of me."

"Waddaya mean, it's part of you?" Johnny Boy asked. The hatcher resurfaced, again knocking the three humans to the ground, covering them with dirt, roots, and multitudes of underground insects, some as large as a man's arm. Jack was the first to dig his way out. He saw the stiletto fall, along with dirt that cascaded from the hatcher. Obsessed, Jack didn't hear the hail of gunfire, courtesy of his comrades fighting their own battle with a common enemy. The beast flew through the air, traveling in a high arc, then back to the ground and into its subterranean tunnels.

Jack dropped to his knees. "I've got to find it!" He dug greedily with his hands, moving large quantities of soil with each scoop. Jack felt something hard hit his stomach as he scraped dirt toward himself like a madman.

"There it is!" He grabbed the object and yelled in triumph!

Standing, Jack readied himself for battle, yet unsure how to attack such a formidable foe. The hatcher emerged from the ground close enough to brush against Jack, knocking the stiletto from his hands.

"Nooo!" he bellowed as the hatcher reentered the ground twenty feet away. Jack peered through the hole.

"Don't you do it!" Johnny Boy demanded. It ain't worth it."

Jack saw the gleam from the stiletto and dropped beneath the surface.

Several moments later, another volley of gunfire ensued as the hatcher resurfaced, this time with an unexpected guest.

"It appears as though we gotta fight . . . and I mean a fight ready to commence," Jack said.

The numerous penetrations through the soil had compromised the tunnel ceiling, making a collapse imminent. Fortunately for Johnny Boy and Link, the amount of dirt they displaced dropped them into the tunnel without causing a total collapse.

"Move," Johnny Boy barked, "and I mean now!"

Link was first to his feet. He helped his partner up, and they made for stable ground. Had the situation not been so serious, it would have been laughable to see the two men slip, slide, and stumble down the tunnel.

Once they reached an area where the floor wasn't littered with debris, they slowed their pace to a fast walk. As their breathing returned to normal, their on-edge status dulled, and they began to relax.

Link smiled. "I reckon we dodged a bull—."

A concussive blast, followed by violent shaking, persuaded the men to revisit their place on the floor. Johnny Boy rose to his hands and knees, barely able to maintain that position with the movement of the floor. "Jack," he screamed, "Jack, where are you!"

He started to repeat himself when Link jerked his arm, causing Johnny Boy to reconnect with the ground.

"We gotta find Jack," Johnny Boy protested. "He's just a kid."

"We ain't gonna find nothin' or nobody til this place calms down," Link said. "Now lay there and keep that big mouth 'o' yourn shut til this shakin's over."

****

Jack grabbed the blade and began to run before ensuring a solid grip on the stiletto. The knife slid from his hand as the ceiling collapsed and disappeared under the falling debris. Without hesitation, his knees hit the ground and his hands ripped into the material covering his only weapon.

Where are you? He dug furiously, cutting his hands and splitting fingernails, and jammed several fingers in search. His heart jolted as he pulled the blade free from its entombment. Before he could stand, another wave of dirt and debris rained from the ceiling, covering Jack.

I can't believe it's gonna end like this. Through layers of dirt, he felt something sliding along his back. *If I'm goin', then you're comin' with me.* He pushed the button on his stiletto. The blade shot from the casing's end as Jack thrust it deep into the hatcher. The surprised creature didn't realize what had happened until the latter two-thirds of his body had been split in half lengthwise.

Jack jumped to his feet and ran down the tunnel, shaking off a thin coat of dirt. He climbed over mounds of rubble, pausing only a moment to look back.

Via a multitude of tentacles, an unseen undulating Sim stood beside the injured hatcher, offering comfort to the stricken reptile.

Writhing in pain, the hatcher released a mournful death squall that could bring the strongest to their knees. Moments later, the ceiling above the hatcher collapsed, ending the nightmarish wail.

Applause broke out, causing Jack to jerk his head around.

"Not half bad for a young'un what's still wet behind the ears," Johnny Boy said.

"I ain't sure a young'un could do such as what I just seen," Link said. "That thar young'un lookin' like he can handle hisself jest as good as most any man I done and ever seed."

Grin arc rue, Sim thought the ancient phrase still used today by his race, denoting camaraderie among newfound friends. Although they knew nothing of Sim's feelings, he paused, absorbing emotions he found initially disturbing, then quickly warming to the same feelings emanating from Johnny Boy, Link, and Jack. Sim didn't pretend to understand this new way of thinking. *It makes me feel complete and part of something larger than myself. It is as if I am becoming a willing participant in time. I will remain hidden and follow discretely, despite making contact earlier.*

"I don't believe I've been as happy to see someone as I am to see you two now," Jack said. He crawled over the last mound of dirt, slid down the other side, and then made his way up a short, steep incline before the three were united. Link took hold of Jack's hand and shook it like a wild man.

"Good to see ya, boy . . . yessir, doggone good to see ya." Link continued to shake the boy's hand with no sign of letting up. Johnny Boy rolled his eyes.

Then, the ground beneath them started to drop. Johnny Boy, Link, and Jack ran until hitting a four foot wall.

"What in tarnation!" Link exclaimed. "Where in the world did that come from?"

"Remember the drop?" Johnny Boy asked.

"Yeah," Link said, "what of it?"

"That's how far we fell," Jack said.

"Link," Johnny Boy barked, "come 'ere . . . now . . . up we go!"

"What!" Jack shouted. He found himself being lifted to the ledge above. "What are you doing?"

"Shut up!" Johnny Boy ordered. "Just get ready to catch another one." Before Link could collect his thoughts, he felt a head push through his legs, lifting him onto Johnny Boy's shoulders. The tunnel began to rumble and shake, nearly taking the double stack of humans to the ground. Johnny Boy managed to keep his footing and slammed into the dirt wall.

"Take his hands," the man on the bottom commanded. Jack pulled Link's hands while Johnny Boy pushed his boots. Link's knees touched the upper landing, and he immediately lay on the ground, hanging his arms over the edge of the wall.

"Grab my hands," he yelled. Johnny Boy's fingertips touched the two hands reaching down to save him. As the four hands clamped together, the ground beneath him dropped another foot leaving Johnny Boy suspended in the grasp of the other.

"Hold on," Jack screamed. The boy crawled onto Link's back and grabbed Johnny Boy's right wrist. Before Jack could establish the same connection on the left, Johnny Boy's hand slipped from Link's grasp, causing the precariously dangling man to swing.

Link reached down. "Give me your hand."

Johnny Boy reached up, and then . . . .

"Nooooo!" Link yelled

They watched their friend fall to the landing below. He stood and waved.

"Still here," he laughed.

Then Johnny Boy disappeared into the darkness as the landing gave way.

Sim levitated into the flow of soil and debris. He was there but visible for a millisecond before melding with the surrounding fall of dirt. Present but never seen until a time of his choosing.

CHAPTER NINETEEN

Dalon Con, Krabb and Sketch

"This here's mighty fine eats," Sketch said. Particles of food flew across the room as he spoke. "Tain't never gnawed on a critter such as this."

"Yessiree, this is some kinda tasty meat," Krabb echoed, saliva tainted with grease and bits of masticated flesh running down his chin. "Whatcha call this stuff?"

"First, allow me to say that it warms my heart to see you find such enjoyment in this meal I have prepared," Dalon Con said. "Now, to answer your question, the animal you are dining on is cabot. It is the most common and intelligent animal in the forest. Due to its resourcefulness and the fact that it is nocturnal, the cabot is also the most difficult to capture."

Krabb pulled the bottom of his leather wrap up high enough to reach his face. When finished, he wiped the remnants from his garment against the cobblestone. He looked at Dalon Con, puzzled. "We're smack dab in the middle 'o' Defeated. If them critters are smart as you say and live out amongst the trees, how in the world did them toothsome varmints end up 'round here?"

Dalon Con smiled. "Very observant, my friend; however, there are times when things normally unattainable are made available." Krabb and Sketch stared at Dalon Con, dumbfounded. "I understand how confusing this must be;" He continued, "nonetheless, I charge you to meditate on these words I've spoken, for every good thing comes from the Great One."

"What in tarnation is a 'meditate'?" Sketch asked.

"It means you think on it long and dang hard." Krabb elbowed Sketch. "I been a tryin' to learn you some smarts fer all the years we been together, and you still makin' me look stupid." Sketch was gasping after Krabb's unexpected elbow, which turned into wheeze-filled laughter until he could speak in short, choppy phrases.

"We been—lookin' stupid—ever since—we knowed each other—and I'll be danged—ifin ya gonna throw—all that stupid—on me by maself," Sketch said, his breathing now recovered, allowing him to increase his rant, "ya carn sarn, no excuse fer a ten-pound bag 'o' ignorant, and a brain full 'o' mush to boot." Sketch moved closer to Krabb and began to poke his comrade's stomach. "And let me tell ya one more thing– ya keep messin' with ole Sketch and ya gonna get somethin' on ya that river rock and hot water won't take off...ya heared me, ya big galoot."

Krabb placed his hands on Sketch's shoulders, staring directly into his eyes. "Ya 'bout done?" Krabb asked.

Sketch sighed. "Reckon I am." He ran his index finger under his nose and then sniffed. "Let's get to followin' somebody what really knows somethin'."

"Sure nuff," Krabb replied.

"Well," Dalon Con said, "I see you brought your dispute to a swift resolution."

"Yeah," Sketch said...

"We have a spat now an agin," Krabb said, "but they never 'mount to much."

"Ya cut ma talkin' off one more time," Sketch grumbled, "and we gonna be right back at it."

"Sorry," Krabb said, "I be payin' better notice hows I be a treatin' ya, but ya gotta know it might take a spell, soz ya gotta work with me."

"Looky thar," Sketch said, "that orange streak movin' 'cross the sky."

Dalon Con smiled. "They are seen from time to time." Sketch shrugged, and Krabb paid the anomaly little attention.

"Wait a doggone minute," Krabb said, turning to face Dalon Con. "What's this I hear 'bout a Great One?"

"Yeah," Sketch joined in, "and what's so great 'bout Him?"

"You raise some interesting questions," Dalon Con said. "Let us sit and parlay."

"Soundin' good to me," Sketch said. "Let's get started. We done and wasted too much time already."

"Yessiree, Mr. Dalon," Krabb said, "we's waitin' on you."

"If you waitin' on me, then you backin' up," came an ominous voice.

As usual, each time a chance to speak of the Great One becomes available, the darkness bent on evil finds a way to postpone this valuable conversation; Dalon Con thought, *however, this delay will last but a short time.*

"That don't sound good to me," Sketch said. He dropped to his knees and elbows, trying to remain low and mobile.

"You right, fer sure," Krabb echoed.

Dalon Con stood his ground. The voice originated from one of the shadows formed by the tunnel's lack of lighting in some areas. "Show yourself. Only a coward uses the cover of darkness to stalk his prey."

"That's mighty big talk fer a little man what's all dressed up nice 'n fancy," the Shadow-Walker said. "Did yer mama get ya all spiffed up an send ya out to play with them two belly crawlers you hangin' with?"

Krabb rose to his knees. "Who you callin' belly crawler?" he demanded. Thinking better of his outburst, he dropped back down to his elbows.

A deep guttural, "Ha, ha, ha," resonated from the shadows. "Ah, the belly crawler speaks. Will wonders never cease."

Dalon Con pushed his staff (masked as a cane) forward and tapped it on the ground. The vibration, as before, spread throughout the cobblestones. "Advance and speak, demon seed."

Thundering footfalls preceded the creature as it stepped into the light. Its body was covered with random multicolored streaks. Each extremity was massively formed like the trunk of a tree. There were no feet; the legs widening at their base provided ample stability. Two fingers on each hand permitted large objects to be grasped but disallowed any fine motor skills. “What do you want with me, holy man? I have no quarrel with you.” The creature’s neck bulged as it spoke. Its head widened from the neck up, ending with a flat top. The facial features were disturbingly human-like.

“Make yourself known to me,” Dalon Con commanded.

The abomination turned his head slightly to the left. “Shadow-Walker is sufficient, and as I have said, there is no quarrel with you.”

“I am Dalon Con, and my quarrel stems from the very fact that you exist.” He sensed a presence closing in from the left and another from the right. He felt no reason to dread these new arrivals.

“I see the lines are drawn;” the Shadow-Walker said, “the first move is yours.”

“There *are* no lines,” Dalon Con replied, “and rest assured, the first move is in no way your decision. I will strike in my time.” On his left stood Sketch, and to his right, Krabb. The thought of his new acquaintances standing by his side warmed him, but he also knew of the danger and the protection he must provide.

CHAPTER TWENTY

Gabriel and Bile

Once again, Gabriel was being whisked through the tunnels at a high rate of speed. He'd grown used to this mode of travel and quite fond of the time he spent with Bile. The big man would reach such speeds that he had to begin slowing before he could safely come to a stop. The amount of time needed would depend on the speed attained. *We must be coming to a stop. It feels like he's starting to slow down.*

****

Bile stopped in front of a ladder made from rebar laid into the stone wall. The ladder ended at a forty-eight-inch round piece of steel. "Goin' up," he announced. He scaled the ladder and pushed the round cover off the entryway.

"We ain't gonna' fit through that hole at the same time. Crawl up ma back and through that hole soz I can foller and get outta here, too."

"I sure didn't miss this place." Gabriel said, when they were back above ground in the heart of Defeated.

"'Pends on how ya see thangs. I'ma wantin' ya to pay attention to what I gotta say. Ya look 'round and see a dirty, good-fer-nothin' chunk 'o' land covered in stone pavers. Brick buildins is everwhere, makin' fer alleys, tunnels and ever sorta nook 'n cranny fer critters to hide in." Bile looked at the boy. "Now, tell ole Bile ifin that ain't what you's a thinkin'."

Gabriel peered into his companion's eyes. "That's exactly what I'm thinking."

"Now, here's where you and I's gets to thinkin' a might different." Bile dug a piece of sludge rat from between his canine and incisor. He tossed the piece of chewed flesh back into his mouth and continued to speak. "When I looks at all them stones, bricks, trash and the like, I don't go gettin' scared."

"You don't?" Gabriel asked. "Why?"

Bile laughed. "Ain't nothin' to be 'fraid of, 'specially when you's pert near the meanest thang in the *entire* city 'o' Defeated." Gabriel furrowed his forehead, considering Bile's statement. The color began to drain from Gabriel's face. He wobbled as he wove his head around to look at Bile.

"You telling me you're not the meanest one in Defeated?"

"Nope, there be another I dast not vex, but I ain't never been known fer keepin' ma nose where it don't belong, even if it do bring a heap 'o' trouble with it. I figger since I gotta go some time, it might as well be a time I do the choosin' and doin' somethin' that gives me a load 'o' fun."

"What might that be?" Gabriel asked.

"Fightin', yessir, they ain't nothin' better'n a good ole beat down, even if the one stretched out happens to be ole Bile hisself."

Gabriel stood, staring into Bile's face, his eyes beginning to well. "Not so sure I like that."

Bile looked at Gabriel, not knowing what to make of the youth's sentimentality. "Let's get outta here and I'll show ya some 'o' those better places I told ya 'bout."

"I'm ready for that." He stood there staring at the ground and kicking the dirt, causing dust clouds to rise and settle back to earth.

"What's up, young'un?" Bile asked. He knelt, bringing himself to eye level with Gabriel.

"I want to ask you a question, but I'm not sure I want to know the answer."

"I always been one to get whatever's buggin' me off ma chest, so go ahead and spit it out."

Gabriel didn't hesitate. "I want to know who has the power to lay you out."

Bile sighed. "You were in his company when I stole ya away."

"Then it didn't hurt to ask."

Bile shrugged. "I guess not." He stared deep into Gabriel's eyes. "From now on, Dalon Con will evoke the sense of an enemy in your heart. I want you to remember that name." Bile stood and extended his arm. "You know the deal, young'un."

Gabriel settled into his usual place on the big man's back, his face pale and emotionless as his mode of transportation began to pick up speed.

CHAPTER TWENTY-ONE

Dalon Con, Krabb and Sketch

Dalon Con spread his arms to the side. "Get behind me, brave ones. You have no part in this dispute."

"Ain't no such a mess," Krabb stated, "you is one 'o' us now."

"And ain't nobody left somebody when that thar nobody needed somebody," Sketch said. "Now thar be somethin' you kin stake yer underbritches on."

Dalon Con could not help but smile. "Very well, friends. We shall go forth together."

"Ya heared that?" Krabb asked. "He said we was friends."

"Pardon me," the Shadow-Walker said, "as much as I hate to interrupt this love-fest, I believe there is another matter of business to debate before you three begin to . . ."

Dalon Con's staff left his hand, becoming one with the Shadow-Walker's skull, then returned to its owner before the giant could recover from the initial blow. "Hold your vile tongue, insidious slug, lest my next strike removes the few cells that remain in your cranium!"

The Shadow-Walker back-pedaled into the tunnel wall. "Uhhh," he moaned, his hand plastered to his forehead.

"Well, looky thar," Krabb exclaimed, "that big feller jest kinda done and bit the dust."

"Yeah, boy," Sketch echoed.

Dalon Con raised a finger. "Never allow your opponent to lull you into complacency, for this can only lead . . ."

Even as Dalon Con spoke, his words were beginning a life of their own. With little time to prepare, Dalon Con spun to face a full frontal assault from the Shadow-Walker. The giant knew there was no chance of overtaking Dalon Con, even by surprise. His only hope was to abscond with one of the two that traveled with him. The Shadow-Walker jagged to the right. Dalon Con drew Krabb and Sketch toward him. Sketch was wedged between the wall and Dalon Con, while Krabb was more vulnerable in front of Dalon Con.

"Miiine!" The Shadow-Walker screamed as he collided with the three.

"No!" Dalon Con roared. He brought his staff across The Shadow-Walker's shoulder and knelt, curling his arm further around Sketch and Krabb. As his fingers touched his abdomen, he felt nothing. Sketch was safely tucked into the crook of Dalon Con's arm, but Krabb was nowhere to be found.

Dalon Con and Sketch turned to see The Shadow-Walker with a small body tossed over his shoulder and two despair-filled eyes staring back, as both disappeared down the tunnel.

Before Sketch could process the recent events, he found himself on Dalon Con's back, nestled in a warm, invisible sling that held him securely.

"Hold tight," Dalon Con said, "our velocity will now increase exponentially until a noise much like that of extreme thunder ensues." After a short pause, Dalon Con spoke again. "Perhaps you should cover your ears." Sketch placed a finger tightly in each orifice as Dalon Con accelerated.

Sketch ducked his head as a white cloud began to form around Dalon Con. The cloud streamlined, trailing white streaks behind the two men before violently dissipating in an ear-splitting "crack." Sketch watched the tunnel walls going by. "They jest 'bout smooth as can be, and them funny lookin' lights . . ."

"Those funny lights," Dalon Con interrupted, "are the street grates that allow the topside ambient light in. The great speed at which we are traveling creates a visually smooth appearance on the tunnel walls."

"I hope Krabb is ok." Sketch said, accompanied by a sudden look of wonderment. "It's quiet!" he exclaimed. "It's so dad-gummed quiet I kin talk without yellin'."

"Indeed, it is, small one, but that shant last much longer. You see, it was necessary to attain this great speed in order to keep up with The Shadow-Walker. The loud noise you heard was the breaking of the sound barrier as we traveled faster than the speed of sound itself."

"He kin run this fast, jest like you?"

"No, he cannot. However, he has been in this city of Defeated for many years and has learned by way of dark friends and seldom-traveled routes how to quickly move anywhere in the city."

"Faster than the speed 'o' sound, huh?"

Dalon Con nodded, although his affirmation went unnoticed.

"You must know where he be a goin'," Sketch said. Even though he was looking at the back of Dalon Con's head, he could see the corners of his mouth wrinkle on both sides, indicating a wide smile.

"Do not forget, Sketch, I, too, have been around."

"I bet you has . . .yessir, I jest bet you has."

"Hold on, Sketch." The cloud reappeared with the thunderous "boom." The roar of the wind returned, then subsided as they endured the lengthy process of slowing to a halt.

Sketch jumped down and ran around to face Dalon Con. "Well, I reckon wherever we was headed is the place that we is."

Dalon Con placed his hand on Sketch's shoulder. "Yes, it is as you say. This is the same place that we is."

"Well, which way is we a goin'?"

"One moment, please," Dalon Con said. He dropped and began to search through the tunnel on his hands and knees, pressing into the corner formed by the walls and floor coming together until he reached a spot that gave way. "Here it is." Dalon Con stood as a small, rectangular-shaped piece of wall disappeared into itself with a hiss. Two feet to the left of the missing piece, a wall section large enough to allow a man to pass through opened.

"Well, I'll be hornswoggled," Sketch said. "That jest about takes the ca —" The little man's voice quickly trailed off into silence, via Dalon Con's grip and sudden vault through the passageway onto a metal slide.

Both openings closed, cloaking any sign they ever existed.

CHAPTER TWENTY-TWO

Gabriel and Bile

A short hesitation and a barely audible "hum" told Gabriel that Bile was beginning the deceleration process. Once Bile came to a complete stop, Gabriel shimmied down his back. The boy noticed a hint of greenery encroaching upon the drab cobblestone. "Hey, I can see the tree line."

"Yep," Bile replied, "I used to come to this here place as a young'un, jest for the peace and quiet." Bile's forehead furrowed as a sad expression crossed his face. *But that was a lifetime ago.*

"So what are we waiting on," Gabriel said, unaware he was inching toward the distant foliage with each breath.

"Slow down, jest a minute," Bile warned, breaking his contemplation. "If you'd hold them horses 'o' yourn, I gotta quicker way to git from here to there. Ya game?"

"I'm waiting on you," Gabriel replied.

Bile knelt and pressed on several cobblestones until he found the correct one. The stone dropped out of sight into the ground. Several feet away, a hole big enough to accommodate a large man opened in the ground. A series of cobblestones slid back, revealing the portal.

"Now, who's waitin' on who?" He snatched Gabriel up in his arms, landing on the metal slide moments later. The misplaced cobblestones slid back into their original positions, looking like they had never been disturbed.

Gabriel lay on his back atop Bile. From the moment he found himself clutched in Bile's grasp, he experienced a brief bout of confusion. Gabriel realized he was moving at an accelerated rate of speed through a cylindrical system of four-foot diameter pipes. "We're moving so fast I can hardly breathe!"

Bile acknowledged Gabriel's protest by clamping a single hand over the boy's chest to hold him down, then using his other hand to block the intense flow of air from directly striking Gabriel's face. This created a calm vortex behind Bile's hand, allowing Gabriel to breathe easier.

"Much fun," Bile's voice boomed.

Gabriel signaled affirmative by tapping the oversized hand covering most of his thorax. "This is amazing," an astounded Gabriel said to himself. The pair traveled for miles at unimaginable speeds, all courtesy of the force of gravity. The interior of the cylinders was lined with random glowing lights that had no detectable beginning or end. Mesmerized, all Gabriel could do was stare at the reflective light show, and because of their downhill slide, the stationary ceiling appeared to move at a frightening rate. After fifteen minutes of travel through the psychedelic slide, a wave of nausea forced Gabriel to close his eyes.

"Whatsa matter, boy? You comin' down with a case 'o' the pukes?"

"Grrb aggh, " Gabriel managed to force his stomach contents back down.

"C'mon now, ya can do better than that." Bile grabbed the young man by his shoulders and began to shake. The pipe section they were now traveling took a 70° dive. As the unlikely pair's descending speed increased, they were unable to move. Vertigo returned with a vengeance—a reprisal encompassing both man and boy alike. Seconds after they reached terminal velocity, Gabriel and Bile hit a series of hills and valleys designed to slow any nomad daring to venture this way. How unfortunate that the younger of these two travelers was unaware of the importance of entering these tunnels with an empty stomach.

"Raaaaalllph," Gabriel sounded, as a dark chunky liquid poured from his mouth. The flow barely missed Bile's face as the stream left

Gabriel's mouth, traveling backward into the reverse current of air. Moments later, with one upward surge, both figures popped from the tunnel through a screen of vegetation, landing in a marsh-covered swamp.

"Well, at least it broke our fall," Gabriel said, his arms extended to each side, dripping mud. His face and hair were covered with errant ribbons of sludge moving downward, following the contours of his face.

Bile shook his head and hands, slinging mud in a 360° pattern. "I reckon," wiping two handfuls of slop from his cheeks, "first thing we gotta do is get outta this mudhole."

"I'll second that," Gabriel replied. Bile stared at the young boy. *What's that sposed to mean?* he wondered. Gabriel could feel Bile's gaze of puzzlement and could not help but call him on it.

Maybe I shouldn't do this, Gabriel thought. Before he could act on this notion, his mouth was already open. "Can't help but wonder if you've got something you want to say to me, that you're not saying."

Bile lowered himself to a squat position in front of the boy. "Ya said, 'I'll second that'. . . . what's that mean?"

Gabriel smiled. "It means that I agree with you."

"Why don't ya jest say so, 'stead 'o' spittin' outta bunch 'o' fancy words?"

"I thought I did, and while I'm at it, you spoke of this place like you'd been here before, and now I'm not so sure."

"Ya got that head 'o' yourn on straight. I be a might older'n you, so's the fact is, I been here, but the years run together and it's been awhile."

"How many years we talking about?" Gabriel asked.

A serious look crossed Bile's face. "Don't rightly know." He said, scratching his head. "Near as I can tell, a couple three hunderd year, give er take."

"Like you said," Gabriel replied, stunned at Bile's revelation, "we gotta get out of this mud hole."

"Since we here, let me show ya somethin' first."

****

The slime-covered object made a popping sound as it cleared the surface of the mud bog. Two large fingers gripped the mucus-covered shell. "Now, pay attention, boy." He shook the shell, removing unwanted secretions.

"What are you going to do with that?"

Bile looked at the boy and smiled. "Et it."

Gabriel suppressed a gag, forcing the little left in his stomach back down.

Bile held four dark mottled shells in one hand, then slapped Gabriel in the back with the other. "Whatsa matter, boy, got no stomach fer scumdauber?"

"Never tried it." Gabriel found himself standing, his right forearm covering his mouth and his left hand supporting it. Bile slid a thumb and index finger into a small pocket sewn into the front waistband of his pants. He removed a thin black object that opened with a hinge in its middle. "A knife?" Gabriel questioned.

"Yep," Bile said. He pushed the blade into the edge of the bivalve and, with a twisting motion, separated the shell. "Mmmm." A stream of drool flowed from the corner of Bile's mouth. He scraped the mound of material from inside of half the shell with his teeth; it disappeared with a slurping sound. He dispatched another, opened and consumed the third, and then popped the shell on the last. Bile paused and glanced at Gabriel. "You et." His voice muffled as bits of flesh fell from his mouth when he spoke. Bile jutted a hand toward Gabriel. It contained a palm-sized half of a shell, full of what could only be called a hot mess.

"Eat that?" Gabriel asked. He poked the jelly-like mass with a finger and cringed.

"Et!" Bile screamed.

Gabriel jumped, reaching toward the repulsive form lodged within the shell.

"Now!" Bile barked, reinforcing his prior statement. The boy jerked, grabbed a handful of orange snot, and crammed it into his mouth. Expecting the worst, Gabriel clamped his eyes shut and swallowed. His facial muscles relaxed into a smile.

He scooped handful after handful until half of the scumdauber was gone.

"Not bad, looks like ya took-a-likin to that water-suckin critter right off."

"Burrrp." Gabriel's smile widened.

"Ettin' full 'o' import 'round here." Bile looked up into the canopy, the light beginning to wane with the onset of dusk. "Gotta keep yer strength up; this place'll suck the life right out-n-ya. Let's get a move on and find somwheres to bed down fer the night." Gabriel nodded, unwilling to gather any relevant words together.

****

"Wake up, boy," Bile barked. "Time be wastin' and we gotta get a move on."

"More sleep," Gabriel moaned.

"Not today," Bile picked the boy several feet off the ground and dropped him.

A " hmph," along with a dull thud as the air left Gabriel's lungs, followed by a "hzzz," marked the labored return of the evacuated oxygen.

"Now, get up."

Gabriel managed to pull in a full tank of air.

"I can't wake up," he wheezed. He proved his point by falling back asleep.

"I telled ya this place'll suck the life out-n-ya." Bile threw Gabriel over his shoulder. "Gotta get this young'un out an underneath this canopy." He sniffed several times. "Wouldn't take much to put me down." Bile wound his way through the anesthetizing foliage and into clear air. He sat Gabriel down and rested until the drowsy feeling subsided. "Up, boy." He began to shake the young one. "You done laid 'round 'nough; now git up."

"Ahhh," Gabriel groaned, "I wanna sleep."

"Sleep?" Bile said. "Sure, sleep all ya wants." He seized Gabriel by the ankle and started to walk. After dragging Gabriel's limp body through a changing landscape of rocks, dirt, and animal holes, the young man was wide awake.

"What are you trying to do to me, you're ripping the back of my head off?" Gabriel raised his head, supporting it with both hands. He could feel warm liquid oozing between his fingers. His leg fell to the ground.

"Ya ready to git up n' walk?" Bile was bent over, one hand on each knee, talking to a boy rubbing the back of his head as the last vestige of light disappeared. "Let me take a look." Bile grabbed a tuft of the boy's hair in each hand. The big man twisted and turned Gabriel's head in several directions, trying to find even the smallest amount of light to make the scalp visible. After several attempts, he let go, pushing Gabriel's head to the side and rising as he did so.

"We needin' a fire. Can't see nothin' less we gotta fire. Git up boy and c'mon, we gonna start us a fire." Bile headed into the dark, waving his hands in front to detect trees and sniffing loudly, searching for a particular fragrance.

"Help," Gabriel muttered, in a tone so low he could barely hear it himself.

CHAPTER TWENTY-THREE

Hayden

Hayden continued to travel until he saw most of the town from the air. "I am satisfied the calamity did not start within this period of time. I see nothing unusual beginning or having taken control," he thought for a moment, "other than the lengthy conversations I am having with myself." Hayden smiled. "I suppose there could be worse company to keep."

With the ambient light waning, Hayden made a final broad sweep over the town, then turned east and back to the cave to attempt a short vault into the future.

****

"Back home again," Hayden said, touching down close to where the temporal door should be. He pressed on the bar of the small black box he carried. The doorway thrust from the ground and came to life. Startled, the man stumbled backward. "I'm getting too old for this," he groaned, "and I still haven't passed the century mark." Hayden stepped into the spidery light and disappeared as before.

The portal's orange glow within the cave was visible from the outside, its intensity heightened by the onset of nightfall. A pair of eyes glanced toward the cave opening, catching the fading luminescence. Moments later, a momentary streak of light flashed across the sky.

"Hmm," the watcher said. "Orange seems to be a popular color tonight . . . yes, very popular indeed."

****

Even though Hayden traveled through every moment in time instantaneously, the journey consisted of color with regular temporal portals. Occasionally, he'd catch an unintelligible glimpse of an era between Burrus Plax's beginning and end.

"So confusing," he whispered. "How thankful I am that minds greater than mine determined a method to control my movements through time." He passed another portal showing molten rock. "Primitive though this method may be, *none at all* would most assuredly prove to be much worse."

****

Hayden appeared within the carbon frame inside the cave. After several steps, he turned and watched the frame disappear into the ground. The sun shone brightly just above the horizon and he took a moment to notice his surroundings, aware that his short trip had covered years.

"Little has changed. The trees are larger and the ground foliage somewhat overgrown. It would appear as though I have traveled only a few years forward in time." This gave him great comfort, knowing his leap had not surpassed its intended distance.

He tore off a tiny piece of greenery from the nearest bush and rubbed it between his thumb and index finger until the chlorophyll stained his fingers green. "How long," he mumbled. He tried to grasp the concept of time travel—where he started, where he'd been and where he was now.

"Too much," he said, placing a hand on each side of his head. "Multiple timelines, existing in all simultaneously. It is all just too much to comprehend."

Hayden hovered close to the ground, then raced upward until above the tree line. The small air jockey paused and then moved on, careful not to loiter in any one place too long. "How many times shall I repeat this scenario?"

****

"Hello, old friend," Hayden said as he flew into a familiar urban setting. "Though you are no friend of mine." Making his rounds throughout the city, he stopped at the one residence he'd entered on his last appearance. The weather stripping had been replaced at the bottom of the door, so another means to enter would have to be found.

After several hours, an opportunity made itself available in the form of a repairman. The visitor, wearing denim overalls and carrying a wooden toolbox, reached for the top of an outdoor light fixture, removing a small, flat brass object. Placing and turning the narrow end, equipped with jagged edges, into a corresponding hole in the door, the entire assembly swung inward.

As the man walked into the kitchen, opening two small doors underneath a water delivery device, Hayden floated unnoticed into the room to begin his own investigation. The Dalleon cell remained in its same location. Then, he inspected the pictures on the wall. *I am detecting a difference in age among the subjects of as much as twenty years.* Hayden scrutinized the photographs closely. *There are also additions that were absent on my first visit.* He stared at the facial structure of the younger subjects—*offspring.*

The noise of the front door opening, then beginning to close, interrupted his analysis. Hayden, taken aback, rushed toward the front door, but the portal slammed shut before he could slip through the last remaining crack. He hovered, dumbfounded. Then he heard a clicking sound. The door opened and the man walked in.

"I almost forgot," the man said aloud. "They wanted the key left inside, since they'll be gone a couple of weeks."

The tiny flying man slipped through the doorway and out into the open. Hayden was terrified at the thought of being trapped in the residence for two weeks. *Surely, death would have overtaken me,* he shuddered in a moment of panic, *not to mention my people's fate.* He cut his exploration of Carpathia short and started back to the cave.

Upon arrival, Hayden immediately raised the time portal door and set out again, hoping to find an answer for this planet's ruin. Night had fallen, and the same eyes that watched him leave on his last journey were there, paying close attention to this departure.

CHAPTER TWENTY-FOUR

Jack and Link

"I don't believe what I'ma seein," Link said. He wiped away a tear and shuddered. "What is I gonna do without that knucklehead to set me straight when I do somethin' stupid?" Link began to cry in earnest.

"C'mon!" Jack grabbed Link by the collar and jerked him clear as the ground began to crack and then collapse under the weight of both men. "Run!" Jack barked.

"Give a feller a chance, why don'tcha." Link placed his hand on the unstable ground to keep from falling after Jack nearly pulled him off his feet. The two made a mad dash, barely ahead of the collapsing earth. Link stopped, leaned over, grabbed his knees, and began to draw air into his oxygen-starved body when the encroaching crevasse stopped its advance.

"Not yet," Jack said, tugging the man's collar. "Just because that crack in the ground ain't chasing us, it don't mean it's not still coming."

Link knocked Jack's hand away, then came to a halt. "You think that thing that swallered up Johnny Boy is really comin' afta us?" Link's expression bore the look of a man facing a firing squad.

Jack peered deep into Link's tortured eyes. "I wish I could tell you something that would make you feel better, but the truth is, I don't know. But I do know we have to keep moving." Link nodded, and the pair proceeded at a brisk pace.

Link spread his arms for balance. "The ground be a shakin' again, this time worserer than the time afore."

"The crevasse has increased its forward speed and rate of collapse." Link and Jack ran as a massive mound of dirt pushed skyward in front of them. Then, as the earthen hill exploded, Link and Jack dropped into a void, missing the concussive shockwave that would have certainly ripped them to shreds.

****

As Sim watched the explosion, he reflected, *I've seen much in the past day or two that I have never seen before. A way to live and carry myself that changed shortly after the fall of Burrus Plax. However, such a vast distance of time has passed, and it seems as though these memories belong to someone else. I will make myself more presentable, and then, over time, I will introduce Sim to the world.*

****

"Looks like we're at the bottom of the hatcher's tunnel," Jack said.

"Is that what this is?" Link asked.

"One and the same... one and the same." The two men dug their way from a shallow tomb. As Jack raked his fingers through the crumbling material, he touched something small, heavy, and cylindrical. Wrapping his hand around the object, Jack detected an internal split, barely noticeable but complete. A fleeting sense of lost stability sailed through his consciousness, nestling deep within his subconscious, waiting to sprout and grow. Jack had but a moment to experience being split in two.

"You okay?" Link asked.

Jack blinked several times. As the sensation started to fade, the divide left a feeling of despair so oppressive that he found it hard to stand under its weight. As soon as the overwhelming impression hit Jack, it subsided into a surreal thought that dissipated with a pop.

Link hesitated, then mumbled, "Not sure at what I'm looking, but something."

"If it's all the same to you, we need to way out of here before this tunnel ends up on our heads— again."

Jack was unaware that Nexus and the Other had taken residence within him, splitting his inner being into two. The two would eventually converge when the time had been decided. Until then, two halves of one young man and two halves of a single world dangled precariously over an abyss supported by a nearly invisible thread.

****

"Over here," Link yelled. A three-foot-wide ramp formed due to the hatcher's tunnel widening and the mountain's destruction. This ramp was tight to the collapsed tunnel wall and led from the floor to the ground above. "Can we use that to get outta here?"

Jack patted his friend on the back. "Good eye; let's take a closer look." Link and Jack took several steps, the shadows cast by the walls of the hole making it more difficult to see. "It appears pretty rough and the dirt's gonna be loose," he said, "but I believe you've found our only way out." Link jumped, placing his fingers on the edge of the ramp. His hands sank into the crumbling soil, dropping his body to the ground.

"Loose!" Link barked. He pushed himself to a standing position and glared at Jack while rubbing his hip.

The ground then rumbled loudly, jerking back and forth in quick succession, throwing both men to the ground. The earth continued its attack, heaving and tossing the men like pebbles. Then, a deafening silence.

"You's ok?" Link rubbed his arm.

"That was no tremor," Jack said.

They moved to where the ramp was at a more manageable height, and each one planted a foot simultaneously. The soil compressed eight inches before being firm enough to support their weight.

"Not too bad," Link said, slowing. He proved his point by extending his arms to the side and taking several hard-fought steps up the ramp.

"Keep moving, we're not out of danger, yet."

As if on cue, a pulse of air pushed from above at regular intervals, increasing in intensity until Link and Jack were knocked down and pushed deep into the loose dirt. Shielding his eyes from flying debris, Jack glanced upward and saw two massive wings hovering overhead.

"The ramp," Link yelled over the roar, "it's blowing away."

Jack didn't need to hear; he could feel the dirt disappearing beneath his body.

****

"Hold on!" Jack yelled. To what they didn't know. How long did they have before the ramp was gone? Jack looked for their salvation—a rock, anything where he could firmly place his feet.

Then, amidst the churn, a reptilian-like head propelled out through the bottom of the pit and into the air.

The hatcher!

The sheer force of its exit and body mass launched the hatcher into the flying aberration, where it clamped onto the underside of the hovering creature, causing it to move away.

"I thought that blamed hatcher was dead," Link said.

"Be thankful it wasn't," Jack replied. "I think we'd best use this time to get outta this hole."

Link nodded. "Ima followin' you."

****

"Look," Jack exclaimed as they stepped from the ramp onto solid ground. "The hatcher has pushed the sharp side of his tail into that flying thing's chest and sliced it from stem to stern."

Link shared that the flying aberration was a shower—a plain gray reptilian bird that appeared to predate history—that measured thirty feet from tail to beak and had a wing span of close to seventy feet.

"For something that just got split wide open," Link said, "looks like he's no worse for the wear. In fact, it appears that stupid thing is having a good time." The hatcher and the scower were interlocked by the hatcher's tail.

"I don't believe this," Jack said. "That crazy bird has shoved his beak slam through the hatcher's neck, and now it looks like they're dancing in midair." The two creatures began to circle counterclockwise, rising high into the air.

"If they get much higher," Link said, "they'll be out of sight and out of our hair."

"Ya think?" Jack replied. "That just may turn around and bite you on the backside."

"Wadda ya mean?"

Jack nodded upward. "Take a look." The hatcher and scower were spiraling toward the ground. The impact threw a plume of dirt and debris several hundred feet into the air, leaving a crater fifty feet deep and seventy feet wide. Even though Link and Jack were nearly a quarter mile away from the cataclysm, both men dropped to a prostrate position, feeling the concussive jolt vibrate through their bodies. Jack jumped to his feet, followed by Link. Rising through the sinking cloud of dust was something never before seen.

"What *is* that?" Link asked.

Jack froze.

First to appear was the head, triangular-shaped with two spiral protrusions at the rear of the skull. Both had sharp, pointed ends and faced rearward. Another horn-like projection, identical to the ones on the skull, attached to the end of the bottom jaw and pointed straight down. Link pulled his attention away from the strange entity. "Well do I get an answer?"

Jack shook his head. "Not until I have one to give . . . and I mean something that's believable, which is not what I am seeing around here."

The creature's partially opened mouth displayed a cavern full of disturbingly human-like teeth. The octagon-shaped eyes were set deep into sockets with a boney ridge following the contour of the outer edge along the eye socket. The eyes changed color from fiery red, slowly fading to cobalt blue. The nasal passages were elongated ovals, constantly dripping a green toxic fluid.

"I do believe we should expect a visitor," Jack said.

A dumbfounded expression crossed Link's face. "Wadda ya mean?"

"Our new friend seems to be heading this way," Jack replied.

Link jerked his head in the direction of the oncoming creature. "Have you ever seen such a thing?"

"Not recently," Jack said, "leastwise, not when I was sober." He knelt, attempting to get a better look at the beast's underside." He cocked his head, trying to make sense of what he was seeing. "Two arms, hands, three fingers, and opposable thumbs," he mumbled.

"Why all the concentration?" Link asked.

Jack extended his arm, palm out, signaling Link to remain quiet. At the same time, he continued to determine if what he was looking at was really there: two legs, both with raptor-like feet and talons, a pliable translucent membrane connected to each arm and stretched to the corresponding leg, forming a wing, enabling the creature to glide. Its twelve-foot-long tail was identical to that of a whale, except it split in two and fanned out, widening the gap between the two sections. The space between the two tail sections was adjustable according to any varying requirements desired by the winged creature.

Jack scratched his head, allowing Link to question his friend. "Back with us, I see."

"Not sure. I'm watching a copper-colored flying freak, flap what could only be described as a horizontal aquatic tail, up and down, propelling it through the air." Jack turned to look at Link. "Please tell me you see the same thing."

Link nodded. A high-pitched squall emanated from the flying creature, causing Link to cup his hands over his ears. Jack stood tall with a stoic expression. He removed the nexus and turned toward Link.

"What's wrong?" Link asked, moving backward as he spoke.

Jack did not make a sound and was on top of Link in an instant. Before Link could make any sense of the events taking place, he lay in two pieces on the ground, his eyelids blinking as his life's blood poured from his body.

Then, Jack moved toward the beast, who was circling to land. Nestled deep within Jack, one had now come to claim the other.

****

A pair of eyes opened, joining a second pair that had previously been deposited within this realm of darkness.

"Who are you?" The first pair asked, sounding identical to Johnny Boy.

"I thought I was Link," the second pair replied, "But now I'm not so sure . . . and you sound like my good friend, Johnny Boy."

"Well I reckon I do sound like your good friend, 'cause I am Johnny Boy . . . least wise that's who I was up 'til now . . . but like you I'm not sure."

"What do you figure has done and happened to us?" Link asked.

"Don't know, but you can bet I'm gonna find out."

"I weren't be so sure, cause you might not find'er so easy after all . . . and by the by, you kin call me Byrnes . . . and all my friends, least wise thems what ain't dead, calls me Mama Byrnes."

A black cloud, invisible except where it passed over the white sclera of each eye (the only hint of light in this dark environment), encased the four ocular organs.

"Johnny Boy," Link implored, "Whereja go?"

"No worries," Rave said, "You're among special friends."

"And before you know it," Murph said, "We'll all be one big family."

"Well said," Dub chimed in.

"Nooo!" Link's scream was abruptly silenced as the black cloud enveloped everything into a suffocating darkness—a void where voices protesting their fate were felt but not heard.

CHAPTER TWENTY-FIVE

Dalon Con and Sketch

"Yee haw," Sketch yelled. "We is a rockin'em now." Sketch was wedged firmly between Dalon Con's legs as both men navigated the ins and outs, ups and downs, and the sudden left-to-right jerks experienced during their journey down the slide.

Sketch was enjoying the ride, behaving like a child on a roller coaster, until their speed suddenly increased, causing him to grip Dalon Con with a death grip. Closing his eyes, he buried his face deep into Dalon Con's chest. Moments later, the kid returned with the same youthful exuberance.

"I can see thar's a bunch 'o' slides jest like we's on to both sides, but it seems like near as I can tell, somebody done and puked a pretty good amount, that away." Sketch pointed to the left with his index finger.

After a fifteen-minute ride, it came to an end.

"I taint sure ifin I'm glad the ride's over or do I wants to tackl'er agin," Sketch said, staring up the path they had just traversed. He looked to Dalon Con. "Could we do er agin?"

"I am afraid that will not be possible. We must make all haste to a location, that until now, has yet to be seen by human eyes."

Sketch ceased his childlike drivel. "Wadda ya mean, not seen by nary a two-legged critter, like me?" He spat and then wiped his mouth with the backside of his hand. "Just what kinda eyeballs is we 'spectin' to see?"

Dalon Con couldn't help but smile. "On your feet and I will weave you a tale of recent descent, as we travel."

"Sakes alive, I ain't heared me no story in a hunderd year er more," Sketch said, the childlike excitement returning. "Git on wit it, Mr. Dalon."

****

"You illin', boy?" Mr. Marcus asked. "Ya been leanin' up against that shovel more than you been usin' it. Ya ain't old enough fer the dirt to have a hold on you yet."

"No sir," Dain said. "It's the stories about . . ." a distant rumble in the rock strata interrupted the conversation. The rumble took on a life of its own, changing to a growl. It advanced slowly toward the group, gaining in volume as it progressed. Mr. Marcus and the two young men started to laugh when Dain dropped to his knees and covered his head, afraid the apocalypse was upon them.

"What's the matter young'n," Marcus barked, "big bad monster comin' to get ya?"

"First timer, eh?" Neell said, kneeling to help Dain to his feet.

"Don't tell me ya believed them bedtime stories 'bout ole kranker flyin' through solid rock to git little ole you." Marcus squalled, then burst into another fit of laughter, bracing himself against what he called his discipline stick. The underground cavern was shaking and, by some unseen force, supporting a thirty-mile-per-hour wind. Marcus smiled at Dain, and then, all but the smooth metal brain bucket he wore was gone, along with his unknown cohort.

"Well, I guess that's one way to do it," Neell said. He scanned the immediate area. "Might not be a bad idea to follow suit."

Mimicking a child, the hollow sound of Marcus's voice oozed from his helmet. "Run little ones. The kranker is hungry and close behind." After a short pause, a hysterical cackle ensued, prompting the young men to obey the voice.

****

Dain and Neell collapsed from exhaustion. "At…least…that…ungodly…voice…is…gone," Dain garbled, the droning of Marcus still fresh in his mind. Neell stared at Dain, satisfied to wait until his breath returned before speaking.

Rolling to his knees, Neell placed both hands on his thighs and sat back on his haunches. "Well, here we are."

Rising to his feet, Dain glanced at Neell and then surveyed his surroundings. "Where do you suppose *here* is?"

"Outta that cave," Neell replied, relief in his voice. He pulled a blue-green leaf, examined both sides, and let it fall to the forest floor. He failed to notice a dozen minuscule scientists, camouflaged in blue-green lab coats, moving under his boot's arch support and heading toward the recently vacated cave. These miniature bipeds, known as the Odobi, resembled normal human beings. The Odobi was a race devoted to the scientific study of catastrophic changes in established civilizations, whether good or bad.

Dain paused, affixed on a symmetrical breach in a plank wall. "See that narrow opening just ahead?"

Neell nodded. "Appears too well made. . . not natural, like you'd expect."

Dain smiled. "Wouldn't want to keep'em waiting now, would we?"

Neell furrowed his eyebrows. "Probably not the proper thing to do. I expect we'd best get to meetin' and greetin'."

Dain sighed. "I reckon so."

****

The opening had been cut into a four-inch-thick wall constructed of vertical wooden planks. Neell ran his hand along its edges, admiring the workmanship. "Smooth."

"Why the oval shape?" Dain rapped the wall with his knuckles. A metallic sound rang out and then came the answer to Dain's question. The response came in the form of a twelve-foot-long insect.

"Down!" Neell yelled. Both men ducked as the creature skittered overhead and through the oval.

"So that's it!" Dain exclaimed. "The entrance is cut to fit the creature's tail."

"That *would* keep any larger animal out."

"Yeah, it would, but out of what?"

"Do I detect an adventure in the making?" Neell inquired.

"Nope," Dain said, "just a little look-see for starters."

****

The tail swept across the opening, removing a clump of Dain's blonde hair and ripping a portion of his gray cotton shirt collar. He threw himself sprawling backward. The next thing he saw was a hand reaching down to help him up.

"Good reflexes," Neell said. "When I saw that tail slice across the opening about the time you popped your noggin back through, I expected your headless corpse to be the next thing on the ground."

Dain shook his head as he brushed off his clothes. "It's not that, not that at all." He glared at Neell. "Something warned me to pull back out of the opening before the jayrack removed any body parts I wanted to keep."

"Something warned you?" Neell asked.

"Yep, and before you get started, it also told me that thing in there is called a jayrack, and not only is it called a jayrack, but we got to go in there and pay it a visit."

Neell stood leaning against the wooden fortress, a perplexed expression on his face.

"In there?" Neell thumbed toward the enclosure. "And just how do you reckon we do that?"

"Look," Dain replied, "that's just what the voice said."

"The one inside your head?" Neell asked. "The voice. . . it's a voice now?"

"No. . . not so much a voice," Dain countered, the frustration evident in his speech. "It's not audible, it's just there."

"So, you're beginning to hear—"

"Finish that sentence, and you'll leave your share of blood on the ground."

"Whoa!" Neell said, both arms straight out, palms forward. "Didn't mean to step on your toes."

Dain looked at Neell with a puzzled expression on his face. "Don't know what got into me."

"Maybe something that has no business mucking around in your head has you on edge."

Dain raised his eyebrows and nodded. "Could be, but we still need to find a way in."

"We've got a perfectly good hole right here," Neell said.

"Yeah, we do," Dain said, "and the last time I had my head through that hole, I nearly lost it."

Neell scratched the back of his neck. "There is that," he said, struggling to suppress a grin. With the idea of tunneling under the wall firmly in mind, Dain began digging beside the four-inch-thick barrier. To their astonishment, the grain of the wall opened up, its fluid motion swallowing the young men before they could even think of escape. Unable to protest, Dain and Neell were pulled into the living wood and oozed through the wall into a containment area.

****

One look at the malevolent scenery told both men they didn't want to stay. They prepared to slide through the oval in order to escape what felt like their final internment.

"I think we should go now," Dain said.

"Don't have to tell me twice." The bottom of the oval penetration was five feet from the ground. Neell grabbed the bottom edge and pulled himself up. He dangled his left leg through the hole, then moved to include his right. Hearing a moist crunch, he turned his head toward the noise. What had once been Dain was now a twelve-foot-long red smear traveling diagonally across the wall.

Before Neell could react, the human-like hand rose from Dain and swiped down the wall again. This time the red smear contained the upper half of Neell's body, while his lower half fell outside the area, where, within minutes the limbs—bone and all—were devoured by numerous scavengers that roamed the forest floor.

****

"Now that thar's a story," Sketch said, his voice tinged with a mix of nostalgia and regret. "I mean to tell ya, it is." His shoulders slumped, and his demeanor dropped as he added, "I done and forgot 'bout my bestest bud, Krabb." Tears began to cascade down Sketch's face, branching off as the flow increased.

Suddenly, the system of underground caves began to rumble, and the northwest wall of Dalon Con and Sketch's enclosure cracked. Then a hole appeared, filled with black, so dark that even light failed to escape.

The figure maintained its shape as it moved through the opening, then dropped onto the cave floor with a disturbingly fleshy sound. Eight large, human-like fingers gripped the sides of the opening as it pulled itself into the cave. Then, a large, disheveled man leaned over and placed Krabb on the cavern floor.

"If I'm not mistaken this here belongs to you," Smort said, "Thought I might bring'em back, since I found him to be the reason a shadow-walker was having such a good time." He laughed a bit then removed his hands. "He be all yourn."

"As far as a goot story goes, I believe I done an heard better," Krabb said, "talking 'bout that there tale 'o' the Corstrum and them two silly boys what got all smushed up."

"Krabb!" Sketch hollered, throwing his arms around his protégé and nearly falling from his perch. “Where ya done and been, ya ole wind bag?”

“Don’t rightly know,” Krabb replied. “I were jest here. I were gettin’ rousted pretty good by this thing a ma bob, before this here fella,” Krabb threw a thumb in Smort’s direction. “Stepped in and pulled me outta the sitcheation, whilst making a mess outta that thar shadda-walker.”

Smort blinked, then stared at Dalon Con. “You,” he remarked, moving toward the stoic old man who appeared as a thirty-year-old-suit.

“How are you, Smort?” Dalon Con asked, “Things are a bit different since we were last thrust together.”

“As much as I hate to agree, you treated me right proper, but that don’t mean I’ma just gonna roll over and be your patsy . . . no sir. You’ll have to keep on your toes ‘til I come ‘round to your way of thinkin’ . . . ifin I ever do.”

“I am aware, doing what I ask,” Dalon Con said, “that in your eyes relieves you of control regarding your life; however, nothing could be further from the truth.” Smort stared into the wizened face, losing enough of his inhibitions to submit.

“I will comply,” Smort said. Dalon Con smiled, pulling Smort’s head down making it possible to whisper into the big man’s ear. A minute later Smort grinned, touched his benefactor on the shoulder, then slid through the stone corridor, and into the foliage.

Minutes into his journey, Smort collapsed inward and found himself being pulled at an incredible speed in an unknown direction.

CHAPTER TWENTY-SIX

Dalon Con, Krabb and Sketch

"We have arrived," Dalon Con said. Krabb's mouth dropped open, and he turned to face Dalon Con. "Ya mean to tell me that ya done an brung us to the very same spot ya been gabbin' 'bout since we left?"

"Your statement is true," Dalon Con replied, "the very same spot."

"But why would ya ever do such a thin'?" Sketch asked.

"Not to worry, my friends," Dalon Con said. "Those who are ignorant of the ways of this place, known for millennia as the 'Corstrum' or 'place of meeting', are destined to reap its rewards, no matter how horrendous they may be."

"Then ya gots me and Krabb's back on this here one?" Sketch stood, his shoulders slumped and eyes beginning to tear.

Dalon Con placed his hand on Sketch's back. "Do not concern yourself with such things; I will keep you and your comrade safe. However, once we enter the Corstrum, you must never leave my presence." He gazed at Sketch and Krabb with an endearing expression. "If you do, even for a moment, I can no longer guarantee your safety."

"Hmmf," Krabb grunted, "I'll be bleevin' that'un whenced I can lay these eyeballs on 'er."

Sketch moved toward Krabb and placed a hand on each of Krabb's upper arms. "We gots to give him a chance," Sketch begged. "He'd never let the harm come at us."

Krabb stared at the ground. "Jest get 'er started so's we can get out'n this here hole." Dalon Con pulled each man close and walked toward the wooden structure, stopping when all three were in contact with the wall. The grain in the wood began to separate, creating large, malleable pockets.

“What in tarnation?” Krabb exclaimed.

“Close your eyes,” Dalon Con said; then all was silent as the three humanoids were pulled through the wall. Dalon Con was the first to appear inside the Corstrum, followed by Sketch and Krabb. A single glance inside prompted the two men to grab their benefactor.

“Have ya ever seen such a sight as this here place?” Sketch asked.

“Not in nary a time I kin ‘member,” Krabb replied.

“Squaaa!” emanated from hundreds of small flying reptiles. Dalon Con quickly wrapped his robe around his two wards. Although the garment was invisible, the comfort it brought to Sketch and Krabb made its invisibility insignificant.

“Looky there,” Sketch cried out, “them flyin’ whatever they is can’t be no more than twelve inches long.” The soaring creatures had bat-like wings and a tail that comprised a third of its entire length.

“What scares me is them stickers what slices everthin’ it touches,” Krabb said. Razor-like spikes protruded from the creatures bodies, causing blood to splatter as they collided with one another. Severed reptilian fragments rained down, covering the ground except where Dalon Con stood. The twitching segments were quickly devoured by underground carrion feeders.

“What you reckon they want?” Sketch asked.

“Ain’t got no mind ‘bout that,” Krabb replied, “but I sure is glad we is where we is.”

“They are part of this world.” As the trio walked, Dalon Con placed one hand upon Sketch and the other on Krabb. “The Great One did not give you a heart of fear; you would do well to remember these words.”

As the boxed-in area narrowed, a foul stench permeated the air. “Stay close,” Dalon Con said. Krabb and Sketch tightened their grip.

“Hag! You have summoned me to your hellish retreat,” Dalon Con snarled. “Speak and do not tarry. My patience flees at the stench that is you.”

The ground rumbled, and several sharp projectiles flew out of the foliage. Dalon Con calmly held up his hand. "No," he said softly, and the stone daggers fell harmlessly to the ground.

The air grew increasingly acrid, making it difficult to breathe. Then, an acidic mist slithered along the ground, dissolving everything in its path.

"Noooo!" Krabb whimpered as the mist crept closer.

"Enough!" Dalon Con boomed. "No more games, Hag. Show yourself."

A rustling of leaves, followed by a deep alluring voice, emanated from the darkness ahead. "The Nexus and the Other are now as one," Hag hissed. "You have failed, old man."

"Your declaration is as empty as your threats."

"Ah, but I smell fear. It surrounds you like that old cloak. No, not you, but . . ." Hag inhaled deeply. "Yessss. Little ones. They are not as foolish as you. They sense my power. Perhaps they . . ."

"Take this as a warning, Hag." Dalon Con slammed his staff on the ground, briefly illuminating the black void causing Hag to shriek in pain. "The light is coming. You cannot stop it. And know this—if you summon me again, prepare."

"Prepare? Who are you to order us?" Hag shrieked. "This world is ours! In the end, you *will* serve us."

"I serve only the Great One," Dalon Con said quietly as he turned to leave. "An in the end, you will die."

"Spew your trivial threats," Hag bellowed. "We will see who prevails." The sound of wailing laughter grew as Dalon Con, Sketch and Krabb pushed through the wall a second time.

"That crazy galoot has done and scared the bejeesus outta me," Krabb confessed.

"It twere a bit unnervin'," Sketch agreed.

"Remember," Dalon Con said, "fear has no place here."

****

Many options, Smort thought, *much to consider . . . so very much to consider. I feel a connection with the three I follow. Yet, I recall the vile teachings I succumbed to as Burrus Plax evolved into the despicable planetary mess it is today.* Smort caught a glimpse of Dalon Con, Krabb, and Sketch. Brevity ruled as he smiled, but then his lips fell. *It is best to remain aloof until I come to terms with my emotional conundrum.*

Smort cocked his head, both eyes squinting while he gazed forward. *My intellect seems to have increased exponentially . . . this change on a scale I never would have imagined . . .* "how strange," he said, as he made a complete split from his alternate persona.

****

The primary version of Smort traveled blindly for an undetermined amount of time, coming to an abrupt halt in a considerable amount of soft gray flesh.

"What be this mess I'm in, and somebody best have a good answer afore Smort starts a tearin' this place to pieces."

"Even with ample time you were unable to carry out a simple assignment," Hag said, "and since Dalon Con continues to live I have enlisted another worthless operative to carry on in your stead."

"What have you done," Smort roared, "I will not be replaced."

"This is the first utterance from your mouth that rings true," Hag replied. "I will not replace you; however, you *will* die."

"Ahhh," Smort squalled as folds of gray matter turned him to liquid to be assimilated by the material encased in Hag's cranium.

****

The three men, their faces illuminated by the warm glow of the fire, sat on rough-hewn logs, enjoying a meal of cabot and thargrass, as the sun dropped below the horizon.

"Thems was some mighty fine eatin'," Sketch said as he tossed a scrap of meat into his mouth and wiped his lips with his sleeve.

"Twernt so bad," Krabb said, "but I done an had better."

"Well I ain't never heard one old coot complain so much in all my born days," Sketch said.

"I'm glad you enjoyed our bounty supplied by The Great One." Dalon Con said.

"This here Great One ya keep goin' on and on bout," Krabb interrupted, "that's what he were gonna bug ya 'bout, weren't ya, Sketch?"

"I would be happy to tell you of the Great One," Dalon Con said. "It is no bother; in fact, it is the very reason for my existence. Firstly, the One I speak of is the Creator of all and everything that was created."

"Hold on right thar," Krabb said. "Ya mean to tell me that this here feller done an made everythin'?"

"That is correct," Dalon Con said, his excitement growing. "The Great One also watches over His creation, wanting each of us to fellowship with Him."

"Just a minute," Krabb said, standing and pointing a finger at his now-perceived opponent. "Ya sayin' that this here feller done an made me, too?"

"Yes," Dalon Con said, "just as he made me, Sketch and every other creature that walks this planet."

"I be a thinkin' you done an gone too far," Krabb said.

"Now, you jus hold on thar, ya carn-sarn fussbudget," Sketch said. "Yo pappy sho-nuff named ya right when he comed up with callin' ya Krabb, 'cause you 'bout tha orneriest man I eva runned into."

"You ain't gonna talk at ole Krabb like that—"

"Shut that jabber hole up, and shut it right now," Sketch demanded. "You's gonna listen at me and you's gonna listen til I's done." He leaned over nearly nose-to-nose with Krabb, poking him in the chest with a boney finger as he spoke.

"We done an been together pertnear eighty year now, and all that time I put up with yo cantankerous gripin' an complainin'." Sketch placed his hand on Krabb's shoulder. "Now, ya knows I loves ya jest like ya was ma brotha, but I gots to tell ya, we done an been together so long cuz can't nobody else stand to be 'round ya." He paused his rant, waiting for his partner to absorb his words. "Krabb, we be a needin' to listen to this man. He be a good man. Ifin it weren't fer him, weuns be supper fer worms and all kinds a critters. So once in yer life shut that trap an open them ears 'o' yern."

Krabb slumped. "I know I ain't easy to be 'round, and I'm much obliged you seen fit to hang wit me all these year. I guess I ain't had me much 'o' an upbringin' and it done an stuck with me since I was jus a little feller."

"Sometimes, it helps to cleanse the soul and relieve oneself of a heavy burden," Dalon Con counseled, "especially, when friends want to help bear that load, making it lighter for you."

Krabb stared at the ground, making random designs in the dirt with his foot. "Never found much time fer tellin' folks ma biness." He raised his head and looked at Dalon Con. "Sides, I ain't a wantin' to 'rupt yer story."

"No," Dalon Con replied, "the Great One's ways are not our ways, and I believe this has happened so that you may find relief."

"Why in tarnation would He do such a thin'?" Krabb asked.

"The Great One's love for each of us is immeasurable," Dalon Con said.

"Go head, Krabb, spin yer yarn," Sketch said.

"Feels kinda strange, me doin' the talkin'," Krabb said, "but here goes. Ma daddy twern't worth much. From the time I were able to 'member, alls he do is sit 'round and smoke tarweed. Ma mammy– she were the one that birth me– took care a all us young'uns." Krabb hesitated, thinking about his siblings. "All we et was what Mammy killed. She pulled out the guts 'n tossed a chunk 'o' meat on a slab 'o' iron what had a fire under it. Ifin ma daddy smelt that thar meat afore us young'uns could sup, he'd stumble into the cookin' place, jest full 'o' the meanness. We'd get mighty hungerful with nothin' to et that night."

"I sure fer goodness didn't know ya had it so rough," Sketch said.

Krabb produced a grim smile. "I'sa jest started. One night, Daddy stumbled into where Mammy was a cookin' and touched that hot piece 'o' metal. He got even worst at walkin' and came close to fallin'. Mammy took 'vantage 'o' him and pushed Daddy down on that hot metal an then helt the side 'o' his face onto it. She were pressin' hard, and Daddy were 'bout to fry up like a slab 'o' fresh skint meat." Krabb stared into the distance, his voice silent, and eyes brimming with tears.

"Is you ok?" Sketch asked. "I knows ya gots to be illin', talkin' 'bout such a mess." Krabb glanced at Sketch and then toward Dalon Con before resuming his gaze into nothing.

"If this is too much," Dalon Con said, "we would understand you wanting to curtail your recollection of events."

Krabb sniffed and wiped his eyes. "No siree, this here tale needs a tellin', 'n I'm bound to tell it."

Dalon Con smiled. "Carry on at your discretion, my friend."

The comment warmed Krabb. "Daddy managed to knock Mammy away an snatched up a piece 'o' metal she used to cook with. His head were stuck to that thar cookin' metal an he had a job scrapin' what were left 'o' his head." Krabb smiled at the pain he knew his father had to endure.

"Once he unstuck the side 'o' his face, Daddy had the same thin' with his hand, 'ceptin' all the fingers was cooked and twern't much to scrape off. That's when he headed fer Mammy." Krabb pulled a rag from his back pocket and blew his nose. "I ain't got the heart to teld ya what he done to Mammy." He sniffed again. "But he kilt her right thar whilst all five 'o' his young'uns seed him do it." Krabb looked down and shook his head. "It weren't no call fer him ta do her like he done."

He looked up, his face wet with tears. "He just kept goin' on at her, even afta she were dead."

Krabb wiped his eyes again. "I'ma thinkin' that thar day all us young'uns figered Daddy were gonna pay fer what he done to Mammy."

Dalon Con threw several pieces of wood on the fire, attracting unwanted attention. "Pardon me, it was not my intention to interrupt your tale . . . please, continue as you are led."

Krabb nodded. "Thank ye kindly, Mr. Dalon." Before he could begin, the ground started to shake. A hole appeared just within the boundaries of the fire's light. It started no more than a foot in diameter, then slowly widened.

As the fray began, only Dalon Con noticed a white blur exiting from atop a tree and moving laterally, disappearing a millisecond later. *That one I know,* he thought, a wide grin spreading across his face. "Sim."

"What in tarnation," Sketch asked, "be that thar hole pokin' itself outin' the ground?"

Dalon Con sprang to his feet. "Both of you, to my side!" he commanded. Sketch and Krabb heard him but remained frozen, struggling to comprehend the chaotic scene unfolding around them.

"Now!" Dalon Con barked. His two wards obeyed and soon clung to the familiar furry robe.

The hole had reached three feet in diameter when a large hand appeared, pulling at the edges to widen it further. Then a second hand emerged, and together the fissure expanded to over six feet.

"Them big hands is 'bout to put the fear in me, I don't mind tellin ya," Krabb said, a slight tremble in his voice.

"Do not fear," Dalon Con said. "Size is of no consequence."

"I don't know," Sketch said. "The way it's a lookin' ta me, them thar hands might be full 'o' that conquency you was a gabbin' 'bout." Dalon Con could not help but smile. He glanced skyward. *What a wonderful sense of humor.*

Hands pushed up through the hole, followed by arms and a head full of thick, brown hair. An unexpectedly kind face smiled and said, “Don’t leave, I’ll be right there.” His palms pressed on the edges of the opening and brought the rest of this massive man through the hole where he sat on the edge. Pulling his legs from the opening, the well-muscled eight-foot-tall man stood up and brushed the dirt from his denim pants, long-sleeve pullover shirt, and high-top leather shoes.

“He’s a sight more nimble than you might ‘spect fer a feller that big,” Sketch said.

“Uh huh,” Krabb mumbled.

Once satisfied most of the dust was gone, the large man made a beeline for the old man.

“Dalon Con?” he asked. “Please tell me you’re Dalon Con.”

“I am he. Now, what may I do for you?”

“I’ve been looking for you and have wandered among the dregs of society, seeing strange creatures and city streets that would make a dead man puke.”

“May I inquire your name?” Dalon Con asked.

“Where are my manners?” the large man replied. “Of course, folks call me Falum.”

“You have yet to answer my question,” Dalon Con said. “How may we help you?”

“Mr. Dalon, there is something that’s after me. I don’t know what it is, but I knew if I could get to you, not only would I be safe, but I would be able to help you when this evil arrives.” Falum peered at Dalon Con. “I don’t mean to say that you’re unable to handle this situation on your own, just that I’m willing to help.”

“Worry not,” Dalon Con said, placing a hand on each of Falum’s arms. “Your words do not insult, and I am grateful for your assistance.” He smiled at Falum with a sparkle in his eye. “I have an ally, One who is stronger than any other. There is no end to the strength, power and love of this One.” Dalon Con lowered his arms and placed his hands on Falum's hands. "I have known of your coming for some time now. The Great One gave me no details, but left me to discover them myself, for which I am grateful. In this short time, you have proven your alliance to our cause, and for this I am indebted to you."

"I am grateful for your words," Falum said, "but I think we should leave this place in all haste."

"A wise move," Dalon Con said, "for we are not yet ready for a confrontation."

CHAPTER TWENTY-SEVEN

Gabriel and Bile

Gabriel's hand slid up his chest and grasped his throat. He felt a rubbery cord around his neck, the same diameter as his pinky. What he didn't know was that a long, slender creature called a garrote had surfaced from the ground near his neck, looped over, and slithered back into the soil on the opposite side. Emerging several feet away, it began to gorge on the blood oozing from his head. This served two purposes for the garrote: it could feed leisurely while simultaneously strangling its prey, preventing premature coagulation.

Gabriel began to fade from consciousness as oxygen deprivation overtook him. He saw a light growing steadily larger and assumed it to be the one he'd been told of, manifesting itself when someone is close to death. But instead of peace, he felt panic. As Gabriel's eyes lowered for the last time, a shower of sparks partially revived the boy, raising numerous blisters on his face. His revival was made complete when the garrote split apart, releasing his neck. A domino effect expanded Gabriel's trachea, allowing his diaphragm to spasm back to life, filling his lungs. He shuddered violently several times, his body greedily using the air and gasping for more. As Gabriel's head cleared, he heard a familiar voice.

"Ain't much more then an apitzer," Bile said, "but it'll do." He dropped his torch and snapped the garrote in two. Shoving half of the snake-like creature into his mouth, Bile began to chew the rubbery flesh. He swallowed and then began to gnaw on what remained of the blood sucker.

"Ohh," Gabriel moaned.

"Well now," Bile said, masticated flesh spewing from his mouth, "I see yer still a kickin'."

Gabriel raised his arm several inches off the ground. His fingers dangled, then fell, sending up a cloud of dust.

"Attaboy," Bile said. "Climb on, we needs to be a gettin' outta here." Bile reached down, tossed Gabriel over his shoulder, and traveled at his usual high rate of speed.

Gabriel touched the back of his head, feeling a sticky mess where the blood had clotted in his hair. Then, the rocking motion in Bile's stride lulled him to sleep.

****

When Gabriel opened his eyes, he was lying flat on his back. A flickering, orange light danced from the low-cropped foliage.

"Well, looky here, somebody wakin' up." Bile, stirring red coals at the bottom of a shallow fire pit, hocked up a phlegm ball and blew it into the hottest part of the fire, smiling as the wad of slime sizzled.

"I guess you could call it that." Gabriel, his head aching, rolled over and pushed himself to all fours.

"C'mon, I saved ya some grub." He grabbed a fist full of three-inch dark-colored irregular-shaped pieces from beside the fire. Gabriel crawled to the flames and sat opposite the big man who tossed him some of the food. As the boy gathered a half dozen pieces, he closely examined one. *Wide one way, flat the other, and kinda squishy.* Bile noticed Gabriel inspecting his dinner.

"Et boy," Bile snarled. "There be big doin's ahead, and you gonna need 'xactly what that thar food puts in ya."

Gabriel reluctantly took a bite. He raised his eyebrows. *I guess I can get'em down,* he thought, nodding at Bile. *Not eating them sure isn't worth getting beat up over.* "These things have a name?" Gabriel asked.

Bile thought a moment. "A feller showed 'em to me afore I kilt him. They growed on dead tree stumps, and I'm a thinkin' he said they was some kinda room . . . like a mushed up room." Gabriel found the last one Bile had thrown at him and popped it into his mouth.

"It'd be better cooked."

"Shut up 'bout the food. Didn't I say we got big doin's ahead?"

Gabriel nodded. "Fill me in."

"We is joinin' up with a feller what's gonna help us get rid of that Dalon Con."

Dalon Con's not a bad guy. In fact, he saved my life. I'd better find out why this is happening. "I heard you mention him before," Gabriel said warily. "But why do you want to kill him?"

"Ifin ya knowed me at all, ya know I don't need no reason. But since you's helpin' me do it, I s'pose you kin know."

"Helping you, I've never killed anyone!" *I don't count that filthy witch, Mama Byrnes as a person.*

"Ya be a knowin' what they say," Bile smiled. "First time fer everythin'." Gabriel slumped, so many thoughts running through his head that he wanted to scream. "Don't worry none, boy; ole Bile's here to tell ya that a good killin' ain't nothin' but fun."

Gabriel sat quietly, staring at the ground.

"Time to go, boy," Bile said. Before Gabriel could process the statement, he was plucked from the ground and on Bile's back, moving toward their next destination. Gabriel feared the next stop would include a showdown with Dalon Con, and a feeling of melancholy washed over him. Dalon Con had rescued him from the white death. Gabriel had been taken in, readied for travel, and protected by Dalon Con until Bile had snatched him away.

Gabriel stiffened. "If Dalon Con is such a force to be reckoned with, how was Bile able to pilfer me from Dalon Con's very grasp?" He immediately knew the answer. Gabriel seethed, his breaths coming in short, rhythmic bursts. "Dalon Con allowed it to happen." Then, he smiled. "Jerk me around . . . I don't think so," Gabriel whispered. "You will pay, Mr. Con . . . Yes . . . you *will* pay."

****

"Where are we?" Gabriel asked when Bile came to a halt before a sizeable wooden barrier.

"A place where folks git together and meet."

Gabriel rolled his eyes. "Does it have a name?"

"Ain't rightly sure. I knowed it starts with cor and then sump'm else, but I ain't sure what."

Gabriel turned on Bile. "What do you mean, 'I ain't sure?" he screamed. "Do you know anything, or are you just a big stupid oaf?"

Bile dropped to his knees and drove his fists into the ground, one on each side of Gabriel. The concussion caused Gabriel to wobble. Regaining his footing, he found himself face-to-face with an animalistic Bile who snorted and growled with each breath.

Gabriel stepped back and extended both hands. "No, Bile, I was out of line." He took a second step backward as Bile inched closer to the boy. "I couldn't control myself;" Gabriel pleaded, "I was overcome by rage." Bile slowed his advance.

Gabriel curled up on the ground and wrapped his arms and hands around his head. His entire body shook, waiting for the end. When it didn't come, he dared to open one eye and peer through a small crack between his fingers. Bile was on his feet, arms by his side, both fists clenched. Gabriel closed his eyes again and waited.

"Up, boy!" Bile ordered in a shaky, guttural tone. Gabriel unfolded his arms and reared back onto his haunches.

"I said, UP, BOY!" Bile roared.

"Yessir, Mr. Bile, sir," Gabriel stammered. He jumped to his feet, stumbled, and fell flat on his back.

Bile stared at the boy's blunders. Slowly, his anger faded, and a smile tugged at the corners of his mouth. Then Bile laughed.

CHAPTER TWENTY-EIGHT

Jack and Torast

Jack patted the creature's head and rubbed its scale-covered throat. "Strange, but I'm just now realizing that I've been waiting for this flying . . . whatever it is, for many weeks."

"*I take exception to being referred to as a, 'whatever it is.' Please call me Torast.*"

Jack stared at this giant flying reptile who possessed the power of speech without uttering a word. Occasionally, a thought seemed to travel from his brain to his mouth, only to be pulled back before it could be loosed.

"*Nothing to say?*" Torast asked.

"When I can put together a sentence that has anything to do with what I've seen, then I'll have something to say."

"*Cease your fascination with me and allow your mind to drift.*" Jack closed his eyes and relaxed, listening to Torast's droning. "*Our unification, something that was planned long ago, will soon be complete. Without your knowledge, you will quickly advance a number of years, both physically and emotionally, to fill this role. We will soon join two others, one called Bile and the other Gabriel. They will assist in the destruction of a common enemy. Bile is a loathsome and depraved creature. All that remains of his humanoid ancestry is his bipedal appearance, and even that, at times, is questionable.*

Gabriel is his complete opposite. He has been inundated with spiteful impressions from his first guardian, causing bouts of rage and then great depression. These emotional fluctuations have been brought on by the love he harbors for his next benefactor, which will prove to be a deadly combination. You should by now know that this benefactor and our common enemy are one and the same."

ack opened his eyes. "Dalon Con," he whispered, his eyes briefly glowing a brilliant orange. Turning to Torast, Jack began to scale the side of the beast, using the hard protrusions as a makeshift ladder until he reached its back. He swung his leg over and settled into a natural depression that fit his buttocks and supported his back. Jack extended his arms, grasping two perfectly placed handholds.

"Let's get to it, my friend," he said.

Torast pushed, lifting his thorax from the ground and straightening his legs to their full length. Arching his back, he squatted to tense his leg muscles, pausing to allow the tension to build. Then, with a powerful thrust, Torast pushed upward and forward with all four limbs, propelling himself and Jack several thousand feet into the air.

The noise was horrendous. Moments into the flight, their forward speed generated a deafening explosion as Torast breached the sound barrier. Jack quickly realized he could communicate with Torast telepathically. "*Whoa,*" Jack exclaimed, *"what's going on, big boy?"*

Torast shifted a series of locked tendons along his back. *"Since you asked, I enjoy stretching seldom-used muscles and the fresh air in such an open area is liberating."*

As the aquatic-like tail began to contract and release, the legs shifted away from his body, allowing his wings to unfold and support the massive weight. As the tail and wings synchronized, they took over the tasks of support and propulsion.

"Can you share with me our destination?" Jack conveyed to his winged companion.

"Eventually, to a meeting place called Corstrum," Torast relayed. *"For now, there is much preparation to be made before our showdown with Dalon Con."*

"Does this Dalon Con deserve the respect we have accorded him?" Jack silently questioned.

"And more," Torast conveyed. *"Even with reinforcements, I fear our meager force shall not be enough."* Torast's attention was drawn to something he saw in the distance. *"We have reached our first destination; prepare to descend."*

"Preparation?" Jack wondered. *"How could I possibly know how to prepare for something I've never done?"*

"There are many things at your disposal you would come to know, if only you would consider each situation as it arises," Torast silently replied. *"It has been this way since our link became complete."*

Jack brought the words *'prepare to land'* into his mix of thoughts. Immediately, the landing procedure and his part in this process became clear. *"Ready for descent."*

"Very good," the flying reptilian mentally replied. Torast moved his four legs inward, folding his wings tight to his body. As his tail moved into an upward position, he began a steep dive. Jack pulled back on the two handholds, causing a boney shield to rise, protecting him from the wind that would surely tear him apart.

"Wherever we're going, you must be planning on getting there in a hurry."

"I am simply moving at the speed gravity dictates," Torast expressed.

Jack began to reply when his telepathic message was interrupted by a sudden reduction in speed. With Torast's wings extended, they slowly circled their intended landing area, marked by a two-hundred-foot circle cut in the middle of a forest.

"So, this is our destination?"

"It is as you say, our destination." Torast extended his legs downward, and they compressed, acting like shock absorbers when he touched down.

"I'm not getting a clear picture of this landing area," Jack said, "only hits and misses set in shadows."

"I know marginally more than you," Torast replied, "enough to bring me here and a few other unexciting details."

"Why the six-inch diamond-shaped stones covering the ground of this opening?" Jack asked.

Torast tapped the stone floor with a single talon. "There is no ground beneath these stones."

"One of those unexciting details you failed to mention?" Jack asked, his expression exhibiting a smirk. Torast nodded.

A jolt caused Jack to jerk forward in his seat as the two-hundred-foot-diameter stone floor sank beneath the ground. When completely out of sight, trees emerged, removing all evidence that anything other than the foliage had ever existed.

****

After several hundred feet, the stone floor came to rest at the bottom of the shaft.

"*This* is our destination," Torast said, stepping through an arched doorway that led into a large, well-lit interior room. Jack scanned the area from floor to high-domed ceiling.

"Wow," Jack said, "this place is covered from top to bottom with the diamond-shaped stone." He squinted, trying to zero in on one of the stones. "It's luminescent; that's how this place gets its light."

"This place was built by the ancient ones," Torast said. "They were the race of beings who preceded this era, driven underground by followers of the one whose name I dare not speak." Torast's voice quivered with agitation. "Azoff is an unwilling member of the sect that forced the Sarack to assist them in their earlier atrocities."

"Does this have anything to do with our connection?"

"It has everything to do with our link. However, this is something we will speak of at a later date. I wish to continue relaying to you knowledge of the ancient ones and, moreover, their indirect relevance to you and me in this age."

"I'm listening," Jack said.

"As I've mentioned, the ancient race, known in their time as the

Sarack, were unjustly accused of every manner of atrocity through no fault of their own. Many were imprisoned, tortured, and destroyed. The survivors of this ethnic cleansing retreated underground and enlisted the Thack in building what you see here and much more." Torast moved further into the subterranean lair. "The Sarack no longer exist as they once did, but the expanse of catacombs they created is still in use. In fact, a sacred article was wrapped in cloth and placed here by the very Sarack we speak of today, to aid us in our endeavor to save this world."

"By whom?" Jack asked.

"There are those who have found their way into this fortress for the sole purpose of shelter, using the many portals, just as we did, to gain access." Torast paused before resuming his tale. "And those I would rather not acknowledge, lest they appear."

"If you're uneasy about something roaming around down here, big fella" Jack said. "then I'm scared to death."

"Worry not," Torast said. "If such a thing were to happen, we would have prior notice."

Jack scratched the stubble on the side of his face. "How so?"

"We would see a multitude of creatures fleeing before the storm," Torast said.

"Well, that's reassuring. The storm... certainly no menace there," Jack muttered. Just then, a small mammalian creature with antlers skittered under Torast and disappeared down a perpendicular tunnel.

Several seconds passed before a three-legged sub-humanoid, a bulbous aquatic creature paddling through the air, and a pair of actual snakes followed the same path as the first.

"We're standing in the middle of intersecting tunnels," Torast observed, stepping back to clear the path for new arrivals. Then they watched as a flood of various creatures filled tunnel.

"I can only assume this is what you meant by 'prior notice,'" Jack said. "What now?"

"I have no plan," Torast said. "I am merely waiting for an opening."

"An opening for—" Jack began, but Torast interrupted, leaping into the fray and plowing through the oncoming rush. The torrent of creatures pummeled them from the side, nearly knocking him over.

"Is there a plan now?" Jack asked telepathically after they safely reached the other side.

Torast picked up speed as he raced through the tunnel. *"Yes,"* he conveyed. *"In fact, you are experiencing its inception even now."* Suddenly, a sonic wave tore through the tunnel, causing Torast's rear legs to sway before he regained control. Then, a cascade of debris fell, pelting both man and beast.

"Hey, big fellow," Jack relayed, *"if you have it in ya, I reckon this would be a good time to get us outta here."*

"Your suggestion rings with many truths."

"I'd wager there's hope for you yet." Jack sensed a sudden surge in speed, accompanied by a subtle up-and-down motion. Jack realized that Torast had harnessed the power of his tail to propel them even faster. A second pulse, this time ominously close, surged through the tunnel towards Jack and Torast. The motion of Torast's tail, combined with his massive form navigating the tunnel, created a rush of air that barely managed to diffuse the impending sonic wave.

"Brace!" Torast roared, his voice piercing the ambient noise. Jack tightened his grip and lowered his head as a third wave caught the fleeing pair, throwing them several hundred feet down the tunnel ceiling until they came to a scraping halt.

Aaaa," Jack moaned. He opened his eyes long enough to see movement in the shadows. Torast lay still, except for the expansion and contraction of his chest.

The shadow moved erratically—scurrying along a wall, stopping abruptly, and then scampering sideways. Then, it stopped and remained still. Silence enveloped the space in an oppressive cocoon until, without warning, the creature exuded a deafening midrange roar. Jack and Torast lost consciousness, sending them into a pattern of seizures.

Caught by the full force of the sonic wave, Sim lay seizing in a pouch pocket formed between the left and right sections of Torast's tail. *Things are not as they seem. Regardless of what the world surrounding my being is trying to convey, I have a use, albeit small but nonetheless significant once I locate my associate.*

CHAPTER TWENTY-NINE

Gabriel and Bile

Bile and Gabriel hastened toward the wall until they were mere inches from the barrier. The grain in the wood opened, pulling them into its folds. Seconds later, they appeared within the enclosure.

"We be here to see Hag," Bile announced.

One of the flying reptiles hovered in front of the big man's face, cocking its head from side to side.

"Whadda *you* want?" Bile growled. When the creature continued to hover, Bile snatched it from the air, its spikes digging into his hand. "Ahh!" Bile shook his hand violently, attempting to dislodge the beast, but the miniature animal's spears locked it tight.

Lifting his hand, Bile bit the head off of the creature and turned to spit it out, but it was firmly attached to the roof of his mouth. Bile thrashed about, sending splatters of blood in all directions.

"Arg ths pntrs klt he il ay," Bile garbled, his tongue now skewered and unable to move freely. He dropped to his knees and then to all fours. But, before his hand hit the dirt floor, a second reptile landed where Bile's free palm would land. As soon as the spikes penetrated, the giant stumbled to his feet.

He thrashed wildly, attempting to bite off the second head. With each attempt, he lacerated his skin. In seconds, Bile was blind and lying on his back. Only three fingers remained on formally huge, powerful hands that were now conduits channeling life's fluid from numerous wounds on Bile's face.

Bile!" Gabriel yelled, "Let me help you."

The big man grimaced, raising a hand in acceptance as Gabriel moved closer. Then the boy kicked the injured giant until he heard ribs crack. Bile stared wide-eyed for several moments, then sighed his last.

Within milliseconds, a horde of parasites began their grizzly work. Soon, nothing remained of the man called Bile, save for two filthy garments even the cadaver beetles wouldn't touch.

"Not much of a loss," Gabriel spat as he kicked dirt across the offensive clothing.

A deep voice emanating from a cave spoke.

"Actually, more of a gain . . . wouldn't you think?" A deep voice hissed.

"Who's there?" Gabriel asked. "Show yourself."

"So demanding for one so young," the deep voice chuckled.

"Are you to speak from the darkness as a gutless one?" the boy taunted."

"Mind your tongue, young one, else I will remove it for you." A concussive shockwave exited the cave, knocking Gabriel unconscious, bursting both eardrums

Then, multiple gray tentacles snaked through the cave entrance, encircling Gabriel and pulling him into the darkness.

****

Gabriel moaned. He was lying face down, his head to the side. He attempted to lift his head to survey the dimly lit surroundings but screamed in agony, slowly easing back down. "What happened?" he groaned.

"You crossed Hag," a familiar voice answered. "If it happens a second time, the punishment will far exceed anything you are presently experiencing . . . understood?"

Gabriel lifted a hand, signaling affirmatively. A large foot impacted the ground, sending vibrations that hit him like a hammer would a melon.

"Speak!" the voice roared.

"Yes," Gabriel murmured amidst unbearable pain. *Why does everything sound so distant?*

"Very good," the voice replied calmly.

"May I ask who I'm talking to?" Gabriel whispered. "And please speak loudly; my hearing is all but gone."

"Of course . . . I am Hag," he hissed."

"Bile spoke of you."

"Ah, yes, it seems your friend met with an untimely demise."

"No friend of mine," Gabriel spat. "He kidnapped me from Dalon Con."

"Ah, yes, it seems your friend met with an untimely demise."

"No friend of mine," Gabriel said. "He kidnapped me from Dalon Con."

"And, what of this Dalon Con?"

"Also, of no use," Gabriel said as a diversion away from the old man.

"Well, it appears as though you are in need of companionship."

Gabriel's pounding headache had eased enough that he pushed himself onto his knees. Gently wiping the sand from his face, he slightly raised his head.

"Out of curiosity," Gabriel said, "How did you manage a floor made of sand being far from the seashore?"

"The loose sand is a byproduct of abrading stone during cave excavation."

Still having not seen the one called Hag, Gabriel was reluctant to raise his head further.

"What is the matter boy, Hatcher got your tongue?"

"No," Gabriel said, attempting to quell the pain he knew would arrive once he moved his head. He looked up until he saw the face of a massive creature looming directly overhead.

"At least you are trying, although the attempt is pitiful, at best."

"Uh huh," Gabriel mumbled.

Hag was a slimy gray four-legged amphibian-like creature, with a ridge of 80-foot tentacles running down its back. Each leg had five toes, devoid of nails, claws, or talons. Its flat, round head had a wide mouth full of sharp, white teeth, marking it as a carnivore, while side-by-side slits served as its nose. Its face had no remarkable features other than the wriggling, thin eyebrows with their own parasitic agenda.

Yet, what held Gabriel's attention were the two bulging eyes that glowed blaze orange.

Hag's chuckle dripped with sarcasm. "Well? Have you completed your inspection?"

"If you mean, have I studied your appearance, then yes."

"Excellent! Now, on to other matters."

Gabriel furrowed his eyebrows. "What matters?"

"There are always many things to discuss. First and foremost, my inability to travel outside this cave."

"Then how did you get here?"

"There is a way, of course; however, it is not the preferred method."

"Explain."

"There are carriers, which exist for one reason and one reason only." Hag extended his neck, bringing his face within several feet of Gabriel, "to safely transport Hag wherever he wishes to go."

"What is the preferred method of travel?" the boy asked.

"Close your eyes. I need you to think of your parents—the six short years you shared with them and the great love with which they surrounded and embraced you."

Gabriel's heart soared. Not only did he remember those precious years, but he felt his parents' presence. He was four years old again, sitting in his daddy's lap. Gabriel's mother was preparing the evening meal, singing as she cooked.

"H-how can this be?"

"Now, open your eyes," Hag said, bringing Gabriel from his reverie.

"Why did you bring me back?"

"I need to inquire of you once again."

"Of course," Gabriel agreed, hoping to see his parents again.

Rest assured, you will, just not as you now hope.

"Stare into my eyes. Watch their intense heat and then remember Mama Byrnes." Gabriel's hands clenched into fists, and his jaws tightened, causing his teeth to grind. His corneas burned, pulling in Hag's fiery eyes.

"Do not fight, boy." Hag hissed.

"That witch, my only regret is that I can't kill her again."

"Remember what did she did to your parents? To you?" Hag poured more fuel on the fire that raged within the boy.

"She murdered them!" Gabriel raged. Then, he dropped to his knees and pounded the cave floor. When the soft sand did not quench his fury, he stood and plunged his fists into the cave walls.

"Remember, Gabriel. Always remember." Hag's voice faded into nothing.

Something pushed the boy back through the stone wall. He dropped his hands, his anger fading, and turned. Dizziness swept over him as he stared at the wall.

"I feel as though something has been ripped from me." Gabriel knelt and steadied himself with one hand. Tears dripped onto the dirt as he remembered his parents. But, Mama Byrnes . . . *something feels different.*

Suddenly, Gabriel's head shot up, his face streaked with tears. "What have I done?"

Hag's preferred method of travel is fueled by another's rage. Now, the beast has directional control over a fast-moving emotion.

CHAPTER THIRTY

Dalon Con, Sketch, and Krabb

"My vision is more than adequate to lead you through the darkness." Dalon Con glanced toward the faces of each ward in the waning firelight. "I cannot be sure what manner of evil has taken up the cause against us, for our nemeses number many."

"I wish I could help determine what follows us," Falum said. "As I fled, there were no tangible signs, only a sense of dread in pursuit."

"I shoulda done and knowed we'd be smack dab in the middle 'o' some such nonsense agin," Krabb said. "And why fer did this here big feller come a pushin' through tha ground? Can't he walk on top like everybody else?"

"Krabb," Sketch said, "I tried to told ya ta hesh and let Mr. Dalon and this big feller take care 'o' what needs plannin'."

"Although, not always," Dalon Con said, "each one may have an aspect that is of use to whatever situation they are in."

"Why the need to travel underground, Falum? It seems counterproductive that you would use such a method."

"Not at all, Mr. Con," Falum replied, "I was merely mimicking the mode of my pursuer."

"That don't make a lick 'o' sense," Krabb said.

"Please elaborate," Dalon Con said. "You are human and unable to bore through the earth as a means of travel."

"What are you saying?" Falum asked.

"That you are, indeed, the pursuer," Dalon Con said. "Come to me, small ones." Sketch and Krabb nestled within the inner folds of their protector's robe.

"Surely, you don't believe that," Falum said.

"Lie no more and show yourself," Dalon Con commanded.

"As you wish, old man." Falum placed both hands on top of his head. Short black claws exploded through the end of each digit, sinking into the big man's cranial flesh.

"Looky," Sketch said, "he's gonna rip the hide right ofin hisself."

Falum pulled his hands apart, splitting the hair, skin, and skull. A slender snout erupted through the opening, revealing the remainder of the head and a long snake-like neck. Forelegs followed, pushing down on what was Falum's body as if it were a tight-fitting set of clothes.

"That pile 'o' blue beast don't look so all-fired bad ta me," Krabb said. The creature's head appeared to have no mouth, just a small opening underneath the upturned horn that protruded from the end of its snout. Two forward-facing eyes seemed to float in a halo of white light. "Have another look see, I liable to change ma mind," Krabb said. "Cuz these old eyes ain't never seed such."

Standing upright, the creature stood fifteen feet high with its neck fully extended. His hands and feet bore sharp claws, and an eight-foot tail, not needed for balance, was covered with spikes, making it a formidable weapon.

"Its body taint got one scale on it atall," Sketch said, "but it are right shiny."

"The beast you see before you is covered with interlocking plates," Dalon Con said, "plates that are nearly indestructible."

"You ain't zactly makin' us feel any better," Krabb said.

"My comment was not meant to enhance your feeling of well-being," Dalon Con replied. "I want both of you to wrap your arms around one of my legs, placing your feet atop the foot." Dalon Con then produced several pieces of rope, securely lashing them to his legs.

"I've been ordered to watch you closely," the creature said. "You stand before me an old man, posing as one much younger . . . I fail to see any threat in you."

"Name yourself, one who speaks," Dalon Con demanded. "And, know this: you may try this old man; however, use discretion lest your words turn and bite."

"The one who speaks is known to all as Vitch," the beast laughed. "And you should know this: discretion is not my way, for defeat is a stranger." The creature slid sideways, his movement so quick it was barely perceptible. Dalon Con matched his foe's lateral shift, purposely lagging just behind.

"Exceptional, for one so feeble," Vitch said. "But not fast enough. Perhaps, you should stop for a much needed rest." He tilted his head back, reeling with laughter. The laughter abruptly ended as Vitch whipped his neck toward Dalon Con, releasing several gallons of thick, cream-colored fluid.

"Enjoy, old man." The area bore the acrid odor of bile, the fluid turning into a thick congealed substance seconds after making contact.

Yet, the vile liquid missed as Dalon Con effortlessly evaded the attack.

Vitch repeated his attack with the same results.

"I taint bleevin' what Ima seedin'," Sketch said. "Ever place that smelly mess be a touchin', is sendin' up smoke."

"Beats me," Krabb said. Before the words left his mouth, several trees hit by the liquid struck the ground.

"Looky thar," Sketch said, "that slime done et rite thru them trees."

"Be still, old man," Vitch warned, the frustration evident in his tone, "or, when I catch you, no mercy will I show."

"I look forward to it," Dalon Con replied, further infuriating the demon. He then leaped onto the beast's neck, wielding his staff as a weapon and striking Vitch's head several times.

Vitch roared in pain and swiped at the old man with its claws. Dalon Con leapt into the air and delivered a final, decisive blow, sending the beast crashing to the ground.

"Are you all right?" Dalon Con asked his two wards.

"We doin' okay, Mr. Dalon," Sketch said, "but it do get a bit unnervin' with all these goin'ons."

Vitch groaned.

"I realize my physical prowess is no match for you," Dalon Con mocked. "However, I would invite your comments on my performance so far."

Vitch growled, then rotated his head like a drill bit. Within seconds, the creature disappeared into the earth. The ground trembled, sending vibrations in every direction.

"Brace!" Dalon Con yelled as he dropped into a squat position.

A rotating horn broke through the ground just as Dalon Con sprang to thirty feet, twisting and returning to the ground, where he held his staff above his head, ready to strike.

"Be still," Vitch bellowed, his frustration turning the white light surrounding his eyes red.

"I was not aware I had moved," Dalon Con quipped, knowing it would further enrage his combatant.

Vitch responded by vomiting toward Dalon Con. The old man again took to the air. Traveling in a slow arc, he covered over one hundred feet, before gravity pulled him back to earth.

The beast followed with a constant flow of acrid slime, coating the trees and their foliage in its wake.

Vitch screamed. "You cannot defeat me!" The creature slammed his fists into the ground several times, blood pouring from his eyes. Vitch reared back, extended his neck, and sent forth a deafening roar. "You *will* not defeat me!" the beast squalled. Overwhelmed by anger, he bore into the ground a second time.

"I cannot stress how important it is," Dalon Con said to Sketch and Krabb, "that you hold tightly; your very lives depend upon it."

A massive vibration shook the ground. Dalon Con squatted, placing his hands on the ground. Then, He rose and took two steps back. When the horn erupted through the ground, Dalon Con jumped and wrapped his arms around the creature's neck. He slammed his staff against the top of the monster's head, bringing them both to the ground.

Dalon Con immediately sprang from his perch and began to run.

Vitch spewed a stream of liquid that moved closer and closer to its target. Once Dalon Con sensed the slime only inches away, he sprang up and back, again landing on the base of Vitch's neck. He continued his trek by running down the center of his adversary's back.

The flow of bile flowed across the back and sides of the creature, who wailed in pain. Then all was silent.

Dalon Con leaned over and unlashed Sketch and Krabb.

"Come out and enjoy our temporarily safe surroundings."

The three walked around the bubbling corpse of Vitch.

"What a stench." Krabb held his nose. "Didn't thin' nothin' could stink wors'n than your britches, Sketch."

The trio laughed. Then, a sharp crack, followed by rustling foliage and a thundering slam, shook the terrain. The corrosive liquid started the surrounding forest to fall at an alarming rate.

Dalon Con swept his arms around his wards as a tree hit the ground several feet away. Sketch and Krabb resumed their perches, arms locked around their mode of transportation's legs in a death grip as the destruction began.

"I don't mind tellin' ya, I is 'bout plum tired of being scared, Krabb."

"Taint no shame," Krabb said, "cuz I'ma right with ya."

Timber rained down, the scene mimicking a war zone with no escape. The trio was surrounded by the acidic slime-covered plants.

"I'ma fearin' we be goners," Krabb said.

"Do not let fear take your hearts, little ones." Dalon Con moved erratically until the barrage lessened.

"Perhaps our foe grows as tired as myself." Dalon Con said just as an errant limb knocked him to the ground, pinning him between two downed trees. Then, a massive tree began a downward trek toward them, obliterating everything in its path.

"Mr. Con!" Krabb and Sketch yelled.

A white apparition appeared, encircling Dalon Con and his two cohorts, pulling them with barely enough distance to call a fragment between tree and ground.

Dalon Con smiled. *And once again, Smort, be you friend or foe?*

CHAPTER THIRTY-ONE

Hayden and Max

Hayden attempted to blink. Unable to do so, he yawned, rubbed his eyes, and found the reason for his inability to open his eyes—an inordinate amount of gunk buildup on his eyelids. He gently pried his eyes open using his forefinger and index finger, affording sight and a tremendous amount of relief.

The elevated humidity explains why my eyes were glued together, but why is this the only time period I have experienced this effect?

Hayden pondered the question, then smiled. *If I pose a question that defies an answer, does the question become rhetorical?*

He chuckled at his ponderance, munching on a nutrition bar as he collected his belongings.

Crackle. Crackle. Shhhh.

Hayden fumbled for the black box, dropping it twice before firmly grasping it.

Broken static filled with intermittent periods of silence.

"Come on, come on." Hayden lightly tapped the side of the device. It was check-in, and he so needed to hear a familiar voice. As if on cue, Wakke's voice boomed clearly through the communication device.

"Hayden—regard my words as you would life itself." Wakke's voice was followed by a short period of static, then silence. Hayden's heart fell. "It was good to hear my friend's voice." The small man sighed. "I feel sure I will hear it again."

After several minutes, he abandoned hope the message would come through. That would be one problem he would discuss with the Odobe scientist who created the device—reliable reception.

Smiling, Hayden lifted off with a renewed sense of optimism. Curious about the increased water's origin, he flew toward the cave's entrance.

Once in the open, he felt unusual vibrations emanating from the earth. Climbing to a higher altitude afforded him a wide-angle view of the landscape. Flying a grid, he found nothing out of the ordinary. Then, the surface soil began to rise.

At first, the pattern appeared random—two vertical strips, each several feet wide and twelve feet long, rose from the ground. Yet, while one end remained attached to the soil, the other floated in the air.

Well, this is unusual; then again, it takes much more to bring about surprises in the past. Hayden frowned, frustrated. *I have no idea whether I am in the past, present, or future.*

This was another point to discuss with the scientists. However, after his journey was over, he doubted if time travel would ever be used again. There were too many unknown dangers.

Yet, even for this futuristic being, the phenomenon below was strange. It continued its dance, creating shorter horizontal strips. Then, one large portion connecting the vertical and horizontal sections broke away.

Free from the earth, the device rotated slowly until the vertical projections pointed downward. Hayden's heart beat faster, and his eyes widened at the strange metamorphosis. *It looks like a twenty-foot-tall stick figure.* The vertical appendages bent forward, stopping at a ninety-degree angle. The sides curled underneath themselves and split into five sections on their ends.

"Feet!" Hayden exclaimed. *The dirt has transformed into an anatomical body part.* As the conversion process increased, huge hands flexed into fists, the torso broadened, and the being appeared to be testing its legs.

"The metamorphosis is nearly complete," Hayden breathed.

As the newcomer was dressed in an earthen robe, laced sandals formed on his feet. Then, the giant creature smiled through his heavy beard and spoke.

"I am Max, small one—welcome." His voice was deep and resonant. He extended his right arm until his open palm was underneath the hovering time traveler.

Hayden hovered, his mouth open. "You know who I am?"

"Of course, Hayden. Please, there is no need to fear."

Hayden looked at the open hand. After a moment, he set himself down on Max's open palm. The giant retracted his arm, lifting his hand until it was several inches from his face.

"How could you possibly know my name?"

"I know most things in regard to this world."

"I do not understand," Hayden said. "Who are you that you should have such information?"

"I am the very heart of this world," Max said, "the world I named Burrus Plax."

"I did not mean to question your sovereign claim to this planet. I merely wish to understand."

"It is not a question of sovereignty. Simply put, I *am* this world and this world is me." The giant changed from soil to stone, then converted to wood, iron, water, and then back to earth.

Before each transformation, Max stretched out his hand to different locations of the landscape: stone for stone, water for water, earth for earth. By pushing his hand into the soil or wrapping his fingers around the nearest tree, his composition instantly matched the element.

"How can it be that you *are* this world, yet manifest yourself as the form I see before me?"

Max smiled. "It was a gift granted through grace by the Creator."

"The Creator?" Hayden questioned. Before Max could reply, he cupped his hands around Hayden, pulling him to his abdomen. As the giant ducked his head and curled both knees into his chest, a ball of fire struck and obliterated him from sight.

CHAPTER THIRTY-TWO

Gabriel and Roan

Gabriel ran, not slowing, until he reached where he and Bile had entered. The giant's rags lay on the ground, but there was no sign of the carnivores who devoured him nor the flying razor blades. Then, the sound of wings sent Gabriel racing for the supposed entrance.

The deadly reptiles swooped down, slashing his forehead. Gabriel swung his arms wildly, trying to fend off the onslaught until he remembered the barbs. He sure didn't want one of those things stuck to him. He didn't have time to stop for a weapon—they would slice him to pieces.

He ducked as a piece of reptile flew over him, its deadly spikes dripping with blood.

That is one saving grace. While trying to attack me, they are killing themselves.

Gabriel winced as the enemy caught him on his left calf. He felt blood running down his leg but stayed the course. Only a few more meters. Just as two large killed charged him from the side, he slammed his body into the wood, forcing his way through.

****

Gabriel walked deeper into the forest. "At least I'm alone." *No one to bore me with stories or beat me for no reason.* When he stopped to relieve himself, something shoved him from behind, causing him to splash the front of his pants with urine.

He whirled around. *Something followed me from Hag's domain.* "Show yourself demon seed."

"I am no associate with Hag."

"Then show yourself," Gabriel demanded.

"I am not your subordinate. I answer to no one."

Gabriel scanned the ground, searching for something he could use to defend himself.

"Nor do I play games."

Gabriel scowled. "You've spewed enough about what you don't do," the boy said, his anger growing. Then, he noticed a possible weapon within reach. "Of course, this only applies if you are capable of doing anything."

"Ahhh!" A violent strike from the invisible assailant took Gabriel to the ground.

Gabriel sat up, wiping the blood from the corner of his mouth. "Well, now, it seems my friend can actually accomplish something."

"I am not your friend."

Gabriel smirked. "Do you understand the concept of 'hits like a girl'?" He heard the slight rustle of leaves before being kicked in the gut. "Evidently, he does," the boy wheezed. "or at least understands what it means to be a wimp."

There was a slight stirring to the right. The entity was becoming careless. "Is that all you have?" Gabriel taunted.

"I will now show you what I have," the invisible one screeched.

Heart pounding, Gabriel rose to one knee and placed his right hand firmly around the end of a three-inch limb. He closed his eyes as the rustling leaves moved closer. He swung, hitting something solid to his left. Then swung downward in a two-handed overhead high-flying arc.

"Crack!"

A dull, full-bodied thud sounded in front of Gabriel. Dead leaves flew upward and then gently settled back to earth, forming a rough outline of an invisible creature lying flat on its back.

Suddenly, a vibrating tempest tore Gabriel's hands from the limb and threw his body to the ground. He jumped to his feet and saw what appeared to be lightning moving erratically over the creature. He advanced as close as he dared.

"The arcs of light are breaking down." As the light disintegrated, a solid area started to take shape. Gabriel pressed a finger into the newly formed space. The intermittent light ceased, leaving a four-foot-long bipedal creature covered from head to toe in smooth jet-black skin. Its two arms supported hands with four fingers and no thumbs, and its face possessed minimal features other than white inset ovals for eyes.

Gabriel knelt for a closer inspection. *I hope this thing is dead.* He slid a fingernail under one of the facial plates, and it fell to the ground, breaking into several pieces. Underneath were crushed teeth and a cracked jawbone.

"Didn't know I hit you that hard." Gabriel rose to a standing position. He shook his head several times. "What *are* you?"

"A temporal thief," a voice from behind said, "and from the looks of it, a dead one." Gabriel whirled to face the newcomer—a six-foot-tall man dressed in tanned leather pants and a long-sleeve pullover shirt of the same material. A wide leather belt held numerous unknown items. Two more belts, identical to the one around his waist, were attached diagonally on his chest, crossing at mid-thorax.

"Name's Roane." He waited for a reply, and when no response came, he spoke again. "I can only assume that your confused expression means an explanation of my appearance would do you a world of good."

Gabriel nodded. "An explanation would be good." Gabriel glanced at the stranger's attire. "What are you wearing on your feet?"

Roane lifted one of his legs. "Don't know what they're called, but they sure have come in handy since I found them." Unknown to them, but they were black and white high-tech running shoes.

"Found them?" Gabriel said. "Where?"

"Not sure," Roane said. "A while ago, I was walking through a field of three-foot-tall prairie grass and tripped, landing face-first on these. Been using them ever since."

"How long is 'quite a while'?"

Roane furrowed his forehead and lowered his eyebrows in thought. "About fifty years, give or take."

Gabriel turned, pointing at the prostrate creature, then looked back at Roane. "How about this dead, whatever you called it, laying here?"

"Temporal thief," Roane replied.

"Okay, what is a temporal thief, and exactly what does it do?"

"A temporal thief steals time. It never appears unless someone is experimenting with time travel. I say experimenting because very few understand how to journey through time without upsetting the natural order of their surroundings.

"This creature steals moments of time and stores them in his cache until releasing them out of order. Random temporal discharge causes the maximum amount of chaos possible, which is what it wants."

"What can we do?" Gabriel asked.

"Just as *you* have done," Roane said. "We kill them."

"Them! You mean, there is more than one?"

Roane nodded. "Each time one is claimed through death, which rarely happens, another takes its place."

"So, it's never-ending. Kill one, and POP! Another arrives. Great, just Great." Gabriel looked at the dead temporal thief. "I there no way to kill them, I mean permanently?"

"Only when time stops," Roane said. "Come, our search begins."

CHAPTER THIRTY-THREE

Jack and Torast

Torast tried to raise his head, but it fell, causing a thunderous boom and vibrations that encompassed the immediate area.

"Ohh," Jack moaned, placing a hand on each side of his head. "Quiet, please, quiet." Tormented by the hard floor that had been his pillow for the last sixteen hours, he slowly pushed himself into a sitting position. Leaning against the wall, he waited for the dizziness to subside.

Within moments, a skittering shadow passed above his head. Jack crawled to where Torast lay, the large one still making feeble attempts to right himself.

"The sound of tiny feet crawling across the cave wall at breakneck speeds and the sporadically-appearing shadow piques my interest, but at the same time, makes my skin crawl," Torast said.

"Every time that thing touches me, it's like fingernails down a slate writing board." He demonstrated his disgust by slapping at the creature each time he felt its claws make contact.

using him to land on his back.

"Hey!" Jack protested.

"This is not the most desired way to achieve hydration." Torast looked at Jack. "However, when desperate measures are required, they must be exercised." Torast placed a hand over the young man's eyes. "Now, relax."

A narrow proboscis unfurled from beneath the creature's chin. With his free hand, he placed one finger on Jack's neck.

"Do not struggle," Torast warned when Jack flinched. "There will be no permanent damage."

Permanent? Jack stiffened.

A thick liquid dripped from the tip of the unrolled tube. Then, Torast directed the proboscis into Jack's throat and momentarily pressed on his patient's trachea, allowing the tube to slide into the esophagus and down to the stomach. Moments later, he removed the tube, curling it back into his body.

"I'm assuming nothing you did was detrimental," Jack stated. "That being said, it wasn't half bad— kinda sweet."

"Good, the fluid will also supply any nutritional needs." He stared at Jack with what could only be called a concerned expression.

"What are you looking at?"

"Making sure."

"Making sure of what?" Jack frowned.

"Our metabolic systems are likely quite different," Torast said. "If the discrepancy is too great, the liquid could be fatal—or even explosive."

"Well, wouldn't that have been good to know before you injected me with that stuff?"

Torast nodded. "All appears well, as I do not see any body fragments hanging from the ceiling or walls."

"That *is* a good thing." Then, something familiar touched Jack's head, causing him to jerk. "Oh yeah, and that annoying gnat is driving me nuts." Jack swatted at a shadow above his head.

"Perhaps it will slow down long enough to explain its actions."

"I am the Guardian," a creature announced.

"Well," Jack said, "you stopped, and on top of that, you can speak!"

The Guardian was a three-foot-long lizard, but it was covered in close-cropped fur instead of scales.

"What do you guard?" Torast inquired. "These tunnels spread through most, if not all, of Burrus Plax."

"With my great speed, no distance is out of reach." The creature was adorned with alternating black and silver stripes, which camouflaged perfectly with the cave's surface. A boney ridge with no apparent function protruded from its skull.

"Don't take what I'm about to ask the wrong way," Jack said, "but with your small size, how is it you're able to defend such a vast network of tunnels?"

"No offense taken by your short-sighted comment," the Guardian said. "However, if you delve into your recent past you will recall, a sonic pulse disabled you, your companion, and a stowaway, that has gone undetected until now."

Jack glanced at Torast. *"Stowaway?"* he thought.

The Guardian stepped closer, "The blow that you remember, I delivered."

"Why such a show of force aimed at ones of no consequence?" Torast questioned. "Also I detected the stowaway as soon as he touched down but saw no reason to bring such an insignificant happening to light."

"Since the ones who created this planet-wide labyrinth have forsaken it for a time," the Guardian said, "it falls upon me to keep this underground lair free for the ones who will occupy these halls again."

"You sound as though there is a prophecy yet to be fulfilled." Torast said.

"The prophecy you speak of is foreign to me," the Guardian said. "I am but an expendable pawn destined to die in defense of this stronghold."

"Not much of a life," Jack said, "or death, for that matter."

"As I have said," the Guardian began, "life for me is immaterial. I am born to die and there is always another ready to take my place."

"Who holds the secret to these catacombs and the prophecy?" Torast asked.

"Have you not heard me?" the Guardian said. "I know nothing of this prophecy you speak or this place other than I am to give my all in its defense."

A small stream of water began to trickle through the middle of the tunnel. Torast and Jack turned to the Guardian.

"The dampness you see is the only adversary for which I have no defense." Then, all eyes widened at the next sound heard.

"This is my world!" an enraged voice roared, followed by a deluge of water that filled each tunnel in the massive system.

****

A massive geyser erupted from the subterranean tunnel, unceremoniously tossing a sizeable flying beast, an average-sized young adult, a ball of tentacles, and a small furry reptile onto the planet's surface.

"Ohh," Torast moaned, "one more time getting slammed to the ground by some erroneous source."

"At least this time it wasn't *as* bad," Jack said, glancing toward the Guardian as he rose to a sitting position on top of Torast. "It helps when you can ride it out on top of . . ." Jack poked his finger into the beast's skin, providing ample protection for a rider. "As I was saying, something that gives like my friend here."

"I must agree with Jack," the Guardian said. "With my small size, I tend to bounce from the surface of the large one, once contact with the earth is made. This makes my experience pleasurable."

"Well, I am ecstatic that, in my pain, one was able to find pleasure." Torast said.

Jack patted Torast with his hand. "Time to get up, big boy." He slid down the live mountainside, landing on his feet. Feeling something on his shoulder, Jack turned his head to the right. "Having more fun, are we?"

"When one sees an opportunity to solve a problem," advised the Guardian, "it is usually prudent to take advantage of said opportunity."

"Well put," Jack said.

"Do you wish me to leave?" the Guardian asked.

Jack felt the presence of such a powerful being comforting. "No, ride as long as you wish."

"Thank you," the Guardian said, relieved, "it is good to have an opportunity to conserve energy. This will enable me to cut my feeding times by half or more." The ground trembled as Torast rolled to his feet.

"Which way?" Jack asked.

"Straight ahead," Torast replied, "until I have recovered sufficiently to take an aerial route."

"Shouldn't you stay here in order to guard the system of tunnels?" Jack asked the Guardian.

"Once the chambers are free of water, I will return," the Guardian said. "As this will take a significant amount of time, I will travel with you until I can return."

"What of the creature with multiple tentacles?" Jack asked.

"He has gone for now," Torast said, "but is sure to return, revealing his intentions at that time."

Several miles away, another geyser spewed out an imposing figure that was visible until the water surrounding it drained off its body, ushering the figure into the realm of the unseen.

CHAPTER THIRTY-FOUR

Dalon Con, Krabb and Sketch

Three haggard figures emerged from a devastated section of downed forest into a sparse grassland.

Krabb looked into Dalon Con's eyes.

"It sure seems like I done and seed just a little sump'en rite a'fore we was moved. The way I seed it, we were a-pushed out and underneath that rat-big log that were gonna squish us."

"You speak true, small one," Dalon Con said, "the one who saved us, I have been aware of for some time as he follows step for step. Be not alarmed I will allow no harm to befall you."

He discreetly checked his surroundings. *Something lingers from the Smort I briefly knew, something both good and bad.*

"As soon as this recent arrival's objectives become apparent, I will share them with you. But I want you to remember that had it not been for Vitch, our rescue would not have been necessary."

"What do that got to do with anythin'?" Krabb asked.

"Just remember," Dalon Con said, "for the Great Ones ways are not our ways."

"Well, looky thar," Sketch said. "it peers the sun be a comin' up." The group stopped as an orange light streaked through the sky.

"Don't look like no sun, I eva seed," Krabb said. "I swear we coulda all done an got kilt and you'd still have somethin' stupid to say."

"Jus speakin' ma mind," Sketch said. "Cain't help ifin them thoughts ain't as smart as you figure they ought ta be."

"Yeah, yeah," Krabb grumbled, throwing a hand toward Sketch, signifying dismissal.

"Is there any need you two should go on so?" Dalon Con asked.

"You heered him," Krabb said. "He talk so much ma ears get ta hurtin'."

"However, he states goodness in the face of adversity," Dalon Con said. "Why does this bother you so?"

"Why is it?" Sketch asked. "We beens buds fer near 'bout long as I kin 'member."

Krabb lowered his head, kicking at the dirt surrounding a dried clump of grass. "You be right. We has been buds all these years. And all these here years you be a spoutin' all this goody-goody mess." Krabb raised his head, his eyes meeting Sketch's. "I wished I was like you is, but it just ain't in me." Once again, he lowered his head. "I cain't figure why you'd be a puttin' up with an ole grump like me, anyhow."

"We been through thick 'n thin an done an stayed tagether no matter what, so's I don't see no need to start a changin' now."

"I guess you be right," Krabb said, "so's I reckons we oughta get on with it."

Sketch looked at Dalon Con. "He neva was one ta make a fuss afta arguin'."

The old man smiled. "Then I suppose we should get on with it."

"Where is we agoin', anyhow?" Krabb asked.

"On this world," Dalon Con began, "there are but three cities, all of which bear different names from the ones they were given when constructed. One you know as Defeated, and the two others are Grave, once known as Blanche Aries and Rash, called Single Duality. Humans continue to inhabit Defeated, although if its name had ever been changed, there was no record of this happening."

Dalon Con knelt, bringing himself to eye level with his wards. "Each of these settlements, may be devoid of human life. However, it most definitely will be occupied by someone or something." He looked at Sketch and then Krabb. "That is where we are going."

****

Dalon Con, Sketch, and Krabb stood before a twisted mass of shank trees, a variety of flora that grew to a height of thirty feet. It produced foliage on its top five feet. Growing in all directions below were six-inch-diameter limbs with a dark blue hue.

"Where is we?" Sketch asked, a wary look on his face.

"Wher'eva we be," grumbled Krabb, "I ain't thinkin' I cares too much fer it."

"If you look closely," Dalon Con said. "sections of bricks and mortar can be seen between the limbs."

"Ya mean yer tellin' us that this here's one 'o' them other cities?" Krabb asked.

"Yes," Dalon Con said, "this is Grave." He knelt before the two small men. "As we have done in the past, I am asking you to do so again. Stay close to me. For no reason are you to leave my side."

"Is we agoin' in thar?" Sketch asked. "Please tell me we ain't."

"Entry is necessary to gather accurate information."

"What we be a needin' accuate' formation for?" Krabb asked.

"Maybe that ain't none 'o' yer bizness," Sketch said.

"There are no secrets here," Dalon Con said.

"You ain't gettin' me in that devil hole," Krabb said. "No way, no how."

"I will not force either of you to go," Dalon Con said. "However, I can offer you no protection if you choose to remain." He took several steps toward the overgrown township.

Sketch looked at Krabb. "After what I done an seen, I ain't stayin' here."

"I reckon Ima right behind ya," Krabb said.

Dalon Con smiled when he felt the pressure of four small hands touching his unseen outer garment. "Nice having you both along for the journey, even though we will certainly entertain a pause before our passage can begin."

"It's right much gooder to be here with you ta clutch tight wence I be a feelin' such an urge," Sketch said, staring at the new arrival, "like rat now."

Krabb looked at Sketch, then up at Dalon Con, "yeah, what he said."

"I cannot express how important it is for you to stay as close to me as possible."

"I be hatin' to repeat maself," Smort chuckled, "but why in the world would'ja be wantin' a Krabb when ya could be a havin' a Smort?"

As the large bipedal man approached, Krabb and Sketch clutched tighter to the robes.

"If I am not mistaken, we have been through this scenario before. Why would you bring about the same, knowing the outcome from the first?"

"Maybe Smort be stupid, but we know, ain't no way that that could be true." Smort scratched his rear end through the fabric and picked his nose with a free hand before returning to his rant. "Now this be the way this here sitcheation's gonna go. I'm a gonna commence smashin' heads, startin' with the ones lookin' at me." Smort grinned at Krabb and Stitch. "Now, you three kin can fight ole Smort or watch whilst I crack some skulls. What's it gonna be?"

"I cannot explain what is happening nor why," Dalon Con said, "however, your lack of short term memory will be to your detriment if you persist."

"I reckon we'll see," Smort said, charging.

****

Smort lay safely tucked away, thirty yards from the nearest wooded foliage. His position offered the daily sunlight he would require during his recovery.

Dalon Con, his eyes glistening with unshed tears, couldn't help but voice his frustration. "When will they learn. Even now they repeat the same scenario, it having happened just days before." He stared into the distance, his forehead creased with worry. "Perhaps," he said, his voice filled with a mix of determination and resignation, "No, it is more than that. After Grave, new doors must be opened, but that is for a later time."

Raising his staff, the wall of limbs cracked and splintered. Then, Dalon Con and his two wards stepped through the opening and disappeared into the shadows of Grave.

CHAPTER THIRTY-FIVE

Hayden and Max

The fire dispersed, leaving a swirling funnel of thick smoke. As the haze thinned, a mound of blackened earth emerged, its surface shifting like something alive. Before the first wave of smoke had a chance to clear, a second fireball slammed into Max's back, echoing the force of the first impact. His skin darkened and hardened as he absorbed the fiery energy, transforming into a charred, rocky form.

"No more!" he roared, his voice a gravelly growl. Flicking his wrist, he launched a shimmering liquid projectile that solidified mid-air into a jagged spear, shattering the organic missile into pieces.

Rising, he transformed his hands into smoking cannons. With a primal yell, he fired, the blasts smashing through the incoming rounds, reducing it to a smoldering heap.

In the distance, a fixed-winged avian-like creature hovered, its smooth blue and gray skin reflecting the light. It had oversized eyes, a long pointed beak, and fire spewed from its rear for propulsion. The creature's grotesque form included an organic weapon system, adding to its bizarre appearance.

Max's unwavering focus released projectiles with precision. Each impact tore segments from the airborne menace, sending fragments of its flesh through the air. The creature's retaliatory fire ceased, but Max's onslaught continued.

With a final, decisive strike, a defensive projectile struck the creature's left wing, tearing it from its body and sending the smooth blue body hurtling toward the ground, where the mangled flying aberration exploded.

As the dust settled, Hayden hovered nearby, absorbing the aftermath of the chaos. The remnants of the avian creature smoldered in a heap, a testament to Max's relentless attack. Within moments, Hayden floated in front of Max's face.

"Good to see you," Max breathed.

"You as well. In the spirit of what I have witnessed, I must also say it is good to be seen."

Max chuckled, then produced a boisterous belly laugh. "I take it you are suffering no ill effects from the ordeal."

"Not at all. What manner of creature has the ability to perform as the one you destroyed?"

"An Areck," Max said, "it is a hybrid creature bred for naught but evil purposes."

"Why did it attack?"

"I have pondered the same question, for any harm done to me would have to pass through this world first."

Hayden glanced toward the smoldering remains. "That seems very counterproductive. To harm to the very world one inhabits."

"Not for the Arecks," Max said, "For they, like many creatures on Burrus Plax, are bred to die. It has no means to ingest nutrition or liquids; its only capability is the intake of air." Max took a moment. "We must search for the one who sent the Areck, and rest assured, he will be the same as others we are still actively looking for."

"Where do we begin?"

"Beneath the settlement of Defeated, of course."

****

The forest started to thin, and the occasional cobblestone could be seen through the ground cover.

"This will be where we enter the lair," Max said.

"Underground?" Hayden asked.

"Evil abides in the cover of darkness."

"From what I have witnessed in Defeated, evil has spread beyond its subterranean confines."

"This is true. But, what lies concealed beneath Defeated begat what resides in the city."

Hayden had been riding on Max's shoulder since they left the ruins of Areck. He now stepped onto Max's extended open palm, and once again, Max carefully curled his fingers around his small companion, securing it against his chest.

"Hold on, little one, and worry not—you are safe." Max sank into the ground.

The downward motion was smooth and lasted briefly, ending with a gentle bump. Then Hayden sensed the ligaments in Max's fingers tighten until the giant broke into a small underground grotto.

The underground grotto exuded an unsettling air, a chilling stillness that seemed to swallow every sound. The walls were rough and jagged, carved from ancient stone, with water trickling down in eerie, rhythmic patterns that echoed through the cavern. A faint, flickering light cast ghostly shadows that danced across the walls, creating the illusion of movement.

Once released, Hayden activated his propulsion unit and landed on Max's shoulder.

"I am getting used to this particular perch—" he quipped in the oppressive stillness. "Stellar view."

Max chuckled softly, the sound swallowed by the surrounding gloom.

"This *is* where we are supposed to be, isn't it?" Hayden asked, peering into the unsettling darkness.

Max nodded. "Now we must carefully locate the occupants, lest we be detected."

"Shouldn't we hide? Are these not the very ones who intend to do harm to this planet?"

"Most likely you speak the truth," Max conceded. "However,

there remains the risk that those who wield control through financial superiority are disconnected from the day-to-day operations."

Hayden nodded. "Then, as before, I will follow you . . . or perhaps, ride along is the correct term."

"Take these words I am about to speak and forget them not. They may supply knowledge in times of need, just as I am asking you to supply me with any questions you may have. Max smiled. "As we travel, I will remain camouflaged, even as you ride. You must not move. Some avian-like predators would have you partially digested before you realized you had been taken."

"Will the low ambient light in the cave not hamper your ability to recognize the quarry we seek, or the predators that seek me?"

"We are fortunate, indeed," Max said, "to enjoy this level of light. You see, whatever occupies this subterranean space also requires a certain amount of luminescence. It is this combination of devices that has produced this light, however dim it may be."

Without another word, Max disappeared into the cave floor like a swimmer cutting through water.

As they moved deeper into the grotto, the oppressive atmosphere seemed to press down on them, a silent reminder of the dangers lurking in the darkness.

CHAPTER THIRTY-SIX

Gabriel and Roane

"What exactly are we looking for?" Gabriel asked as they stood at the edge of a small creek.

"What we seek will soon find us." Roane nodded. "Ready?"

"Sure. Well, don't get wet," Gabriel laughed.

The two men jumped the brook at the same time. But, midway across the two-foot-wide waterway, Roane was suddenly pushed into an ocean by a thirty-foot rogue wave. He grasped at the water, struggling to get to the surface, but each time he broke through, another wave slapped him down. His head grew dizzy, his strength weakening. As he broke through the water again, he felt something hit the top of his head and then slip across each shoulder. Grabbing the rope, he tied it around himself, letting his would-be rescuers pull him to safety.

****

Gabriel was inches from touching down on the far side of the small creek. But as soon as his boot landed on the grassy bank, the ground changed to a thick layer of fine gray powder, causing him to slip.

What just happened? He scanned the area for Roane, but the man was nowhere to be seen. Sitting on his haunches, he ran his fingers through the ultra-fine dust that became airborne at the slightest touch.

Never seen anything quite like it, rubbing a bit of the powder between his thumb and forefinger. *Where am I?* A series of explosions, followed by an earthquake and a searing light in the midnight sky, told Gabriel what he needed to know.

What the . . .? Burrus Plax doesn't have volcanoes.

A massive explosion drew his attention to the horrible truth. An entire mountain exploded in a gigantic fireball, followed by a fast-moving ash cloud.

That's a pyroclastic flow traveling more than four hundred miles an hour, and it's headed straight for me.

Gabriel started running. *How am I ever going to outrun this thing? Better still, how do I know so much about volcanoes?*

****

Gabriel and Roane fell to the ground at the same time.

"Well, looks like we cleared the creek," Roane smirked, his arms around his knees.

Gabriel sprang to his feet, jerked left, right and then paused, not knowing what to do.

"Volcano– run!" Gabriel squawked.

"Calm down. What I said would find us . . .has done just that."

Gabriel dropped his arms. "Found us? What do you mean, *found* us?"

"The temporal thief stores sections of time then places them out of order to cause chaos."

"Yeah," Gabriel replied, "but you said that . . . that . . . that—"

"Temporal thief?"

Gabriel took a deep breath and nodded, "—was dead!"

"I also said another would replace its deceased brother," Roane said, an '*I told you so*' expression on his face. Gabriel plopped down on the ground beside Roane.

"So, that was the replacement?"

"Yep," Roane said, "that was him." He reached over, placing a hand on Gabriel's shoulder. "What we just experienced was a greeting from our new friend."

“So, at any time we can be whisked away to God knows where an possibly die?”

“Pretty much,” Roane said, leaning back on one elbow.

“Anything else I should know?” Gabriel asked.

“Let me see if I can translate,” Roane replied. “Our buddy wants us to know he'll be around, just in case we need him, and, for an added bonus, he'll be around especially when we don't.” Roane looked at Gabriel. “I think I'll stop there; I wouldn't want to ruin any surprises.”

“Thanks a lot,” Gabriel said, “you don't know how comforting your words have been.” He tossed a pebble into the stream. “So, what now?”

“I'm thinking,” Roane said.

“Oh joy,” Gabriel replied, “another layer of comfort.”

“We could always—”

Suddenly, Gabriel and Roane found themselves on a round, flat, four-foot diameter plateau. The plateau was supported by a much slimmer stem, about ninety feet tall, that swayed back and forth, gaining momentum with each tilt. Surrounding their perch in all directions was a boiling sea of lava with random rock projections. Tornadoes of fire swirled intermittently, dropping from the boiling mass of burning clouds.

“I can't take much more of this,” Roane yelled over the roar of the bubbling rock and twisting firestorm.

“Judging by the way this plateau is beginning to tilt,” Gabriel said, “we won't have to.”

The plateau tilted, and Gabriel and Roane fell toward a fiery river of lava.

Both men hit the ground simultaneously, rolling into the creek. Gabriel was the first to crawl out, collapsing in the sparse vegetation. Close behind, Roane dropped to the ground beside Gabriel. Narrowly missing immolation, smoke rolled from their hair, curling upward until dissipating in the atmosphere, helped by the wake of a temporal thief as it passed.

****

“Well, somebody sure told me a lie,” Gabriel said. He shook his arm, flicking off as much water as possible. “There might be fish in this stream, but I’m not fast enough to catch them.”

Still on his knees, he stretched his back. “I can see several, but just can’t—” Something flew past Gabriel’s left side into the water, lodging firmly in the bottom. Two hands grasped the homemade spear and pulled it with a skewered fish attached from the stream.

“Excuse me, I thought I’d catch a few gunner fish to eat.” Roane placed his foot on the scale-covered creature and pushed. The gunner slid from the spear and began flopping on the ground. Within fifteen minutes, it was joined by four more.

Gabriel nodded. “Impressive.”

“If you can see them, then they can see you. Keep your shadow off the water. Then you’ll have a better chance. Or better yet,” He smiled, holding up his spear. “Find and alternate solution.”

Roane scaled one fish with a small, sharp, flat metal piece, filleted one side, and looked at Gabriel with half of the fillet hanging out of his mouth. He continued his work, then extended a piece toward Gabriel, who accepted Roane’s offering. Gabriel moved the fillet around in his hands before reluctantly taking a bite of the raw fish.

“Well?”

“Tolerable,” Gabriel said. “I preferred cooked.”

Roan nearly spat out his bite of fish. “Cooked?” Roane made a face of disgust. “If you think gunner fish is tolerable raw, try eating it hot. Yech!”

****

Gabriel and Roane lay on the ground, staring into the sky.

"So what's the plan, if you have one," Gabriel asked.

"Not sure," Roane replied. "There's something I must find before we can begin our journey in earnest."

Suddenly, the star-studded sky cracked and fell, dissolving into nothing before it hit the ground. Following the vanishing shower, the sky turned a vibrant shade of blue, interspersed with wisps of cirrus clouds.

Roane jumped to his feet, followed by Gabriel. They were in a field of short, cropped, yellow flowers. A line of trees was visible several hundred yards away.

A barely detectable vibration traveled through the ground's surface, gradually increasing. "Roane, I believe we have a problem—again."

Roane was facing the opposite direction of the tree line, pointing.

"Look, you see that boiling mass of dirt headed our way?"

"Does it have anything to do with the ground shaking?" Gabriel asked, an unsettled expression on his face.

Roane nodded. "And the thunder."

Gabriel frowned, his expression anchored in impatience. "Well?"

"It's a herd of raycon."

"Impossible. They've been extinct for a century."

"We're traveling through time, Gabriel."

"Then how could you possibly know about raycons?" Gabriel asked.

"Because I am over a century old, that's why," Roane spat. "They stand twelve feet tall, have four legs and three horns, each one bigger around than your thigh. And you don't want to be anywhere near a hear that is stampeding." His eyes scanned the oncoming herd. "Once they get moving, there's nothing that can stop them."

"What do we do?" Gabriel asked.

Roane turned to Gabriel. "Run!"

CHAPTER THIRTY-SEVEN

Jack, Torast and the Guardian

Torast lumbered through what was once a forest, the small trees steadily thinning until it became an arid grassland. The dry vegetation crunched under the creature's great weight.

"Comfortable?" Jack asked the Guardian. The lizard was stretched out along a boney ridge that formed the front edge of Jack's cockpit.

"Yes."

"You don't talk much, do you?"

The Guardian glanced at the human and shook his head.

"Prying for information, are we?" Torast asked.

"For all the good it's doing," Jack replied.

"Some things are best left alone. For the answers you seek will be revealed in their own time."

"How can you be sure? This one leans toward the stubborn side."

"Beings of all kinds struggle to hold their tongues," Torast said, "especially when they possess knowledge that others seek. The temptation to share becomes too strong, and they are torn about how to divulge it."

"I suppose."

Torast's right foreleg forced its way through the crust, stopping when the underside of his shoulder made contact with the ground. Stepping to the revealed an underground chamber.

"Something smells good," Jack said, "somewhat sweet."

The Guardian did a quick 180 to get a look into the hole.

"This occurrence is not at all a favorable development." Torast cocked his head. "Sounds emanate from within the chamber."

Suddenly, a swarm of eight-legged insects poured out of the abyss, darkening the sky. They were twice the size of a male human and covered with black and red stripes. Their short legs had one joint, ending with a single claw. Jack and the Guardian sprang from Torast's back. Jack laid face down on the ground, his hands protecting his head; the Guardian lay next to the human, pressed as tightly as possible against Jack's side.

"The oraphix make an appearance each millennium for a single day in which to eat and mate." Torast said, quickly moving from side to side, carving a shallow niche in the dirt to protect his vulnerable abdomen. "That time appears to be today."

"What is an oraphix?" Jack asked.

"An omnivorous insectoid that appears each millennium, as you heard Torast say," the Guardian replied. "Each oraphix will feed on any living thing so that it may acquire the strength it needs to mate before it dies."

"What about Torast?" Jack asked.

"Torast's body is impervious to their strikes, save for his abdomen," the Guardian said. "Yet, there is one who could deal these ravagers a great blow."

"Whoever or whatever it is," Jack replied, "we need here in the worst way."

"The entity I speak of is an actual part of this world," the Guardian said. "It is capable of appearing in any form it wishes."

"It seems to me," Jack said, "that this being you speak of would not attack another natural part of the same world."

"That is true. But the oraphix are not native to Burrus Plax. They were brought here for one purpose—to annihilate every living thing. However, the creators of this plan underestimated the resistance they would encounter. And after the oraphix completed their initial sweep of the planet, the orchestrators of this bloodbath arrived to claim their prize, only to be annihilated themselves. Then, having mated, the surviving oraphix laid larvae that burrowed deep into the ground, waiting for a thousand years to pass."

"Well, the longer we lie here, the greater chance of *our* annihilation. We need to do something to stem the flow of bugs."

"Indeed," the Guardian said. His movements were a blur; he skittered to the top of Torast and blasted a sonic pulse directly at the column of bugs. The flow stopped immediately. The Guardian then jumped to the ground and raced to the edge of the opening. He continued sending the sonic pulses directly into the chamber, unsure if this attack would neutralize the remaining creatures. After several minutes, the Guardian ceased his assault, cocked his head and listened intently. Thirty minutes passed with nothing but silence emanating from the hole. In the meantime, Jack had scaled Torast and returned to his natural cockpit.

"Anything?" Jack yelled.

"No," the Guardian said, raising a forearm in a gesture to silence Jack, then his head shot up toward large balls of white light appearing in the distance, along with several explosions.

"What's is that?" Jack asked.

"Oraphix that have found a food source," the Guardian said upon returning to his perch.

"I know I'll regret asking, but what does that mean?"

"We have effectively removed enough of the insects to slow their reestablishment during the next mating ritual."

"That's good, right?"

In a way," Torast replied. Just then, a herd of dazon stampeded toward the three beings, each with an oraphix attached firmly to their back. The aggressor had a tube inserted into the back of the dazon's neck, extracting its life's fluid. This produced a white circular light that exploded when the prey expired.

Then, the doomed antelope shriveled and dropped to the ground—a pile of dried skin and brittle bones. As its prey fell, the male oraphix attacked the female by landing on her back in mid-air and driving its single-jointed legs deep into her thorax. Mating would take place, the pair hitting the ground dead, forcing their larvae out, completing the entire ritual in a matter of seconds. The newborn then burrowed into the ground, feeding on tree roots and other prey for the next thousand years when it resurfaces.

"We should keep moving," Torast said. "With the battle of light still in force, it offers enough cover for us to escape."

****

The sky lightened, and rays of sunshine appeared over a distant treeline. Torast continued to lumber along, laden with a human and a small furry creature. He was moving down a gentle incline.

"I've been meaning to ask you a question," Jack said.

"I am right here," the Guardian replied, attempting sarcasm for the first time.

"Keep trying, you'll get it," Jack said. He raised one eyebrow and thought for a moment. "That's right, a question." He turned his attention back to the Guardian. "How long do you think it will be before the tunnels will be dry enough for you to resume your vigil?"

"Excellent question," the Guardian said. "I cannot offer a definitive answer, for there are too many variables. Will the water be able to drain or will it have to evaporate? Perhaps the one who flooded the chambers will take a notion to repeat his actions."

"All viable possibilities," Jack agreed. "You indicated there was one who could deliver the oraphix a decisive blow."

"You are correct," the Guardian said. "This being is also responsible for removing us from the system of tunnels using a burst of water."

"Who is this powerful adversary?"

"Do not be so quick to call this one an adversary." The Guardian blinked several times. "His name is Max."

CHAPTER THIRTY-EIGHT

Dalon Con, Krabb and Sketch

Sketch and Krabb dug their fingers into Dalon Con's fur garment, shutting their eyes as the old man quickened his pace.

"The buildings are in unusually good shape," Dalon Con said, his eyes adjusting to the dim light. A steady hum originated from deep within the heart of the city.

"I bees too ascared to look," Sketch stammered.

"Ima thinkin' Mr. Dalon are a headin' fer that hum we's hearin'," Krabb groaned, "and I ain't zactly sure I want him to get thar."

"No need to fear," Dalon Con said. "It is imperative that we discover under what guise this supposed dead city is operating."

"Don't look like she operatin' to me atall," Krabb said. "What makin' ya think she is?"

Just then, several hundred feet away, an orange fireball blew a door off its hinges and into the street. The door was accompanied by a man in a white lab coat, flames leaping from his back. This was followed by a string of curses and three other men beating out the flames with blankets.

Dalon Con glanced at Krabb.

"Taint no need in even be goin' thar," Krabb said. "Jest leave'r be."

Dalon Con smiled.

****

The large figure sat upright, shaking his head and spitting out the coarse saw dust that coated his mouth.

"What happened to me," Smort said, constantly pursing his

lips and blowing out tidbits of the sanare tree. He grabbed his head trying to compress the pain coursing through his cranium with little success. *Need water.* Crawling downhill on his hands and knees, the dehydrated Smort finally reached a clean source of hydration in a fast moving stream. He submersed his head letting the cool water ease his headache. Then rose and began gulping water from his cupped hands, remembering what brought him to this state. When he could hold no more, Smort rolled to the side and fell asleep to a near comatose point. His body absorbed the H^2O, continuing the healing process as he dreamt of revenge aimed at Dalon Con.

****

The trio crept behind a vacant house directly across the street from the target location.

"As we move around the corner of this structure," Dalon Con said, "we should be able to see into the dwelling, and, hopefully, determine what caused the fire and ensuing explosion."

"Ya sure we gots to move?" Sketch asked.

"Yeah," Krabb added, "I'ma kinda startin' to like thins right in this here spot."

"Where I go, you go, unless . . ."

"Lead on," Both Sketch and Krabb said.

"There is quite a bit of activity inside the house." Dalon Con watched through the open doorway as several men in white coats hurriedly rushed around the room. "It appears they are concerned, about what I do not know." He watched three men carrying a fourth into the dwelling where the explosion force originated. Within seconds, the door returned to its original position in the jamb.

"Curious," Dalon Con said.

"I ain't never seen such a thing," Sketch said.

"Grhmpf," Krabb grunted, "I reckon we be agoin' ta find that hummin' now."

"You do an excellent job of reckoning," Dalon Con said.

The trio slipped between the houses, across the street, and toward the door that only minutes earlier was lying in the street. Placing his hand on the knob, Dalon Con gave a gentle push, setting the door in motion.

"It don't look lika dad blame thin' happen," Krabb exclaimed as they entered.

"Though we know it did," Dalon Con answered.

"Leastwise, I thunked it did," Sketch said.

What I truly fear, Dalon Con thought, *is that a temporal disturbance has occurred here, erasing the damage with a change in the timeline.*

"We must leave now, lest a temporal event catch us unaware." He herded Sketch and Krabb out the entrance. Once they reached the center of the street and away from the front of the dwelling, Dalon Con slowed. "Are you all right? It was not my intent to force you to move at such a speed when we entered the building; however, probabilities necessitated a hasty retreat."

"Mr. Dalon," Sketch said, "if ya get ta thinkin' we's a movin' too slow, then ya push us any which away ya think be best."

"Sides, we's 'bout happy as happy kin be jest gettin' outta that place," Krabb said. "And now I ain't feelin' so bad 'bout huntin' down that hummin' noise."

****

Several hours later, the old man stopped in the heart of the city. "We are closing in."

Sketch agreed. "That hummin' be gettin' louder."

They moved cautiously, finally coming to a halt in the middle of a vacant lot. "The sound of working machines is right under foot." Dalon Con pointed toward the ground.

"What now?" Sketch whispered.

"I am unsure of what we will face," Dalon Con said. "It is imperative we rely on surprise when confronting the unknown."

Several miles away, a bright light, followed by a thunderous sound, caused them to turn toward the commotion.

"Is that—?"

"Yes," Dalon Con interrupted, "it is the very explosion we witnessed not long ago."

Krabb opened his mouth to speak, then changed his mind. Dalon Con's hand rose to silence the small man. "When we entered the dwelling and saw that the room was free of damage, I knew a temporal thief had gone back, retrieved a small section of time and replaced the timeline in the room. In this way, the room would appear as though nothing had happened until the carnage we originally witnessed played through a second time."

"So yer tellin' me that this here thin' . . . this tempal crook, is a-takin' chunks 'o' time and movin' em 'round to make thins look differnt?" Krabb asked.

"And this here time keeps a movin' 'cept where the crook done an knocked a slab 'o' it out an slapped er somewheres else," Sketch added.

"Yes," Dalon Con said, "and the same timeline, which, in our case was the fireball and the four men, just repeated itself in the blast we recently observed." He stared down in wonder at Sketch and Krabb.

"No disrespect 'tended," Sketch said, "but why is ya lookin' at us thata way?"

You misunderstand the meaning of my gaze." Dalon Con knelt, bringing himself to eye level with the tiny men, "it was out of respect and surprise at the amount of knowledge you possess."

"That's awful kind ta say them nice thins 'bout us," Sketch said, "but we ain't got no idea why we know'd all them thins."

"They jest kinda come to us," Krabb agreed.

"This distorted concept of time," Dalon Con said. "is where the answer lies."

He sighed and gazed around. "First, we must find a suitable location to enter the underground lair."

"We be with ya all the way," Sketch and Krabb said.

Dalon Con smiled. "I know."

CHAPTER THIRTY-NINE

Hayden

Hayden watched the humanoids in white lab coats move from counter to counter, checking devices, specific gravities, and other such items.

"Ezra, come," one of the men called. "There are anomalies I cannot explain."

"How can I help, Malik?"

The first man pointed to a computer touch screen. "These two images just appeared. One remains constant, while the other fades in and out. It is my assumption it is an anomaly within the machine—a ghost."

Ezra nodded. "I believe your first instincts are correct; however, the constant image could be more problematic."

"Agreed. However, it could also be an anomaly of a different sort. Then again, it may be an intruder."

"Regardless," Ezra said, "as a member of the Odobi race, which has and will endure for untold millennia, I will discover the source of this confusion."

"Odobi?" Hayden stammered. "That's impossible. In this timeframe, Burrus Plax hasn't reached the age of the Odobi. With the different timelines crisscrossing this planet, there's no relative time source to anchor us—only one of a constant nature."

"A conundrum at best, is it not," Max said.

"You do not know how good it is to hear your voice, old friend." Hayden looked toward the sound, locating a convex impression of

Max's face on the floor. "And to look upon you again."

"It good to see you too, little one."

"But shouldn't we be more discreet. Your voice is rather . . . noticeable."

"My voice is relative to whom I am speaking. What sounds loud to you may be undetectable to others." Max directed his attention toward the scientists. As for your confusion, I can only offer a hypothesis—what we are witnessing is grounded within a temporal disturbance."

Hayden stared at Max. "You speak of time . . . moreover, you speak of movement through the fabric of time."

"It is as you say." Max rose through the floor until his shoulders appeared. He brought with him a hand, palm side up, for Hayden to use as a landing platform. Hayden took advantage of his new perch.

"You know the problem," Hayden said. "Yet, you have no idea as to a solution?"

"The idea of the involvement of time is pure speculation on my part, which is why any solution is beyond my conception."

"But you state as fact that this is a temporal event."

"Even though I know very little of time travel," Max said, "it is the only logical conclusion one can draw. We will search deeper into this supposedly dead township, for this city contains many unknown disruptions. This path will most likely take us further below this city."

"Allow me to continue in your stead," Hayden interrupted. "I feel this mode of travel will prove of great assistance as we continue our explorations. I will continue to travel within your curled hand to where you think the greatest concentration of energy lies."

"Enough said." Max's hand closed around Hayden as he disappeared below the floor. Hayden felt irregularities as Max traveled through different strata.

Though they traveled horizontally, Hayden felt like he was moving upward found himself in a space much larger than Max's curled hand. As he looked around, Max slowed to a stop.

Hayden approached two small openings where light filtered in. *I am seeing through Max's eyes.*

The view gradually clarified, revealing a large, well-lit room with high ceilings. Several silver-colored barrels stood side by side with less than an inch between them. Each container had copper wire loops around the top and bottom and additional loops two feet from each end, resembling large springs.

Whatever these are, Hayden thought, *I sense great power.*

"You are correct," Max replied.

Though essentially inside of Max's head, Hayden jumped at the sound of the giant's voice.

"My apologies." Max softly chuckled. "I will be careful from this time forward."

"No need, it is I that should apologize to you for the way I have acted. Do you bring information?"

"Yes, these cells store pure energy and are linked together. The room you see here is one of many."

"What need would anyone have for this amount of power?" Hayden asked.

"Thus far, it is a mystery, even to me," Max said. A humming sound ensued and began to grow. "The ambient light grows as the sound grows."

It was then that Hayden's small black box crackled to life. "Hayden," Wakke said, "I can only hope you are able to hear and decipher this message. You must not—" Several seconds of static interrupted the transmission. "—Drade has managed to—" Once again an influx of static wiped away any intelligible speech. "—Please signal acknowledgement of transmission receipt—" One more period of static ensued. "—Or all may be—" The message ended and Hayden's receiver went silent. He pushed the "message received" button.

"No answer." Hayden shook the box. *What did Wakke say? Something about Drade? Drade.* "That's it!" He turned toward Max. "It is the only answer that makes sense and covers all."

"Calm yourself, small one, and tell Max your sudden revelation."

"All the pieces fit together. In my timeline, we were aware that time travel was possible. Albeit illegal, this project was government-sanctioned.

"I represent the Odobi in the present—my present; however, what we have before us is a *future* race of Odobi—how far into this future, I have no way of knowing. The only way this future race could be here at this point in time, is through time travel. And that could only have been divulged by an Odobi from their past, who used this technology to travel into the future. They then supplied the scientific community of the future the technology, along with the coordinates to our specific point in time or as close as could be determined."

"Your theory explaining how the next race of Odobi made it into this space in time is possible, even probable;" Max said. "This would explain your differences in size. However, if we delve deeper into this reasoning the scenario makes no sense. Who is this Drade?"

"One our most brilliant scientists. To keep the story short, he felt our use of time travel was pointless. His idea was to advance beyond our knowledge. And to do that . . ."

"Is to remove you from the equation. That is a dangerous game, indeed," Max said.

"This act will nullify any contributions my race makes to this world, this time. And those barrels we saw with the copper coils no doubt supply the extreme amount of power required to make time travel possible."

"Therefore, making it easier for the evil that is so prevalent to complete their takeover of Burrus Plax," Max said.

CHAPTER FORTY

Vrollic

Muffled voices argued in a domain so dark that no light could penetrate, and none existed within to escape the oppressive gloom. Multiple entities spoke simultaneously, rendering their comments unintelligible.

"Wasa matter wit ya carn sarn devils arguin," Mama Byrnes said, "Keep on, 'n' I be given ya somethin' to arg-ya 'bout." As Mama Byrnes spoke the last half of her proclamation, the demon that claimed sole occupancy of Byrnes for many years shed the voice of the seedy old woman.

"What is ya doin' a goin' in and outta me ya no good varmit?"

"Your parents sold you for a day's rations," a deep voice said.

"You tellin' a lie, ya scurly devil."

"I have no reason to utter an untruth, and for your information, not that it will matter much longer, my name is Vrollic."

"Whatcha meen when you spew that mess outta your lying pie hole, that it twon't be a matterin' much longer?"

"That you and your six cohorts are soon to be assimilated into my being, adding your unique qualities to my essence, increasing my strength many times over."

Mama Byrnes bristled. "Ya got 'bout an odd way of speeching to regular folk whence you bringen thangs to mind like cohorts. I taint even got no idea what a cohort is, so why don't ya get to 'splaining so we both be a knowing."

"With pleasure," Vrollic said, "Broan, Murph, Rave, Dub, Johnny Boy, and Link. These are all your cohorts, and now you may add yourself to that list."

"Whatcha thinkin' 'bout, addin' me to that list' a' cronies? I taint like them."

"You speak true when you state you are not like the other six, for you are much worse."

"Vrollic, or what'air yer name be. Is you tellin' me I is badder than them thar peoples you drug into this here place whence you were inside ma head. It twere you what caused these folks to do what you claimed I did? And what about this here assamillyation?"

"It is what it is," Vrollic replied, "and now is the time for the 'seven' to become one. Each will represent their malevolent portion embedded in the whole."

Even though surrounded by an intense solid black in the dark realm, all could feel themselves beginning to rotate. They sensed an integration, as multiple entities melded together—twisting, turning, contorting—until a single creature emerged.

Vrollic grew to twice his size in the void, standing over sixteen feet tall in a crouched position. His body was basically humanoid, with an overall increased musculature. A frontal overlay protected his organs, and a single plate across the back of the thorax covered his spinal column. Smaller plates of the hardened skin wrapped his head, face, and neck, lending additional protection to his cranial and facial areas. Vrollic's skin was composed of microscopic dull-gray scales, except for the soles of each foot, which were similar to cloven dayvine hooves.

"Looka thar," Johnny Boy exclaimed, his eyes widening. Four wings sprouted from the monster's back, each carrying a vibrant hue as they unfurled.

"Well now," Broan said, "It be a lookin' like one of them curved knifes, you knows, I bleeves they call 'em talons whence they be on somethin' that kin fly."

His hands, now transformed, were a sight to behold. Four fingers and a thumb, each adorned with a boney ridge and five talons, ran the entire length of his hand and down the back of each digit. His feet, too, had undergone a metamorphosis. The big toe, now accompanied by a suitably sized talon, was followed by four progressively smaller toes, forming a solid mass.

The creature's back and posterior of its four extremities were splattered with a bright green bioluminescence streak finished with jagged edges. The outside of these serrated pulsating reliefs was surrounded by a bright purple, changing to red before ending in an azure blue that blended perfectly into Vrollic's gray skin.

Vrollic paused after standing for effect.

"You are the seven I have chosen, purposely to increase my strength."

"What could one as powerful as you possibly gain anything from assimilating me?" Rave asked.

"My power increases exponentially by harvesting from seven subjects instead of one. So if you have any information to share, do it quickly. Once the integration is complete, you will cease to exist."

Terrified voices filled the air, gradually fading until only a haunting silence remained.

"Time's up," Vrollic said with a chilling chuckle, "you lose."

CHAPTER FORTY-ONE

Gabriel and Roan

Looking straight ahead as he ran, Gabriel could see Roane pulling ahead at an alarming rate. Roane slowed, allowing Gabriel to pull alongside.

"Can't run any faster, eh?" Roane yelled.

Gabriel looked over his shoulder and then at Roane. "You see that cloud of dust gaining on me?"

Roane glanced back and then nodded.

"Don't you think if I could run any faster, I would?"

Again, Roane nodded.

"Then, shut up!"

"You got it," Roane mumbled, accelerating and outpacing his companion.

"Don't think I can make it to the tree line," Gabriel huffed. He glanced back and then wished he hadn't. There was a raycon not more than thirty feet behind, every bit of twelve feet tall. The coarse hair that pushed outward from its mane nearly dragged the ground; however, its most disturbing characteristic was the three horns protruding from its head. Gabriel was beginning to wear down, yet summoned a burst of energy as he obsessed about the horns piercing his body.

"Hold on!" Roane dropped back to offer assistance, his voice just audible above the roar of the thundering herd. A startled Gabriel nodded as Roane moved behind, placing both hands on his lower back.

Gabriel instinctively grabbed the creature's rough mane while Roane wrapped his arms around Gabriel's waist.

"Are you all right?" Roane yelled into Gabriel's ear.

Gabriel nodded.

The herd had reached the tree line and plowed into the forest. Branches scratched and clawed at the two men. Trees fell, trapping a number of the raycon beneath them.

"Look out!" Gabriel warned. A tree, twelve feet in diameter, made contact with the side of their raycon's head, taking the animal to the ground and tossing Roane and Gabriel into the same creek where this miniature scope of time-tripping had started.

"As fun as this has been," an exasperated Gabriel said, "I wonder how much longer this temporal thief is going to jerk us around, because I've had enough."

"I think we've seen the last of it," Roane said. "The thief has made its presence known. Unless we do something that interrupts the fabric of time, we will see it no more."

"At least that is something," Gabriel huffed as he collapsed onto the bank. "Any notion as to where we go from here?"

"No idea," he groaned. Reaching round, he searched for a puncture wound in his buttocks, then sighed with relief. "No blood. No extra holes," he whispered. "Good way to travel, but next time, let's get a saddle. Those ridge horns are a pain in the . . ."

Roan looked at Gabriel. "You ok?"

"I cannot explain this sudden urge to reunite with an old friend," Gabriel said, "and the desire grows stronger every day."

"Who is the old friend?" Roane asked.

"Dalon Con. I was raised by an evil witch who killed my parents and turned me into a slave. After I escaped Dalon Con rescued me." Gabriel continued his story of escape and kidnapping. "Fortunately, Bile died, due to his own arrogance. I suppose I helped. Wasn't sure if I was glad to be rid of him, or if I wanted him back in my life."

"Sounds like a confusing time," Roane said. *He's finally starting to grasp for the only thing that will truly save him. I hope he will see the need to begin our search for Dalon Con.*

"Confusing doesn't begin to describe the mess I was in," Gabriel said. "It hasn't been that long since my separation from Bile, and, even though I know what must be done, I cannot force myself to do so."

"My friend," Roane said, "only you can make that decision."

Gabriel nodded slowly. "We should search for the one I've mentioned favorably."

"And who might this one be?"

"Dalon Con."

"Any notion of where to begin?"

Gabriel shook his head. "It's been so long since I've seen him, I'm unsure if he exists."

"You mentioned your feelings were indicating your need to follow Dalon Con," Roane said. "Is this still the case?"

"Through the static of Bile's influence, I believe that to be the case."

"Has Dalon Con left you any indication of where he might be?" Roane asked. Gabriel was already deep in thought. He turned his head to the right until his eyes connected with Roane's, and a wide grin spread across his face.

"I know where he is."

"Well," Roane said, "you're not going to keep it to yourself, are you?"

"That's all I've got, I'll know more when we get closer."

Unseen by the two, and washed out by the midday sun, a streak of orange light passed directly overhead.

"Do we have a direction to follow?"

"That's part of the problem," Gabriel replied, "we have several directions that will lead us to our destination. Two of the roads are easily traveled, while the remaining two are fraught with danger, including the possibility of death."

Roane glanced at Gabriel. "Lead on."

****

The smooth road made their journey effortless. But it was too easy.

"So far, so good," Roane said. "Maybe we made the right choice."

"I guess we will find out—"

Suddenly, a hollowed-out cylinder made of bone, four feet in diameter and nine feet tall, fell over the top of Roane, encasing him in an organic tube. Before Gabriel could react, he found himself in a similar predicament.

"I guess we have our answer," Roane's muffled voice said.

"Yeah, I guess we do. So, any suggestions as to get out of this predicament?."

"My first thought was to push this . . . this . . . thing over and crawl out the end, but then I realized that whatever dropped these cylinders over us is more than likely still around."

"And?" Gabriel questioned.

"Do we really want to meet this creature?" Roane asked.

"No, but we can't afford to hang around in these prisons." Gabriel strained to extract his arms, but they were wedged too tight. "I can't move."

"I think that's the idea. Well, we either stay where we are and die or confront what's waiting for us on the other side—and possibly die. Which death do you prefer?"

"There is another option." Gabriel began to count. "One, two, three!"

CHAPTER FORTY-TWO

Jack, Torast and the Guardian

The unlikely trio continued to move across the wasteland. "Have either of you seen such a spectacle as this?" Torast asked.

"Not in my lifetime," Jack said.

"As bad as this may appear, I have seen much worse," the Guardian replied. The ground was littered with oraphix due to their mating ritual but also because they'd underestimated their prey. The skin and bones of the hapless victims lay strewn among dead oraphix.

"Well, the one saving grace," Jack said, "is that I won't be around to see another generation released."

Satisfied the plague of insects was over, Torast pushed his great mass to a standing position. *I mustn't forget the entity that rode up in the space between the right and left half of my tail.* Then, he turned toward his companions. "We should continue the journey before the proper outcome is no longer attainable."

Jack and the Guardian mounted their transport.

"Question. I seen no tools to speak of in Defeated. If my reasoning is correct, would be a need for tools, even if that need were minuscule."

"There *is* no need for tools," Jack said. "*Tools* are for taking a life, it's a case of beating plowshares into weapons. As sad as that is, it's the only explanation I can offer."

Just then, the Guardian rose and cocked his head. "Listen," the Guardian said, "you must hear it." Jack cocked his head, trying to mimic the position of the Guardian.

"I hear nothing but the dry grass under Torast's feet."

"Push that sound aside and concentrate," the Guardian said. Jack attempted to follow the Guardian's instructions but to no avail.

"No good," Jack said, "still nothing but the crackling of dry—wait, I hear something." He looked at the Guardian. "Or moreover identify with it."

"Tell me what you perceive," the Guardian said.

"An entity with multiple legs or possibly tentacles," Jack replied.

"He speaks of moving water, confusing it with tentacles from some unknown beast," Torast said. "The banks of the sea are but a short distance away."

"The water is close, though that is not what I sense. But the new creature resides *in* the water. It must be found before it can inflict any negative impact as is often the case when newcomers invade this region."

"And the fact there's a large quantity of water nearby leaves the possibility, albeit highly improbable the oraphix may re-hydrate," Torast cautioned.

****

"The waves no more than two feet in height." Jack and the Guardian walked to the water's edge, where a school of tiny fish swam.

The Guardian slid through the water, gobbling up the small fish until the entire school had been devoured.

"Hey!" Jack protested. "I'm hungry too, you know."

"The aquatic creatures you refer to," Torast offered, "are not to be eaten by anyone of human descent."

"What about our silver and black friend there?" Jack asked, wagging a thumb in the Guardian's direction. The furry, striped reptile moved ashore and began to shake, removing the unwanted moisture.

"Get enough to eat?" Jack smirked.

"It will do for now." With one final shake, the creature sprayed Jack with water.

"I suggest you board," Torast said. "We will follow the coastline until we reach our destination."

"And where is that?" Jack said, using a sleeve to wipe off moisture from his face.

"When I am made aware," Torast said, "then you will know as well."

"Of course," Jack mumbled.

Once he and the Guardian returned to the familiar cockpit, Torast lumbered along the shoreline.

"Enjoy your meal?" Jack's stomach grumbled. "They looked delicious."

"The fish you speak of are unlike any other in these waters," the Guardian said. "They have no formal name and are simply referred to as 'death'." The reptilian turned its head toward Jack. "Had you partaken of even the smallest morsel of this marine creature, you would cease to be."

"Good to know, but that does nothing to put food in my stomach. Is there anything that swims that I'm allowed to eat, without it becoming my last meal?"

"Of course," the Guardian said, "everything that lives in this water, save for the aquatic death, is acceptable for your nourishment."

"If I may interrupt your conversation," Torast said. "Others of unknown origin also occupy the sea, but in such a way that they use the water as we use the ground."

"A boat," Jack said, "and a rather large one, at that."

"I have seen such a thing," the Guardian said. "However, it was many years in the past, perhaps before the last oraphix invaded this world."

How old is this fuzzy lizard? Jack wondered. *A thousand years, or more, is a long time.*

"Nothing such as this has crossed my path," Torast said. "I am at a loss whether to make contact or give this one a wide berth."

"I don't know where you two have been," Jack said, "but, not so long ago, numerous vessels sailed the seas and rivers of Burrus Plax."

"Listen," the Guardian hissed. "There is commotion aboard the floating object," the Guardian said. "Eight bipedal figures and two animals are moving in our direction."

"I see two smaller boats," Jack said, "but they are too far away to make out the occupants." By now, Torast had come to a halt to assist in identifying the objects coming their way.

"Two hack-cats have been employed as propulsion for the boats," Torast said. "One beast to tow each vessel. The owners of this flotilla are members of the Scariff clan." Torast discharged a massive snort.

"Something tells me that the "huff" Torast just expelled is more than a simple release of air," Jack said.

The Guardian looked toward Jack as if to agree. "I sense growing anger."

Torast explained that this particular Scariff was a splinter group, splitting from the main clan several centuries ago. "This division came about through the desire to conquer and enslave."

"May I assume this event transpired?" Jack asked.

"If you make this assumption, you would be correct," Torast said. "The original Scariff clan was a benevolent society. Soon after the split the people were enslaved and assimilated into this offshoot. The malevolence that fed this dark side of the Scariff continued to grow, turning these beings into ruthless murderers, committing all manner of unspeakable atrocities."

"Can they be stopped?" Jack asked.

"There has been no valid reason to attempt such a dangerous task," Torast said. "They occupy a small territory in and around this body of water. As they have shown no desire to expand their area, no one has considered it necessary to take such a great risk."

"What of these hack-cats?" Jack asked. "They don't sound like the friendliest of critters."

"These are one of the worst this planet has to offer," Torast said.

"Heed the words he speaks," the Guardian replied, "for this beast shall not be trifled with."

Torast described the creature, noting its impressive fourteen-foot length from tail to snout and a body covered in tiny, armor-like scales overlaid with dense, dark fur, making it nearly invisible in water, with the three-foot-long, flat tail serving as a rudder. The hack-cat's large eyes provided perfect vision in and out of water. "It has nostrils for breathing, but no mouth. Instead, it has two twelve-inch tusks for holding down prey. This is because the creature is multi-esophageal."

"A multi-what?" Jack asked.

"This animal has four legs," Torast continued. "At the end of each leg is what appears to be a paw with retractable claws. However, on the underside of each foot, there is a round orifice containing a swirling mass of teeth. It has taken the Scariff many years of breeding this creature to achieve this murderous end."

CHAPTER FORTY-THREE

Dalon Con, Krabb and Sketch

"The appearance of the temporal thief tells us we are in the correct location. That being said, it also places anyone who would trod here in grave danger."

"Mr. Con, Ifin I'ma understandin' 'xactly watcha sayin'," Sketch said, "shouldn't we be a high tailin' it outta here?"

"The temporal thief is here to protect something of great value," Dalon Con said. "I have no way of knowing what this *something* is, only that it affects the flow of time." He knelt in front of Sketch. "And Unfortunately, leaving is not an option, small one."

"I done and figgered that already," Sketch said.

"By my way 'o' thinkin'," Krabb said, "we ain't got no way ta know ifin it's now, later or afore."

"Correct," Dalon Con replied, "however, you can be sure the temporal thief will stop at nothing to prevent our finding what he seeks to protect."

"What kinda thins kin he do to stop us?" Sketch asked.

"The beast can attack in a physical manner, but prefers to allow time to do its work for him. In this way, the thief can avoid any danger to himself."

"So yer tellin' me," Krabb said, "we kin put a hurtin' on that thar tempral thingy, Mr. Con?"

"Yes. The thief is vulnerable to attack. Its only defense, other than traveling along the temporal line, is losing itself in distorted time. These are voids lacking temporal matter that remain once the thief removes what he desires and replaces it with sections that do not fit."

Dalon Con stood. "It is time to move deeper into the city."

"An bet we's goin' underground," Krabb huffed.

"Yes," Dalon Con said.

"I knew you wuz gonna say that."

****

The surroundings felt far from inviting. The dense foliage above filtered the sunlight, casting a murky blue pallor. The ground, littered with loose and shifting cobblestones, made navigating the uneven terrain increasingly difficult.

"Excuse me, Mr. Con, but I's been steppin' on loose cobbly stones an they is gettin' worser," Sketch said.

"Hold!" Dalon Con stopped, leaving Sketch and Krabb balanced precariously on a line of cracked and loose stones. The man knelt, fingers tracing the defective masonry, assessing the instability of the path ahead.

"Of course." Dalon Con lifted his head and looked at Sketch. "I believe you may have found that which we have searched for, and, may I say, excellent work."

"That thars a rat good piece 'o' findin'," Krabb said.

"Ah, twernt nothin'," Sketch said, puffing out his chest.

Dalon Con slid four fingers into one of the wider cracks. "We should be able to remove a sufficient amount of cobblestone to use as an entrance. I feel air and sense a significant amount of activity beneath our feet." He clamped his fingers and thumb around a stone and wrenched it out with a sharp "pop," holding up an octagonal-shaped piece of pavement.

"This method will suffice." After they removed a four-foot area of stones, Dalon Con instructed Sketch and Krabb to remove the exposed soil. "However," he cautioned, "remain standing on the stone walkway as you dig." Dalon Con instructed.

After an hour, the hole was too deep for them to reach the bottom.

Dalon Con punched his cane into the dirt at the center base of the hole, creating an opening.

"Well, looky thar," Sketch said, staring over the edge of the hand-dug pit. "They's a bright light shinin' up through the opening."

"With the stream of light being little brighter than our ambient light, I feel we have chosen a safe place to enter," Dalon Con said.

"Each of you stand on one of my feet, then grab my legs tightly," Dalon Con said. When Sketch and Krabb were ready, Dalon Con jumped into the hollow, crashing through the tunnel ceiling to the cavern below.

****

Dalon Con headed toward a bright light that led into a larger space one hundred yards down the corridor, stopping three feet short of the entrance.

"I can hear a significant amount of activity within the room," Dalon Con said.

Dalon Con hesitated a moment. *I sense something.* He then whispered, "Sketch, Krabb. I will need both of you to assist me. My cloak must remain tightly closed. I am counting on you."

"A dang sight hard to grip when ya can't see whatcha grabbin'," Krabb said.

"That's fer sure," Sketch replied.

Interesting. An unseen creature, nestled in the shadows, watched Dalon Con with interest. *Very interesting, indeed.*

Dalon Con pulled his head deep into the recesses of the cloak's hood and concealed his left hand within the robe's sleeve. All but invisible, Dalon Con stepped into the middle of the doorway.

Dalon Con knew that the temporal thief had reasons for keeping them from this place. The men in the room, not of this timeline, worked with incomplete, altered technology. Due to their flawed knowledge, what they perceived as a single trip was, in actuality, multiple excursions to Burrus Plax.

As Dalon Con stepped from the doorway back into the tunnel, he sensed the presence lingering just out of sight—its essence both foreign and oddly recognizable—brushing the periphery of his awareness. The air grew heavy, and the flicker of time seemed to pause in anticipation of what was to come.

"You know who them fellers is, don't cha?" Sketch said.

"I believe so," he nodded. "These scientists would not be among us had they considered returning to their time," Dalon Con said. "What escapes me is how they obtained such technology, which was discovered and abandoned many years before they existed."

"How can ya know that's why they's here?" Sketch asked.

"The appearance of the temporal thief alone tells me that time travel, or, moreover, the ability to traverse a timeline from beginning to end, is why they are here," Dalon Con said. "Without this information, these scientists will be unable to return home. I fear, in their zeal to experience temporal travel, they have not taken into consideration any negative consequences."

"So they be stuck here?" Krabb asked.

Dalon Con nodded, tapping his lips with his index finger. "How these scientists received this technology remains a mystery; however, multiple trips were made, and we know the answer *will* show itself."

"Mayhap them fellers whats sposed to be here," Sketch said, "you know. Give them some 'o' this technacolgy to bring them here on purpose."

"Thus, keeping Odobi of the future in this timeline," Dalon Con said. "And continue perfecting temporal travel, while maintaining a captive maintenance crew and an entrance portal away from prying eyes." Dalon Con paused, pondering the situation. He began to nod. "The upper echelon of the tiny Odobi in my timeline could easily monopolize time travel". . . He smiled. "Well done, my friend."

"Do that mean we got this here probum licked?" Krabb asked.

"Perhaps, little one. We shall see," Dalon Con said, as the group moved deeper into the tangled blue flora.

CHAPTER FORTY-FOUR

Hayden and Max

Max exhibited an expression of concern. "Tell me of this one called Wakke, and what has he to do with you."

"I feel shame for what I have hidden from you," Hayden said. "Wakke is a friend and co-worker. We, as you know, are members of the Odobi. We came to Burrus Plax eighteen years ago." He paused, considering his old friend.

"Wakke remains in the same timeline in which we began. I however, have not a clue where I reside in time, other than I am in a timeline that precedes Wakke. I have no way to communicate with him other than pressing this button on my controller, which tells him I still exist." Hayden moved in a sizeable circle, several feet in front of Max.

"The Odobi's sole purpose is to gather scientific knowledge. Once we discovered the condition of this world, we set out to find what brought about the vile, lawless society that Burrus Plax is today."

"And?" Max asked.

Hayden explained that Odobian society had once harnessed the power of time travel. Then, without explanation, temporal experimentation was abruptly outlawed, the technology concealed, accessible only to a privileged group of scientists. Resuming time travel became a covert operation, secretly sanctioned by the government. Yet, only a few officials and travelers knew about the mission to Burrus Plax. This venture, driven solely by a thirst for knowledge, eclipsed any consideration of the consequences their actions might entail.

"You know not of the damage you may have wrought upon this world," Max's eyes ablaze, "however, *you will* learn."

"Does this mean we are through? I have started to value your friendship."

"My anger burns, but someone such as you, who bears no malice toward others, I also consider a friend. Rest assured, we are not through."

"Thank you," a calm assurance settling around Hayden.

"You are thinking of more than just yourself. Perhaps, the Odobi have a chance."

"A chance," Hayden repeated, "please, explain."

"To learn to care for someone or something other than yourselves." A smile spread across Hayden's face.

"Perhaps," Hayden said, "I am finding it comes naturally, but stems from my time spent with you."

"Good," Max said, "we will keep these things—"

The ceiling directly above their heads began to crack and loosen.

"Hayden, to me, now!" Max closed his hand around the airborne Hayden and disappeared into the cave's floor as the cave-in ensued. However, Max found it strange that the barrage of debris was not pounding the ground above his head. He immediately propelled himself to the surface.

"Blue sky," Hayden said in surprise. "The stones didn't drop; something removed them from above." The penetration through the ceiling suddenly turned black, and an incredible suction pulled Hayden from Max's hand.

"You will not take my friend!" Max roared and allowed himself to be pulled into the vertical abyss.

Hayden screamed into the deafening wind, bouncing off the side walls of his prison as he moved upward. Then, an overwhelming sense of comfort returned as five familiar digits curled around his body.

What Hayden could not see, and Max had detected for some time, was the sixty-foot-tall creature pulling the two through its six-foot-wide snout. At the end of this feeding tube lie six grinding pads, waiting to pulverize its next meal.

"If I am not mistaken," Max said, "we are in the unpleasant company of a dragbeast."

"Possessing minimal intelligence, relying mainly on instinct." Then, the dragbeast rumbled and shook violently.

"Sounds as though something is approaching," Hayden said, "And that something is of considerable size."

"The dragbeast's proboscis uncurls when it feeds, sucking its intended meal into its mouth to be ground to mush."

"So, in short, we are about to become food for a big, stupid bug."

"What you have alluded to would most certainly ring true, had I not taken on the attributes of the stone as we left the underground cavern." With no warning, Max plowed his stone fist through the jaw of the dragbeast, flooding the area with light. "Better?"

With each blow, the dragbeast's makeup becomes more discernible. One giant orb acts as the thorax. The second orb must be its head. Its brain can't be any larger than the tip of my smallest finger. wo eyes are facing forward, and two are facing to the rear, along with a pair of antennae.

Max shook his head. *What could one so stupid need with antennae?*

Suddenly, the world shook violently.

"Max," Hayden yelled, "what's happening?"

"Did I fail to mention, the dragbeast is capable of flight?"

****

Flames shot from underneath a giant orb, which slowly began to rise into the air. Once it cleared the ground, the flames became straight columns of fire, pushing the organic vehicle skyward. The dragbeast's back withdrew from the rest of its body and split into four sections, each of which spread apart, forming four wings, one end of each attached to a central point. The assembly began to rotate, adding lift and directional control.

****

"No," Hayden replied, "you did not mention the ability to fly. What do we do now?"

"We will remain here until the dragbeast lands."

"Why can't we leave now?"

"Currently, I am made of stone and could offer you no cushioning upon landing. I am afraid that could prove fatal . . . Unless."

Without warning, Max wrapped his fingers around Hayden and leapt from the opening in the dragbeast's cheek, their bodies plummeting towards the unknown.

CHAPTER FORTY-FIVE

Gabriel and Roan

Roane and Gabriel start back and forth in their bone prisons. Roane was the first to tumble onto his side. He wriggled the length of the tube, slowly extending his head.

Thud!

"Roane," came a muffled voice through the dense bone. "Can you hear me?" Roane forced his head outside of his enclosure.

"Move to the end of your cylinder."

"Which end?"

"Either!"

The two enclosures lay perpendicular, six feet apart, and Roan could see both ends of Gabriel's. He watched Gabriel's bone rock, and then he wriggled halfway out.

He turned and smiled.

Then Roane's eyes widened as a furry, prehensile tail shot out from the foliage. "Go back in, now!" he screamed.

But it was too late; the creature wrapped itself around Gabriel's torso and jerked the young man into the air and out of sight.

Roan pulled himself from his chamber and gazed into the trees, searching for any sign of his missing companion.

"No!" Then he turned and screamed at the top of his lungs. "Don't tell me you're only going to take one of us!" He paced erratically, yelling his threat until all became silent.

****

"Hey, Roane. Looks like we're back together."

"Yes, it does. Unfortunately, we are a hundred feet up a tree."

"There is that. Any ideas?"

Roane scanned the surrounding forest.

"We're in a spot where several large limbs come together, forming a bowl. The foliage is so thick that leaves are all we can see."

"Any clue as to how we're going to get down?"

Roane shook his head. "Maybe, after I learn how we got up here."

"The thing that yanked me out of the bone, threw me in here. It all happened so fast, I never got a glimpse of what it may have been."

"Nor did I," Roane stood shaking his head in frustration. "The only explanation I can muster—and this is going to sound crazy— is a childhood legend."

"Okay." Gabriel said slowly. "Well, it's a start."

"Did your parents tell you bedtime stories?" Roane asked.

"I had such a short time with my parents before they were murdered, I can't say for sure."

"I didn't realize your childhood was so painful."

"That tale is for another time," Gabriel said. "Please, continue."

"My father loved to tell stories, and one story we heard, more often than not, was the tale of a creature known to us as a thack. Until now, we believed the thack was a story designed to scare children. I never even considered that it was true."

"What makes you think this is a thack?"

"Every night, my father would light a candle, signaling it was bedtime. Once in my bed, my father would start to weave his tale. He'd put his head closer to mine to maximize the mystique he had already created."

"Why would any parent want to scare a kid before bedtime?"

"Funny that you should invoke the word 'kid.'"

"What do you mean, 'kid'?" Gabriel asked, a challenging tone in his voice. Roane cocked his head.

“How old are you?” Roane asked. Gabriel scrunched his forehead in deep thought.

“I'm caught in a strange paradox. I feel like I'm in my early to mid-twenties, yet a nagging voice insists I’m merely sixteen," Gabriel mused, his voice tinged with uncertainty.

“Looking at you, I would guess you are in your mid-twenties,” Roane said.

"But how?"

“Being in close proximity to the temporal thief and multiple timelines has affected your age.” Roane then held up his hand, "I know; that is a tale for another time." Crossing his legs, he continued.

Roane shifted nervously. “As I said, Father could make an already eerie room much worse by placing his head in close proximity to mine. And as the candlelight danced off his facial features, he would begin.”

****

“It was nearly midnight when the mist settled over the town of Clayson,” Laben began, his voice low and foreboding. “Everyone was asleep, unaware of what was coming their way.” As his father spoke, young Roane pulled his covers up to his chin, eyes wide with anticipation.”

“A presence approached the first house. You could hear the timber cracking as a thack tore off the roof with its sharp, clawed forelimbs.

"Grrrr," Laben growled, raising both hands and curling his fingers like claws, swiping menacingly at the air.

Terrified, little Roane pulled the covers up further, until only his eyes peeked out. “Standing on the small portion of the roof that remained, the thack slowly uncurled its long tail, letting it drop into the house. Then, one by one, it wrapped the appendage around each occupant and devoured them.”

By now, Roane’s face was completely hidden beneath the covers. His father leaned in, and with a sudden, startling motion, ripped the covers from his son's head, screaming . . . "And now he's coming for you!"

****

"Nice father you've got there," Gabriel said. "Sounds like the witch that raised me."

"Indeed," Roane replied. "However, there was something strange during this time, that, in my later years, I could never understand."

Roane gazed out over the tree line. "My father was a warm, kind man. I truly loved him, but an alternate persona took over when he lit the candle each night."

"Mama Byrnes smoked cigarettes wax shavings she scraped from a candle." Gabriel ran a hand through his hair. "Thinking back, despite being as mean as she was, after a few hits from her cigarette, she turned into a vile creature, the likes of which I have never seen."

Roane's voice grew tense. "It seems, Gabriel, we share more than we thought."

"At least, it offers a possible explanation of what placed us in the top of this tree, though I am hoping you are wrong," Gabriel said.

The tree shuddered, sending a shower of leaves to the ground.

"What now?"

"I think it may be your idea of what placed us in this tree," Roane warned.

CHAPTER FORTY-SIX

Jack and Vrollic

The sky and surrounding scenery began to melt and then dropped out of sight. In its place were the two boats, now only a few yards from the shoreline. The air was thick with the smell of salty seawater and the stench of the cat-like creatures who paced anxiously in the shallows, stirring up thick, brown mud.

"Let me guess," Jack said, "the hack-cats have come out to play . . . isn't that nice."

Vrollic, watching the unfolding situation, was strangely attracted to the malevolent players. *I know not what the scenario before me entails or to what end it will be beneficial, only that I feel a kinship with the participants.*

"Perhaps we should pay closer attention to what lies ahead," the Guardian warned.

Two cloaked figures waded toward them. These once-human creatures employed, or in the case of the hack-cats, bred others to do their bidding.

"Get on board with all haste," Torast said. "The light wanes, and we must leave before dusk." The Guardian quickly scurried aboard, followed by Jack, who settled into his familiar cockpit.

"One of the creatures is swallowing a mouthful of some unknown substance," Jack noted.

"No time for that now; we'll deal with it later," Torast said.

"Brace yourself, furry one," Jack quipped. "If I remember correctly, we're in for a wild ride."

Torast extended, then compressed his legs to their maximum just as a black paw sank its claws into his side just below the edge of Jack's cockpit. Releasing his compacted limbs, they launched into the air with a hack-cat still attached.

The creature gnawed against Torast's outer layer of protective skin as a second paw moved into the cockpit.

"Hold tight!" Torast growled over the deafening wind. The sonic barrier gave way, allowing the flying creature to extend his wings and engage the vertical movement of his tail.

"It's still here," Jack yelled, dodging the hack-cat's sharp claws. Then he realized it was no longer necessary to raise his voice. *Guardian*, he thought.

"I can do nothing to help," The Guardian shouted, "Since we travel at a supersonic rate, my sound expulsions will have no effect. It is for the same reason we are able to converse. We move at a rate faster than the sound that follows us."

A thought crossed Jack's mind. *Of course, the Nexus.* He wasted no time in retrieving the implement from his waistband. Before he extended the evil blade, The Guardian regurgitated into the hack-cat's mouth, releasing a pound of deathfish. The monster's eyes rolled over white as the beast dropped from Torast.

"Will falling from this height kill the beast?" Jack asked.

"The fish I spat into its mouth killed the beast," The Guardian stated.

"Nothing will remain," Torast said. "Good work for one so small."

"What happened back there?" Jack asked. "I mean, there were two boats headed our way, and, in an instant, they were upon us with hack-cats ready to rip us to pieces."

"There is a legend concerning a creature called the temporal thief," Torast said. "This being could shift increments of time to confuse."

Jack tilted his head. "When you said timelines, did you mean time travel?"

"Yes," Torast said. "We should set down soon. I am in need of nourishment and I could use assistance finding a suitable place.

"What should we look for in a landing area?" Jack asked.

"Flowering trees of any type would be welcome."

"And a clearing in which to land?" The Guardian asked.

"Not necessary," Torast said. "I shall create my own."

****

Torast, guided by hunger, took only minutes to set down in the delectable stand of foliage. Jack and The Guardian waited patiently while Torast destroyed tree after tree, taking each one flush to the ground before beginning to eat another.

"When do you think he will finish?" Jack sighed.

"I have no way of knowing."

Jack looked at the fuzzy small creature. "Do you have a name? I mean other than what you do."

"Yes," The Guardian answered, "however, it may be too difficult for you to pronounce."

"Let me be the judge of that," Jack said.

"Abekilecridstatymunmo."

Jack suppressed a smile. "Ok. I'll have to admit that is quite a name. Perhaps we can compromise."

"It seems as though you have equipped yourself with a suggestion."

"How does "Abe" grab you?" Jack smiled.

The Guardian raised his eyebrows. "I believe that will do."

"Then, Abe it is," Jack announced. "When our vegetarian friend finishes his dinner, we'll let him know about the official name change."

After what seemed like hours, with a dozen or more acres cleared, Torast lowered himself into a slight depression in the ground and promptly fell asleep.

****

The massive reptilian opened his eyes, welcoming the sunlight.

"Well, now," Jack said, "our friend awakens."

"And from a much-needed intake of nourishment and rest," Torast added.

"Abe and I," Jack said, throwing a thumb in The Guardian's direction, "enjoyed a nice breakfast of cabot and greens, but as far as sleep goes" . . . Jack looked at the ground and shook his head several times. His eyes rose to meet Torast's. "Man, the way you snore, there's nothing within ten square miles of this place that was able to sleep last night."

Torast seemed to blush. "It is expected after consuming such a large meal, and I apologize for keeping this knowledge to myself."

"No harm done," Jack said. "There are nights I've gone without sleep."

"I require no sleep to speak of," The Guardian (Abe) said.

"There is one thing I must ask of you," Torast said. "You mentioned the word 'Abe' as if it were a viable being. Who, or what, is an Abe?"

"Abe is our little, furry friend's re-given name," Jack replied.

Torast managed to contort his expression into one of puzzlement. "How could the one known to us as The Guardian become this one you called Abe?"

"In actuality," Abe said, "my name is Abekilecridstatymunmo; however, with the difficulty that comes with its pronunciation, Jack shortened the name to Abe."

"Abekilecridstatymunmo," articulated Torast, "I experience no difficulty when pronouncing this name."

"You wouldn't," Jack mumbled. "Ok. Let's get back to business. What of the Scariff and the remaining hack-cat?"

"They have been trailing us since our departure," Torast said.

"Why?" Jack asked. "What could they possibly want from the three of us?"

"Two," Torast said. "If you will allow yourself to delve deep into your subconscious, then, you will know." Jack's eyelids were closed before Torast finished speaking.

****

Jack felt himself floating past familiarity with no preset essence. He opened his eyes. "The Nexus," he whispered, "identical to what I carry, but the one I am viewing runs as far as my eyes can see . . . why?" He heard a barely audible noise at regular intervals, which grew in volume until the word it delivered could be understood.

The Other, it proclaimed. Like a surge of electricity, the word jolted through Jack, compelling his eyes to snap shut. In that moment, he understood—the Nexus was him, Torast was the Other, and the convergence of the four into one was imminent. His eyelids flew open with such force that his head was thrown back. A new entity stood before him. Jack, now a towering version of himself, was united with a diminutive form of Torast.

"Who *are* you?" Abe nervously skittered around the new arrival.

"My importance is yet to be seen."

An unseen multi-tentacled cephalopod wove its appendages through scales, affixing itself with suction cups. Sim settled in, attuning his body color with the enlarged biped.

Wait 'til they see me, surprise, surprise, and yet I sense this form will not last.

****

Vrollic watched as Torast launched himself and two passengers into the air and out of sight. "We will meet again," he whispered.

CHAPTER FORTY-SEVEN

Dalon Con, Krabb, Sketch and Smort

"Don't rightly know who you is or who you thunked you is," Krabb said, "but round these here parts, you don't bad mouth nobody." He took several steps away from the protection he had come to rely on. "Specially one setch as Mr. Dalon."

Perhaps I should endear myself to this band of mercenaries, Smort thought, *until I can determine the strength of the one called 'Dalon Con.'*

"I agree and also apologize for my previous comment. I regret making such a statement and attribute my lack of judgement to the prospect of fighting one more powerful than myself." *Mayhap this 'Dalon Con's' legendary strength is no more than that . . . naught but a power that dwells within the hearts of man.*

"We must leave this place and continue our search elsewhere," Dalon Con said. "Vital information awaits us." He glanced toward the new arrival. "Smort, travel with us. No doubt your services will make a definitive impact."

"It will be my pleasure," Smort said, "to work with ones that up until now I have followed through stories and word of mouth, never planning to meet. May I inquire to *our* destination?"

"To the last abandoned city, Rash."

With that, the trio, followed by Smort, began a journey that would bring unexpected results.

****

Krabb awoke, not recalling he had fallen asleep. It took several minutes to shake the cobwebs from his head. "Well, I'll be. That thar

Mr. Dalon done and tied ma hands tagether so's I won't fall off." Looking to his left. Sketch had fallen asleep, but, unlike himself, his tied hands were sliding down Dalon Con's right leg and his feet were about to touch the ground as it flew by.

"Sketch!" Krabb yelled, "wake up, now!"

Sketch jerked at the desperation in Krabb's voice. Their eyes locked as Sketch's feet hit the dirt, pulling him down, his loosely tied hands hands hooked around Dalon Con's ankle.

"Krabb!" Sketch yelled. His hands pulled free and then he was gone.

"No," Krabb wailed, "no, not my Sketch… he is all I gots!" Then, a blast of wind, and two hands lifted up the small man, placing him back onto his riding perch.

"Where ya done an been, ya crazy galoot?" Krabb said. "Ya plum scared me near ta death."

"Did ya miss ole Sketch?"

Krabb turned, and even though he couldn't see Smort, he said, "Thank you."

Dalon Con slowed his pace when he noticed an anomaly ahead. *What I have seen is no longer visible; however, I sense its presence.* Then, a flicker of light caught his eye at the periphery of his vision. Driving his cane into the ground, Dalon Con initiated a controlled spin. As he whirled, he felt a barrage of impacts against his body—a steady stream of small human hands reaching for his legs. *They must be after Sketch and Krabb.* However, each time the hands reached out, they were repelled by his invisible, spinning cloak, which shielded him with its continuous motion.

"What are goin' on?" Sketch asked. "Them little bitty hands is afta somethin."

"I ain't neva seen so much mess as we done an been into," Krabb replied.

“Watch out!” Sketch screamed. “They’s comin’ afta ya.” A single pair of arms reached through the bottom of Dalon Con’s robe and snatched Krabb from his perch. Seconds later, Sketch was gone.

Dalon Con ground to a halt. “No, I have lost them.” Tears began to flow as he tried to find a clue as to the whereabouts of Sketch and Krabb. “I have lost the ones I was given to protect.” He looked toward the heavens and spoke to the Great One.

Several moments later, equipped with a renewed sense of purpose, Dalon Con used his senses to follow his missing friends.

Soon, a caravan was visible through a thin stand of trees, easily trackable by the light of the full moon.

“I must be atop a plateau or elevated area, such as a hilltop, to see the ones I trail so clearly.”

“Excellent vision,” a voice said. “You have a distinct advantage over your quarry.”

Dalon Con whirled, facing the sound of the new arrival. A man, six and a half foot tall, stood in the shadow of the unusually bright moon. His blond hair was cut short, and a bushy mustache that ran down the newcomer’s face ended at his jaw line. “Do not trifle with me,” Dalon Con warned. “Paramount is my mission, and I will tolerate no interruptions.”

“Your task is of no concern to me,” the new arrival said. “My name is Dune, and I am tracking humans of a tiny stature, known as the Odobi. My curiosity was piqued when you appeared to be following the same race of people.”

“I know of such a people.” Dalon Con said. “However, the Odobi *I* track are the same size as you and I.” His staff began to glow a warm yellow, lighting the immediate area.

Dune ran his hand through his thick, blonde hair. “Temporal thief—mean anything to you?”

“Yes.” Dalon Con turned to leave.

“Why are you tracking the Odobi?” Dune asked.

"They have absconded with two close friends that were placed in my protective care." He glanced at the man who followed him. "I would ask you the same—why are *you* tracking the Odobi?"

"To learn more about them," Dune replied. "When you mentioned the race of large Odobi sized the same as you and me, I knew you had been to the abandoned city Grave."

"Grave," Dalon Con said, "I know little of the happenings there. What can you tell me about this once thriving town?"

"There was a time I called Grave home," Dune said. "For nearly a century I lived and worked in what I considered to be a thriving town, and, indeed, a thriving town it was." Dune took a seat on the ground, and pressed for Dalon Con to join him, but he continued to walk. "There's a question I want to ask."

Smort, becoming enthralled with the conversation, said nothing; however hung on each word uttered.

"What is on your mind?" Dalon Con inquired.

"Why is a young man such as yourself, in these wilds wearing nothing more than a thin suit of clothes, a noose around your neck and carrying a cane?

Dalon Con smiled. "Things are not always as they appear."

Dune nodded. "As for my tale, I was a resident of what used to be called Blanche Aries until things began to change, including the name. Now, as to the change—the transformation was gradual and as though a dimmer switch had been turned on to its brightest setting and then slowly decreased."

Dalon Con listened carefully, gauging Dune's words with what he knew to be true.

Dune moved nervously, having to recall his past. "The came about gradually and instantaneously; however impossible it may seem, that is the way it happened." Rubbing his temples, Dune's eyes narrowed into slits, as he concentrated. Several moments later, he shook his head and looked at Dalon Con. "I cannot explain the dissolution of Blanche Aries even though I lived through the transformation."

"I believe you," Dalon Con said. "Would you elaborate further on how this manifested itself?"

"The demeanor of people—changed. Not everyone, but, I dare say, a majority of the population drifted into darkness, and morality dissolved."

Dalon Con sighed. "Turning to the most vile human atrocities: murder, rape, and unspeakable carnage were forced upon those who remained of sound mind."

Dune nodded several times. "That it was, my friend, that it was."

Dalon Con slowed and retrieved a flask, three cups, a piece of flint, and a small steel knife. He pulled several handfuls of dried grass and gathered a bundle of twigs and larger pieces of wood to sustain a fire.

"I'll have to say, I'm rather interested in what you're planning to do next," Dune said.

"Very simply, I am going to warm a beverage for you, that Smort and I to enjoy." Dalon Con struck the flint against the knife, causing a shower of sparks.

"Woe!" Dune exclaimed, jerking back from the sudden light. Dalon Con repeated this procedure twice more, causing the tender to smolder. He picked the bundle of smoke up with both hands and began to blow until it burst into flames. Setting the burning tender on the ground, he piled the kindling and several large pieces of wood.

"And, there you have it," Dalon Con said. He allowed the fire to burn down, loosened the flask's lid, and placed the container in the center of the hot coals.

"Impressive," Dune said.

After several minutes, Dalon Con removed the flask and filled three cups. "Savor this," he said, handing both men a container.

Dune's eyes widened, and a grin spread across his face.

A large forearm slid across a set of lips. "Still the best thing ever to pass through my lips," according to Smort.

"I should have saved my words until after I tasted this wonderful elixir," said Dune.

"It pleases me to see you enjoy your beverage so," Dalon Con said. "Would you share with me your introduction to time travel?"

"I spent quite a bit of time traveling . . . in and out of Blanche Aries. Well not so much traveling through time, but taking a sufficient amount of time to travel. It was my home, though I felt less safe the longer I stayed. It got to the point where I was spending more time in the surrounding forest than at home. The looting had gotten so bad, I would have to fight during the day to retain the meager belongings I still held, even though this small amount would remain mine but for a short time." Dune took a sip from his cup.

"You were pushed from your home and into the less hospitable surroundings?" Smort asked.

Dune nodded as he swallowed. "Yes, but I never strayed far from Blanche Aries, especially after they arrived."

"After who arrived?" Dalon Con asked.

"I didn't know at first," Dune said, "but after locating their whereabouts, I listened to their conversations in the underground stations they had prepared. It was then I learned they were the Odobi you knew, residing under the city of Blanche Aries."

"This is not the work of the temporal thief," Dalon Con said. "Had that been the case, my encounter with the Odobi who absconded with my friends would have been a mere rift in time."

"Exactly," Dune said, "but both races co-exist within the same timeline."

"An anomaly pieced together awaiting someone to take a short journey into the chasm of an incomplete timeline," Smort said.

"Making what we know to be true," Dalon Con said, "a theoretical impossibility."

CHAPTER FORTY-EIGHT

Hayden and Max

Max landed feet first. The moment he touched the ground, his bodily makeup changed from stone to soil, and Hayden was propelled into Max's soft dirt hand.

"You appear none the worse for wear, small one," Max said.

"This condition stems from being in your capable hands. No pun intended."

Max chuckled, "since you find my hand so capable, stay as you are, for I feel as though we are being summoned to Grave." Large fingers folded and interlocked over Hayden and the two, large and small, were underway again.

****

Max sailed under the ground but stayed close to the surface to monitor any above-ground activity. On his third rise, while moving through a short-growth, he noticed dark sludge bubbling from one of the hills that lined each side of the valley.

Small one, have you ever laid eyes upon a neslecon?

I cannot say as I have.

Max came to a stop, his hand holding Hayden above ground. He opened his fingers, causing the small one to squint at the bright sun.

"Do you see the viscous fluid flowing from the hill on the left?"

Hayden checked each rise until the sun's glare reflected off the discharge. "Yes, I see it."

"That, for all intents and purposes, is the first of two developmental stage of a neslecon."

Hayden viewed the sludge. In its place stood what would become a flightless avian.

"That creature is huge!" Hayden exclaimed. It appeared to have three twelve-foot-high legs, each with a three-toed foot and a rearward appendage. "I have never seen a bird with retractable claws. Look, it is anchoring itself to the ground."

"Firmly attaching itself to the ground is necessary for its upper portion will experience violent changes as it forms." The neslecon's body consisted of an oval of flesh several feet thick that sat atop the three lower appendages.

"The legs are filling with color," Hayden said. A deep red, almost black pigmentation crawled in segments up the legs, stopping at the top. The body then doubled in size, resembling a kernel popping into corn, but instead of flesh, it was covered in smooth, iridescent feathers, lighter than the legs. A skinless tail emerged, extending several feet above the ground. Another burst at the tail's end formed a solid, two-foot diameter ball with boney spikes protruding. The tail whipped around, smashing the ball through a large range-leaf tree before burying into the ground.

The vibration continued to increase until even the neslecon traveled back and forth, swaying six feet with each directional change. A reptilian head with mammalian features shot skyward. This unnatural cranium was attached to a long, slender neck that bobbed and weaved in a serpentine fashion.

Hayden's eyes widened as he gazed at the creature still growing before him. "I have never seen such a head on any beast." The neslecon's cranium was like that of a snake, its snout bearing a resemblance to a wolf with an elongated muzzle. "It is covered with scales and the face with thick fur is all colored the same deep red. But the teeth, what a horror. They were like nothing he had ever seen, a chilling sight that sent shivers down his spine.

Craaack!

What sounded like an immense thunder clap sent a shockwave from the fully-formed newborn creature.

Hayden immediately found himself in the dark, moving downward.

Turning his attention back to the neslecon, Max understood the cause of the uproar. *The beast has developed an additional two heads, a total of three, each pointing in a different direction. Every tree has been blown over and the low foliage is gone.*

We must tarry no longer.

Why? I am safe, am I not?

Yes, but this creature is unlike all others, small one. The nelecon feeds on time scraps provided by the temporal thief.

Max found himself in the far north of Burrus Plax. He wrapped his right hand containing Hayden with his left and cradled both close to his abdomen to shelter the little one from the cold. Max sank into the snow. "Are you all right, small one?"

"Yes," Hayden said. "To what do I owe the pleasure of once again residing in the dark of your hand?"

"It seems the temporal thief, in order to welcome the neslecon into this world, has paid us a visit."

The temperature had dropped significantly, and a creature made of ice and about half the size stood upon the high ridge.

"Are we safe?" Hayden asked.

"Yes, for now." Max retreated into the snow twenty feet to escape the fierce wind. "We are in the great north. And I cannot change from soil into any other medium that would allow us to escape, because snow and ice cold, in your case, would be too dangerous."

Suddenly, everything went momentarily black.

"Ahhh!" Hayden grabbed both sides of his head as a flood of pain slammed into him. His world was flooded with light, and he covered his eyes against the glare. A voice began to pierce the deafening silence.

"Small one," the muffled voice said, "small one, are you still with me?" Hayden felt a gentle nudge against his back.

"Max," he groaned.

"It appears the time thief has given the neslecon its first meal. The two will now travel together in a symbiotic relationship. The temporal thief will provide nourishment in the form of tattered time fragments, and the neslecon will add another layer of protection to the temporal thief."

"Hayden," Wakke's voice cracked, "please signal if you can hear me." The transmission was replaced by static. Hayden sent a response signal. "Hayden, was that you?" Wakke pleaded. "I picked up a minute deviation in my communication line, but . . ." Hayden pressed the bar several times.

"Nothing," Wakke reiterated, despair swirling in his voice. "Hayden, if by chance you *are* able to hear me, you *must* keep a vigil for Drade." The next few seconds were filled with static. ". . . eighteen years of constructing the portal, Drade collected from . . . highly secretive technology." Static, and then the device went silent.

"If I am not mistaken," Max said, "the eons-old saying goes: 'and the plot thickens'."

****

"I cannot say I understand fully," Smort said, "only that you have been placed within my being as a connection, to what, I do not know."

"You have been transferred through time to assist with the desolation of Burrus Plax," Drade said.

CHAPTER FORTY-NINE

Gabriel and Roane

Gabriel scratched the side of his face. "If the thack in your bedtime stories as a child devoured everyone in the house, then why are we still alive? Wouldn't he have eaten us instead of depositing a substantial meal in this tree?"

"Unless, he's saving us for later."

"That was an alternative I would just soon not have considered."

"Have you noticed this tree is still shaking?"

Gabriel nodded. "It's getting worse." The movement of the tree abruptly stopped, causing the foliage in one area to dance wildly.

"It must have heard you, something's coming our way." A large, gray, mammalian head pushed through the foliage, its skull measuring six feet in length and probably two and a half feet in height and width. The face was reminiscent of a rodent but with kindness exuding from this being's eyes.

"Is everyone all right?" it inquired.

"I suppose," Roane said. He kept a wary eye on the newcomer, unaware he was inching backward.

"A-Are you what my friend here would call a thack?"

"I am," the creature answered.

"Then, why aren't you devouring us?" Roane stopped his retreat and moved closer to Gabriel.

The large mammal lowered his head, resting it on a limb. "I see you have fallen prey to the false stories you were told as a child."

"They didn't seem like stories when my father told them," Roane said.

"Did your father tell the tales at random times, or were they saved until bedtime and used along with a candle?"

"How could you know about the candle?"

"It was, and still is, the cord that works to bind the Nexus and the temporal entities together as one, making it the 'other'."

"So, am I correct in assuming your aim is *not* to eat us?" Gabriel inquired.

The creature nodded. "I am Azoff."

"You mentioned time travelers and the Nexus, use the candle to bind themselves together." Roane said.

"This is true;" Azoff stated, "however, even though the Nexus and one known as the Other have joined together, the connection between the Nexus and the travelers remain unstable."

"What does that mean?" Gabriel asked. "And, please, use everyday language so even *I* can understand."

"With pleasure," Azoff said. "The time travelers who have come from the future to thwart the past cannot be successful unless the union between themselves and the Nexus is made complete."

"Enough. If you do not intend to kill us, we have a more important scenario which requires our immediate attention." Roan said. "Like, how do we get down?"

"Why *did* you drop us into this tree?" Gabriel asked.

"It was not within my plans to devour either of you," Azoff said, "rather, I took every precaution to keep you from being devoured."

"Yeah, well I was brought up on horror stories about the thacks, that you a malevolent race." Roane asked.

"We are none of the sort," Azoff said. "Our kind have been persecuted from the beginning, stemming from the evil in our midst. And not just any evil, mind you, but an evil with intelligence."

"And the Nexus?" Gabriel added.

"As for the Nexus and time travelers, I do not know. Always remember, the Great One's ways are not our ways."

"The Great One," Gabriel said, "Dalon Con spoke of this one."

"As will we," Azoff said. "However, if you wish to depart, you and your companion must climb onto my back. Use the fur as handholds, stay close together, and hold tight." Roane And Gabriel wrapped their hands around a clump of fur behind Azoff's head, finding it long, coarse, and easy to grasp.

"Whoa," Gabriel exclaimed as the thack quickly slipped up the tree. "I didn't realize we were this far off the ground!"

"But why are we going up?" Roane yelled.

The thack stopped just below the highest point where foliage grew, allowing an unobscured view. Then, Azoff dug his claws into the tree, pushing and pulling his mass causing the tree's top to sway. Within seconds, the trio were airborne.

"Ahhhh!" the men screamed.

Azoff spread out his legs where a translucent membrane acted as wings.

"We're gliding," Roan said. "At a breakneck speed."

"Not just gliding, we're actually losing and gaining altitude."

Protruding from Azoff's underside, just below his prehensile tail, was a textured, flat, rubbery appendage. It moved from side to side, acting as a rudder. Gabriel observed closely. As Azoff accelerated, Gabriel noticed that the lower third of the tail remained stationary, stabilizing the creature's body while the upper third flexed powerfully, allowing him to steer in any direction.

Gabriel felt a steady drop in altitude. "We're descending."

"The sun is low in the sky," Roane said. "I'd wager that has something to do with it." In less than a minute, the trio safely landed.

"You may dismount." Gabriel looked at Roane, puzzled, and Roane returned the gaze. "Merely slide down. My fur will slow your descent until you reach the ground."

"I didn't realize you were quite so large, big fella," Roane said.

"Or, could it be that you are so small?" Azoff replied.

"I think he got you on that one," Gabriel said.

"It would appear so," Roane replied, "So,where do we go from here?"

"Excellent inquiry," Azoff said. "We begin our search for the one Gabriel knows well."

An expression of excitement exploded across Gabriel's face. "Dalon Con!"

"It is as you say," Azoff replied.

"Gabriel, you said you would be able to sense him as you moved closer to his proximity. So, can you?"

Gabriel stared at the ground. "I am not sure." He gazed at the circle of trees, then nodded—slowly at first, then more vigorously, as he raised his head. "Yes. I know where Dalon Con is, or at least, where he is headed." Gabriel furrowed his forehead. "But it doesn't make any sense."

"Explain," Azoff said.

"I am gleaning a word from an unknown source," Gabriel said, "but it is totally void of understanding."

"Give us the word," Roane urged.

"Rash," Gabriel said. He shrugged his shoulders, then dropped them in resolve.

"Of course," Azoff said, "one of the last abandoned cities on Burrus Plax."

"Perhaps, not as abandoned you thought." Roane said.

CHAPTER FIFTY

Abe and Rakke (Jack/Torast)

The newly transformed being knelt and scooped a palm full of dirt into its hand. He raised the appendage, tilted his hand and watched the soil pour out.

"What shall I call you?" Abe asked.

"I am Rakke," the thing replied, "however, that shall be no concern of yours." Suddenly, the creature took a swipe at The Guardian.

Abe was nearly a quarter mile away, before Rakke could complete the sweep of its arm.

"The tiny scamp is of no consequence. Leave it to die, as it most surely will." The new creation extended its right, scale-covered foot, taking his first step as the creature, Rakke.

The new creature's copper armor scale-like plating similar to Torast. Yet, he was human-shaped– even the face resembled Jack's. Yet, his tail remained, although much smaller. *I cannot help but wonder if it —*. Before the Guardian could finish his thought, Rakke's legs compressed and he shot upward several thousand feet.

Abe watched a bright copper-colored dot, made more noticeable by the sun's reflection. *It appears Rakke has inherited Torast's method of thrust. Should be no problem keeping up, although I do not understand the force that is compelling me to do so.* Abe stared at Rakke, moving across the sky until he was nearly out of sight. *I suppose I shall follow until the will to do so leaves. Something is telling me that abandoning the chase is not an option.*

****

Vrollic raced to follow Torast/Jack. With his keen sight, he easily scanned the movements of this new creature.

It seems the small furry one is no longer with this associate. A trail of dust quickly approached from the Southwest. "Could it be?" he whispered. *Yes, yes it is. The small one apparently follows the creature.* Vrollic fell in behind as Abe passed, determined to follow him to his destination.

The one who follows me has been within close range for some time, Abe thought as he continued to follow Rakke. *I will allow him to continue his pursuit by keeping my speed at an acceptable level he can match. Yes, I will allow this until I deem otherwise.*

****

Rakke extended his arms, releasing both wings, then flattened his tail. Then, he was not alone. "Who is there?"

Who you are not, a voice replied. *I am what remains once the essence of merging Jack and Torast has been extracted. You may call me Bridge.*

Rakke realized the voice he was hearing was inside his head. "How is this possible? I am able to hear you speak, yet the sound comes from within."

I am within, because I am you.

"What good are you to me?" Rakke growled.

None, as far as you are concerned, but necessary, nonetheless. I am any notion of a positive nature that remains with you . . . I am your conscience.

"I neither want nor have need of you. Get out!" Rakke barked.

Bridge chuckled. *You have no way of ridding yourself of me. I AM you.*

"Laugh, funny one, for if I take such a notion, I will tear myself to shreds to be rid of you. Now, leave me to myself without the benefit of your council. Now, I wish to hear nothing more from you, or I will carry out my threat.

****

Rakke began a steep dive over a large saltwater lake, then plowed headfirst into the water and began to swim into the depths.

"Ahh," Rakke bellowed as he surfaced thirty minutes later. He stepped onto land carrying two handfuls of fish. Lowering to a squat position, he savagely devoured his catch. When done, he stepped back into the lake, dove, and swam straight down for nearly a mile.

And just where are we going?

"We are meeting a very close and dear friend."

And should I know this friend?

"Since you are, or at least claim to be, my conscience, then you should know him well. In fact, we have reached the entrance to his abode." Being able to see through Rakke's eyes, Bridge identified an opening with an arched top cut into a stone cliff through the murky water. The path was clear, with no door to block the way.

Rakke swam through the water just as he would through the air. "Things are not always as they appear."

Please elaborate.

"In time," Rakke replied, "in time." For the next hour he continued to move peacefully through the water-filled corridor, his copper-colored skin, which also acted as armor, illuminating the surrounding area. Rakke's sense of danger began to heighten.

I sense an abrupt change about to take place.

"Now, what have we here?" Rakke brought his extended arms forward with the back of his fingers touching something akin to an organic spear.

"I know you are close," Rakke said. "Show yourself and I will—" A massive head appeared from the gloom just as Rakke disappeared into the body of a giant eel.

****

Abe and Vrollic

The Guardian and Vrollic came to a halt at the edge of a large freshwater lake.

"Well now," the Guardian said, "at last we meet."

"It appears so," Vrollic said.

"May I assume you are in pursuit of Rakke?"

"You may, for in fact, what I feel is a deep kinship with the one you call Rakke and the two that proceeded his metamorphosis."

Abe stared at Vrollic. "It would appear we are beginning this relationship at odds." Abe began to circle Vrollic at a snail's pace.

"Any ideas on how to accommodate our differences of opinions?"

"No accommodation. Evil is evil and never given a pass no matter how attractive you may twist it to be."

"What a shame, I had hoped we may develop a bond, for which—" Vrollic lashed out, bringing his hand down hard where Abe stood.

Abe grinned as best he could with his reptilian face as he zipped well out of harm's way.

"Your speed saved you this time, but beware, I rarely miss twice."

"Well, I guess I will just have to make the best of things, no matter how bleak they appear." In less than a second, Abe was nearly half a mile away, waving from atop a hill.

Vrollic boiled at the taunt and the thought of this insignificant creature getting the best of him in such a simplistic way. He turned, faced the lake, and waited for Rakke.

CHAPTER FIFTY-ONE

Dalon Con, Smort and Dune

"Imagine, if you will, a phrase that has no clear origin, yet has been whispered across the vast expanse of the Milky Way for thousands of years. This phrase, my friend, is a key to a concept that challenges our understanding of time. It suggests that *time is not a fixed entity, but a fluid, ever-changing force.*"

"I'll have to admit," Dune replied, "you have me stumped, because I don't have an inkling as to what you're talking about."

"I have simply stated that time is relative to the timeline in which we reside. This makes time travel possible. The phrase also states that time is not constant."

"I think I'm beginning, and just beginning, mind you, to understand." Dune scratched his head. "So, you're saying no matter where, or, better yet, *when* I am, time is constant to that when, making time overall relative?"

"Well done," Dalon Con said, "however, that seems not to be the case in all situations. For, if it were true, two far-removed generations of Odobi could not survive in the same timeline."

"So, now you're telling me time is relative *and* constant," Dune said, shaking his head and rubbing the back of his neck. "Back to confusion."

"I apologize for your bewilderment," Dalon Con his voice tinged with a hint to regret. "Time *is* relative; however, because of someone's clever manipulation, in the instance of the Odobi timeline, it remains constant."

"Not just the Odobi timeline," Dune said, "but ours also, since they are one and the same."

"It seems that the short period I have been here time bows to no one," Smort said, "but exists to serve itself."

Curious, Dalon Con thought. *The one called Smort states he has been here only a short while. I must ask myself where is here: in this place, on this planet, or occupying this when. And what constitutes a short amount of time for this being? I have an idea, but cannot prove it to the world or myself as it is only a feeling. I will play along and let time reveal this one's essence.*

"Dune, your statement shows wisdom. Not only do we and the Odobi share a timeline, but many other beings occupy the same space along with us."

"It seems to me, a man can use all the friends he can get," Dune said. "And, for this very reason, I am going to help you retrieve your friends from the Odobi that stole them away."

"It gives me great pleasure to call you friend," Dalon Con said. "Smort, yours is a very interesting take, one of which I have never entertained; however, I now feel your thoughts bear serious consideration."

****

"I'd say your two friends have just about had it," Dune expressed as they approached the caravan encampment.

Sketch and Krabb were huddled together, encircled by at least thirty small Odobi. They looked identical to their counterparts, except for their dress, which consisted of a cloth wrap that covered their bodies from the waist to the knees.

Dalon Con's rage grew as he surveyed the situation. A fire burned inside the circle, and the two men were sitting on the ground just to the left of the blaze.

"Mine!" one of the Odobi would yell before running through the circle and slapping Sketch and Krabb alternately on their face and head. Dalon Con took one step toward the fray.

"No," Dune hissed in a loud whisper, "we go together, but first, you must listen to the Great One and release your rage."

He speaks the truth. Dalon Con glanced at Dune and immediately dropped to his knees, covered his face with his hands to his face, and sobbed.

****

"I ask your forgiveness for my actions," Dalon Con said.

"I see no need for you to ask such a thing from me," Dune replied.

"I have received pardon from the Great One," Dalon Con said, "forgiven myself and seek the same from you."

"Now, I understand," Dune replied. "Forgiveness is for the asking, which you have done, and I gladly extend it to you."

Dalon Con smiled and nodded. "Now, we must assist my wards lest they come to harm."

"The language you speak is understandable," Smort said, "but what you say is foreign to me."

"We will speak later," Dune said. "First we must attend to your friends."

"Could you use some assistance addressing these important elements?" Smort asked.

"Yes, and gratefully so," Dalon Con nodded.

****

The circle of Odobi had closed in around Sketch and Krabb. The fire waned but still supplied adequate light.

"I will end this now!" Dalon Con raised his staff, ready to plunge it into the ground, when a brilliant, amber-colored flash, followed by a steady light, caused Dalon Con to whirl to his left. There, Dune held a three-bladed weapon with a single handle in each hand. The center blade was two feet long and narrow, with a twelve-inch blade on either side, four inches apart. Each weapon produced its own glow.

"Now, we go," Dune stated.

"Yes," Dalon Con smiled. "Now we go."

"And I will follow," Smort said, "in hopes I may be of some assistance."

"You will know," Dalon Con said, "just follow your instincts."

As three men neared the circle of Odobi, the small humanoids began to chatter, ceasing their assault on Sketch and Krabb. The circle divided and backed away from the giant intruders. Several picked up sharp sticks, jabbing at the air in a threatening manner.

"Awful good to see you there, Mr. Dalon," Sketch and Krabb sighed.

"Your riding platform awaits," Dalon Con said, opening his invisible garment. The two small men stumbled onto Dalon Con's feet and wrapped their arms around his legs. Their eleventh-hour savior released his robe, allowing it to flow down, encasing Sketch and Krabb in their place of security. Dalon Con then turned his attention toward the Odobi.

"You will assail neither good nor bad ever again." He raised his staff vertically and plunged it into the ground. An amber lightwave spread from the staff's end at an immeasurable rate, obliterating the Odobi.

Dalon Con stood momentarily as the fine black dust that was once the ancient Odobi settled onto the ground.

"Nice," Dune said. His weapons lost their luminescence as he pushed them down into his boots. The knives flattened and conformed to his legs.

"Not nice. Necessary," Dalon Con sighed. Then, inhaling deeply, we turned toward Dune. "I have seen the subterranean workings of the Odobi in Grave. We will now travel to Rash, for I suspect much of the same abides beneath that city, as well."

"And, if it does?"

"If we inspect both Grave and Rash, this should tell us which one was overtaken first," Dalon Con said. "As for Defeated, I know not whether the Odobi have yet to establish a foothold, or if it was the first city to come under attack and is now the central hub for operations."

"I know little of these cities," Smort said, "though I sense I will be of more assistance once we arrive."

"I reckon we best be gettin' on to that thar Rash," Krabb said.

"How are you when it comes to running?" Dalon asked Dune.

Dune smiled. "Try to keep up."

"Smort, what say you?"

Smort smiled, looking first at Dune and then toward Dalon Con. "Wait not for me, either."

****

"Here we be agoin' agin," Sketch said.

"Yep," Krabb replied, "and both them thar new fellers be keepin' up purdy good."

"There is something different about these two," Dalon Con said. "Dune is in this world, but not of it. Smort has a malevolent beginning, yet is confused now that he is being overrun with diverse ideas."

"Might be because of that thar Great One you be a spoutin' from time to time," Sketch said.

"So, when is ya gonna fill *us* in on this here Great One?" Krabb asked.

"First, there was one, then, at times, there are two," Dalon Con said.

"What in tarnation do that mean?" Sketch asked.

"In time, small ones," Dalon Con said, "in time."

"Is you know'd how many times ya done an told us that?" Krabb asked.

Dalon Con chuckled. "Indeed."

"He's right, Mr. Dalon," Sketch said, "ya done left us hangin' so many times, I don't know whitcha way ima goin'."

"I know what I have stated, and, in some cases, what I have not stated may be confusing. However, bear with me a while longer, and your confusion will clear."

"Ifin you say so, Mr. Dalon," Sketch said.

"We is with you," Krabb said.

Dune accelerated until he was running beside Dalon Con. "Trouble awaits us ahead."

"I, too, sense a malevolent presence looming."

"Everyone, down!" Dune bellowed. He dropped to his knees and removed the three-bladed knives from his boots. Dalon Con went down and rolled onto his back, keeping Sketch and Krabb safe. Smort dove head first, his arms outstretched onto the ground. The heels of his palms dug into the earth.

"Now!" Dalon Con exclaimed. Dune's weapons, one in each hand, began to glow. He raised them alternately at regular eight-inch intervals. Each time a blade ascended, a resounding snap was heard as if a taut rope were severed.

CHAPTER FIFTY-TWO

Hayden and Max

"The one you talked to over the small device, Wakke," Max said, "who is he?"

"He is one of my own kind," Hayden said, "and lives on this world far from where we stand."

Max was quiet for a moment. "I do not sense this man."

"He, resides on this planet, but in a different time."

"Ahh," Max nodded as he rose to a standing position and began walking at a leisurely pace. "There are but three cities on this small planet of Burrus Plax: Defeated, Grave, and Rash. And in each location, I have detected a disturbance in the fabric of time, some stronger than others. The appearance of the temporal thief, and, most recently, the neslecon, have solidified the notion of time travel."

"Why did you not tell me before?" Hayden asked.

"I knew of your plans, but could not grasp for the eighteen years it took you to construct the time portal. I was also aware that you were the time traveler, and I was cognizant of the one you call Wakke."

"Then why question me concerning him?"

"These were but vision yet to transpire. Once you explained the origin of your friend, all fell into place, especially, when I saw the orange streak in the sky each time you traveled through the portal."

"You indicated our next destination would be Grave," Hayden said. "How could you have known to choose Grave?"

"Being bound to certain parameters, a best-guess scenario was all I had. Now, I know our destination will be Rash, and on that you can rely." Max nodded at Hayden, then he closed his hand and disappeared underground, making his way toward Rash.

****

Max, how long will be before we reach our destination?

Quite a while, small one. But what is this . . . I hear a lack of patience from the small one I have come to know so well?

It is not so much a matter of patience but a matter of necessity.

Max felt Hayden's embarrassment at the request. *Ahh, now I understand. You must perform this task to remove waste products from your body.*

I wear a bodysuit to dispose of the waste material automatically. However, even it has a limited collection capacity and must be emptied from time to time.

He felt his capsule on the rise. Seconds later, Max's fingers opened next to a tall stand of trees with a lush, green canopy. "What an alluring smell." Hayden inhaled, held his breath, and then slowly exhaled.

"The heady aroma stems from the trees themselves. If one tarries too long, the scent will overtake him and he will never leave, eventually becoming food for the forest."

"Well, that's a pleasant thought."

"Perhaps you should tend to your business, and then we will take our leave." Hayden nodded, levitated, and disappeared behind a tree.

Several minutes passed. *Although I am not familiar with the process the small one is undertaking, I have waited long enough.* Max reached the tree Hayden had chosen for relief with a single step and peered around the trunk.

Where has the small one gone?

Dropping to his knees, Max closely examined the base of the tree but couldn't get close enough. *This is of no use.* He moved a hand toward each eye, scraping a trench around each socket. With one eyeball between each set of index fingers and thumbs, he pressed them into the soil and slowly moved around the tree. After progressing halfway around, he stopped.

"A tunnel with drag marks along its floor!" *They appear to be from*

Hayden's propulsion unit and head downward at a steep angle. In an instant, Max was two inches tall, sliding down the newly made tunnel that dumped into a large open area. He hit the floor and returned to normal size.

"Small one." A minuscule dot moved toward Max's face, when he raised a hand to strike at the newcomer, it replied.

"You would not swat a friend, now, would you?"

"It is good to see you, small one. I was afraid I had lost my friend."

"It will take much more than a small hole for this world to rid itself of me." He settled into Max's hand.

"Good words," Max said. "However did you came to be in this place?"

"As soon as I moved from your sight, I landed and began the sanitation process," Hayden said. "Immediately after I completed disposal, this tunnel appeared and I was sucked down, ending up in this chamber."

"I understand. Even though at my present size, I felt no such pull of air, once I reduced my mass to fit into the tunnel, the pull was evident."

"What of the cannibalistic nature surrounding this forest?" Hayden asked.

"The desire to remain here, considering that these woodlands dine upon one's flesh, is greatly reduced in this underground area, small one. We can travel from this dark place using this underground route. It appears to be large enough to prevent me from having to make contact with the soil, which may affect you in a negative fashion."

"If the less contact we have with the soil and roots means the less chance I have of contracting any unwanted pathogens, then all the better," Hayden said.

"So be it." He closed his hand around Hayden and began his travels through the existing corridor.

****

Max. I wonder what formed this passage?

I have been pondering that very question since I dropped into this subterranean area. Not long ago, I removed a giant beast, a young man, and a small reptile—called The Guardian—from a system of tunnels that extend throughout Burrus Plax. However, these tunnels were carved through rock. Though I do not know who constructed this vast network of corridors, it is similar in every way, save for the stone construction.

Though I cannot confirm the ambient light originates from a similar crystal that covered the stone corridors. That is why I believe both networks of tunnels were constructed by the same beings.

Excuse my ignorance, Max, but if you and this world are as one, how can it be possible that you would not know all the happenings on Burrus Plax?

That is the greatest conundrum of all. It is as though a portion of my memory has been stolen."

I need to ask a favor. For the sake of my original mission, I must check on an anomaly I stumbled upon during my first trip through Defeated. Would you mind if I took a short leave?

Of course, small one. I will take you there myself. No one with friends should be alone. Max said as he slowly turned to the southwest.

****

"Please, wait here; I will return shortly," Hayden said as they arrived in Defeated.

"Take care, small one," Max said. "I will be here when you return." He smiled and threw Hayden a wink, something the small Odobi had never seen but felt comfort at its display.

****

Hayden arrived at the home he had entered twice before. It appeared unkempt and much older. He had no trouble entering the building, as there were numerous holes in the windows and rotten wood to provide an opening. David and Susan appeared considerably older, and their health was noticeably compromised. They resided in squalor, eating a foul-smelling meal at a dining room table.

"This tastes pretty bad," Susan said.

"Yeah," David garbled as a hand flew to his mouth to catch the vomit spewing out.

"Looks like you've got it again."

"Don't have much longer in this hole."

Susan smiled a grim smile. "That's the one thing we have going for us." They took each other's hands and touched their foreheads together.

Tears began to well in Hayden's eyes. *I have to find the Dalleon cell.* He moved into the living room and immediately heard a small metal object make contact with the floor.

What is that?

A misty black fog was visible on the other side of the room, with the coveted item in between. Hayden made a mad dive for the small golden circle, barely visible on the wooden floor. He reached the object and wrapped his fingers around one of the handholds, lifting the Dalleon cell. As he did, a black fog flew past, missing its chance to retrieve the coveted item.

Hayden pushed the levitation device and sped through a hole in the window. *Most assuredly, the black evil is following me.* He tried twisting the hand controls further, but they would not move. *The houses are flying by; however, I feel an urgent need to move faster.*

Hayden flew another mile. *I can see the tree line, where I believe Max to be.*

"Max, where are you?" Hayden whispered. The black dust touched his flight pack, causing an electrical disturbance throughout his body. His controls froze, and he slammed head-on into a solid panel. Then, a hole, slightly larger than Hayden's body, crumbled from the center of the panel.

"Max!" Hayden cried as he flew through the opening provided by his friend. As Hayden passed, the opening filled with a thick liquid that contained the black dust and held the malevolent substance fast, solidifying the material as it fell to the ground.

"I see you made it back," Max said.

"And, let me say, I have never been so happy to return."

"Did you complete your mission?"

"Yes, I did." A wide grin crossed Hayden's face.

Max returned the smile. "That pleases me. However, your being away brings about a time deficit that we must overcome on our journey to Rash."

"Then, by all means, let us leave."

Max increased his speed twofold. *I believe the problem is the temporal thief. He has placed a small portion of my memory somewhere along the same timeline. For this very reason, I now recognize that lost information is critical to our success.*

So we have no choice but to locate what you have forgotten, Hayden thought.

As you say, there is no other choice.

CHAPTER FIFTY-THREE

Gabriel, Roane and Azoff

"We will remain here for the night," Azoff said. "Nocturnal dwellers in this area of Burrus Plax are not the welcoming kind. I am an omnivore and able to find food beneath my feet; however, I realize your nutritional needs may not follow the same criteria."

"I have no idea how to secure food," Gabriel said.

"Looks like Roane to the rescue. What would you like for supper?"

"I'm starving," Gabriel said. "I'd be willing to try those fancy shoes of yours."

"Don't think so," Roane said, digging through the containers attached to his three belts. Then Roane glanced up at Gabriel. "Don't just stand there gawking. Gather some firewood before all the light's gone."

"Take care as you reach into the grass," Azoff warned. "This time of evening you want to make sure of what you're picking up. It could bite you."

Gabriel nodded and started scavenging for dry wood. After dumping a pile of firewood of various sizes beside Roan, he set out for more.

"Time for bigger pieces," Gabriel mumbled to himself. He scanned the ground as he moved forward. "That one's about the right size." Gabriel bent over and wrapped his hand around a two-inch limb; the limb then wrapped its end around him.

"AHH!"

"It appears as though your friend did not heed my warning," Azoff said.

Gabriel was dragged up one of the tallest trees.

“We must go.” Roane leapt onto Azoff’s back.

“Go!” Roane barked, holding the torch aloft. Azoff ascended the tree behind the flailing Gabriel.

“A sagnith has absconded with Gabriel,” Azoff shouted to overcome the surrounding noise. “This creature has six legs and is more on the order of an insect. It nests underground; however, to keep its domain’s entrance secret, the sagnith uses a indirect way to get there.”

“And once it reaches its destination?” Roane asked.

“It will take its catch back to the nest and share the bounty with its brothers and sisters,”

“Not a pleasant thought.” Roane reached into a small pocket along the side of his hip and removed a slender, metal object.

“We must be quick. The daylight is almost gone and I fear I may lose him.”

The sagnith moved erratically between trees, up and down, yet rarely on the ground. Azoff was within several feet of his quarry, anticipating the bug’s next move.

“You are mine.” Azoff clamped down gingerly on the small bug, pinning him against the tree so as not to injure Gabriel. Roane headed in the opposite direction and sliced the metal blade through the insectoid several times. With one final stroke, he skewered the creature in place. The dying creature released Gabriel, who scrambled onto Azoff’s back.

“What are you doing with that?” Gabriel grimaced at the blood-dripping insect on the end of Roane’s blade.

“Never know if something is edible unless you try it first,” Roane smiled.

“This is true in most cases,” Azoff confirmed, “and I happen to know the sagnith is considered a delicacy among most of the inhabitants of Burrus Plax.” The thack took several more steps across a span of trees, then dropped to the ground.

"Looks like we're home," Roane said.

"And not a moment too soon for me," Gabriel replied.

"I can only suppose that your statement is some form of sarcasm," Azoff said. "Certainly, you cannot consider this small parcel to be any one of our homes." Roane and Gabriel smiled in an attempt to subdue their laughter. Azoff moved close to the firelight and began to forage on the forest floor.

****

"Like this," Roane said, giving Gabriel a lesson on how he thought their six-legged meal should be cleaned and prepared. He separated the carcass into three equal pieces. Roane tapped Gabriel's shoulder. "Come with me."

Roane pulled a pellet out of one of his pouches, pressed the thick substance over and around the end of a piece of wood, and thrust it into the fire, giving it a moment to ignite. Then, the men searched until finding several flat rocks of various sizes.

"We'll lay the largest one on the fire and support the edges with the others."

Gabriel placed the last stone. "That does it."

"I've never smelled anything so enticing." Gabriel wiped his mouth.

"Agreed," Roane said, "but the longer I cook these legs, the more brittle they become."

"That is a sign your meal is done, and, from the aroma, I would say you have cooked it to perfection," Azoff said.

Gabriel pilfered a small piece of flesh and placed it in his mouth. He said nothing; instead, he closed his eyes and savored the experience.

Roane slid the cooking stone off the coals and took a taste. He smiled and nodded. "Exactly right." The men ate ravenously.

Then, Roane looked at Azoff. "Aren't you going to join us?"

"Excellent meal," Azoff said, "thank you."

"You're welcome," Roane replied. "I suppose we should get some sleep."

Gabriel enforced Roane's suggestion by yawning deeply.

"Let's gather more wood to stoke the fire," Azoff suggested. "I will assist—as a protective measure."

****

Gabriel opened his eyes, blinked several times, then attempted to wipe the hair from his face.

"What's wrong? Have a face full of fur?" Roane sat beside a newly tendered fire.

"Feels that way," Gabriel replied. "Have I been lying up against Azoff all night?"

"We both have," Roane said. "If it wasn't for our furry friend here, curling in front of the fire, we most likely would not have seen this morning."

"Walk around to my side that faces away from the fire," Azoff said.

Gabriel's mouth dropped open at the pile of dead bodies—reptiles, mammals, insects, and things with unknown classification.

"Each could have killed you last night," Azoff yawned.

"How could you have gotten them all?" Roane asked.

Suddenly, nearly a dozen claws pushed through Azoff's hair along his back, then moved downward as if on cue.

"What is that?" Gabriel took a step backward.

"A symbiotic relationship of sorts," Azoff replied. "These parasites offer their protection in exchange for all they care to eat."

"It doesn't appear they ate," Roane said.

"The dead creatures you have seen," Azoff said, "are what remained after they fed."

"Excuse us for a moment." Gabriel and Roane stepped away from Azoff.

“This is the first good look we have had of Azoff,” Roane whispered. “Do you see what we’ve been riding and eating with?”

“I do. He favors a rat, save for the long tail—”

“And Azoff’s blunt nose,” Roane interrupted.

“His front feet are huge,” Gabriel said. “And with the size of those claws, it’s no wonder he was able to move through the trees like he did.”

“How about that mouth? I bet it could chew through rock.”

“Well, I’m just glad he’s on our side.”

Roane nodded. “Yeah.” Then, the two men walked back to within earshot of Azoff.

“So, what is on the agenda today?” Gabriel sat by the fire to eat breakfast.

“I assume we look for your mutual friend,” Roane said, nodding at Azoff.

“That is correct,” the large rodent said, “and I believe we should not tarry. A hasty exit would serve us well, that is, if you two have completed the descriptive conversation you were having on behalf of my presence.”

The men’s faces flushed.

“Do not let this trouble you,” Azoff said. “It is normal to question the unknown. Now we must take our leave.”

CHAPTER FIFTY-FOUR

Rakke and Bridge

The silver flash continued its steady pace through the underwater tunnel. Its stomach full, the eel enjoyed a sense of well-being, or at least as much as the simple-minded creature could appreciate. Suddenly, its left side jerked and bulged out several inches. Another jolt caused the snake-like swimmer to slam into the tunnel wall. This pattern continued as the snake was thrown in every direction until it split apart. Finally, all that remained was a few strips of flesh and debris-riddled water. From out of the carnage emerged a copper-colored figure. Rakke filled his mouth with another piece of eel flesh. "Excellent meal," he garbled.

Might I assume we are now going to see your friend?

Rakke swallowed. "You may assume whatever you wish. Now leave me be; there is much to ponder."

You know not where you are going. However, just as all of the others have learned, your time will come.

Bridge found he was able to sleep by closing his eyes and relaxing. *Although I still don't understand the ins and outs of closing eyelids that don't feel like they belong to me*—this was his last thought as he dropped into a light sleep.

Rakke seethed with anger.

****

Vrollic could not bear waiting for Rakke to return. *Too long. Maybe short increments of time, but I have had all I am going to take. My speed is exceptional. I will circumnavigate this waterway until I locate the one called, Rakke.*

****

Bridge's eyelids popped open, as Rakke slowed his forward progress. *It appears the waters are receding or we're beginning to rise above its level.*

By now, Rakke was standing, walking up an incline, still enclosed in a stone corridor.

It's growing brighter. Bridge had no way of knowing, but felt sure he was scratching his head. Puzzled, he began to contemplate his present situation until Rakke interrupted.

"In case you are wondering, we have reached our destination."

And where is here?

Rakke stepped through a doorway and into the sun.

By chance, Vrollic saw Rakke step into the sunlight and enter the Corstrum. *The malevolent presence I sought earlier in this search has elevated to pure evil. It courses through my being, entering my very soul. My body grows stronger through the manifestation of this newfound addition.*

As his eyes became accustomed to the overwhelming light, Bridge saw a courtyard surrounded by a heavy wooden fence. "This is the Corstrum," Rakke announced.

Is your friend not here? A hiss came from the very cave Rakke used to enter the Corstrum.

"He has arrived. Hag resides in this cave."

Sim hastily detached and bore into the ground upon hearing that the Corstrum had been reached, followed by the name Hag. *This time, hiding was much more secure.*

"It is good to see you for the first time, as you were meant to be," Hag hissed.

"I feel we are at a point where travel is possible," Rakke said. "What I require is a destination."

"The system of tunnels that were dug by the thack millennia ago is where we are bound."

"To what end?" Rakke questioned.

"The compassionate thack occasionally use them for shelter. They purposely made the underground system to benefit all the inhabitants of Burrus Plax."

"Yet, these beneficial tunnels are flooded and are of no use until the water recedes." One corner of Rakke's mouth curled upward.

"Why the smile, you are here for our benefit."

Rakke groaned. "And what is that to me?"

"That which I have said, is nothing to you," Hag replied. "That which I have *not* said, is everything."

"I didn't meet with you to play games," Rakke said.

Hag looked at Rakke. "The fact is you have no idea why our meeting was arranged, only that it would benefit you."

"What you state is fact. Now, it is time to state the profit."

"The system of tunnels extends over sixty feet below the surface," Hag said. "What we seek is a place where the tunnels meet. That is where the entity we seek is concealed."

"Did you not hear my words? The tunnels you continue to beleaguer are unusable," Rakke spat.

"Do not try my patience regarding matters I already know. The moisture contained within the chambers is being dealt with even as we speak, Although, it is not known if the methods used will have any effect."

"Then we should be on our way." Rakke stood, feet shoulder-width apart, arms spread forty-five-degree angles to the ground with hands open and palms out. Hag extended two tentacles and coiled them several times around Rakke's thorax. Then, the two beings started to vibrate, sending out a high-pitched whistle that carved ruts in the cave wall.

Hag started to flicker, growing fainter with each cycle until he was seen no more.

The blending complete, Hag laughed. "Escape from my prison is *now* a viable option."

To remain concealed, Sim listened to the exchange between Rakke and Hag from a subterranean position outside the tunnel. Then, he felt himself changing.

My transformation has begun. Sim flexed a new appendage that included five digits, enabling him to grasp objects.

****

Jack, Torast, Bridge, and Hag collectively appeared as the one called Rakke. Each of the four, except Bridge, had the power of speech and the ability to move appendages, facial muscles, and all other body parts. Although Rakke had been created from the essence of others, he was a separate entity and, therefore, had his own voice. Bridge was limited to conversing internally with Rakke.

Rakke lifted his legs, testing out his musculature. He raised his hands and flexed his fingers. "Good, yes, very good."

"As I mentioned earlier," Hag said, "it is time to leave."

****

Rakke circled above the ground, preparing to land. "This is where we belong, is it not?" He felt Hag's affirmation and landed close to one of the round entrance portals of the tunnel system.

"The hole you see is one of many entrances and exits to and from the system of tunnels," Bridge said.

"From here on, only one of us will speak," Hag declared. "It is too confusing with each of us trying to speak when we have the same information. I believe this task should go to Rakke."

"So be it," Bridge said for the benefit of Rakke.

"So be it," Jack said.

"So be it," Torast said.

"Shut it!" Hag ordered. "If there was ever a case for silence, this is it. Only Rakke speaks!"

Stepping forward, Rakke shielded his eyes from the brilliant light emanating from the hole. "The light of day emanates from this place." Once his eyes acclimated to the unnatural light, he jumped feet-first, sliding down the nearly vertical sides of the entrance, landing in chest-deep water. He stared at four tunnel openings, decided, and began the quest for the intersection and their ultimate prize.

A skittering sound quickly moved in and out of earshot, echoing throughout the passageway.

There is a strange familiarity to this creature, Rakke thought.

The Guardian came to a stop, thirty miles from the creature he used to call friend. *Jack had just given me the name of Abe. Then he and Torast became one and attempted to end my life.* Abe felt a pain inside, though he was not injured. It was a strange sensation that he took several minutes to ponder while covering nearly two hundred miles through the tunnels.

Could what was created be undone? Jack. Torast. Abe sensed the creature lumbering down corridors, searching.

I will monitor the creature from a short distance. And hope.

****

Pushing the thought of the Guardian from his mind, Rakke continued his mission. He couldn't help but run his fingers along the walls, fascinated by their structure and the light they exuded, enhanced by the amount of water the tunnel carried. *Even with our great strength, I fear finding an entity smaller than my hand within thousands of miles of corridors will be impossible. Although, there may be a way.*

He leaned back his head and sniffed. *It is faint, nonetheless detectable unless this new aroma is naught but a ruse.*

CHAPTER FIFTY-FIVE

Dalon Con, Krabb, Sketch, Smort and Dune

"Could you ascertain what material you were cutting?" Dalon Con asked.

"They were taught strands," Dune said. "Steel wires made of steel that on a . . ." He paused, not knowing what to say.

"There is no fear in this place;" Dalon Con said, "speak freely."

"I believe what Dune hesitates to speculate," Smort said, "is the steel wire is the material an anchor uses to construct its web."

"Ya heerd that?" Krabbe said. "We fixin' to git et up by some great big ole bug."

"Keep'er down," Sketch whispered harshly. "We done an promised Mr. Dalon we'd shut it."

"Is this creature not indigenous to Burrus Plax?" Dalon Con inquired.

Dune shook his head. "The anchor is instinctively attracted to worlds that other off-world creatures themselves have been drawn to. The anchor's intellectual prowess is that of a rock; however, their instincts for finding food are second to none."

"So their interest is due to the influx of creatures brought here as a result of time travel."

"Yes," Smort said, "though not for the time travel, but for the increased amount of prey to feed on."

"Make no mistake, the anchor is as bloodthirsty a creature that places strands of razor sharp nearly invisible wire to slice its prey apart," Dune looked at Dalon Con "even if the target is moving at a casual stroll. Then, a black cloud drops over the recently deceased and absorbs the flesh in seconds."

"Leaving naught but a dark smudge in the shape of the hapless victim," Smort added.

"A shadow beast," Dalon Con breathed.

"Exactly," Dune nodded. "We cannot be sure what shape the anchor takes, as its shadow is distorted by the sunlight. Even though it is a shadow—"

"—it can be a formidable opponent." Dalon Con finished, "rising from the ground to fight as any other being."

"Mr. Dalon," Sketch said, "you is a scarin' me a powerful lot."

Krabb chimed in. "Yous is layin' tha fright all ova me too."

"Worry not, small ones," Dalon Con said, "no one shall lay a finger on you, lest they go through me first."

"My protection is extended to each of you no matter the cost," Smort added.

A formless mass slowly lowered itself above Dalon Con and Dune.

"Grip my legs as tightly as possible," Dalon Con whispered, then glanced toward Dune, whose hands slowly moved toward his weapon.

Dalon Con, Dune, and Smort continued to converse in a casual manner, seemingly oblivious to any danger. Dune inched his hands imperceptibly down his thighs, until he perceived a starting point. His mild pattern of speech never wavered yet his eyes spoke volumes.

Dalon Con glanced to the left, moving nothing but his eyes. Gripping his staff, the end glowed a bright amber. Dune curled a hand around each weapon's handle, bringing his knives to life. Smort curled his digits into fists that grew to a massive size.

Dune vaulted upward, plunging his tri-bladed weapons forward, while Dalon Con thrust his glowing staff at the black, fluid form. Smort slammed his enlarged fists together, running toward the black mass that now hovered just above the three men.

"This devil stays just out of reach," Dune growled. "It possesses agility and an intellect I knew nothing of."

"Step aside," Dalon Con barked. "There is one who will deal with this scourge in time; however, until then…" He raised his staff and blanketed the anchor with a blast of amber light before vanishing completely.

Dune laughed. "The anchor is much easier to destroy than I would have imagined!"

"Not dead," Dalon Con said. "Our shadow beast has made a hasty retreat. I know of no way to eliminate these creatures."

"The smell of ozone permeated the air after the anchor had been encased in your staff's aura," Smort said.

"That is worth consideration," Dalon Con said, "for we may encounter this being again."

****

Suddenly, Dalon Con found himself sliding down a glacier at breakneck speed. Ahead, he saw a straight cutoff, indicating the glacier's end. By the time this notion settled into his brain, he was soaring through the air several hundred feet above an ice-filled sea.

A dusting of falling snow landed on an invisible creature that crawled on a ledge directly below.

It appears as though my last breath may be drawn under frigid circumstances. However . . .

"Die, malevolent beast." Dalon Con crushed the temporal thief's skull with his staff before hitting the icy water.

****

Dune was falling. Ten feet away, was a sheer stone cliff, and, six hundred feet below, nothing but ice and stone. *I never thought it would end this way.* Before Dune slammed into the ice-covered ground, he extended his arms and shut his eyes.

****

Smort sat in a bathtub full of hot water. *How odd,* he thought, splashing warm fluid on his face. *There is no need to complain, for this water is wonderful.* In front of him was a window, where he saw Dalon Con and Dune plummeting to their deaths. He stood up, causing the small shanty to rock and slide forward off the edge of a cliff.

It looks as though I am now headed for my own demise.

****

Dalon Con, Dune, and Smort hit the dirt at the same instant.

"What happened?" Dune gasped.

"Move, now!" Dalon Con bellowed. The men scattered as a tri-headed neslecon dropped from the sky and drove its three heads into the ground. Within seconds the three muzzles reappeared, each carrying a ragged-edged piece of broken glass. Extending their necks skyward, they began to digest their meals.

"A vile creature known as a temporal thief absconded with a small section of this timeline and replaced it with another," Dalon Con said. "However, this will be the last timeline this temporal thief *ever* invades." He tossed the dead temporal thief onto the ground.

"It appears time travel *is* possible," Dune conceded. "So, where are we now?"

"We have returned to where we faced the anchor," Smort said.

"Yet we are not out of danger." He nodded toward the hillside. "The neslecon still lingers, waiting, I imagine, for the new time thief."

The neslecon's three serpentine heads pecked at the ground. Each time one of the heads tapped the soil, a piece of material that looked like a purple shard of glass appeared in its mouth. Once finished with its meal, the three heads of the neslecon began to work their way upward into the air, following an unseen straight line.

"Them snake-headed devils is now a pullin' them thar chunks outin the air, chompin'em up and swallerin'em down," Krabb said.

"It looks as though our three-headed friend is cleaning up the edges of a temporal passage," Dalon Con said.

"A temporal passage?" Dune asked.

"A panel set into the timeline that the temporal thief uses to interrupt small sections of time by replacing them with alternate time units."

"Is that what happened to us when we briefly entered another world?" Smort asked.

"The temporal thief did cause the anomaly," Dalon Con said. "However, neither you nor I entered a different world, rather another timeline. You see, a timeline consists of many panels set into predetermined temporal slots. The thief steals panels of time. At his own choosing, he replaces a present-day panel with a section from the past, momentarily shifting us out of our timeline.

"However, with each passing second, the replacement panel becomes less stable. What you are witnessing is the destruction of our temporal excursion."

"That is why our trip to a different timeline was so short," Smort said. "It could only last as long as the panel, and, once the panel destroyed itself, our trip ended."

"You are correct;" Dalon Con said, "For us, the time deviation has passed; however, even now, the temporal beast is penetrating timelines. All are vulnerable to attack so long as the neslecon feeds."

He tapped the ground with his staff. "From the time the panel is destroyed, until replaced, the creature is vulnerable."

CHAPTER FIFTY-SIX

Hayden and Max

"How could the temporal thief abscond with a portion of your memory?" Hayden asked. "If you are physically linked to this world, then a mental connection must also exist."

"Of course! Small one, you have most likely answered your own question." Max's eyes brightened. "Your communication device," Max said. "I thought little of it until now, but each time you conversed with your countryman, I felt a slight unnatural sensation. I must have been a minuscule amount of energy leaving my body."

"So you think Wakke had something to do with the energy transfer?"

"I do not think so. During one of your communications with Wakke, he insisted you keep a vigil for the one called Drade. But, what if that wasn't the truth. In one of the transmissions, Wakke told of Drade's eighteen-year-long pilfering of your time portal. Then, Wakke's instruction to keep a vigil for Drade was nothing more than mind control emanating *from* Drade to throw a wrinkle in our thought process."

Hayden tapped his forefinger against his lips. "So you believe Drade is your memory thief?"

"I do," Max said. "In the warnings you received, most were unintelligible due to static. I believe this was the work of a temporal thief."

"How could Drade even know how to steal someone's memory?"

"From what I gleaned from your communication with Wakke, Drade was not acting like his usual self. This would lead me to believe a possession of the mind had taken place. Once the possession of

Drade was complete, the thief could school Drade in all he needed to know, including the removal of my memory."

"But why?"

Max smiled grimly. "Burrus Plax is ruled by a rarely seen evil, one intent on stealing the souls of every being on this planet."

"I have never thought of such a thing as a soul," Hayden said. "You have started a fire that burns within—perhaps that is *my* soul."

"What you feel is the Great One, and yes, it *is* within your soul. The Great One is also known as the Father and Creator."

"Creator," Hayden repeated, "how intriguing—creator of what?"

A wide smile spread across Max's face. "Everything you have ever seen, including you and me."

"I do not understand," Hayden said. "How can that be poss—"

Suddenly, the ground began to crack, numerous fissures spreading for miles in random directions.

"Hold on, small one. These understand not who they are about to embrace." Max closed a hand around Hayden as he had done many times before. The small one's world turned black as the two dropped into a crevice.

Max kept one hand firmly closed around Hayden and lifted the other. "Take your leave, noxious beasts, lest I remove each of you in pieces." A thunderous underground clap told Max these creatures were not at all who he'd originally thought them to be. This was a single being who traveled to this place via Max's anger.

Max dug his free hand and both feet into the side of the crevice to slow his fall. "Brace yourself, small one." Max had traveled thousands of yards underground by the time his speed had decreased, then he dove into the cliff wall.

I apologize for the rough treatment you must endure, Max said. *However, tracking and eliminating the foolish one who has taken it upon himself to quell our passage is necessary.*

Max stopped moving through the hard-packed earth and

concentrated on the organic generator in his abdomen. Within seconds, he released energy pulses that traveled through the ground and then detonated, clearing a section half a mile wide and three miles deep. He then rocketed toward the surface, pinning Hayden down with the sudden increase of g-forces.

"Interesting," Max said as he surveyed the landscape. "I must apologize, for I will be repeating the barrage you experienced a second time."

Hayden covered his ears. "Do as you must; I will survive."

Max dropped deeper into the earth. *Brace yourself, small one.* His abdominal generator discharged pulse after pulse, and then he moved to a different area and depth and continued the barrage.

A deafening squeal broke through the concussive noise of the final destroying pulse. Moments later, a giant thud permeated the ground, rocking Hayden from side to side in Max's hand.

Max said as he ruptured the sound barrier four hundred feet below the surface, sending tons of rubble, along with himself, sprawling upward. Landing flat on his back, he jumped to his feet and opened his hand. "The evil is near, small one. Our way will soon become more hazardous. We will be forced to hunt the creature I have just exposed."

"I have been with you through many dangerous situations," Hayden said, "What have you unearthed?"

"I cannot be sure," Max replied, "but I believe they are the same creatures that constructed the vast systems of tunnels under the surface of Burrus Plax." Max closed his eyes and shook his head. "Too many stolen memories cloud my judgment of what is accurate. Although, I believe I have found a portion of them.

"During the short time we spent in the air, I glimpsed what I believe to be shards of my missing memory that are now scattered across the ground. If you recall our earlier conversation, the thief would have placed my memories at random points along the timeline and, it appears, hid them underground."

"And your bombardment brought them to the surface. So we gather your memories and then to the city of Rash, correct?"

"Rash will have to wait," Max said, "until we locate the memories that were taken from me."

"And once we gather what is here, how do we find the rest?"

"The temporal thief leaves a trail I should be able to track," Max nodded. "The problem will be picking up the trail after the sonic blast. Although it will manifest itself again, we do not have time to wait for this to happen."

CHAPTER FIFTY-SEVEN

Gabriel and Roan

"I have to say, this is a step up from walking," Gabriel said as he readjusted his grip of Azoff's thick hair.

Another thack, Cash, was enlisted by Azoff to bear Roane. "Two steps," Roane replied as the pair walked side-by-side along the bank of fast-moving river.

"Any other ideas about finding Dalon Con, Gabriel?" Roane asked.

"No. Just the word Rash, and there's something else—something I can't explain."

"Let me in on your confusion," Roane said. "Between the two of us, perhaps we'd have a better chance of how to proceed."

Suddenly, the thacks stopped. Two massive fish-head creatures blocked their path about a hundred yards ahead. The tops of the heads sloped upward, ending in a boney ridge. Oversized teeth, round at the base and gradually tapering to a point, erupted through the gums. These aligned with the teeth in the upper jaw. Both heads were attached to necks that extended into the river.

"They don't appear aggressive. Are they dead?" Dune asked, his hands moving toward his weapons.

"Not dead. Scalese," Azoff said. "An abhorrent beast with a mean disposition. They are sizing us up as opponents and will strike soon if they deem us not to be a threat."

"Do we wait until they decide?" Gabriel asked, "or do you have something else in mind?"

"Of course," Azoff replied. The thacks jumped high enough into the air to uncoil their tails, releasing the prime source of propulsion, and then the pair were soon circling above the surprised scalese.

Both of the creature's heads shot upward. They grabbed Roane's thack by his rear leg while the other latched onto his snout and began to pull the doomed creature toward the ground.

"Jump, Roane!" Azoff barked. He moved toward Cash, allowing Roane to climb over and ride in tandem with Gabriel. The three watched as the thack was ripped to pieces and devoured by two heads of the scalese.

"It came completely out of the water," Gabriel said. "Both heads, along with their thirty-foot necks, are attached to a small, round body."

"Quite a contrast to the rest of the silver-scaled beast," Roane said.

"Azoff, I am very sorry about your friend," Gabriel said.

"Worry not about Cash," Azoff said. "He passed in an honorable way, saving the life of another."

"Perhaps we should move to a greater altitude to avoid the same fate," Roane offered.

"Normally, yes," Azoff replied, "and we will do just that, once my brother is avenged." Before either Gabriel or Roane could protest, the thack dropped into a steep dive toward the creature.

"Looks like this is it," Roane yelled into Gabriel's ear.

Azoff swooped around one of the scalese's heads, prompting the aquatic monster to raise its dome and follow him. He then repeated the maneuver with the other head, eliciting the same response. With both heads in motion, Azoff deftly led them in opposite directions, causing their necks to entangle in confusion. The creature, now disoriented, began to attack itself. Azoff ascended to a higher vantage point and watched the chaotic spectacle from above.

"Now, watch the two senseless beasts take care of the problem for us," Azoff spat as the creatures started to rip each other apart.

"I think it's about over," Gabriel said. "One of the heads is hanging on by the spinal column, and that half of the creature is no longer moving."

"Does the death of one head affect the other?" Roane asked.

Azoff nodded. The dead scalese was overrun by scavengers, both in the river and on land.

"Again, our condolences on the loss of your friend," Gabriel said softly as they flew away.

"Thank you," Azoff said, "but we must concern ourselves with the living and finding Dalon Con."

"Gabriel mentioned Rash, but also something he couldn't explain," Roane said.

"Gabriel understands the concept of Rash, yet his mind is clouded with thoughts concerning a deep connection with the old man who appears as a thirty-year-old-suit," Azoff said.

"So, Rash has something to do with our next stop?" Roane asked.

"Rash *is* our next stop," Gabriel stated, "unless you want to spend time looking for a place that has no name and, most likely, doesn't exist except in my brain."

"Rash it is," Azoff said. "Gabriel, please point me in the right direction." Gabriel pointed north/northeast, and Azoff banked in that direction, increasing his speed.

****

After traveling through the night, the sun broke over the horizon. "There, Azoff, that clearing just ahead and to the right," Gabriel said.

The sleeping thack shook his head and became alert. "I see it."

"How can you fly when you're asleep?" Gabriel asked.

Azoff chuckled. "It is rather strange, isn't it? All I need do is think sleep, the direction I want to travel, and the self-flight mode engages, taking over whenever I doze."

"That can come in handy," Roane said, followed by a long yawn.

"So nice of you to join us," Gabriel said.

Roane stretched and yawned again. "Are we preparing to land?"

"We are, indeed," Azoff replied. "According to Gabriel, we are getting close to our destination."

"You mean Rash?" Roane asked.

"Yes," Gabriel said. "Though I have no way of knowing its exact location."

Azoff continued to circle, coming closer to the ground with each revolution, "Hold on tight."

Several moments later, Azoff orchestrated a smooth touchdown. Roane and Gabriel slid from their winged mode of transportation and onto the ground.

"All right, Gabe" Roane said, "it's your turn."

"I will have to admit," Azoff said, "I have awaited your method of location for some time now . . . please proceed."

"You two are expecting something you're not going to see," Gabriel said. "I can look at each of you and honestly say, I do not know how to find Dalon Con."

"Well," Roane said, "I guess we wait."

Gabriel furrowed his brows and looked off into the distance, remaining this way for several minutes. "That's it!" Gabriel exclaimed and sped into the surrounding foliage.

"We'd better follow," Roane said, climbing onto Azoff's back.

"Once again I bade you, hold tightly. The trees hold little room in between for one my size, and we'll most certainly have to climb."

Gabriel slipped through the dense forest as if it were not there.

"Look to your left and just ahead," Roane directed. "He's dodging trees as if he knows where they are before he reaches them."

"I see him," Azoff huffed. "However, it is all I can do to match his speed."

Azoff leaped from one treetop, rolling one hundred eighty degrees and pushing off another, only to repeat the roll and use the following six trees to catch up with Gabriel. Roane was nearly knocked off several times.

"We may have another problem," Roan said.

"And what may this other problem be?"

"There is a disturbing amount of parasitic life on the forest floor, more than able to harm Gabriel."

"Then it would behoove us to follow Gabriel from the ground," Azoff said. "In this way, we may offer more protection to our comrade." Azoff began his descent using his body to decimate trees, giving himself adequate room to land. Each time he impacted the wooden obstacles, Azoff grunted in pain.

"Are you all right?" Roane asked.

"It is not the way I would wish it to proceed, however, it must be done." Thirty feet before man and rodent touched down, a bright amber bolt of light spidered along the ground on either side of Gabriel, Roane, and Azoff.

This way, an inviting voice welcomed.

CHAPTER FIFTY-EIGHT

Rakke

"Many a mile," Rakke said as they trudged through the tunnel. "Many a mile from where I stand and then some."

This causes much distress, Bridge replied. *You do not appear to be the kind who would let such a small thing as distance bother them so.*

"In this case, speed is of the essence, concerning our coming together. The one known as Torast is of such great mass that he burdens this combined body with his weight. Having hundreds of miles, possibly a thousand or more to travel, this added weight will significantly slow our ability to reach the intersection."

What will you do about this unexpected hindrance, not to mention the massive amount of water?

"We keep moving, until we locate the intersection, we keep moving."

There are many other ways, Bridge said.

"None I am willing to entertain," Rakke replied. "Your ways take me in the opposite direction from where I wish to go." He began his trek, moving as fast as his legs would allow.

You would do well to try my way.

"Why must I listen to your constant need to change what I have set in my mind to accomplish? Hag has instructed all to be silent, save for Rakke . . . and *I am* Rakke!"

We have already established that I am your conscience, Bridge said. *No one holds dominion over me… no one but the creator, and until he instructs me otherwise, I will speak when I choose.*

A brief sonic blast lasting several milliseconds echoed throughout the chamber. Rakke whirled around, dropping several feet and sending a wave through the tunnels as he did so.

****

"Excellent," Abe said, "it does indeed affect this one." He traveled forty miles in the blink of an eye. "Yes, this revelation is outstanding." He glanced back. "Thankfully, I can move along the ceiling and avoid the flood." Then he was gone.

****

There is another life form occupying this maze of tunnels.

"Many life forms make these chambers home," Rakke replied.

Yes, Bridge said. *But this one causes uneasiness in you that I haven't noticed with any other creature here.*

"Perhaps, this would be an excellent time to rest your voice."

No. I see no reason to rest. In fact, I have much to say that you will find quite interesting.

"Of this I have no doubt."

Another sonic pulse rang through the tunnel system—this time much closer.

As I have conveyed, there is a better way to relieve your anxiety.

"Keep it to yourself, as I have also conveyed." No sooner had the words left Rakke's mouth than he found himself flat on his back, being dragged through the water down unknown corridors by an invisible assailant.

****

Unusual, Abe thought, *the one made from two is being dragged through the very tunnels I was created to protect . . . yes, interesting. I will keep a close eye on this situation.*

****

Comfortable? Bridge asked.

Rakke growled. "Know this, funny man—the day will come when I will rip your head off, leaving mine intact."

Interesting. It speaks, yet it makes no sense. Bridge was doing his best to aggravate Rakke into taking any irrational action.

Rakke chuckled, then focused on the entity propelling him through the passageway. "I warn you. It is unwise to drag one such as I through these tunnels. Release me!"

The entity stopped, dropping Rakke into the water.

"Do not try that again, for you will then feel my full wrath. Do you understand?"

Several moments passed without an answer.

"Well, I see the coward has fled." Rakke attempted to rise but was forced back to the ground by the powerful unseen entity. Then, the attack came to an abrupt halt.

"I will have to say," Rakke gasped. "Had you not ceased this ill-advised abduction, I would have taken matters into my own hands." Rakke again pushed himself up, standing defiantly, only to be driven down to a sitting position on the tunnel floor. This time, his head completely submerged, and his back wedged tight against the stone wall. Rakke's body armor, considered indestructible, carried a significant indentation across his right shoulder.

How are things going? Bridge chuckled.

"Get . . . away . . . from . . . me," Rakke burbled as he struggled to rise from the water.

Okay. Let us see how that works for you.

"Who is this one that wields such power?" Rakke commanded the others within him.

The entities that made up Rakke started speaking to each other. Yet, Jack kept silent, feeling a kinship with this newcomer.

"I believe it to be the creature that is one with Burrus Plax," Hag said.

"How do we handle such a being?" Torast inquired, "Having breathable air will not be a problem for up to an hour. But after that . . ."

"Silence. I will talk to this one." Hag hissed. "Son of Burrus Plax. You would do well to know your place before—"

"Hold your tongue, slime devil," Max roared as his watery hand grabbed Rakke by the throat, jerking him out of the water. (Invisibility made possible by his contact with the surrounding water.)

"We should go," Hayden whispered to Max.

The creature was released, and he sank to the watery floor in a crumpled heap.

****

After several minutes, Rakke brought his head up enough to breathe. "I will now stand," Rakke said, then pushed himself to a standing position.

Good for you, Bridge said.

Vrollic said, "I wish to talk."

"Now you wish to talk!" Rakke seethed, glancing in the direction of the voice.

"I am not your attacker. If I had been, you'd be no more." The towering newcomer, his calm demeanor contrasting with his imposing stature, hovered several feet away, his own luminescence casting an ethereal glow.

"Who are you, and do you realize the danger in which you have surrounded yourself?"

"My name is Vrollic, and I wish, as I have said to talk with you and the others that join in making you complete."

"You will *not* travel —"

"Your knowledge of us intrigues me," Hag interrupted Rakke. "You will travel with us, for I sense you know much more than you should."

Rakke scanned Vrollic for several moments and then spoke.

"You are with me," he said, rising to his full height. "And as we converse we will also search for a round bronze medallion built into the center of a crossroad, though the intersection we search for is one in the midst of thousands."

And the plot thickens, Bridge thought, humor heavy within his statement.

CHAPTER FIFTY-NINE

Dalon Con, Krabb, Sketch, Dune and Smort

"Tell me how, you can catch and cook the cabot at will," Smort said, smacking his lips. "*I* cannot get any closer than a hundred yards to one before it bolts."

Dalon Con chuckled. "Practice and a little help."

"I think we should turn our attention back to the anchor beast. Knowing more of this foe may help in battling it in the future." Dalon Con stirred the coals of the fire.

"There is no way to know exactly where the anchor originated," Smort said. "It is believed it the offspring of two unrelated species. Other than that, we've learned very little about the anchor's life on Burrus Plax."

"And any idea when the anchor made its first appearance on this world?"

"No longer than fifty years." Smort grabbed the last piece of cabot.

"Fifty years," Dalon Con said, "interesting."

"Why is this interesting?" Dune asked.

"It may mean nothing," Dalon Con mused, "or it may answer many questions."

"Ya heerd that," Krabb said. "They's gonna ast more questions."

"Hesh up," Sketch said, "when Mr. Dalon gots thins ta say ta ya, let'm talk."

"Perhaps it would be best to listen to the small ones." Dune covered his mouth, suppressing a wide grin.

Smort looked at his hand, brought it close to his mouth before deciding otherwise and dropping the appendage to his lap.

Dalon Con noticed Smort's actions. *It's almost as if he was birthed a short time ago and knows little concerning simple everyday occurrences.*

"We know the ability to travel through time has been brought to Burrus Plax." Dalon Con continued, "We haven't the time to discuss details; however, during the eighteen years it took the first-time explorers to build the temporal doorway, it is possible that the anchor and the first temporal explorers' appearance are related."

Dalon Con stood and motioned to Dune and Smort to do the same. He took two steps, then sensed a presence above his head. "Small ones, to me!" Krabb and Sketch wasted no time.

"Move, now!" Dalon Con's voice thundered, his command echoing through the air.

The group raced out of the way as an arsenal of eight-inch bone darts embedded themselves into the ground.

"What in tha world be agoin' on now?" Krabb asked.

"Got ma eyes closed up too tight ta know," Sketch said.

"We need to separate," Dalon Con yelled. "I will take care of the rest."

The group ran in an erratic pattern as they sped along the pathway, confusing the flying creature. Several attempts at skewering its prey missed their target. Dalon Con slowed when sensing the assailant cease his onslaught.

"What was that?" Dune puffed as he jogged up to Dalon Con.

"I cannot be sure, but I would say it is a maritime," Dalon Con said. "I have heard they exist, but I have never seen one until now."

"It seems we are drawing more and more creatures from other worlds," Smort said, "not just the anchor."

Dalon Con glanced at the orange streak dancing through the clouds from the corner of his eye. "That indeed seems to be the case," he said. "I wonder how many are directly related to the influx of temporal disturbances."

Dalon Con glanced at Sketch and Krabb. "Are you all right?"

"Yes sir, Mr. Con," Sketch said while Krabb nodded.

Dalon Con inhaled deeply, scanning on the horizon. "Let us continue to Rash."

****

The maritime quivered as it began to drop, splashing into the Scale River. The severely dehydrated creature began to absorb water until its weight had increased threefold. Its regeneration complete, it dove eighty feet to the bottom of the river and moved on a predetermined path. After several hours, it stopped when it came to a steep bank, entering a cave many times its size.

"I see you have arrived."

****

It was well past Sunrise when the group stood at the entrance to Rash. Like its sister city, Grave, the buildings were overgrown with shank trees, leaving all coated in an eerie blue light.

Dalon Con placed a hand on Sketch's and Krabb's shoulder. "Do each of you remember our trip into the city Grave?"

"I sure duz a member it," Sketch said.

"Don't bleeve I ever ferget," Krabb replied. "It be why I is so scared now."

"We made it out unscathed," Dalon Con said. "I cannot guarantee the same results here. However, I will do everything in my power to keep you safe."

"That be good nuff fer me," Sketch said.

"Good nuff fer me, too," Krabb echoed.

"We will keep this identical to our trip into Grave," Dalon Con said, "which means you will stay as close to me as possible." Sketch and Krabb both tightened their grip.

"Good," Dalon Con said. They made their way around the first row of shank trees.

"There be that dadblasted hummin' agin," Krabb whispered. "I reckon I ain't got no choice but to listen at it."

"So listen at it, quiet like," Sketch said.

Within moments, the trees thinned and they were walking along a cobblestone street. They came upon what had been the front entrance to a family's home. Light shone through where the weather stripping had rotted along the bottom of the door.

"Do you remember when faced with this situation in Grave?" Dalon Con asked Sketch and Krabb.

"You betcha," Sketch said, "we helt that thar none visible robe tight so's nobody could see us walkin' in the room."

"Perfect," Dalon Con said, "for we are about to repeat that day."

Dalon Con turned toward Dune and Smort. "I would ask you to stay here until we return,"

Krabb and Skecth then grabbed the seam of Dalon Cons garment and held the edges tightly together. Just as before, he appeared as a transparent but slightly blurry entity. Concealing his hands and head, Dalon Con reached for the tarnished brass knob.

The door swung inward two inches, the hinges not making a sound. He entered the room and then spoke softly.

"I kin still hear that hummin'," Krabb whispered as Dalon Con walked toward another room. At the far end of the space was a doorway through which a much brighter light emanated.

"Four men working," he said, "and two more coming into the room carrying what looks like three-foot-square pieces of blue glass." Dalon Con moved closer. *This laboratory is nowhere near as advanced as the one in Grave.*

****

"You know what those glass squares were, don't you?" Dune said.

"If our past experiences are any indication, then I believe them to be sections of time the temporal thieves harbored for their own use."

"That thar inklin' ya was atalkin' 'bout," Krabb said, "taint as far-fetched as ya thunked it was."

"Please, explain," Dalon Con said.

"This happen quite a while back," Krabb said, "so'd I's might have some trouble memberin' everythin' right off, ifin that's okay. But, near as I can 'member I had me this steady girl . . . I bleeve her name be Maudie." Krabb rubbed his chin and looked at the morning sky, pondering his past. "Yep, that was her name all right. We was gettin' right friendly. She'd even let me kiss her on the jaw." Krabb looked at Dalon Con. "That's when things changed, real sudden like."

Krabb explained that he called after Maudie one day as she strode by, asking where she was going. Maudie remained silent, quickly walking away with a three-foot- piece of glass tucked under her arm. He walked after her, then quickened to a slow jog, determined to catch up with his girlfriend.

But when he touched her shoulder, Maudie whirled on him, demanding he leave her alone. "When I asked what had done gotten inta her, she jest yelled fer me ta leave her alone. I ask agin what be wrong an she turn on me, sayin' 'Only thin' done an gotten inta me, is you an ifin ya don't want me gettin' in ta ya, ya best be abackin' off!' Done near broke ma hert."

"Bein' 'bout as hard-headed as they come, I started runnin' faster till I caught up with that girl," Krabb continued. "But when I reached out, I touched the edge 'o' that piece 'o' glass she were atotin' and she turned her head alookin' at me 'bout the time that thin she were acarryin' hit the ground. After that, I taint real sure what happen, 'ceptin' I were drownin' in mud fer as these old eyes could see."

"What about your friend, Maudie?" Dune asked.

"Never seed her agin," Krabb said, "but I be atellin' ya one thin'—the girl I were achasin' twern't ma Maudie. Somethin' done crawled inside an made her plum mean as a snake."

"The fact that you found yourself in a mud-covered world *would* lend more credence to our speculation. The squares we observed in Rash, were, in fact, out-of-place units of time used by the temporal thieves," Dalon Con said.

"You are indeed correct," Smort said. "This area was remanufactured to process time panels making them more stable, therefore more useful to the temporal thieves with their longer life."

Dalon Con nodded toward Smort. *Hidden truths are emerging from this one.* "We have a long journey ahead. Let us take in nourishment before leaving."

"Let me guess—" Smort smacked his lips. "Cabot."

Certain aspects of this planet were preprogrammed into Smort's brain before sending him out into the world. All else was left for him to learn as the need arose. This leaves the next item of import to be the one who set this in motion.

CHAPTER SIXTY

Hayden and Max

"Again, I hate to beleaguer the subject," Hayden said, "but how can we physically hold a piece of your memory in our hands?"

"It is not as difficult as it seems, small one. It is simply a matter of touching the shard of memory and it will return."

"But if *I* touched the shard, would your memories return to me?"

"That is impossible, for my memories are not yours." Hayden put a finger to his mouth, looked down, and began to nod. After several moments, he looked up.

"I am beginning to understand. However, how do we search for these missing bits of your consciousness?"

"I wish there were a mythical or magical way to perform a thorough search but none of these exist. We will have to rely on our eyes to detect and our hands to retrieve, returning each to its rightful place within my memory."

"How can we physically search? I am so small and you are nowhere near the top of the trees where many of the shards lie."

"Do not be so quick to question." Max rose many feet above the tree tops as he spoke, his girth equaling his height as he grew. "I will search the top and you, small one, the bottom."

"Understood, however, do not allow yourself to outpace me as I may never find you again."

Max laughed. "Worry not, for I will stay with you each step of the way."

Hayden was amazed at the number of tiny pieces scattered on the forest floor. *Curious,* he thought, *all I need to do is touch one of these pieces . . .* As he did so, the shard disappeared.

"Whoa, it works!"

"Thank you, small one, you have restored a valuable thought."

"My hope would be to convey that you are welcome, but I know you would never hear my voice from such a great distance."

"Worry not, small one," his voice full of delight, "for I can hear your words clearly and, might I add, they have never sounded better."

Hayden hovered low and touched three separate shards. "I'll have to admit, it makes me feel much better knowing you are so near."

"I am glad this brings you comfort and thank you for my three recent acquisitions . . . I suppose you could say that I am bringing back memories."

"Excellent attempt at humor." Hayden laughed.

"It is good to see you, small one," Max said as he reduced his size.

"Has your memory returned?" Hayden asked as he hovered in front of the giant.

"Portions have, I now remember a race of creatures known as the thack who carved the stone tunnels to house visitors. The thack also provided a small, furry one called the Guardian, for service at first, as there were many rooms, and later for protection, when the population turned toward evil. However, the essential segments of memory I search for have yet to return."

"How is that possible?" Hayden asked. "Certainly, we recovered the majority of the pieces."

"We gathered, perhaps, a third of what was lost," Max said. "We must now locate the rest." He extended his hand, giving Hayden his usual place to land. "Small one, we will never collect my memory in its entirety. The infinite number of pieces makes the task impossible; however, we will recover enough to give us the answers we need."

"I am saddened," Hayden said, "about the fact that you will not retain what could be, pleasant memories."

"Do not concern yourself with such things," Max said. "If thoughts or scenarios that used to be memories within my consciousness are no longer there, then it is as if they never occurred."

Hayden nodded. "So, where do we look for another cache of your memory shards?"

"Our search has already begun. Come close. Three-winged creatures are circling above our heads." Hayden instinctively started to move his eyes upward. "No," Max said calmly, "look only at me.

"The carthon have exceptional sight, down to detail on one such as you. Thankfully, their hearing is not as keen."

"What do they want?" Hayden asked.

"Purely reconnaissance. They have been following us for some time. I initially was not sure of their intentions, but their lack of concern told me what I needed to know.

"They are known as the Cue, an intellectual group of flying reptiles consisting of many species that hire themselves out to anyone who can afford their services."

"So, someone is paying to know our whereabouts." He took to the air, levitating until he floated in front of Max's eyes. "Any ideas?"

"Indeed. At least, I have a partial idea brought back by my restored memory. However, I cannot identify who hired the Cue until we locate the next cache of memory."

"We should begin that task immediately."

"As I have said small one, we have already begun and, perhaps, we may bring a bit of confusion to the Cue who still circle above our heads. Take a seat and brace yourself." The large biped dropped beneath the surface of the ground in less than a second, leaving the three circling reptiles perplexed and diving toward the earth to locate the objects of their surveillance.

"It is all right with me," Max said, "if you utter the words."

"Do you mean the phrase, 'here we go again'?" Hayden asked.

"Yes, I do."

"I already have."

"Good, then I must ask you to once again brace yourself." Max dove deep into the earth.

Hayden covered his ears as the pressure changed. He swallowed hard, temporarily relieving his discomfort. "This must be the greatest depth we have reached since we began traveling together."

"You are correct, small one. It is also the greatest speed we have achieved."

"Why have we resorted to such extremes?"

"To escape the Cue. There are too many unknowns, the most important being: who hired these winged reptiles to track us?"

CHAPTER SIXTY-ONE

Gabriel, Roane and Azoff

The maritime telepathically communicated with the anchor.

I arrived but a short time ago and have made contact with several inhabitants, whether indigenous or foreign, I know not.

Good, the anchor conveyed. *Call me Adlar. What became of this meeting?*

The group I encountered was more formidable than I expected, leading me to believe that the theft of a temporal vortex may be more difficult than I first thought—perhaps an impossibility.

The anchor rose several feet in the murky depths. *Impossibilities are not an option. If this presents a problem, maybe your trip has been for naught, for you will surely die before you can move.*

Where would you like me to begin? the maritime yielded.

****

When Azoff landed, Gabriel and Roane quickly dismounted, searching for the source of the amber light.

"I know what I saw," Gabriel said. "He can't be far."

"Who?" Roane asked.

"Use the name," Azoff said, still scampering to keep up with the two young men.

"Dalon Con, of course," Gabriel said.

"Look no further," a man said. All motion stopped. Gabriel whirled around and saw his old friend.

"You have grown in the short time we have been apart," Dalon Con said. "I sense a period of great distress, though necessary for you to grow within." Unable to speak, Gabriel ran and threw his arms around the young man.

"It seems we have many new ones to meet," Azoff said. "Especially, with two groups coming together." Dalon Con pushed Gabriel to arm's length, though not before kissing him on the cheek. The two stood momentarily staring at one another, smiling at the return of what seemed like family.

"What my furry friend has conveyed is true," Dalon Con said. "We should begin melding the groups together into one."

"I suggest that we keep introductions to a minimum," Azoff said, "so that we may continue our journey to Rash."

"Agreed," Dalon Con said, "I will begin." He looked down at his legs. "Step down, small ones; all gathered here are friends." Two small men reluctantly stepped from his feet. "These men, Sketch and Krabb," said Dalon Con, pointing to each one respectively, "are my friends. Do not let their small stature mislead you, for they are as dangerous as any full-sized man."

"And this is Dune." He placed his right hand on Dune's shoulder. "We have endured much, and, ultimately, stand together." Moving his free hand to one standing on his left, "And this is Smort, the most recent addition to our detachment."

"I am Azoff, one with the family of thack." A murmur ensued from the gathering. "Worry not, for what you have heard of my race is totally false. We are benevolent creatures, concerned only with those who call Burrus Plax home." He motioned for Roane and Gabriel to join him. He placed a paw on each man's shoulder. Azoff introduced Gabriel and Roane, giving a short overview of each man.

"Welcome all. Now, we should be leaving," Dalon Con said. "Dune, Smort, Sketch, Krabb, and I have spent a short time in Rash; however, I think it deserves more investigation, and therefore, we should return."

****

"Here we is ag'in," Krabb said, "standin afore them nasty blue bushes."

"In actuality," Dalon Con said, "what you call bushes are shank trees."

"So, this is Rash," Azoff said. Roane and Gabriel stared into the tangled mess.

"This is what it has become," Dalon Con replied, "however, do not let its dead appearance fool you. For within these crumbling walls, depending on your perception, lies some of the most advanced technology ever conceived or the scourge of the modern world."

"What kind of technology?" Roane asked.

"Fractures in the temporal line," Dalon Con said.

"Time travel," Azoff said. Dalon Con nodded.

"We should go." The furry creature crashed awkwardly through the tangled vegetation. Dalon Con touched Azoff's rear leg, causing the beast to stop, turn, and glance at him.

"We should take all precautions to move about with as much stealth as possible," Dalon Con said.

"If you will allow me to move in front and take the lead, I believe our progress will make greater strides." Dalon Con moved as he spoke. "We will not visit the room housing scientists that were transporting panels of time, as this redundancy will offer no benefit."

Smort increased his pace until he caught up with Dalon Con. "May I speak with you?"

"Of course," Dalon Con said, "empty your soul, for there is no fear."

Smort smiled. "I feel as though I was sent here for a nefarious reason; however, I do not wish to perform such a deed on one I have grown to respect."

"You sound as if you know what this deed entails and at who it is aimed."

Smort shook his head. "It is you, Dalon Con, it is you." The big man dropped his head, staring at the ground as he walked. "I will most certainly die for not completing my mission, but that is of little consequence as I will not take your life." He raised his head and looked at his quarry from head to toe. "Even if it were possible, which now I believe it not to be."

"And who orchestrated this act for you to complete?"

Smort looked into Dalon Con's eyes. "Hag."

****

"Kin ya tell me 'bout that carn sarn hummin'?" Krabb asked, the irritation evident in his voice.

"I believe I can show you the source of your frustration," Dalon Con said. After several minutes of moving over the cobblestone street, he asked, "Can you tell that the noise that bothers you so has increased in volume?"

"Yes sir," Krabb said, "I sure do fer goodness bleeve you is right." After another fifteen minutes of movement, Dalon Con stopped in front of a door.

Before anyone could ask, the door was open, and Dalon Con stood in the room filled with silver barrels with copper coils. "The hum you hear emanates from these units which power this complex," Dalon Con said. "Certainly there are similar components located in Grave and Defeated."

"Yes," Smort said, "identical in every case."

"It looks as though we should take the amount of time necessary to search most, if not the entire, city of Rash," Azoff said, "as it may take a very long time to root out all the secrets it contains."

"Azoff is correct," Dune said, "but, hopefully, we can fall short of encompassing each building here."

"To expand upon Azoff's comment," Smort said, "a complete search would take an inordinate amount of time, possibly causing us to miss vital information taking place in another part of the city."

"We will accomplish both," Dalon Con said, "unlock its secrets without searching through every nook and cranny." Suddenly, a deafening crash ensued, and the entire city and surrounding area shook violently. Beyond where the buildings stood, the ground cracked in multiple places, spidering its way out several miles from the epicenter, which was Rash. Everyone but Dalon Con ducked and looked into the darkness, expecting everything above to tumble down.

"What in tarnation were that?" Sketch squalled.

"Wait here," Dalon Con said. "I will return soon." He was instantly gone.

****

Dalon Con deftly scaled, jumped and flipped his way through the flat foliage that topped the trees. Standing on the tightly woven leaves, he scanned the surrounding area.

If I am correct and Rash is indeed the epicenter, only a small portion of the city remains, with the majority of Rash destroyed. He stood still, able to feel the creature's vibration as it departed the city.

It is moving at a great rate of speed, though I sense it has nothing to do with this dilapidated city or our presence here. Dalon Con heard another explosion and witnessed a debris plume several hundred miles away. *I fear that it may be part of the same disturbance, ridding Burrus Plax of Grave and leaving only two remaining cities.*

For several minutes, he stood, watching the eruptions in the city of Grave. Finally, a muted explosion indicated an underground blast. *This one moves underground as quickly as I can move through the air. He is now too far away to observe with any accuracy. . . Yet, I believe I may know the culprit.*

CHAPTER SIXTY-TWO

Rakke [Abe, and Sim]

I will use the next egress to escape until the water recedes. Though I was bred to be alone, I miss the companionship of others. The Guardian thought for a moment and, seizing his chance, jumped to freedom by way of the next exit. *I do not know how to process these emotions . . . I feel the way I imagine empty would feel.* His eyes began to well. *How strange. Water trickles from my ocular sockets. I will search for ones with whom I feel comfortable.* And then Abe was gone.

****

Rakke pushed slowly through the flooded cavern. "The water dampens any signs the medallion would exude to aid in its location." Rakke continued to move, stopping at each four-way intersection and searching the bottom for the bronze medallion.

Frustrating, is it not? Bridge inquired. *So many locations and so little time.*

"I have no use for you. Bother someone who does not mind your childish games."

It is much more appealing to stay with you. It is almost like we are best friends.

"I have no friends, you illegitimate worm. You will let me be or die!" Rakke roared.

It seems you have forgotten, if I die . . . you die. But that is not the case.

Not wanting to respond but feeling he needed to know what Bridge meant, Rakke spoke. "Explain yourself. Why would you utter the phrase, 'if I die, you die' and then announce these words are incorrect?"

Curious, don't you think? goaded Bridge. *Just plain curious.*

"Do not trifle with me," an enraged Rakke barked, pounding on the side of the tunnel.

Calm yourself. My statement merely meant that your death has nothing to do with my demise. You see, as your conscience, I am tied to you; however, at the same time, I am a member of the spirit world and answer to a greater power.

By now, Rakke had stopped moving.

"Who are you speaking with," Vrollic asked.

"Do not pester Rakke with your useless queries," Rakke snarled. We will have time after I have destroyed this fool who spews nonsense. Now, fool, tell me of this spirit world."

Resume your search, Bridge said, the joviality absent in his voice. *We will converse later; until then, I will make myself known to you, if necessary.*

Dumbfounded by this turn of events, Rakke robotically continued his quest for the medallion.

****

After traveling more than a thousand miles, Abe came to rest in a sparsely wooded area.

Ah, exactly what I need. He made his way to a fast-moving stream and drank his fill. One of the more intelligent aquatic creatures watched this furry reptile consume more than four gallons of water.

****

Miles away, Sim entered the water-filled tunnel system and started swimming downward—drawn by the much-desired bronze medallion. Despite the tubular crossroads numbering into the thousands, Sim knew he would eventually know the answer . . . *and I see that time is now.*

Sim extended a tentacle with a sharpened nodule on its end. *This should do nicely, although it seems more than a coincidence that I should find the bronze circle before I lost the implements to extract my quarry . . . One greater than I led me to the disc, rendering this search and recovery by design.*

He inserted the hardened tip under the edge of the medallion, dislodging the bronze object, and safely wrapping the circular bronze piece with the tentacle. Then, Sim broke the surface of the water and exited through a portal miles away from the one used to enter the system of tunnels. He made all haste into the forest, but stopped to view his surroundings.

Amazing, such beauty I have never seen . . . or perhaps, that I have failed to notice. Let us see what changes this will bring. Even now, the hatred I have aligned with for much of my existence is beginning to wane.

****

A dark shadow within Abe's mind warned this small, furry creature of imminent danger. Abe stood atop a tree a hundred feet off the ground and three miles away. *I can see the culprit, but am not sure of his immediate intentions.*

Several moments later, the finality of the creature's plan for Abe became evident. *I see what appear to be sections of rock twelve inches across, irregular but basically round.* Abe scampered down the tree and then up another, this one two miles closer.

The round sections are attached together like a chain. Abe had never seen a creature such as this. *It continues to slither out of the water like a serpent, colored burnt orange.*

The serpent's most distinctive feature was its large, circular mouth, which opened and closed continuously in a circular manner.

Abe, mesmerized by the display, gathered himself and began to ponder. . . *The beast is rearing up about thirty feet, then randomly driving his head into the ground, which I assume is in search of me. If locating my whereabouts is indeed its aim . . . But why?*

Each time the head plowed into the earth, it left a crater forty feet in diameter and half that distance in depth. This creature was new to Burrus Plax but known to other worlds as a wrangler. Unless Burrus Plax could mount a defense against the wrangler, the planet could unknowingly be doomed due to this single creature.

When the serpent ceased its tirade, Abe scoured the surrounding area. *The destructive power of this one, if it is let loose, could seriously damage Burrus Plax. We must observe this beast closely to see our world is not lost.* From the tree Abe currently occupied, he moved to the absolute top so that his search would not be compromised. He craned his neck upward and brought all of his senses into play.

The sun had risen several hours before Abe awoke, making him realize he had been in this position for nearly twenty-eight hours. He moved his head back and forth to loosen the stiffness.

Must intake nourishment was all Abe brought into his fuzzy mind before attacking the tree that gave him support. Within minutes, the top third of his perch was gone, fueling the creature.

The striped, furry animal scampered down the tree and paused. *I sense one who is in this world, of this world, and a physical part of this world. I am compelled to locate this ambassador who goes by the name of Max and travels with one much smaller than himself.*

Abe slowly turned 360 degrees. *South/southwest would bring me the results I desire.* With that, Abe was gone.

****

The search for this small piece of bronze over an area of thousands of miles, is an impossibility, rage beginning to burn at the futility of his search. Rakke pushed through the water as if it were an enemy until he reached the next egress. *Enough for this search of fools.* Rakke jumped and caught the edge of the round portal. He pulled himself up and out of the tunnel system. "I will continue this search using my intuitive powers . . . if any underling ones who reside inside of me wish to question my decision . . . for your own sake, do not."

One of Rakke's residents lay quietly and then began to snicker. "Do what you will," Hag whispered, "however, your time will come and you will be mine."

"This collective disputes among itself," Vrollic said, "this method will not stand." he continued to follow Rakke at a distance. "Perhaps this division will be my invitation to infiltrate their ranks."

CHAPTER SIXTY-THREE

Dalon Con

It took several thousand feet for Dalon Con to slow down to a safe stop.

"I had a difficult time keeping up with the pace you set," Smort said.

"Ditto and then some," Dune said, panting.

"I will pay closer attention to my speed in the future," Dalon Con replied. He bent over at the waist. "How are we doing?" he asked Sketch and Krabb.

"That were a fast'n," Sketch said.

"I'd ma eyes shut so tight I couldn't see nothin'," Krabb replied.

"May I ask," Azoff said. " I have always been able to move faster than most, but now the speeds I attain have the ability to render me fearful." Even Sketch and Krabb acknowledged the same.

"I believe we have crossed into a planet-wide anomaly, due to the multiple interferences in an arbitrary temporal vortex," Dalon Con said. All but one stared at him with a puzzled look. "The many different interruptions in the timeline on Burrus Plax cause spinoffs of time. When these spinoffs or temporal vortices are interrupted, situations similar to ours may develop." Dalon Con looked at the faces staring back at him. "Does that explanation help?"

"Somewhat," Azoff said.

"I think we should leave it at that," Dune replied. Dalon Con nodded.

"No further explanation was required from your original comment," Smort said, a perplexed expression spreading across his face.

"I thought it was because of these high tech shoes I found," Roane said, lifting one of his feet into the air to give everyone a view.

"How did you acquire these shoes?" Azoff asked.

"I tripped over them while running through the grasslands," Roane said.

"More proof that the timeline is depositing random items across the planet," Dalon Con said.

"Couldn't this constant disturbance, in what you called 'timelines', have detrimental effects on the planet itself?" Azoff asked. When Azoff finished speaking, a rumble began in the distance. In moments, this low rumble had grown into a powerful shaking of the earth, throwing the gathering of travelers about like a handful of twigs.

"I feel sure this event answers your question."

"Affirmative," Azoff bellowed as he bounced end over end past Dalon Con. The quake lasted four minutes, although, to the participants, it seemed like four hours.

"Is everyone all right?" Dalon Con asked as he stood.

A volley of "yeses," filled the air, and then—

"I'm not so sure," Roane groaned.

****

"I found him," Dune yelled, "I cannot detect any injuries at first glance."

Dalon Con, shadowed by the others, knelt to speak with Roane.

"Tell me of your discomfort."

"My left shoulder," Roane said. He moved his right arm, placing his hand on the offended joint. He winced. "Argh . . . that's the one," trying to bring some humor to the situation.

Dalon Con placed a hand on Roane's injured shoulder and slightly moved his arm with his free hand. Roane ground his teeth and closed his eyes, trying not to make a sound.

"Worry not, concerning the state of your manhood," Dalon Con said. "How unfortunate when situations become worse."

"Well, that sure was comforting," Roane said. "You tell a man screaming in pain that it's going to get worse."

"You have to admit," Dune said, "you're not worried about your masculinity."

Smort grabbed his shoulder, his mind racing. *What is masculinity?*

"Calm yourself, Roane," Dalon Con said. "Your shoulder has been dislocated and we must rectify the misalignment."

"Do what you have to," Roane said. "I've had enough pain and am ready to throw my manhood out the window." Dalon Con summoned Dune, Azoff, and Smort to assist him in this medical endeavor.

He instructed Azoff to hold Roane's legs, and Dune and Smort to steady the upper part of Roane's body. "I will count to the sum of three, then realign the joints."

Dalon Con opened his mouth, "One." He stretched and twisted, allowing the ball to pop into the socket, completing the joint again.

"Ahh!" Roane yelled. "That was a far cry from three." He rubbed his shoulder, then moved and twisted his rotator cuff.

"Unusual, though understandable," Azoff said. "Distract the one undergoing the procedure to lessen the pain."

"Are you ready to travel?" Dalon Con inquired. Roane stretched his arm, squeezing different points on his shoulder.

"I believe it will be fine," Roane said. "If I have any trouble along the way, I will let you know."

"Then we will resume our quest," Dalon Con said, and once again was gone.

****

"The daylight wanes," Dalon Con said. "We should take nourishment and converse. As a group that travels together, we should know more of one another."

"It is a bit late to start searching for food," Azoff said.

"Now, don't ya worry one little bit," Sketch said, "cuz this here man kin find food anytime you a wantin' it."

Dalon Con was busy sending a shower of sparks over small pieces of dry wood. As a tiny spark started to grow within the birdnest of tinder, he picked up the bundle and started to blow. "Now, here's where thins get real interestin'." A small tower of smoke rose from the tinder, and as Dalon Con continued to blow, the bundle erupted into a ball of fire.

"And there we go," Dalon Con said. He dropped the ball of tinder, then tossed in twigs to bring the fire up in intensity. Readying the flame to cook, he added larger pieces of wood until the entire area was bathed in a warm, yellow glow. The assembly could not help but clap at the resourcefulness of this young man, dressed so inappropriately.

"There must be sixty pounds of meat on the multiple skewers," Azoff said, saliva dripping from his mouth.

"Dear friends," Dalon Con said, "may I ask you to bow your heads as I thank the Great One for the food we are about to take into our bodies." Everyone lowered their heads, closed their eyes.

"Blessed creator of all things, we thank you for the food you have provided and ask you to be with us during our travels, for danger lurks on each step of our journey. It is in the name of the Living One I make this prayer, Amen. Please, everyone, eat as you will."

****

"I believe that is one of the finest meals I have ever had," Azoff said.

"Sketch done an teld ya that this here man, Mr. Dalon, can cook up some mighty fine chow," Krabb said.

"Thank you, small one. Your appreciation of my food warms me." Dalon Con looked into Azoff's eyes. "Tell me of yourself, large one."

Suddenly, the ground began to tremble.

An effect purposed to render one giddy, split the one into two, then forced the pieces back together, in less than a second, traversed through Dalon Con's brain. He stepped sideways and caught himself, clamping both hands to his head. *I can only assume the same sensation paid a visit to each one of our party in turn.*

He frowned as he glanced toward Smort. *Although I cannot be sure, Smort seems to be the catalyst.*

Dalon Con found himself having to concentrate on the matter at hand. *The impression I received was most certainly a wrinkle in time. Though it may have lasted a fraction of a second, the actual event could have taken hours, days, months, or years.*

Dalon Con paused. *Yes . . . months or even years . . . months or years . . . I cannot remember what the significance of time passage has to do with anything.*

He glanced again toward Smort, bringing about a fleeting memory that dissipated no sooner than it arrived.

CHAPTER SIXTY-FOUR

Hayden and Max

"So what is the going rate for hiring carthons?" Hayden asked.

Max said. "Usually, these creatures work for food."

"That seems harmless," Hayden said. "Do they desire something exotic, or a food source that is difficult to obtain? What exactly do they eat?"

"Bipedal forms of life."

Hayden stared at Max, dumbfounded, and then spoke. "That describes me and the majority of the population on Burrus Plax."

"So we should establish who hired these foul reptiles."

"And as soon as possible," Hayden said.

"I can only assume you have a plan to locate the carthon."

"I do," Max replied. However, it must be done in a roundabout, or even devious, way so as not to arouse the carthon's suspicious nature or give their employers any reason to think someone is onto them. This may result in using tactics I would not normally consider."

"Could these tactics result in the death of another?"

"Yes, which is why this plan weighs heavy on my heart. But it is necessary. For not to do this could jeopardize the population and the entire planet."

"If I ever trusted anyone, it would be you, Max. You can always count on me, as I know I could expect the same from you."

"Then tell me what is bothering you."

"What makes you think you are qualified to diagnose my problems?" Hayden snapped.

Max went quiet, continuing his journey. After several minutes, he said, "I must apologize, small one. I have no right to delve into what you consider to be private matters. I found myself concerned about your well-being."

"I am the one who should apologize for it is nothing you have done, but rather guilt that drives my demeanor."

"Forgive my prying, but what do you have inside that brings about such feelings?"

"My very presence here," Hayden said. "for I fear my temporal travel may have caused problems that, without me, would not exist, including lifelong friends that have turned to darkness."

"Listen to me," Max said, "for I speak the truth." The giant stared into Hayden's tiny eyes. *Thanks be to the Great One, who allows visualization of my precious cargo as long as I maintain physical contact.* "Until our journey is complete, we cannot know whether your presence here is for good, bad, or of no consequence." Hayden's eyes began to well. "Until this time has concluded, we *will* not know, and for that matter, may never know your place in this circumstance.

"I sense that your participation is by design, and, therefore, centered in good," Max continued. "As for your comrades, we all have choices to make and are responsible for what arises due to those choices."

"Thank you for your confidence. Perhaps I should channel my energy toward the situation at hand, rather than my own problems."

Suddenly, Max jerked, feeling a small plug of earth snatched from his back. Hayden, feeling the offense, spoke to Max.

"What happened? I sensed, damage to your body—almost like a dream."

"There it is again." Max slid his arm toward his back again. "I do believe that I have the culprit." Locked in his grip was a two-foot-long, straight beak. "A carthon digging into my back." With a quick snap, he released the dead reptile. A squall echoed from above as the two remaining carthons mourned their brother. "This will take place for a short time before they leave, no doubt in search of their employer."

"How did the reptile manage to get this deep underground?"

"We have been making our way to the surface. The rate at which I was traveling was no doubt too slow for you to experience."

"Since you killed the flying reptile. I've noticed a sharp turn to the left."

"I am tracking the two reptiles who remain," Max said.

"I remember, you mentioned the remaining two carthon were headed to their employer . . . for what reason?"

"The statement I made was purely conjecture. The reptiles in question tend to have a vile disposition." Max extended his arm, curled his hand into a fist, and destroyed a large boulder directly in his path.

"As I said, the carthon's disposition leaves much to be desired. It takes little to make them angry and little more to bring about a physical altercation. When we killed their companion, there was little sympathy but fierce anger.

"You see, these creatures receive no profit for exhibiting sympathy," Max said, "and their anger arises from the fact that the dead carthon is no longer able to work for remuneration."

"A sad existence."

Max began slowing his forward speed.

"Have we arrived so soon?"

"I want you to remain very quiet while I break through the surface."

"Be careful," Hayden said. Max smiled.

"Worry not, small one." Hayden felt himself moving upward, then coming to a stop. After a short pause, he detected a slight upward movement that could only be Max penetrating the surface.

****

Max moved toward the surface, stopping momentarily when he reached the last few inches of crust. Then, his head flattened as he penetrated the last layers of soil, concealing it as it spread while canvassing an area four feet in diameter.

"The light is beginning to wane; however, there is nothing unusual to see, save for what one would normally expect."

Max returned to his usual self and rose until he was standing on the ground.

"Come forth, small one." He opened the hand that had been pressed tight to his chest. As soon as all was clear, Hayden took to the air, elated to feel the fresh breeze on his face.

"It is good to see you, small one, knowing how badly you wished to leave the confinement of my hand." Max raised the usual perch, and Hayden gladly landed in his friend's open hand.

"I am bothered greatly," Hayden said. "Being within your care, especially wrapped in your hands, is normally a great comfort to me. But this time, an intense feeling of anxiety and a desire to escape overwhelmed me."

"I believe what you were experiencing is claustrophobia, brought about by too much time spent within the confines of my hands. This last trip was our longest yet. These periods of confinement have culminated in bringing about these feelings you are experiencing."

"Your words do much to calm my fears. I will feel more at home the next—."

And with that, Hayden was gone.

CHAPTER SIXTY-FIVE

Dalon Con

Dalon Con returned to his position without anyone noticing his absence.

"Any idea of what caused the violent shaking we experienced?" Azoff asked.

"There are many possibilities," Dalon Con, said, "though nothing definite."

"I see," Azoff said, the concern of deception evident in his reply. "There is something not quite right with this one; however, I sense no malice or malevolence." Azoff studied Dalon Con, unable to break through his wall of thought. "Strange," the furry one said, "all I am able to detect is affection for all." Azoff shook his head and began to pursue other avenues.

"What exactly are we looking for?" Roane asked, his voice just above a whisper.

"Not sure," Azoff said, "you would glean more information asking the one called Dalon Con."

****

As the party moved forward, Smort slowed, dallying several steps behind. He continued this pace, taking care not to lag further back to avoid raising any suspicion.

"What is this?" Smort muttered, confusion shrouding his very words. He extended both hands partially in front, his arms bent at the elbows and his fingers curled into a claw-like image. His palms hung in the air several feet apart, facing one another as each exuded a minuscule vibration. *The malevolent basis on which I was formed has come to claim its own, and yet the veil of good has begun its reach into my soul and desires to retrieve the lost. Hmm, I wonder what shall become of me . . . this is something of which I have never before entertained so much as a thought . . . then this is the first instance anyone has cared.* This scenario continued unresolved and unseen.

****

"What we are looking for," Dalon Con said in his regular voice, startling all present, "is anything that does not fit in this setting, no matter how small or insignificant it may seem."

"It seems you fellers is takin' on Mr. Dalon like he be the bad un," Sketch said. "Let me tells ya, this here's sumthin' ya don't wanna be adoin'."

"He done an took good care 'o' me an ma buddy Sketch," Krabb said, "and ya can betcha he be doin' the same fer you if you let'em." Krabb paused a moment, scratching his beard. "But jest like Sketch said, ya don't wanna go agin'em, and that's all I gots ta say."

"Azoff," Dalon Con said, "if you feel there is something we should discuss, or if there is a question of trust, then bring it to me and we will talk it through. Keeping suspicion to yourself only tends to multiply ill will and brings unfounded concerns to everyone involved."

"Forgive my actions," Azoff said. "Though we try not to be, my species is leery by nature, resulting from the negative connotation we have received during simple bedtime stories adults have told their children for thousands of years." Azoff looked around at all gathered. "It certainly is not my intention to mistrust those I do not know; however, many times a candle was used along with these bedtime stories."

A slight murmur echoed through the assembly.

"This seems simple enough," Azoff continued, "but the candle has ties with the Nexus. So often we pass judgement upon those before we know their true circumstances."

"Now I must apologize to you," Dalon Con said.

"That is not necessary.

"When one wrongs another, you are right. To forgive is not a necessity, it is a command. This is not from me, but the Great One." Dalon Con paused and then spoke. "I will leave this for you to ponder. We must be about our passage into Rash."

****

Dalon Con knelt beside Dune, away from the others.

"Going by what you stated earlier," Dune said, "I would categorize this as something that does not fit in with these particular surroundings." The two men were looking at a hollow, clear tube about eight inches long and three-eighths of an inch in diameter. "One end is pointed with a removable blue cap, and the other dons a flat, blue insert." Dune rolled the object around in his hands. "If you look closely, you can see a smaller tube within the outer casing that seems to be filled with a dark, colored liquid." He handed the object to Dalon Con.

Dalon Con removed the cap. "See this." He held the tube between his index and middle finger, and as he moved the point around his palm, it left a blue line everywhere it touched his hand. "I would certainly say this qualifies as outside of what would be considered normal for this area."

"Then we are on the right track?" Dune asked.

"We are indeed," Dalon Con agreed. He placed a hand on Dune's back. "You have done well. It is now time for you to leave."

"I do not understand," Dune said. "Am I not here to assist?"

"In more ways than you know," Dalon Con said. "Look down this rarely seen corridor." Dalon Con extended a finger to give Dune a starting point.

"Which way do I go, and how will I know if I'm in the right?" Dune asked.

“Worry not, for the Great One will guide you and keep you safe in your travels.” Dune stood tall before Dalon Con.

“I am learning to understand,” Dune said, “but it feels like it will be a long journey before I am there.”

“Talk to the Great One as you would a friend, and in all cases, follow His instruction.

We will meet again,” Dalon Con said. He placed an item into his ward’s palm, squeezing his hands tightly around Dune’s fist. “Guard this well. You will know when the time is right to employ the article.” The old man’s arms dropped to his side. Dune nodded then slipped away, with no eyes upon him other than Dalon Con’s.

The old man traveling as an impromptu thirty something moved toward the others to show them the writing implement he had discovered. He spent a good amount of time explaining the piece, giving Dune an extended interval to leave.

Thank you, Great One, for dulling the senses of each one here, including the two attached to my legs, concerning the remembrance of the one called Dune. Dalon Con began to mingle with the others, all searching for anomalies within different areas of Rash. “Here.” Dalon Con said in a loud whisper. All present began to gather around Dalon Con.

“What have you to show us?” Azoff asked.

“I detect the sound of many workers behind this door,” Dalon Con said.

“Shall we enter?” Roane asked.

“First, we need reconnaissance,” Dalon Con said.

****

Smort’s arms dropped to his side, his eyes immediately drawn to Dalon Con. Smort’s gaze moved to each one in the party.

“No one is moving . . . not a single one.” He encircled each member before being enticed to leave. *I do not recall seeing a hallway this clear of shank limbs as to be able to stroll unabated down its length.*

"Well, it appears you made our rendezvous point with no trouble at all," Drade said. Smort's skin tightened and the large man jumped ever so slightly, startled at the unexpected greeting.

"Apparently so," Smort replied, "assuming your statement is true simply because you say it is true."

"I like a man who speaks his mind." Drade finished his statement with a hearty chuckle, "and yes I speak the truth, for no other reason than the truth is what I have spoken."

"Give a subject its mind and it will go on forever." Smort eyed the small Odobi. "I will assume that we are meeting at your predetermined place . . . now what?"

"Your assumption is correct, but first things first. I am called Drade and a proud member of the Odobi clan. We set out to reinstate time travel and construct a functional portal to use as a place of departure."

"What was the reason to reinstate time travel," Smort asked, "it seems the confusion it may trigger in and of itself would cause one to most certainly shy away."

"Not if done correctly, which is what we planned. You see ours was a benevolent society, and our only interest in the preservation of society's run amuck." Drade invited Smort to take a seat in one of two chairs they happened upon, as they slowly made their way, much to Smort's surprise down the hallway.

"We would find a world in trouble, having lost morals, regard for life, cleanliness or any situation that would led to a planetary collapse," Drade said.

Smort massaged the beard on his chin, a doubtful expression crossed his face. "How has this plan played out for you?"

Drade nodded, in sync with his new companion. "Slow at first; however, the new plan sails along smoothly."

"Please explain."

"I'll do better than that, I will show you." Drade rose from his seat, "This way."

CHAPTER SIXTY-SIX

Max and Abe

"I feel as though I have been looking for a creature of the mind, one that bears no physical characteristics, but haunts those with a mental upheaval." Abe scampered around, not knowing which way to go. "Perhaps I *have* lost my mind." he slumped, then dropped to the ground.

"I find that highly unlikely," Max said.

"Who," Abe stammered, making a dozen or more 360 degree turns, "who speaks to me, yet I cannot see?" A great mound of earth, its hand partially inserted into its abdomen, began an upsurge.

Abe's eyebrows rose. "Well, that is one answer and a very good one, I might add."

"I am always appreciative," Max said, "when talking with an individual who has mastered the art of humor." Max paused momentarily. "I myself have little use for it, the main reason being that I am no good at the personal expression of amusement; however, I hope to get better as time passes."

"You are the one I have been destined to meet for quite some time," Abe said, "but am only realizing this to actually take place at this moment."

"Now that we have met," Max said, "where do we proceed from here?"

"This does not seem right," Abe said. "How could I know the answer to your question when we have only just met . . . and yet *I do*." Abe stared into the kind eyes of Max.

"First, I would like you to meet a friend of mine," Max said. He extended his hand, palm up and spoke. “Join us.” Abe leapt onto Max’s outstretched hand. He faced a biped much smaller than himself. This small one is just over a quarter of an inch tall. “Meet Hayden.”

“Pleasure to meet you,” Hayden said, “I have heard of one set aside and called The Guardian, but moreover seen or experienced the result of your sonic blast.”

“This tiny creature is nearly too small to see,” Abe said, “much less, make out any detail, but I will try.” He moved his right eye closer to Hayden. “What strange manner of creature are you?”

“He is one of the many who are directly responsible for bringing time travelers to Burrus Plax,” Max said, “not the initiator, mind you, but one of the pawns in the overall plan.”

“Then he deserves no punishment,” Abe replied. “You said there were many responsible for bringing temporal travelers to Burrus Plax–what of the others?”

“As unfortunate as it seems,” Max said, “they are lost in time.”

“You mentioned pawns,” Abe said. “Are these others lost in a temporal prison because of time travel?”

“You are very close,” Max said. “There were originally eighteen travelers sent to Burrus Plax under the guise of discovering the reason for the fall of this world. In their minds, they wanted to prevent this catastrophe from overtaking other worlds.”

“Noble cause—” Abe said, “something must have gone awry.”

“Time travel had been outlawed many years previous,” Max said, “however, they felt this endeavor important enough to bypass this long ordained law.”

“So, they convinced these eighteen Odobi scientists,” Abe interrupted, “to perfect temporal travel from the old transcripts. This allowed them to travel to Burrus Plax and take whatever time necessary to erect a temporal portal as a base to travel to and from.”

“If not to prevent this same tragedy from happening to other worlds,” Max said, “what was the motive for invading Burrus Plax?”

“Of that,” Abe said, “I am not sure.”

"Resources!" Max exclaimed, "this planet has been blessed with valuable natural resources like no other!"

"What do you mean?" Hayden said.

"Remember the tunnels that were carved by the thack?" Max asked.

"Of course," Abe said, "the material used to coat the interior cave walls was none other than jeweled stone. Because this substance existed nowhere else in this or any other universe, nor was it a natural material, it is available solely on Burrus Plax. "

"It also absorbed light and then dispersed the luminescence throughout the tunnel system." Abe and Hayden sat quietly attempting to understand what they had just heard and seen.

"The vastness of this place will turn you into a babbling idiot if you allow it to do so." Max said. "There is no way to understand, so pay no attention to the mind-numbing drivel with which the evil one fills this place. Rather, focus on the Great One and follow his instruction."

"How?" Abe asked.

"The one of evil spreads chaos and uncertainty," Max said, "while the Great One will inundate you with peace, comfort and a sense of what he wishes you to do."

"For the first time I feel as though I have no purpose," Abe said.

"You have a purpose," Max said. "It may be that it has changed. In fact, I may be able to help you reestablish your purpose."

"How?" Abe asked. "The reason for my existence for millennia was to guard the system of tunnels."

"Are there no other talents you possess?" Hayden inquired.

"There are indeed," Abe said, "powers of defense."

"I would ask you to join Hayden and travel along with us to our next destination," Max said.

"Which is?" Abe asked.

"Being a bit hard to describe," Max said, "we will avoid wasting time with an explanation that can be given while traveling."

"I will allow this," Abe said. Max pressed his hand partially into his abdomen, sank into the ground and then was off.

****

After many miles of travel, Max forced his way through the planet's crust.

"You have a powerful gift," Abe said, "being able to move at such a great rate of speed through any material which happens to make up the section of underground we are traveling through."

"Where are we?" Hayden asked. "I sense dusk is soon to arrive."

"We are a short distance from one of the many tunnel entrances," Max said.

"What is the reason for being in this place?" Abe asked.

"Tomorrow, at first light," Max said, "I will show you an adversary from a distance, as we do not want to confront such an opponent alone."

"Why should we not attack this enemy now," Abe questioned, "under the cover of darkness?"

"This one is made from several malevolent beings," Max said. "It possesses senses that are able to detect the slightest attempts by beings to use deception to move in close."

"Perhaps, waiting until the break of light would be best," Abe said.

"We will take this notion into consideration," Max said. "Tomorrow would be the best time for the intake of nourishment and hydration, if either of you have a notion to do so." He lowered his hand flat to the ground. Abe scampered off the large hand, while Hayden hovered behind.

CHAPTER SIXTY-SEVEN

Dalon Con

"As I have told you, Azoff is my name and I am a proud member of a clan known as the thack." The rodent carved out a shallow depression to make himself comfortable. "How unfortunate that the majority of you believe the thack to be a bloodthirsty group of murderous beings that would abscond with children during the night, when, in fact, we are a kind and helpful species who have made Burrus Plax our home since its beginning."

"What gave rise to the vicious untruths circulated about your kind?" Dalon Con asked.

"The Nexus," Azoff replied. "A weapon with intelligence, set on assimilating the minds of children who reside on Burrus Plax." Azoff smiled. "Yet, this proved to be an impossibility, and the Nexus was forced to acquire a partner." Unaware of his actions, Azoff began to carve a ditch into a piece of sandstone that was buried in the ground beneath his right forelimb.

Roane leaned forward with his elbows on his knees and his fists planted securely on the bottom of each jaw line. "And what did it find?"

"A nearly invisible line within itself with one purpose," Azoff said. "To attach itself to one called the Other."

"Why has it not yet wielded, what I assume to be, great power?" Roane asked.

"Once the Nexus and the Other meld, and I assume they have, certain other powerful aspects of Burrus Plax must be dealt with beforehand," Dalon Con said.

"I been done sittin' here listenin' to ya folks gab," Krabb said, "an I got me somethin' to say." He took a boney index finger and rubbed it under his nose relieving a pesky itch. "There's this other feller nobody's speakin' on. Now when I was a yearlin', I didn't get no stories afore ma bedtime that had critters what kilt ya whilst ya was asleepin'. No siree, bobcat tail. We got nice stories that heped us get ta sleep." Krabb scratched his head. "That's it," he said with recognition. "We had us this great big feller I was tellin' ya 'bout." Krabb stared into the distance.

"What's he doing?" Roane asked.

"He be thunkin'," Sketch said. "Boy, some 'o' you city slickers would git bit by a can seeum with your eyes wide open in the noonday sun."

"I got'er goin' on, I'm here ta tell ya," Krabb exclaimed, bursting into the conversation. "I 'member it real good." He danced a little jig reliving a portion of his excitement and then sat down and began to speak. "We had us whatcha might call a friendly giant. Mama an Daddy would tell us stories 'bout this giant named Max. Oh, there was all kinda ventures and anythin' ya could think 'o' we dreamed 'bout with our best friend, Max."

"An don't you dare ferget 'bout them two little fellers that rode along with Max," Sketch said.

"Ha, ha, hee," Krabb said, slapping the outside thigh on his right leg, "I 'member like it were yesterday. Them two fellers what rode with Max was Hayden an Abe. Boy, what times we did have." Krabb's face began to droop as his thoughts of yesteryears faded and the present began to intrude.

"Yessir," Sketch said, "thems was the days."

"Thank you, small ones." Dalon Con frowned and commenced surveying what he could see in the darkness and what he could sense. "I must ask a question concerning all of you. Does anyone feel as though something has been taken, or perhaps, is just amiss?"

"I feel much the same," Azoff said.

"This notion began growing within me shortly after we came together as one," Dalon Con said. All assembled began to affirm Dalon Con's suspicions. "Please halt your murmurings and bring about quiet." Dalon Con's hand rose and his eyes closed. After several minutes, something struck the ground hard enough to bring trees down and send the group sprawling.

"I'm gettin' a mite tired at all this here ruckus we got goin' on 'round here," Krabb said.

"We must find the source of the commotion," Dalon Con said. "It is of the utmost importance."

"Why all the excitement?" Gabriel asked.

"Gabriel!" Dalon Con said, his voice full of delight. "Where have you been?" Dalon Con reached out to hold him.

"I don't understand," Gabriel replied, "I've been right here."

"Now that you have returned," Dalon Con said, "our timeline is re-established, which allows our correct memories to return."

"Gabriel, you were with us until a short time after our two groups became one," Azoff said. "Your movement through multiple timelines caused the thunderous grounding as you struck the planet's surface."

"I be right good with numbers," Sketch said, "an I figger ya been gone two and a piece of a day."

"Is that possible?" Gabriel asked, looking at Dalon Con.

"Apparently, it is," Dalon Con replied. "For the numbers that Sketch quote are correct."

"I checked the numbers more than once," Roane said, "and they corroborate that you have been absent for two and a half days."

"The Odobi must be experimenting with temporal influences on Burrus Plax," Dalon Con said.

"Unfortunately, something they know nothing about," Azoff said.

"What in this here world is we gonna do?" Krabb asked.

"Continue on to Rash," Dalon Con said. "Though not the place with the highest advanced technology, at least it is connected to the other two cities, one being a former settlement."

****

"Somehow, I just knowd it," Krabb said. "We'd end up back here at this wretched place." The assembly stood staring at the shank trees marking the entrance into Rash.

"No need standing here staring," Azoff said. "Remembering our last time at this place, would you care to lead, Dalon Con?"

"Thank you," Dalon Con said. He stepped into the destroyed shank trees that Azoff had flattened earlier.

"Gabriel," Dalon Con said, "to me." Gabriel increased his pace until he was walking beside Dalon Con. They made their way down the cobblestone street surrounded by dilapidated buildings and the same blue aura that covered the whole.

"Hold on tight," Sketch said to Krabb. "Member what Mr. Dalon telled us?"

"Yeah, I 'member," Krabb said.

"I made the noise they were talking of upon my return?" Gabriel asked.

"Indeed, you did," Dalon Con said. "You see, the size of material that travels through time causing a temporal disturbance matters not. You or a pebble would bring forth an identical force." Gabriel pondered Dalon Con's words for a moment.

"There must be more important things to devote our time to," Gabriel said.

"Exactly what I wanted to hear," Dalon Con said, "and I would like to begin with what you remember. Now, listen closely and follow what I ask. If you have any questions, it is of the utmost importance that you ask them of me." Dalon Con peered into Gabriel's eyes. "Do you understand?" Gabriel nodded. "What do you recall within the two and a half day period we experienced your absence?"

"I recall everything and I recall nothing," Gabriel said. "One of the events seems like nothing, but is everything to me."

"Please convey this experience," Dalon Con said.

"I know that we as a group dined on cabot," Gabriel replied.

"You should know that I cannot confirm that statement," Dalon Con said.

"I know that I myself did not," Gabriel said.

"This statement I am able to confirm," Dalon Con said, "for you were not there dining with us."

"What I have said," Gabriel replied, "and what you have said," nodding in Dalon Con's direction, "we know to be true statements. However, with my ravenous appetite and inability to go an extended time without eating, how is it that I remain satiated?"

"You obviously dined on something, with or without us present." Dalon Con said. "Once you were pulled into a parallel timeline, you were held until it was no longer possible."

"What do you mean 'no longer possible'?" Gabriel asked.

"All timelines have a life span," Dalon Con said. "Once yours ran its course, you had no choice but to return to this timeline."

"Why was I pulled into this parallel timeline that contained such a short life span?" Gabriel asked. Dalon Con rubbed his chin, deep in thought.

"An entity exists that is trying to eradicate each one of us," Dalon Con said. "This entity managed to isolate you by placing your current existence within a shortened timeline, hoping the end of the timeline would also be the end of you. As you can see, this approach failed."

"What about the next attempt?" Gabriel asked.

"That remains a mystery," Dalon Con said.

CHAPTER SIXTY-EIGHT

Hayden and Max

"Hayden, where are you? Have you been taken, if so, who dares perpetrate such an act of cowardice?" Max roared. He pulled his hand away from his abdomen. "Remain within my hand for your own safety while I search for the one called Hayden." Abe nodded. Max placed his hand over the furry reptilian and readied himself to fight.

"The one you call Hayden is unable to speak," a crowish voice cackled. "The one you just held in your hand, you will now have to mount a search for in order to discover if this tiny one still breathes." Max knew the perpetrator had moved from north to south when he snatched Hayden, even if his speed had been incalculable. With a maddening scream, Max dove into the ground, bursting the sonic barrier six separate times before he could no longer be heard.

****

Max could sense the presence of the voice, which he assumed was that of the avian, close by. He slowed his forward speed, gauging by the avian's taunts. Having calmed himself, he made ready for an attack from these infuriating creatures.

"Here he comes, here he comes," the enraging voice echoed. Many others, who were with the one sounding off, began to lend their voices to the oddly mind-numbing lyrics.

"I dare not enter what I perceive to be a cavern or some such grotto," Max said. "I fear the voices would drive me to the brink of insanity." He ran his fingers over the ceiling just inches above his head. "I believe this material may be helpful." Configuring his hand so that his fingers and thumb were pointing straight outward, he placed his fingertips against the ceiling, sensing the hardest rock formation.

Once found, he held his digits there, allowing them to change into the same material. He began to twist his hand to the left, then back to the right, applying pressure as he did so. "With each turn, I see an inch or more of powdered material falling out. When I am through, I will see if I can compose a song that will be as enjoyable to them as theirs has been to me." Shortly after uttering these words, he detected the bottom of the hole, thinning considerably. With one more turn, his hand burst through.

The space once occupied by Max alone filled with a deafening, melodic squall until Max placed his mouth over the opening. He sent a single note into the chamber that cracked the stone ceiling and silenced the avians forever. Then, Max pushed his arm into the breach he'd bored into the rock and removed one of the offending creatures.

"Curious—this creature seems to have nothing organic about it, rather, a body formed seemingly from one-inch-square, hollow, metal tubing." Oval-shaped, it was six inches long and four inches wide, with one open end. It was colored black and covered in tufts of thin, metal strands.

With no warning, an eight-foot-long, sixteen-inch-wide, four-inch-thick piece of black glass shot out of the hole producing an earthquake, bringing a good bit of the cracked ceiling with it. Max searched for a way to open the new arrival until it fell to pieces, leaving one small biped with a device hung over its shoulders that allowed it to fly.

"I was not sure if I would ever see you again," Hayden said, "but allow me to say that it is hard to contain my feelings, now that I have laid eyes on you once more."

"I feel much the same way, small one. Can you tell me of your exploits while you were gone?"

"There is very little I am able to relay, it is as though I was here for everything, yet here for nothing."

"Someone or something is trying to destroy you."

"This makes no sense, Max. I have done nothing to anyone."

"Let us look at this logically. I am impervious to attack," Max said. "At least until this moment, I have faced nothing that could harm me. This does not mean there are entities or anomalies I have yet to meet that cannot do me great harm; however, as I have said, this has not been the case so far."

"Redundancy will not help solve this problem," Hayden said.

"Neither will sarcasm," Max replied.

Hayden hung his head low. "Please pardon my actions. The thought that someone would want to eliminate me is overwhelming."

"I am afraid you are not the only one. What we are commiserating was a failed attempt on your life."

"Do you think that will be the last, or will there be more?"

"The attempt you experienced was a test. I can only assume that the large, rectangular, object you were incased in was a shortened timeline. When this timeline ended, you should have also, but that was not the case."

"Why would someone choose this method to eliminate another?" Hayden inquired.

"As near as I can tell, if this form of execution were viable, once the timeline was destroyed, it would be like the one trapped within had never existed," Max said. "However, I can tell you with much certainty that this has been tried before and with ones in our timeline."

"How could you possibly know so much about what has transpired, without so much as a clue to begin with?"

"The large capsule you arrived in burst into shards shortly after you slammed into the ground. These shards range in size from that of a normal man to microscopic. We assimilate the smallest of pieces into our bodies through breathing as well as absorbing these minerals by way of a simple touch.

“But once these particles enter our body and become a part of what we are,” Max said, “these bits and pieces integrate into our thought process and show us things we otherwise would not know.”

“So you determined through integrating outside sources with our own, what occurred with the failed assassination attempt aimed at me.”

“Very good, small one. We have spent much time away from our original quest. We must now locate the two remaining carthon and track them to their employer.”

“What if they have already reached their destination?”

“We are forced to wait and see where they lie when we reach *our* destination, which I believe will be one and the same,” Max said.

****

The two remaining carthon circled around the top of a plateau. Rakke burrowed up through the elevated earthen works, stopping short of its flattened top.

“Why have we stopped?” Jack asked. “If we are to confront the employers of the carthon, we must not stop until they are found; however location is the easy part of this plan, elimination is where the difficulty lies. Just below the surface of a one hundred foot high plateau is a twelve-foot-tall human-like hybrid, constructed from organic flesh and a malleable metal. What you cannot see is what resides within the heart and mind of the beast, called Rakke. Inside of this monster lies the essence of a young man, Jack, held initially from his attraction to the Nexus; however soon after his abduction the desire for release overcame any hold the nexus claimed.”

“Why do you bother us with useless information?” Hag said.

“Because the carthon employer are just that,” Jack said.

“Just what?” Torast asked.

“The carthon are self-employed,” Jack said, “and leaving this area for what is perceived a more profitable destination.”

****

Sim studied the flora and fauna for what stretched into hours. He blinked several times, breaking from his reverie, and failing to notice the bronze disc he clutched was sending wave after wave of peace through Sim's soul, preparing him for future events. *I make no excuses pretending to understand the changes taking place within, only that I am to be allied with one of this world, Max and ultimately the Great One.*

CHAPTER SIXTY-NINE

Dalon Con

"Mr. Dalon, me an Sketch is rite good at that stuff you wuz a talkin' 'bout," Krabb said.

"Do you mean reconnaissance?" Dalon Con asked.

"That thars 'xactly what I be sayin'," Sketch said. Dalon Con met privately with the two small men, then turned to speak to the remainder of the gathering.

"After meeting with these two brave men," Dalon Con said. "I am convinced that they are the best equipped to take on this challenge of reconnaissance, both because of their size and the knowledge they possess." With that, the two men were gone.

"Is there any way we may assist?" Azoff asked.

"None up till now," Dalon Con said, "however, that could change."

****

"Any idea where we is agoin'?" Krabb asked his traveling companion, having just matched Sketch's speed.

"I gots me a mighty small one," Sketch said, "but it comes from Mr. Dalon, so's I is gonna take it purdy serious." Sketch led Krabb through miles of cobblestone corridors until they entered an area where most of the bricks had been ripped from the building faces. "Foller me close, cuz I'm headed up right quick."

Sketch made an upward turn, scaling the front of the partially destroyed buildings. Krabb followed, making the same vertical turn. After several minutes, the two were traveling smoothly across the face of the building. They appeared to be seasoned performers moving in unison, across, around, and, where possible, through obstacles. A half hour had passed when Sketch began to slow.

"Krabb, this a way," Sketch said, disappearing into a small notch cut into the face of the building.

He continued through the tunnel for quite some time before seeing adjacent roads with intersections at regular intervals. Then, without warning, he found himself tumbling and sliding at a great rate of speed.

Sketch landed in soft grass, surrounded by buildings. Seconds later, a second small body rolled to a stop beside Sketch.

"Well, 'magine meetin' you here."

"Good ta see ya," Sketch said. "I thunked I'd lost ya."

"Take more then that. So, where we goes from here?"

"Mr. Dalon told me ifin I got this fer, ta look fer another small hole, down low and surrounded by green." The two men began to scan the area.

"I think I just mighta fount what we is alookin' fer. Foller me." Krabb took off with Sketch just behind, stopping at a small, square opening nearly obstructed by the overgrown foliage.

Sketch moved through the opening, signaling for Krabb to follow. When Krabb's eyes got used to the dark space, he saw Sketch scraping away mortar, attempting to remove a brick.

"I 'bout got it," Sketch said. "Jest a few more and I gets'er out."

"Gets what out?"

"Somethin' real valuable, 'cordin' to Dalon Con. "See thar, we gots it now." Krabb helped Sketch remove the brick, which produced a thud when it hit the ground.

Krabb retrieved what appeared to be a thumb-sized piece of glass from inside the brick. "We better git." He pushed it into his pocket, and then headed toward the opening and back to Dalon Con.

****

"Right on time," Dalon Con said. "In fact, several minutes early."

"How in this world," Krabb said, speaking to Dalon Con, "would thar be any way you could know all that?"

"There are ways," Dalon Con said with a wide grin, "just as you possess your own."

"Mine ain't quite as fancy as yourn," Krabb said, "but they work."

"Would you care to explain?" Dalon Con asked.

"I'd worm me a way to get where I wants ta get, then I'd go thar," Krabb said.

"In this way it would not have worked for the task," Dalon Con replied. "I received advanced information, reconnaissance. I acted upon this advance information by trusting its source, and what I sought was found."

"What is this here little blue rock?" Krabb asked.

"That trinket was given to me by my grandson," Dalon Con said. "It has been many a year by now." Dalon Con turned the tear-drop-shaped object around in his hands, then held the object up to the sun and admired the cobalt blue color that filtered through the smooth object. "He was living on the planet, Aon. Caladium, that is what he called it. My grandson cited it may be of assistance someday. He made several other comments, but they elude me amidst what we are facing now." He pushed the object into his inside coat pocket and patted the nugget of Caladium from the outside. "Would not want to lose such a souvenir."

"You mean we risked our lives so that you could recover a keepsake from one of your relatives?" Roane seethed.

"It is true," Dalon Con replied, "that I retrieved a present from my grandson, but in no way did I put this group in danger for such an insignificant thing." His booming voice deepened before he spoke. "I provide many areas of assistance for those around me. Your insinuation that I have put others in danger will not stand."

Roane backed away from Dalon Con. "I spoke before all was known; please, forgive me."

"Let it be," Dalon Con said, noticeably rattled by the experience. "We will continue to search the dead city of Rash." He took the lead, followed by Azoff, Gabriel, and Roane.

"One name is trying to work its way back into my consciousness," Dalon Con said.

"Let's hear this name," Gabriel replied.

Dalon Con shook his head. "Once I know, so shall you."

****

"*Dead* city is becoming more appropriate with each block we travel," Azoff said.

"From the scene that appears before us," Dalon Con replied, "your statement contains more truth with each step we take." Suddenly, Dalon Con stiffened. "Stop!" but the words came too late. Each one, save for Sketch and Krabb who traveled with Dalon Con, took a different path.

"Looks like that dad gum tempral crook be lookin' 'round agin," Sketch said. "Don't you reckon he get tired 'o' botherin' us?"

Dalon Con stood atop a round stone, twelve inches in diameter and just over eighty feet in height.

"Mr. Dalon," Krabb said, "they be some mighty big spiders crawlin' up this here pole, and I reckon they got them chompers set on us."

"H-How's we gonna git down?" Sketch stammered. "Everwhere their little bitty feet hit the stone pole, a crack runs from where that foot touched." After numerous taps, the stone tower crumbled, sending the trio plummeting toward a stone floor eighty feet below.

****

Azoff stood on a stunning blue beach, the waves gently lapping at his feet. Suddenly, he felt a light tug on his back. "Hey, down there!" Roane shouted, sliding down Azoff's side. The human marveled at the creature's soft, slippery fur, slicked with seawater. Azoff made a swift quarter turn, sending Roane sprawling to the sand, caught in the gust of Azoff's movement.

"Many apologies," Azoff said, "I did not expect such a violent reaction from a mere turn." He extended a paw.

Before Roane could reach safety beside Azoff, a nine-hundred-foot tsunami surged from the calm ocean, just twenty-five thousand yards away, racing toward them at four hundred miles per hour.

****

Dalon Con's plight shifted, and again, he found himself in the temporal thief's scenario, this time with Gabriel—free-falling toward the earth.

"It is good to see you," Dalon Con yelled to Gabriel. "Though our circumstances are less than favorable."

"How can you be so calm?" Gabriel replied over the roar of the wind that whipped at the old man's robe, exposing two equally terrified men clinging onto Dalon Con. "What do we do now?"

Below them lay several miles of sky with cirrus clouds obscuring the pathway down.

"I don't know how much longer we have." Then, Gabriel offered a tender smile to his friend just seconds before impact.

****

Seven individuals were unceremoniously deposited through the ceiling into a different part of the tunnel system.

"Who's up for that again?" Roane asked, his voice wreaking with sarcasm.

"I go with ya," an excited Krabb replied. "Yes sir, I go with ya as many times ya wanna go, ceptin that tempral crook gots ta stay behind."

Dalon Con said. "The pitfalls we have overcome lead me to believe the Great One has played a large part in our success."

"You started to tell us 'bout this here Great One," Sketch said. "How 'bout now? The darks are acomin' on and Mr. Dalon kin whip up some cabot, then we be set ta gab a while."

"That be cabot ya be asmellin', an she's cookin' up already," Sketch said.

"Please," Dalon Con offered, "seat yourself and we shall eat." Everyone vocally agreed and began to fill themselves.

"What is this?" Azoff said, looking up from his plate made from peeled bark. "Everyone has a steady flow of food, yet Dalon Con is the only one serving."

"Do not stop eating," Dalon Con said. "Service is a large part of the Great One's message."

"Well, I gots me a idea that I done an had me nuff to et," Krabb said. "Let's get ta gabbin'."

Dalon Con said nothing to introduce his subject matter; he just began to speak.

"The Great One is our creator; in fact, he created everything seen and unseen." Dalon Con became more animated as he continued to speak. "He even blessed us with the Living One to cover our transgressions with his blood."

"You're going to stand there and tell me I was created by something I can't see?" Roane questioned. "You may as well tell me I was pulled out of a creek full of mud," finishing his sentence with a chuckle.

"Well, I done an seen this here Great One do some mighty powerful stuff, ifin ya wants ma two cent's worth," Sketch said.

"I know Dalon Con," Gabriel said. "This man has not a lie within him, and I trust him with my life. As for the Great One, he has worked miracles in my life. So, do not talk down to my friend, Dalon Con, and beware not accepting the many gifts offered by the Great One." Azoff stood and did his best impression of a thack trying to shrug as Roane stood beside the four-legged creature.

"I would be happy to entertain any questions," Dalon Con said.

"Whelst, I gots me one," Krabb said, "cuz I'd like ta know what's this Great One do. I mean if he do this here creatin', then why? What's he want a bunch 'o' us 'round anywho?"

"Hesh up," Sketch hissed.

"All answers have questions, just as all questions have answers. But the Great One is not one of confusion." Dalon Con smiled.

"My dear, small one," he said, "the Great One created us for fellowship. He loves us immeasurably and desires our love in return."

"How in tarnation are I spose to love what I cain't see?"

"Just as you cannot see wind, you feel it's touch."

"But wind be damagin', at times, even harsh," Krabb snorted.

"That is true, but it is also gentle. It helps plants spread their seeds and the birds to soar in the sky. When talking to the Great One, begin with prayer," Dalon Con said.

"Ya want me ta talk ta nothin'," Krabb asked, chuckling, "an on top 'o' that, ya tellin' me this here Living One done an died fer me,? . . . I taint thinkin' so, and whats this here Great One gonna do ta me ifin I don't wants ta bleeve?"

"He will turn you over to your own hateful ways and allow you to destroy yourself if that is what you desire," Dalon Con replied.

"I be havin' to say you dun an gived me somethin' to think more on." The instant the words left Krabb's mouth, a large hole opened in the ceiling, and the inhabitants were sucked from the grotto through the opening and returned to Rash.

****

Sim increased his speed as he moved through varying topographies destined for Rash. Fear encased him in its grasp, though the promise of something more outweighed the feelings of unrest.

What this something is, I have no way of knowing what this something is. Yet, an intense desire pulls me in this direction. Sim's appearance as he traveled began to soften. Tentacles drew into his form, replaced with arms, legs, hands and feet. His body stood upright, developing a human-like head, neck, and thorax, mimicking the transformation that was taking place within his very being.

There is a constant barrage of significant alterations to my form, not only my appearance but also my demeanor. I am experiencing what I believe to be a facial expression as the corners of my mouth turn upward. I do not know what this is called; however, it is accompanied with an overwhelming joy. I will eventually realize my journey's end.

Sim came to a halt. *It seems as though a natural covering has been provided to protect my skin, including the odd-looking pads I walk on. Although I would have chosen a different color, it is pleasant to blend into the scenery with my new green skin pigment.* Then, he raised each hand level with his chest and began to clench his digits into fists. *I have seen these before on other beings, but I am now just realizing the advantage of having such implements.*

CHAPTER SEVENTY

Hayden, Max and Abe

"Hold tight," Max said. A slight jerk ensued as the guardian of Burrus Plax dove into the ground as a swimmer would into a lake.

"The last words uttered by Max, 'hold tight', I am aware of its meaning;" Abe said, "however, in this case, I believe its meaning eludes me."

"Much the same," Hayden said. "It may also be affirmation or an 'I am here for you' type of statement." He looked at Abe. "You've been alone for a very long time."

"As I remember my existence," Abe said, "I have always been alone."

"The more you are around these humans," Hayden said, "the more you will acclimate to their unusual patterns of speech."

"I cannot see that ever coming to be," Abe replied, "we are too different."

"You will be much surprised," Hayden said. "It is actually quite a refreshing difference in communication." The three had been traveling for some time before Max began to speak. "I believe we are closing in on our destination, so, hold tight'."

The black box Hayden carried crackled to life.

"Hayden," Wakke said, "I hope you are alive to hear my words. If you have not communicated with Drade, then all the better. Still, there is still a possibility you will meet him in person. If this occurs, beware. Drade has traveled to our future home world, gathered allies who would do evil for profit and moved them to a time in the past or future, I know not where. I cannot reiterate strongly enough: in the unlikely situation your path brings you in contact with Drade, do not trust him. The best to you, my friend, and,—" static overtook the audio emanating from the box. Hayden pushed the button that would indicate to Wakke that he had received his communique.

"Please, receive this message, old friend," Hayden said softly.

"Is this a usual occurrence?" Abe asked.

"Each communication is nearly identical," Hayden replied. He began to explain his own origins to Abe.

"You have had remarkable beginnings," Abe said. "That you can remember your first cell splitting, has no words of description. Would you do me the honor of telling me your life?"

"Certainly," Hayden said. He began his story from his earliest remembrance of life to his bout with temporal disturbances, leading to the present. Abe followed with recollections from his past.

"You also have had an interesting life," Hayden said. "Yet, overall, one of extreme loneliness."

"This has recently come to light," Abe said. "Becoming aware that loneliness exists, I realize there is more to life than existing alone."

"Forgive me for eavesdropping and interrupting your conversation," Max said. "As interesting as it is, I am beginning to sense that we are reaching our destination or one that may be emitting a similar signal."

"Do you have any reason to doubt your senses?" Hayden asked.

"The closer we get to what I perceive to be the area of detection," said Max, "the more uneasy I feel about this place being our destination."

"If any doubt crosses your mind," Hayden said, "then bypass this area." Max had already begun a sharp right turn, reversing their course.

****

The temporal thief pondered the nature of time around him. *Changes are beginning to surface that are not of my doing. The endless timelines that surround me, Tempus, the keeper of time in this sector are under siege . . . this cannot stand! There are beings set to exploit the exclusive system of time excursion set in place eons ago by my operatives. NO . . . this will not stand.*

****

These areas having been spread throughout the planet, the anchor relayed, *are known as timelines, and guarded by temporal thieves.*

What does this mean to me? the maritime countered.

You will presume to preserve the age old practice of restricted temporal travel as I make ready to destroy the temporal thief. Any other objective will meet with swift retribution.

It will be as you have said. In the areas shown, I am supposed to limit temporal travel; however, in what way do you plan to overcome what must be a vast array of protection afforded to the keepers of this system.

The anchor released something akin to a chuckle. *These fools protect this vast complex with one individual. The need to plan is not as high on my list of priorities when laid beside conquer.*

****

"Small ones," Max said, "I will be moving much deeper into the earth to avoid the presumed trouble we were moving toward."

"Maxxx!" Hayden yelled.

Max burst through the surface of the earth, grabbing two dangling legs as he did so. The two legs were attached to a flying creature with twelve pairs of legs and measuring several hundred feet in diameter. It was basically round and built like a turtle, with a hard-shelled top and bottom, both a red mottled color.

The giant dodged the beaks of twelve distinct heads attempting to force him to release his grip. "I sense you would rather I not hold your legs. Then let us see what we can do to bring all to an agreement." Max broke both legs he held in his hands.

The beast, known as an axium, squalled in pain as Max moved from leg to leg, breaking each as he took a hold, then swung to the next target, until all twenty-four legs were useless. The axium, unable to maintain flight, crashed into Burrus Plax.

"I would call that a mess," Max said, walking up to the grounded axium—the majority of the heads still mobile, "I have never seen a brighter red than the colors on that creature's head and neck." He grasped one at the base where it exited the shell and twisted, cleanly removing the head. A spray of pink fluid lasted moments before settling down to a trickle. Then, a blood-red fog rose from the axium, hovered for a moment, and then instantly hurried away. Max raised his hand, releasing Hayden and Abe.

Abe was immediately on the dying creature. "I thought this may have been an axium."

"This creatures purpose escapes me. The Great One possess a grand sense of humor; however, after breaking through the surface and into the fresh air, I am detecting an exotic aroma that I have never before encountered." Max stood tall, inhaling deeply. "The ways of the Great One are not our ways. That could mean the creation of the axium was for this single scenario. A directional locator, if you will, to help us find our intended.

"So, gentle sirs, I ask you to assume your positions." Hayden and Abe took their places on Max's hand.

"Your humorous displays are improving," Hayden said, "however, they still need work."

"Thank you," Max replied, "I will be sure to take that as a compliment. Now make ready for another long underground ride." As before, he dove into the ground and resumed his trek, searching for the audio signal, knowing not how it would manifest itself.

"I fear this will be the case for the rest of this journey," Max said. "As I receive directional changes and alternate coordinates from the dark side of these coalitions, they will advance upon me at an accelerated rate, in an attempt to keep me on my toes and thwart my mission."

CHAPTER SEVENTY-ONE

Dalon Con

Moving another mile into the ruins of the city known as Rash, Dalon Con began to slow, eventually bringing his forward progress to a halt. "Now is the time for quiet," he whispered. "There are lights ahead and the voices of many workers. I am inclined to believe we are on the fringe of a great multiplex of temporal labor."

Azoff looked at Dalon Con. "What are we to do in the situation which we find ourselves? If I may offer a suggestion, I would like to do so, as long as I am not overstepping my boundaries."

"You were never constrained by boundaries," Dalon Con replied, "and yes, solutions from anyone are welcome."

"Thank you for your confidence," Azoff said. "We should send the small ones into the fray to reconnoiter, which will hopefully give us a clearer path to follow."

"Excellent," Dalon Con said. "What say you two?"

"Why ain't we already amovin' ta get that info we need ta smash them world killers?" Krabb asked.

"I be with Krabb," Sketch said. "We's waistin' time dillydallyin' 'round here; let's get a move on!"

"We have our answer," Dalon Con said. "Bring information, as quickly as possible, small ones." Sketch and his comrade moved like a shot down the city street, investigating even the smallest niche.

"They resemble insects," Gabriel said, "crawling on all fours across the floor, walls and ceiling."

"And now they're out of sight in that short amount of time," Roane said. He slowly shook his head. "Amazing how they are able to search such a large area so diligently."

****

"Whatcha say, Krabb?" Sketch asked. "Anythin' yet?"

"Nary a thin', but I heerd that noise Mr. Dalon were agabbin' 'bout."

"Watch out," Sketch wailed, "it's acomin' right fer ya!" Krabb turned to his right as a dozen, spaghetti-like creatures with teeth shot through a window in his direction. "Ya be careful now; they's agettin' closer."

"Jest let me know." Several moments passed before Sketch yelled.

"Now!" Krabb's move defied the laws of physics. As he was scampering over a brick wall, Sketch yelled again, as soon as the creature was within an inch of the little man.

"He be thar!" Krabb jumped up and slowed his forward progress, his 'up' being a ninety degree angle off the wall against which he was running. The creature known as a nodd passed directly under the hovering man.

"Yee haw!" Krabb squalled as he dropped just behind what served as a head for the thirty-foot-long nodd. Krabb wrapped his legs around the loose fibers, effectively pulling them into a bundle and locked his fingers within the strands. He began to ride the creature, digging in his heels and slamming the nodd's head against the wall in an effort to make him want to be rid of the small one. Krabb rode the nodd a mile or more before taking a bite. After chewing and swallowing, he yelled for Sketch to join the fray.

"You be ahavin' all the fun," Sketch said, chewing a mouth full of stringy flesh with pieces flying out as he spoke. The nodd continued to move quickly, still trying to rid itself of the two riders.

"Taint bad eatin', now is it?"

"No sir, taint bad atall." The nodd began to slow.

"It be alookin' like we done an et ourselfs outin a ride." Sketch glanced up and down the length of the creature.

"I bleeve we done jest that cuz thar ain't much left 'o' this here critter, jest chunks missin' out 'o' what used ta be a stringy galoot." Seconds later the nodd hit the ground, nearly dead, and Sketch and Krabb dismounted.

"Shh," Krabb said, placing the back of his right hand against Sketch's chest.

"Whatsa matter?" Sketch whispered.

"I'ma thinkin' we done an run inta that noise Mr. Dalon were talkin' 'bout."

"You's right, Mr. Dalon was awantin' us ta get as much info as we could an bring it back, so's they'd knowed more afore we all pounced on this here place."

"Well then, lets git agoin'." The area was noticeably brighter, causing Sketch and Krabb to realize they'd need to make themselves less visible.

"Whadaya think? Taint much 'round ta camo-whatchamacallit you an me ta make us harder to see."

"Foller me," Krabb said, as he shot down the sidewalk in short spurts, staying close to the wall. Sketch mirrored his friend's movements as they made their way closer to the unknown.

"Looky here," Sketch whispered, "thar be strange scratchin' marks on this here chunk 'o' concrete that peers ta go on fer quite a spell."

"I be aseein' it, and I cain't fer the life 'o' me, 'magine what done an made them marks." They followed the trail of scratches for another mile, with no end in sight.

"I be 'o' the sort what bleeves them scratches will tell the tale."

"So I'ma reckonin' we foller them marks till they end." Both nodded one to another, and they resumed their trek, focusing on the marks etched into the concrete walkway.

"Looky here," Sketch said, "these here marks end at the wall, 'stead of a door."

"Kinda not usual," Krabb said. "You'd be athinkin' them fellers we is chasin' would take the easy way in." Both Krabb and Sketch paused.

"Maybe that thar wall gots a door what goes somewheres else."

"Afore we go atryin' ta open up any wall, let's be acheckin' on that thar noise an light what made Mr. Dalon send us on this here chase."

"I be afollerin' you."

"Ya see that door, a fer piece down this cobbly stone road? The one what gots way more light comin' thru'er than the rest."

"Yeah, I sees it."

"I pointed it out to ya so's we could git thar not speakin' to each other."

"Purdy slick, Krabb, you gots right many more smarts then I ever thunk ya did."

"So's I kin be up ta par honest witcha," Krabb said, "somethin' done an got inside 'o' me. Can't splain it, ain't got time ta gab 'bout it, so's let's jest git in thar an sees whats we can sees." The two small men began to circle the doorway looking for the best way in. This circular search pattern came to an end the instant the door cracked, then fully opened for someone leaving the premises. "This a way." Krabb entered at the top of the door, followed closely by Sketch. Krabb found a piece of equipment large enough to conceal them both. He scampered behind the electronic enclosure, joined seconds later by Sketch.

"From the door to this here hidin place," Sketch said, "taint no more than thirty feet, but that be plenty time ta sees whats I needs ta sees. I looked 'round this here factry er whatever ya call it, an they was chunks 'o' glass all shapes an sizes."

"That be purdy much all they wuz to see." Krabb said. "Ceptin fer the men in white coats what was carryin' stuff to an fro." He looked at Sketch. "We be takin' a once over 'round this whole place. After that, we best be gettin' back ta the wall."

"Please wait," a concealed Sim said.

"Who that be?" Krabb asked.

"I ain't done and seen nobody," Sketch replied, "who thar? You best be atellin' me an my bud, cuz if you ain't I knows somebody be a puttin' somethin' on you that a cleanin' scrub ain't takin' off."

"I wish no trouble," Sim said. He rose from his concealment, his form now visible.

"I ast ya once more," Krabb said, "who you be?"

"My name is Sim, my aim is not to harm, but to speak with Dalon Con."

"Whatcha reckon?" Sketch said.

"We be a takin' him with us," Krabb said.

****

Drade

"Stand back," Drade said, "I'm not precisely sure where the portal will surface." A second later the rectangular frame pushed from the ground hosting an orange electrical spider web within its interior.

"I must assume the function of what appears to be a doorway," Smort said, "is just that . . . a doorway, though to what I must reserve judgement, even though I can compile an educated guess."

"My suspicions tell me that your educated guess would be spot on, so I will endorse your inkling and confirm that a doorway into the miracle of time travel awaits."

Smort stared at the light within the frame. It appeared as a solid entity traveling from left to right, winding around the frame as it moved. Two beings entered the portal, piercing the solid sheet of orange light, each disappearing with a loud pop.

Smort stepped into a brightly lit, clean room. *An unbathed man such as myself certainly does not belong within the confines of an area as this.* He felt a tug against his left elbow. It was Drade dressed in a white plastic jumpsuit, with a clear helmet, and a supply of oxygen for sustenance.

"Put this on," Drade said, "and quickly before you are spotted."

"Where is this place . . . I have never seen such."

“This is an Odobi laboratory of the future.” A door opened, swinging silently on its hinges. A man dressed as Drade and Smort stepped into the room, nodded, then left through a doorway across the hall.

“I was under the impression the Odobi were a race of small stature.”

“From whence we began, you are correct; however, you can see throughout the ages a necessary change has taken place to ensure survival of the Odobi.” Drade stood squarely facing Smort. “It may surprise you to know that I am Odobi.”

“How is this possible, you are nearly as tall as I am?”

Drade smiled. “5’8” to be exact, and the precise reason for this change in height is beyond my pay grade.” He began to chuckle. “In actuality the only thoughts I can muster as to why, would be my exposure to the larger futuristic Odobi.”

Smort shrugged, most of the gesture lost within the confines of the bulky suit. “What more did you want to show?”

“We will step back through the portal and reappear at another point in time where I have discussed a number of the future Odobi returning to our time, for scientific study and the promise of traveling through time.”

Smort and Drade stepped into a gathering of Odobi scientists. After it was determined who would make the journey back in time, a question was fielded from the audience.

“Once we reach our destination,” a scientist asked, “there will be no problems or difficulty returning to our own time . . . correct?”

“This is true,” Drade said, “it will take no more than a day to finalize your travel orders and the maximum of three additional days to schedule and execute your return trip.”

Smort furrowed his eyebrows at Drade’s statement, but kept quiet as his thought process was but an inkling and not confirmed by any means.

“I do not feel that your answers to the Odobi scientists were as accurate as you made them out to be, especially concerning their return trip through time,” Smort said.

"How could you possibly know details," Drade said, "and what would make you think I would have any reason to mislead them?"

"Well, I believe the most appropriate statement you could offer is to answer the questions you asked of me." Smort's body language pushed forth a confident, "gotcha."

"Now that we are back within the confines of our own time," Smort said, "I think it prudent that we should sit and palaver." Drade extended his arm motioning toward the two seats they used previously.

"I can more or less sum up your questions with a few simple explanations," the oversized Odobi said.

"Please, the floor is yours."

"When I was approached at the possibility of being a member of the first team to apply temporal travel to a relevant situation I was estatic. The thought of helping someone in such dire straits absolutely lit a fire within. As the mission was being brought together a figure approached, one by the name of Deep Sink. This abysmal creature, or so I thought, taught me a different way to interpret my surroundings. Although this new way was a bit more radical but as time passed it purposed within my life."

"I do not agree with the manner in which you have branched out; however, I can offer no argument for I am unarmed with any facts."

"Which I believe is the way it will stay," Drade said, smiling. "In fact I can say this with certainty, as temporal travel with these future Odobi is strictly limited to prevent them from leaving this timeline. Now that you are privy to the reason the oversized Odobi occupy areas on Burrus Plax, I must be taking my leave." Drade stared at Smort. "Perhaps you will come around in time, for the true master awaits his day to ravage this world and leave for another."

Smort saw all motion come to a standstill as Drade instantly increased his speed to a point barely detectable. Drade disappeared into the foliage as the surrounding flora closed in around Smort then slammed to a halt as quickly as it had begun.

CHAPTER SEVENTY-TWO

Hayden, Max and Abe

"How do you expect to locate the carthon?" Abe asked. "We have no starting point."

"You speak true," Max replied, "however, we do have one of our five outward senses, that being the sense of smell."

"Never can I remember a time when I have doubted your thoughts or actions," Hayden said, "but I must admit I am having those feelings now. Would you please explain your comments?"

"The sense of smell," Max began, "is the strongest of the five we possess—"

"I would have to argue that point," Hayden interrupted. "The aroma of a flower or a favorite meal is just that and nothing more."

"Extend me the courtesy," Max said, "of finishing what I mean to say without interruption—the same consideration I allowed you."

Hayden bowed his head. "Forgive my interruption. Please continue; you will not be disturbed."

"Close your eyes, if you will," Max said, "even though you are riding in complete darkness, and think of a smell from your childhood, an aroma that brought you great pleasure." Max allowed several moments for the thought to work its way deep into Hayden's and Abe's subconscious. "Now, do the reverse and allow in an odor in that repulses or brings grief." Max gave this more time to percolate in the minds of his two wards before speaking. "Now, do you understand how powerful a scent can be? What at first seems too simple to acknowledge, can bring wonderful or horrid memories back to you in an instant."

"Thank you for bringing the importance of the sense of smell to my attention," Hayden said. "It helps me recall numerous memories, many good, some bad. It also enhances the remaining four senses and warns of taking all for granted, as is easily done."

"I have never paid attention as to whether I even retained such things," Abe said, "and now I think I have never been so grateful for realizing what I actually possess. Even though I was alone, I can recall what I was doing by remembering an odor I was experiencing at the time. Needless to say, this odiferous sense is powerful."

"So you can see," Max said, "where aroma can be a valuable tool, especially when searching for a particular article or being." Max received two emphatic affirmatives. "Do you recall," Max asked, "the last time I surfaced, we were treated to a scent never experienced before?" Once again, Hayden and Abe answered, "yes."

"So the fragrance you just mentioned," Hayden said, "can be tracked by the way the smell smells." A long paused ensued before laughter broke the silence.

"An unusual way to put it," Max said, "but you are essentially correct."

"How will we detect this scent, being so far below the surface?" Abe asked.

"The fragrance," Max said, "will travel into the underground by way of the vegetation, being absorbed along with the carbon dioxide the foliage uses for food. The scent will then exit the plants through their root system and enter the surrounding soil. I have already begun to detect this original odor and can tell that we are still on target to intercept; however, when, I cannot say."

"So until then," Hayden said, "we wait?"

"There is something close to us that we need," Abe said. "The image I am receiving is abstract and foggy, at best, but there is more than one entity that needs us, and on the same level, we need them."

"I have also carried an uneasy feeling for some time," Max said. "I believe our inner warnings may be related. You mentioned there were a number of entities that will rely on us in the future, and that we will come to rely on these same beings."

"This is the impression I have received," Abe said.

"And you can see nothing but abstract images," Max asked, "nothing clear enough to identify?"

"Yes," Abe said, "however…" he paused as if he were seeing something significant in real time. "Wait, there is something. These individuals lie pieces that have yet to undergo the necessary assembly required to be useful. I perceive, even though they carry the fragments, they are unaware of the need to join them."

"I am being led toward Rash," Max said. "Apparently, this is where these creatures reside at the moment."

"Interesting," Hayden said, "I feel as though I am being pulled in the direction of the carthon, possessing the identical coordinates as that into which Max is being led."

"Which means the carthon are in Rash also," Max said. "I believe these new revelations are the key to our ultimate destination, although I do not think we should waiver from our destination to locate the creatures."

"Agreed," echoed Hayden and Abe. "Will you find them the same way we searched for the desirable entities?"

"Negative," Max said, "the carthon will search us out, for they want no loose ends."

"If we travel closer to the surface, won't they to detect us?" Abe asked.

"I have been slowly rising toward the surface for the very reason we have been discussing. Now that you know my plans."

"We are there," Max said, "I feel plugs being taken from my back by the carthon beaks."

"They have found us already?" Hayden asked, a sense of alarm surrounding his voice.

"They have," Max replied. He moved closer to the surface, allowing the wretched creatures to remove larger plugs. In this way the creatures believed they had inflicted irreparable damage upon their enemy.

"Fear not, as I am able to refill the areas much faster than the carthon's feeble attempts. Now watch the prey become the hunter." Max slid his arms rearward until they were even with his back, then raised his entire body until it just broke the surface of the ground. Thinking they had mortally wounded their opponent, the enemy moved in for the kill.

Once their bills touched the back of their quarry, Max snatched a beak in each of his hands and plummeted below the surface, letting the ground do the destructive work. He rolled onto his back, getting a glimpse of a large, metal, man-shaped object before it disappeared. "I believe it is time."

"For what?" Hayden asked. Before Max could answer, Hayden and Abe found themselves drenched in sunshine.

"We will spend some time above ground to give all a much needed rest."

"Thank you," Hayden said, "this will be a much needed respite." Abe nodded his appreciation.

Abe said, "I would like to show you my method of defense, in case you think it may be useful."

Abe instructed Max and Hayden to cover their ears. With slight amusement, they complied. Then, spreading his legs and tail for stability, he issued a sonic blast that carved a eighteen foot trench.

"I pray no one was injured in my demonstration," Abe said. "I purposely held back for just that reason."

"Held back?" Hayden exclaimed.

"Any stronger and I would fear for many of the creatures that reside in this area," Max added. "Rest assured. Your ability as a weapon will be most useful."

"I should say so," Hayden said. "Your abilities could tackle most of the obstacles on Burrus Plax."

CHAPTER SEVENTY-THREE

Dalon Con

"It ain't got no seam," Sketch said. "They be no way to open 'er up."

"Cain't be," Krabb replied. "We kin look at the floor and tell from the scratches them fellers left, that thar be a way in." Krabb ran his fingers over where he believed the edge of the door should be and jumped as his hand passed over this space. His hand made a brief shadow that could've been seen no other way.

Noticing his partners sudden movement, Sketch spoke. "You done an found somethin'?"

"Maybe I did," Krabb replied. "C'mon over here an gimmy a hand."

Sketch joined his friend. "Whatcha want me ta do?"

"See this here spot I be acastin' a shadow over?"

"What of it?"

"Hold yer hands just like ya got'em an watch when I pass ma hand twixin the light an them shadows you is acastin'."

"Don't know what good any a that'll do —"

"Jest hush up an do it," Krabb interrupted.

Sketch passed his hand over the shadows as Krabb had requested. "Well, I'll be, jest as soon as ma hand hits them thar shadows, the edge 'o' what I figgers ta be the door appears."

"An the way I sees it, is you be 'xactly right."

"Now what I sees to be the question, is what'er we gonna use ta pry that piece what acts like a door outta that wall?"

“I don’t bleeve we is gonna hafta,” Krabb said, “cuz if ya look at them scratches we been a followin’, they makes a change winced they reached the door.”

“I tain’t aseein’ what you’s atalkin’ ‘bout.”

“Right cher.” Krabb knelt and began to brush the sand away from what proved to be a square box poured into the concrete sidewalk. The box was equipped with a snug-fitting, metal top that ingeniously slid into the sand and had just been removed from the lid. In this way once this entry point was used, the lid would slide back, concealing the box, and, more importantly, concealing itself with the sand that had been scraped off. Krabb pushed the only button that dwelt within the box. “Be ready to git inside; I ain’t sure how long this here thin’ stays open.” As soon as the brick door reached what appeared to be its highest point, Sketch and Krabb rushed in, a shadow followed, covered by a sense of urgency surrounding the entrance.

“Don’t be alookin’ like we had ta rush,” Sketch said. Before these words left his mouth, the brick door slammed back into position.

Krabb glanced at the base of the door. “See thar,” pointing where his eyes had been, “that’s our way outta here.”

“You mean that thar rope?” Sketch asked.

“I do,” Krabb replied. “But first we best check what these varmits we is alookin’ fer be up to.”

“I reckon this here whole city be covered in this weird color blue,” Sketch said.

“I reckon so,” Krabb replied. “We oughta keep our gabbin’ on the down low, since we ain’t got no idea what we dun an crawled in to.”

“I’m with you on that’un, ‘specially when we got no idea where them galoots is hangin’ out.”

Sim peered around the corner of a decimated brick building. *It seems my quarry are at hand.* He tapped his bottom lip with a forefinger. *Although their acceptance has yet to be seen.*

The two small humanoids moved along using all fours, which allowed them to search into smaller areas they could not reach walking upright. They were amazingly fast, accurate and stealthy.

"You be gooder with numbers and time than me," Krabb said. "How long ya reckon we been alookin'?"

"I figger 'bout twelve ta fifteen hour, give er take with the way time be scootin' all 'round nowadays. An another thin', I'm gettin' ta feel right uneasy 'bout them creatures we's alookin' fer; it's kinda like they might be asearchin' fer us."

"If you be afeelin' that'a way, thence we best keep our eyeballs peeled, but good."

"Let's just keep agoin'. We bound ta run up on somethin'."

"Hold on thar, I bleeve I done an found that somethin' you was talkin' 'bout," Krabb said. He reached for two small brass dowels set into the wall. Popping them out, he handed one to Sketch.

"Whatcha reckon we gonna do with these?"

"You will give them to Dalon Con," Sim said.

Krabb, mesmerized by the shiny object, shrugged, saying nothing. Sketch held out his hand. "Here, you hold'em, we gots ta get back on track."

"I'm which ya," Krabb said. Both men hearing the voice of Sim, but neither acknowledging its presence. They moved up the cobblestone roadway for several miles.

"Ayr ya seein' this?" The road and brick walls were beginning to deteriorate.

"Yeah, and it be gettin right much brighter the more we move." After several minutes, they found themselves surrounded by light.

"Krabb," Sketch said, "we is on the outside 'o' the buildin'; that carn sarn brick door twernt nothin' but a way out."

"We best be makin' tracks ta Mr. Dalon an the others," Krabb said, "Cuz they is gonna wanna know where we is an what done and happened."

****

"More of the same?" Dalon Con said.

"That be 'bout it—" Krabb said, "jest different-sized chunks 'o' what looked like glass gettin' moved from one place ta the other."

"The streets was like the other dead cities," Sketch said, "till we run inta this here wall what had a door ya couldn't see, but Krabb figgered out a way."

"One'st we gots through the brick door," Krabb said, "we moved right many mile down the cobbly stone road an ended up on the outside."

"Interesting," Dalon Con said, "this unusually constructed brick doorway you speak of may have been an ancient escape portal. Why it was there is a mystery, one that may call for further investigation."

"I believe what you will find," Roane said, "is areas like that are constructed to throw ones involved in a contest of search and confront off the path."

"This is more than likely the case," Azoff said. "What better way to lose a predator than giving them something else to catch their attention."

"We will allow them to play their games," Dalon Con said, "then we will make our move. Since the light wanes, we will take nourishment and rest, for I feel tomorrow will be a day filled with strife."

"It is for this very reason," the voice of Sim replied, "I have been sent to aid in the reestablishment of your majority foothold recognized shortly after Burrus Plax's inception." His face was aglow with the light from a seldom seen metal disc.

"I done and heerd that there voice afore," Krabb said.

"You is a rite as rain," Sketch replied, "we heerd his talkin' whence we was in the outside 'o' that brick place wit the door what dropped down."

Krabb pushed a finger into each ear, like he was trying to remove plugs. "We heerd him, but it twere like we dent heerd him."

"Be not alarmed my friends, I have been expecting this one." Dalon Con smiled. "The great one has pulled Sim from the depths of evil lurking in the one called, Hag."

****

Just after dawn, Dalon Con and his travelers plus one were underway. The morning meal had been completed and the calm from the night before dissipated. Words circulating through the group were 'a day filled with strife'. Dalon Con immersed in the possibilities this day held, gave little thought to calming the others placed under his charge.

"Priority must rule this day," Dalon Con said to Azoff. "As much as it hurts, I have no time to calm their fears, when each one's safety comes first." As they traveled, the surrounding foliage, began to thicken, lending an air of closeness to the area. "The priorities of each day weigh heavy, searching for an answer. Oh, what a relief when these are decided, as they have been on this day." Gabriel jumped atop Azoff, at the first sight of a small, green, flying reptile.

"Everyone on the ground, now!" Gabriel yelled. "You must not allow these creatures to touch you, and you must not touch them, for it will certainly lead to your demise." Gabriel, remembering Bile's fate, leapt to the ground and curled into a fetal position beside Azoff. The furry one placed his foreleg along Gabriel's back, pulling him close. All but Dalon Con complied, standing defiant in the swarm of death circling all present. Dalon Con began to walk through the middle of the circling reptiles.

"Even though you were born to kill," Dalon Con said, "you must die." The deafening noise of angry avians dove toward their quarry, slamming into an invisible force surrounding him. Soon, the ground was littered with mutilated carcasses. "These creatures should not be found outside of the Corstrum." Dalon Con stared at one of the dead, flying aberrations.

"What does this mean?" Azoff asked.

"It means that Hag has found a way to venture outside of the Corstrum walls." Dalon Con replied.

"Do anybody know where we is?" Krabb asked.

"Pretty much in the middle of nowhere," Roane said, "although I have found, more often than not, that being in the middle of nowhere on Burrus Plax, means being in the middle of noteworthy nowhere."

"Any ideas?" Azoff asked.

"If Dalon Con thinks Hag has found a way to live in day-to-day Burrus Plax, then that is significant in and of itself," Roane said.

"Roane," Dalon Con replied, "there is more that runs deeper in your comment than what appears on the surface. I am not sure you are aware of this; however, I need you to concentrate and pull it to the surface, for we are going back to Rash."

"I have three names that have been thrust upon me," Roane said, "Max, Hayden, and Abe." I know not who these beings are; however, I am sure they are a necessary link."

"As have I," Sim said, "notably the name of Max has been intertwined in my subconscious, only now coming to the surface of my consciousness as we near our destination."

CHAPTER SEVENTY-FOUR

Hayden, Max and Abe

"Would you mind repeating," Hayden said, "what you mentioned earlier about multiple entities needing to interact with our party?"

"Certainly," Abe replied, "where these notions originated, I do not know, but I feel they were from a friendly source."

"Were they from within," Max asked, "or from the outside of your conscious thought?"

"Both," Abe replied. "To clarify my answer, the notion came to me outside of my body, like a casual conversation. It then moved into my brain in some subtle way. It was very much as if the thought was my own."

"What else?" Max asked.

"One word—" Abe said, "Rash."

"And you are sure you heard the name 'Rash' correctly?" Max inquired.

"I am," Abe replied.

"You know what this means?" Max said. Hayden and Abe were already making themselves comfortable in his hand.

"Back to Rash," Hayden and Abe echoed.

Max slowed his forward progress. "We have reached our destination," he said.

"I detect an anomaly above ground that may be what we are in search of," Abe replied.

****

“We are very close to Rash,” Dalon Con said, “and something is very close to our position.”

“The entities we are searching for?” Gabriel asked.

“I think you are likely correct,” Dalon Con said, “and we should keep a keen eye out for anything unusual, no matter how insignificant it may seem.”

****

“We will surface momentarily,” Max said, as Hayden and Abe felt an upward change in direction and then a sudden stop.

“Ya gotta stop,” Sketch exclaimed. “Ya gotta stop right now!” Dalon Con came to a halt.

“Has ya ever done an seen anythin’ like it in your life?” Krabb said. Both men stepped from their perch atop Dalon Con’s feet and ran toward the man-mountain Max.

“Max, it really be you! I taint seen ya in so many a year —”

“Hesh up yer noise,” Sketch said. “Ya talk Max’s ears plum off an not says nothin’ ta boot.”

Max laughed. “You two rapscallions have not changed in the many centuries we have been acquainted.” He kept his one hand firmly planted into his abdomen and lowered his other for Sketch and Krabb to climb aboard. The three began to converse in a language unfamiliar to everyone present, save for Dalon Con. Once the conversation was complete, Max released Hayden and Abe from his hand.

“See,” Sketch said, “he jes like he were in our dreams, all them years back.”

“He be that,” Krabb said, “and a whole bunch more.”

“I ask that you all gather around so that we may palaver,” Dalon Con said. For nearly four hours those gathered told of themselves and what they knew of the happenings around them. In some cases these conversations led to occurrences many years in the past. At one point a man made from metal was brought into the exchange. That, along with the mention of numerous temporal events, were enough to cause Dalon Con to speak. "We know more of one another; however, what you do not know, but will soon learn, is of the one called Rakke. This one came into being when the Nexus and the Other merged, held together by the innocence of another and the vile existence of evil incarnate. For this reason, we must scour the planet until we find Rakke and destroy this abomination." Dalon Con stepped closer to Max. "First I must bring forward, one that has a special purpose centered around you." A slender biped white and blue in color stepped forward. His features were humanoid and he wore no covering, yet his skin was smooth with the texture of leather, and all reproductive and hygiene centered organs were concealed.

"Sim," Max said, "it is good to finally meet you."

"As it is for me," Sim replied. He produced the bronze medallion, handing the disc to the protector of Burrus Plax. Max rotated the metal circle through his fingers before placing the medallion in his open hand. The disc was absorbed, disappearing into the palm of the large one's right hand.

"The 'cleft,' which is what the disc is called," Max said, "lives up to its name, for it surely does not disappoint." Sim and Max conversed for the better part of an hour. Max broke away and looked toward his longtime friend.

"Dalon Con," Max said, "it is good to see you again, although I will have to admit your appearance is a bit of a surprise." Dalon Con began to laugh.

"I am sure this is so," Dalon Con said. "Rakke has nothing to do with the existence of time travel itself, save for using the temporal disturbance to obtain the parts needed to construct himself, namely the Nexus and the Other. The mastermind of this creature, Hag, resides on this world. Rakke was created to aid in the destruction of your home world, Burrus Plax."

“Why would anyone want to destroy the world on which they live?” Azoff asked.

“It is the only way to retrieve the most valuable natural resource the planet has to offer,” Dalon Con said. “Burrus Plax is unusual in that it contains many of the most valuable minerals in the galaxy, and some believe *that* is worth its destruction. One such as Hag has no problem existing outside of the atmosphere of a planet like Burrus Plax, so its destruction is of no consequence.”

“From my perspective,” Max said, “saving Burrus Plax from harm is of the most import.”

“I believe you will find all here taking the same stance,” Dalon Con replied.

“Then should we not locate Rakke as our first matter?” Azoff asked.

“I have the best chance of locating Rakke,” Max said, “for Burrus Plax and I are one and the same, and this enables me to track this creature no matter how weak the signal.”

“I wish for each of you small ones to travel with ones who are larger in stature,” Dalon Con said. “This will prevent you from being taken by one who would do you harm long before your absence is noticed.” Sketch and Krabb took their normal spots with Dalon Con, while Hayden and Abe opted to stay under Max’s care. Sim chose Azoff as there was adequate room even with multiple riders. The travelers set off with Max taking the lead.

Dusk faded to night and night into dawn before they stopped. Max, Azoff and Roane took a seat on the ground as Dalon Con stood. “Time for nourishment.”

“Let me tell ya,” Sketch said, “you fellers is in fer a treat.”

“An he ain’t tellin’ ya no lie,” Krabb said. “No sirree, taint nothin’ but truth.”

****

"Excellent meal," Max said looking around at those staring at him, who were wondering why this giant man made from soil would need to eat. He felt obliged to answer their unspoken question. "It is unnecessary that I ingest anything for my existence; however, having taste buds gives me a reason to enjoy the wonderful bounty Burrus Plax has to offer."

"That *were* some mighty goot chow," Krabb said.

"That it were," Sketch replied, licking each of his fingers.

"Do you have a plan on how to search for Rakke?"

"I have detected the one you call Rakke," Max said, "or rather, his signature."

"We should hunt this creature to the ends of Burrus Plax," Roane said.

"Admirable sentiments for such a dangerous task," Azoff said. He opened his mouth displaying a wide, cavernous breach full of deadly twisted teeth. After a long while and an odd guttural sound, Azoff closed his mouth.

"Azoff's yawn," Dalon Con said, "confirms that we all need rest before we continue, the exception, most likely, being Max."

"Settle yourselves and take on the rest your bodies need," Max said. "I will keep watch and keep you safe until you awaken." He sat down, and absorbing more material from the ground, grew half again his present size.

"Sleep well, my friends."

CHAPTER SEVENTY-FIVE

Rakke

You look as if you have no idea what you are searching for, Bridge said. *Could this be the case of the one called Rakke?*

Rakke remained silent.

I can only imagine how maddening it must be to have someone who is a part of you, yet against your very being, purposely doing whatever it takes to keep your irritation level at its peak. Once again, Bridge received no reply.

Still not talking, eh? Then how about a sing-along? You know, they say music hath charms to soothe the savage beast. Furthermore, you seem to be a bit testy at this time.

Bridge hesitated for a moment. *I know, just follow me and we'll have you feeling better in no time.* Bridge began to sing in an off-key, high screech. This caterwauling continued for a short time.

"Silence! No more of your childish rants!" Rakke snarled. "You will stop, and you will stop now." When Bridge continued his song, the metal man beat his head against the tunnel wall until rendered unconscious.

Success—Bridge chuckled. *What to do, what to do, when Rakke awakens.*

"Now is my chance," Vrollic said.

"Come aboard," Hag welcomed, "you will be my second, and assist in the takeover of Rakke, who is nothing more than a method of travel."

Attracted to the diverse amount of malevolence Smort found himself tailing Rakke and Vrollic. *Where this will end I haven't a clue . . . I can no longer tell who or what I am.*

CHAPTER SEVENTY-SIX

Dalon Con

"It is time to leave," Dalon Con said after a short rest and meal. "It is good to travel with friends and a full stomach." Max took the lead as before, with Sketch and Krabb paired with Dalon Con and Hayden and Abe under the protective hand of Max.

"Are you getting any further indication that Rakke is in the area?" Abe asked.

"Nothing more than the signal I received earlier," Max said, "and even that is beginning to fade."

"What are we to do?" Hayden asked.

"All we *can* do–" Max said, "continue our search."

"I'ma thinkin' there be a problem with Max and them two little fellers," Sketch whispered.

"What kinda trouble be agoin' on? And if you remember, Sketch, we *is* them two little fellers.

"Ain't got me no idea, why I said such a thing. But I reckon it'll show its ugly head sometime or a nother."

"I cannot tell for certain," Max said, "but I sense an entity we have yet to encounter." A translucent, five-fingered clawed paw took a swipe at Max, bringing with it devastating consequences. "Away from me, vile beast," the giant yelled as he yanked the appendage removing it at the shoulder.

Then, the man-mountain burst through the surrounding foliage, beating the creature with its own foreleg until it no longer moved. Max stood, shaking his head. "Seems vaguely familiar . . . no matter, there is work to be done," Max said, after seeing several more of the beasts, "yes, much more work to be done."

"You have picked a bad place to be on this day," Azoff said. He pounced on the translucent creature with his great weight, compressing his organs and pushing the mush out of its mouth. Its head was sleek with a pointed snout, translucent like the rest of the body, and its cold black eyes seemed to cut through at whatever it chose to gaze.

"Be gone with you!" Dalon Con bellowed, raising his cane and causing the four-legged, slender creature to fracture into small, confetti-like pieces. "I see the carpotheon that remains is on the retreat."

"Should I go after this one?" Azoff asked.

"No need," Dalon Con said, "the carpotheon are a skiddish race that usually feed on carrion. Something has altered this group. I see the same message did not reach the ears of Roane," Dalon Con said.

"Die!" Roane yelled, riding on the back of the last creature, as he plunged a large knife into its spine until the carpotheon dropped to the ground. Roane worked his left leg from underneath the body, then finished the creature off, planting the sharpened piece of metal into its chest.

"Another reason not to pursue," Dalon Con said. The travelers took time to regroup before setting off again. Hayden's communication device unexpectedly crackled to life.

"Everyone," Max said, "stop!" All obeyed, gathering around the man-mountain and the small being hovering above his hand.

"Hayden," Wakke said, "I know you have received a limited amount of my transmissions, for I have received your responses." A long pulse of static ensued before Wakke returned. "I must reiterate that you do not attempt to use the temporal door we constructed. I say this with a ladened heart, for merely having the knowledge of what we have done makes it hard to bare." Another round of static, shorter than the first, interrupted the transmission, after which the transmission was momentarily lost until Wakke broke the silence.

"We were sent here to construct a temporal portal for the purpose of traveling back through time to discover what caused the degradation of Burrus Plax. The ability to travel through time is what caused the travesty we set in motion. I could not have believed such consequences would result from our peaceful experiment." Static took over and the message was permanently lost.

"This must not be," Hayden said. "It was just scientific research; the last thing we wanted to do was injure anyone." His eyes began to well. "Instead, we destroyed an entire society."

"Everyone to their travel positions," Dalon Con said. "I do not like appearing so callous, but we must leave this place so as not to be taken by surprise."

****

"They have been here within the last few hours," Vrollic said.

"That does us no good," Hag hissed. "Unless my arms are wrapped around our quarries' necks, squeezing the life from their bodies, worthless information such as you spew is of no use to me."

"Keep the drool that seeps from your mouth as words to yourself," Vrollic said. "We will continue to follow. I am still able to detect their whereabouts, albeit weak, and strike when we have sufficiently closed the distance."

****

"I detect tension within you that is normally not present," Hayden said.

"Your instincts are correct," Max said. "Rakke, the one we search for, is behind us."

"This means we are now the pursued," Abe said, "and our nemesis, the pursuer."

"You are also correct," Max replied.

"What must we do?" Hayden asked.

"Dalon Con will soon be beside me," Max said. "I have slowed my forward progress, which will alert Dalon Con that there are problems needing to be discussed."

"There is trouble?" Dalon Con asked.

"The one we track," Max said, "now tracks us."

"The signal that Rakke emits," Dalon Con said, "is much more erratic than in the past. This tells me he is motivated by the thought of a surprise attack on his enemies."

"Meaning us," Max said.

"Exactly," Dalon Con replied, "and with his newfound agitation, leaves him primed to make mistakes."

"I had not thought of a scenario such as yours," Max said. "It is good to be within your presence, Dalon Con. There are many things to be learned from one such as you." Dalon Con nodded, showing his appreciation.

"We must increase our vigilance," Dalon Con said. "An attack is imminent and could come from any direction, including above and below." A large, furry creature was now running beside Max. On its back sat two riders, their fingers clutching handfuls of hair.

"Azoff, Roane, and Sim," Max said, "it is good to have you by my side."

"It is here!" Dalon Con bellowed, as their world collapsed around them.

CHAPTER SEVENTY-SEVEN

Dalon Con, Max, Azoff, and all the riders disappeared beneath the surface of Burrus Plax. The ground closed behind them as though they had never existed, a silver foot being the last thing seen. Moments later, Max burst through the outer layer carrying Dalon Con under his right arm and Azoff under his left. Roane slowly rose from the fur which had protected him during his underground tryst.

"You will need more than that to exterminate the ones who hunt you, slime devil!" Max roared.

"More!" Vrollic replied. Towering geysers of dirt and debris violently gushed hundreds of feet into the air. These intermittent geysers kept the travelers guessing which way to move until it was discovered that they never erupted less than fifty feet apart.

"I believe I said more," Max said, "not less."

"I do believe your humoristic attempts are improving," Abe said. Another geyser erupted, sending the group to a distance of twenty-five feet from its base.

"I will accept your compliment," Max said; "however, I do not think humoristic is an actual word, although I have been wrong a time or two in my life."

"Who decides which group of letters is or is not a formal word?" Abe challenged. The travelers found themselves moving again twenty-five feet from the latest blast.

"Someone from the galaxy of Milk and Way, called Webster," Max said.

"Cease your useless conversation," Dalon Con bellowed, "and pay attention to what goes on around you!" This bit of advice could not have come at a more opportune time.

"Azoff," Max screamed, "left, NOW!" Azoff complied, adding a roll to his move left. A sharpened, metal rod, two inches in diameter, pierced the soil and removed a V-shaped chunk of skin, muscle and bone from Azoff's rear leg.

"Keep your eyes down," Dalon Con said. "If you see the topsoil begin to rise, move away until the projectile clears the ground. The geysers were meant to lure us into believing their offense was weak and nothing to fear."

"Nothing could be further from the truth," Azoff said. The sharpened canisters were being released at a much greater rate of speed, causing the travelers to jump from one foot to the other to avoid contact. Max stepped up and removed a hand from his abdomen.

"Please take care of these until my return," Max said. Dalon Con smiled. Max dove into the ground and was gone. Hayden hovered close to Dalon Con's ear, while Abe skittered about, checking what he had not seen.

"This might not be the best time to ask," Roane said, "but would someone tell me what is happening?"

"You are most correct," Azoff replied, "this is *not* the proper time. It would be best for you to stay down and keep quiet." Roane sank into the pleasant-smelling fur, and, taking Azoff's last suggestion literally, sucked his lips inward, placing his teeth over them, top and bottom. Moments later a hollow man of metal burst through the surface and bounced twice before coming to a stop, never to move again. Max followed, pressing his foot into the chest cavity and smashing it flat. "I warned you, metal man," Max said, his voice reaching a deafening crescendo, "but you would not listen!" He grabbed the head and feet, bending them until they touched. Max began to distort and crush the metal creature until it was reduced to a somewhat round object about twelve inches in diameter. "No mistaking where it got you–" Max sank his fist into the metal, driving it underground, "dead!"

"How unfortunate your last word has yet to come to fruition," Dalon Con said.

"The creature called Rakke, I crushed into the ground, how could he not be gone?" Max asked.

"The one we knew as Rakke was but a vessel for the true one of danger, named Hag," Dalon Con said.

"I have experienced the presence of the one you call Hag before," Max said. "It was not a direct confrontation, but the presence of unspeakable evil."

"Your description of Hag proves your truth," Dalon Con said.

"Back away!" Azoff screamed, as another hole was forming a dozen feet from the travelers.

"What is this?" Dalon Con asked Max.

"A portal is being burned from underneath the surface of my planet to where we now stand," Max said. "Ask me no more, for this is all the information I have."

"Max," Dalon Con said, "we follow you away from this place to reconnoiter." Max left without a word, followed by Dalon Con and Azoff. After traveling approximately two hundred miles, the group stopped.

"This should purchase a sufficient amount of time," Max said.

"We have a visitor," Dalon Con said, talking just above a whisper. "Converse just as though nothing is different." Dalon Con made his way over to Max, casually said a few words, then continued to mill around. Max dropped below the surface of Burrus Plax so quickly, it was as though he had not been standing there. No one noticed him leave; even the new arrival made no indication that anything had changed.

"I have noticed Max is no longer with us," Azoff said, having made his way over to Dalon Con. "Is this unusual or by design?" Before Dalon Con could answer, a commotion broke out several hundred feet away.

"Let me go," Jack snarled, "let me go, now!" Max had the young man firmly in his grasp, arms pinned to his sides, making it impossible for him to wield any weapon he might have in his possession. Dalon Con placed a hand on Jack's forehead, and with his free hand he felt around the young man's waistband until his hand came into contact with what he expected to find.

"Stay calm," Dalon Con said with a soothing tone, "until I am able to relieve your person of this weapon and the hold it has over you." Dalon Con talked with Jack for nearly an hour before removing a black cylinder from the young man's belt. He continued to speak, then separated his hand from Jack's forehead.

"There is a familiarity between us," Jack said, smiling.

"Perhaps there is," Dalon Con said, sliding the Nexus into his robe where it was totally concealed. "What is the last thing you remember before this moment?" The smile left Jack's face as he pondered this man's question, his eyes downcast.

"Skateboarding in Defeated," Jack said. "It seems innocent enough, yet also comes with a high price."

"Do not concern yourself with these dark feelings," Dalon Con said. "They will resolve themselves in time." Jack nodded several times.

Suddenly, a one-foot-thick, gray appendage exploded through the ground, with gnashing teeth protruding from the end of the arm. Azoff landed on the creature, sinking his teeth deep into the flesh of Hag and then was gone. Roane rolled off Hag's arm, landing with a sickening thud on the ground.

"Azoff," Roane wheezed, "where are you?" His answer came in the form of a tooth-filled mouth consuming him completely. Max held a hand out, containing Hayden and Abe.

"Guard these two with your life," he said to Dalon Con.

"No harm will come to these small ones," he replied, "unless it first befalls me."

But Hayden stumbled and placed a hand on each side of his head and groaned. "The original temporal doorway . . . has been destroyed by anchor."

****

Adlar, how are we to handle the one we can see only small parts of at any given time, the maritime questioned.

These uprights are nothing to an anchor. They shall die in turn as fast as they attack, although I see no more than one, Adlar expressed.

This being the case, should we not attack?

The anchor contorted what he best thought emulated a smile and then spoke, *Attack, leave nothing alive.*

The two unlikely cohorts decimated Tempus, leaving microscopic bits of the body remaining. Something knocked the maritime to the ground, then seconds later the anchor followed suite.

"Who dares touch an anchor?" the anchor demanded, "you will surely die." The anchor flipped from one side to the other.

"I do not believe this to be the case," Tempus replied, "as you can see, I have made what just as well could have been deadly attacks; however, chose to temper them in order to spare your life."

"Do not temper your aggressions on my account," Adlar said, "for your demise is nothing but a task performed on any given day."

How may I assist the maritime requested?

"You cannot," Adlar roared, "you may stand aside or die!" The anchor deployed several dozen extremities with depressions carved into their ends. Across these indentations stretched a steel like wire, able to slice through most any material.

"A formidable array of weapons," said Tempus, "what do you suppose you will do with them?" His statement issued with an air of joviality.

"This, foolish one," Adlar said, moving three of his extremities toward Tempus from opposite directions. The temporal thief lost two legs and an arm to the anchor's armament.

"Impressive," Tempus replied. Four arms lurched from nowhere grabbing the anchor's limb and folding it back on itself, neatly severing the appendage from its origin.

"What have you done?" The anchor retrieved the severed limb. "This cannot be, it is impossible."

"Obviously not," two separate temporal thieves said. They further solidified this notion by twisting a second extremity to the point where it was easily removed from the anchor.

The new temporal thieves were split in half at mid thorax, then bifurcated from the opposite direction. "Now, what will you do with that?" Adlar asked.

Allow me to help, the maritime insisted, *it appears as though you may benefit from my assistance.*

At the sight of the maritime, hatred burned within the anchor and sarcasm ruled his response. "Certainly, your help would be most appreciated." Adlar raised an arm and sliced the maritime to ribbons. "Bother me no more worthless creature."

The anchor set his sights on the temporal thief finding four more vying for his attention. "How is this possible? I have learned through constant surveillance only one temporal thief is utilized at a time . . . what I am seeing does not happen."

One of the four began to speak. "Wanting to make sure I am proper as I speak, your name is Adlar . . . correct?"

"Correct," the anchor replied, at this point a bit dumbfounded.

"My name is Tempus and may I say it is pleasure to meet you."

"But I eliminated Tempus, according to reconnaissance. My source I maintain was infallible."

"And you would be correct," Tempus said. Several hundred more temporal thieves joined the four and surrounded Adlar, the anchor. "For we are many and we are one. When the remote possibility comes to fruition and one of us is eliminated, another takes his place. The replacements are the same being drawn from another timeline. What you see before you are many entities named Tempus, that have been called from numerous timelines."

Suddenly, two temporal thieves each picked up one of the two severed anchor appendages and began removing Adlar's limbs. The anchor could push up to a dozen out at one time. Adlar was able to strike down several of the temporal thieves before the sheer number of weapons the multitude of Tempora wielded became too much and the anchor was reduced to a stain.

****

Sim ran into the fray at an extraordinary pace, his eyes set on locating Hag.

"Mr. Dalon," Krabb said, "we fount these here two funny pieces 'o' metal back in Rash, stuck in a wall; it just seemed like the right time ta give'um to ya." Krabb dropped the two brass dowels into Dalon Con's hand.

"This appears to be the time for sharing discoveries." Hayden said. "To that end, I have this for you." He extended his arm, palm open, with a small golden disc in the center of his hand. "This is a Dalleon cell; it has a nearly inexhaustible supply of energy." Dalon Con reached into his robe and removed the piece of blue caladium retrieved by Sketch and Krabb from the bowels of Rash.

"Interesting," Dalon Con said, "the two metal dowels you entrusted to me are beginning to rotate." Even Max had postponed his leaving to witness the scenario evolving before him.

"The Dalleon cell is doing the same," Hayden said. Dalon Con slid a panel, making access to the interior of the artifact possible. He then placed the two rods into a corresponding impression in the caladium. As he touched the power cell in Hayden's hand with his finger, it expanded to a size that allowed Dalon Con's hand to grasp the golden circle, which subsequently caused a narrow slot to appear in the caladium when he touched the round piece in Hayden's hand.

"I will relieve you of this, small one, before it becomes too large for you to handle," offered Dalon Con. As he pressed the circular object into the slot, a hole in the center of the Dalleon cell accepted the two rods, fusing both tightly together when their ends made contact. Dalon Con watched in amazement as the door slid shut, making the gift from his grandson a solid piece of caladium with inner workings and great power.

"Now you will die with your world," Hag snarled. A blue and white blur took to the air covering a large area and finalizing its trip on the back of Hag. An arm breached the ground, removing the bottom half of Max's left leg causing the man-mountain to hit the ground, unable to regenerate.

"Now you will believe." A myriad of arms pierced the ground, each one removing a piece of Max until nothing but the tips of two fingers remained. The last casualty went unnoticed as Hayden was pulled beneath the earth, crushed, and devoured.

With each strike of Hag's arms, a crack in the crust of Burrus Plax developed, running for hundreds of miles. Hag paused his assault as Sim plunged two sharpened rods into Hag's back.

"You now see, Dalon Con," Hag began to speak, faltered then continued in an unsteady fashion, "that your beloved world will soon come to an end by my hand. . ." Hag screamed in agony.

"I just wanted you to know that Hag, your childhood, dreamscape nemesis dealt the destructive blow to you and your puny planet. For as long as your consciousness lasts, remember me, for I *am* the candle."

Hag pushed a tentacle through the ground, curling it around an unaware Sim. Before the ensnared biped could respond, Sim lay on the ground in two parts bitten in half at the waist.

Sensing a meal, Smort shot through the conflict ending on his knees over the still warm remains of Sim.

"It would seem that old habits die hard," he said smiling. Smort swallowed ridding his mouth of excess saliva. "The only difference with this meal and one from the past, is I ain't gotta count."

Sim's life fluid pooled in the span between his separated body segments. Smort extended his tongue, to begin his dining pleasure.

As his tastebuds started to tingle Smort's head and shoulders were cleanly sheared away, followed by the bulk of his remains. Pieces of the one known as Smort rained down as Hag ground his flesh, spilling as much as he swallowed.

Strange, my life's blood spills on the ground, Sim thought, *yet I am content, for another lives through me and I through him, purposed by the Great One.* Sim's mouth opened revealing an upper and lower jaw devoid of teeth.

Then, an orange light like that of a spider web filled the area between the rectangular shaped jaw line, and his upper thorax began to vibrate as Hayden from a timeline minutes in the past stepped through the doorway. A dim light penetrated his cheeks then rapidly expanded into a torrent of orange shooting up into the sky breaking the sonic barrier. Then, the body of Sim, being a vehicle for the temporal doorway, was no more.

Even in the midst of dire circumstances, thought Dalon Con, *my heart is light.*

"Now!" Dalon Con roared.

Dune grasped the pellet Dalon Con had given him and burst through the ground. Then the old man tossed him the piece of caladium. It landed between the only evidence that Max had existed, where his remaining fingertips snapped over the blue artifact.

Three unique feet, constructed from nine, large metal-like balls dropped from the sky, slamming into the ground encircling Dalon Con. He raised his eyebrows, expressing a look of surprise. "Unexpected, would you not say?"

"I would have to agree," Dune replied, scouring the appearance of the wrangler's three legs.

"Yet, very familiar," Dalon Con said. He continued to move through the sand, dodging the wrangler's attempts to destroy him. The creature's very foundation made another plunge into the earth and a ghostly image passed through the man's memory. "That's it!" he cried. Dalon Con reached into his side and pulled the ancient piece of cloth procured from the Sarack. The fabric doubled in size four distinct times, making it large enough to cover the wrangler. "You are now the latest death in the saga of my home!"

Leaping into the air, Dalon Con landed on top of the wrangler, covering the beast with the sacred cloth. The material began to slice through the wrangler wherever the smallest amount of force was applied; soon all that remained were twelve-inch slices of the creature.

"Max," Dalon Con said, "Burrus Plax is yours to save. Guard your words, Hag, for you never know when they will return, coming for you." The ground began to rumble and soon the massive form of Max, made entirely from caladium, appeared making his way toward the travelers. The bronze disc could be seen below the surface of the caladium in the center of Max's chest.

"Greetings, friends," Max said. "Please excuse me while I attend to a bit of unfinished business." Max stomped several hundred feet into undisturbed ground before stopping, then turned around and cheerfully announced, "Got it." Max pulled from the ground a slick, gray cephalopod with tentacles of enormous length that dug its incisor-fortified arms into Max in numerous places. With each bite Hag attempted to take, the result was the same—a mouthful of shattered teeth and broken jaw bones.

Max held his hands containing Hag above his head, then proclaimed, "And with this, the creature of temporal dissent's time expires." The giant pulled the distressed creature into pieces, pushing each deep into the ground. Once the last piece of Hag was buried, time stood still as Burrus Plax faded to black.

EPILOGUE

Max sat on the side of a mountain, the overlook high enough to afford him a view of Blanche Aries, one of the three thriving cities—Commerce, Blanche Aries and Single Duality, the only large settlements on Burrus Plax.

"It is good to have a peaceful world on which to dwell, along with hard-working inhabitants to tend to its flora and fauna. While it is confusing, I cannot shake the feeling that there are ones I know, yet will never know." Max laid back, gazing at the darkening sky. "Curious," another orange light streaked through the firmament. "Mayhap, I will discover what it means someday." He tossed a small object into the air, catching the trinket before it could strike the ground. Max admired the artifact's beautiful color as the waning sun punched through a brilliant cobalt blue. He continued to nod his head. "Yes, perhaps one day the mysteries of Burrus Plax will be known to all, including me."

****

"Mayhap what you seek in-so-far as mysteries, one day you will attain," a multi-layered voice said; "however, why would one set their sights so low." Somewhat masked by the bright sunlight, a sixteen-foot winged creature sporting several unique colors and clutching a jeweled jader's skull made for the nearest cover.

"Mysteries are fine," Vrollic said, "though for my part, I would much rather savor a hands on approach."

ACKNOWLEDGEMENTS

Penning a novel is certainly a task in and of itself. In my case it takes a bit more due to my lack of mobility. I offer many thanks to my caregiver, personal assistant, typist and friend, Brenda Schools. She attempts to keep me straight which some say is a lost cause, but she continues to endeavor to persevere . . . Ain't that just about a syllable from being poetic?

Grammar for me is not easily doable, so I bring in the cavalry, A.K.A. Mary Fredette, my editor. Mary takes my punctuation-challenged manuscript and obscure sentence structure faux pas and makes it legible to the reading world.

ABOUT THE AUTHOR

Born in Richmond, Virginia, Lynn Steigleder spent most of his adult life as a supervisor in the field of construction and fabrication. After being diagnosed with multiple sclerosis in 2006, he realized the need to transition into a new career path due to his energy and mobility challenges.

His son suggested he consider writing as a career—having enjoyed his father's short stories. Lynn agreed to the challenge and his first novel, "Rising Tide," in the series of the same name, was released for publication in 2009. The second, "Eden's Wake," and the third, "Deadly Reign," soon followed. "Terminal Core," a standalone was released in 2016.

"Ideas for manuscripts come from every direction," says Steigleder. "Daily events, things I see in nature, or down any path my imagination may lead me."

Lynn writes Christian fiction, science fiction, fantasy, action adventure, and YA.

LynnSteigleder.com